ALPHA HUNTED

KNOTTY & SWEET OMEGAVERSE

CREA REITAN

Alpha Hunted

Knotty & Sweet Omegaverse | Book 1

Dragon Fire Fantasy, Inc.

dragonfirefantasy@gmail.com

ISBN:

ASIN:

Version 2022.06.03 - P.NA

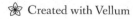 Created with Vellum

BOOKS BY CREA REITAN

THE IMMORTAL CODEX

Immortal Stream: Children of the Gods

Mortal Souls

The God of Perfect Radiance

The Hidden God

The God Who Controls Death

Gods of the Dead

Gods of Blood

Gods of Idols

Gods of Fire

Gods of Enoch (2022)

INFECTED FAIRY TALES

Wonderland: Chronicles of Blood

Toxic Wonderland

Magical Wonderland

Dying Wonderland

Bloody Wonderland

Wonderland: Chronicles of Madness

The Search for Nonsense

The Queen Trials

Alpha Hunted

Beta Haunted (2022)

The Princess and Her Alphaholes Anthology (excerpt of *Wrecked*)

Wrecked

Unsolicited (2022)

Hell View Manor (2022)

CHAPTER ONE

Terence
Ten months ago

The stone tomb stood nearly four feet tall and six feet long. It was easily wide enough to have two corpses lying side by side. Which was fortunate since that's how they were laid. Two on bottom, then one between, and then two more.

It sat on the top of three shallow steps and over the back, draping along the top, was the limp stone figure of a mourning angel. An angel weeping, sprawled over the top of the tomb that held my entire pack.

I was numb at this point. Beyond the time when I could feel anything at all. Deep sorrow. Crippling grief. The blinding pain of loss. It was all there. But on the outside, all I could do was stare. Stare as I had done every day for three hours a day, every day for the past two weeks. Stare at the stone resting place of my five packmates encased inside.

Anger. Denial. Bargaining. Depression. I was still flitting through them all.

I would never fall into acceptance. How could I when everyone I loved the most in the world had died, leaving me here alone?

———

I ALMOST IGNORED the phone as it rang. I was in a hurry to leave. They'd gone without me while I finished some last-minute business so that we were free for the week to enjoy each other. More than two hours had already gone by, and I didn't want to take any more time out.

The phone stopped and for some reason, I paused to glance at it. Why did I feel hollow and empty all of the sudden? I tried to catch my breath but there was nothing there.

There was... nothing there. Where was my...?

My phone rang again and this time I sprang for it. I swiped the button as I brought the unknown caller to my ear.

"Hello?"

"Mr. Andersen?"

I almost told the voice he had the wrong number. I was too distracted, reaching for bonds that I couldn't find. Absently, I said, "Yes."

"This is Officer Marks with the Roanak County Police Department. There's been an accident, Mr. Andersen."

I fell to my knees as tears immediately filled my eyes and I held my breath trying to keep the sobs in as he continued to speak.

"Your pack is in critical condition at Melview Hospital in Roanak. I need you to get here as soon as you are able."

My body shook as my vision blurred, tears streaking down my face as I fell further to the ground. This time I couldn't keep the sobs in. Because I knew, even if he wasn't allowed to say over the phone, I knew by the hollow empty bonds – the remnants of which were starting to fade.

My pack wasn't in critical condition. They were dead. All of them.

―――――

THERE WAS a stone terrace wall behind the grave that made the place feel more ominous than it was. It rose eight feet, holding back the ground from washing away and burying everything beneath it. Beyond it was another wide terrace of graves. I think my grandparents were on that tier.

The stone wall was made up of enormous blocks. There was moss and grass, even a few flowers, growing within the cracks. Along the base was a strip of lush greenery to brighten it up. Bringing more life into the resting place for the dead.

Periodically, there was a door in the wall. Once, when Miles and I were younger, we'd been wandering this same cemetery when there'd been a funeral in progress for a family with one of these crypts. We'd stopped to mourn with them. In doing so, we were granted permission to step inside.

We'd been mesmerized by the eerie silence and the bending hallways that continued to lead into the underground crypt. It was filled with darkness and, as a child, fear. I did what any alpha might. I wrapped my arm around my beta friend and hugged him to me, giving him comfort and shielding him from whatever might be hidden in the dark.

Miles and I had recounted the visit often. As we grew and continued to stroll through the cemetery, we'd often theorize what had been deeper in the dark. We knew it was likely more graves. But the part of us that enjoyed horror movies made all sorts of ideas pop to mind.

I'd briefly considered commissioning one of these crypts for my pack. Miles would have liked that. Though we'd never spoken of how we wanted to be buried since we were a fairly young pack, I was sure Miles would have brought this possibility up. He'd have been excited. He'd have made the idea sound like a quest into a lost crypt. He'd have designed it with medieval touches.

But we'd never gotten to the point in our lives where we thought to talk about death. It was too far away.

———

THE HOUSE WAS large and airy with enormous windows in the walls and ceilings. We'd completely gutted the shell of this place when our pack became five with the possible addition of a sixth. There were five bedrooms, both private and connected. There was a wide-open floor plan on the bottom, broken up by furniture and décor opposed to walls.

There was a heated pool out back because Zack loved to swim. And there was an extensive garden with a stone walk and flowers in anticipation of adding an omega to our pack at some point. The soft, warm femininity filled us with hopes and dreams of a larger family. Children running around. There was room for a great playset and sand box.

But right now, it was outfitted with luxury and comfort for the five, almost six, of us.

Most of the décor was grays on the darker side of the color wheel. There was a lot of rough stone and smooth, modern lines. The large bathrooms were filled with the juxtaposition of smooth round edges of a large soaker tub and donut-like sinks. The sinks had been Foster's addition. He was enamored with them.

There was a little bit of every one of us in each room. Not just the scents but little touches. Color pops and art. Books and technology.

Pictures. A lot of pictures.

Usually there were sounds of conversation. Laughter drifting through the rooms. Intimacy.

Now it was empty. My footsteps echoed. Their lingering scents deeply rooted into each wall, each cushion, each soft and hard surface made bile rise in my stomach.

They'd never be here again. I'd never see their living faces, hear their voices, meet their eyes.

Our once happy home was completely empty.

———

SPANNING the grassy area in front of my pack's tomb were more graves. Traditional gravestones. They were beautifully carved. Not only with the expected names and dates, but with images. Cherubs. Skulls. Gothic touches as well as softer flowers.

Many were filled with quotes or sayings. When Miles and I would walk the paths of the cemetery, we'd often wonder if the additional carvings were favorites of the dead or something from the living they left behind. Sometimes it was clear. Most of the time, it was not.

We had enjoyed this particular cemetery because it was large, filled with trails that snaked within the trees and through the avenues of graves. There was greenery, ponds, benches, and ducks everywhere. The flowers and the grass were well maintained.

It was peaceful and gave visitors the assurance that there was peace in death.

The tomb of my pack faced one of our favorite ponds.

There were large gnarly trees around it, as if they were twisted and tormented as they grew. Our theories on them were not nearly as lighthearted as most of the other places within the cemetery. But the pond itself was almost magical. It felt like it was a window or portal into another place. The trees added to that feel. And the ducks that swam on its surface almost appeared ethereal because of it.

They would enjoy the view in death as we had in life.

I TRIED *to stay in my room. It smelled the most like me and least of anyone else. It was too painful to be surrounded by them when they'd never be here again.*

I couldn't be here. I couldn't stay. And yet, I couldn't bring myself to leave the house either. I couldn't think of anything but my loss.

Once in a while, I'd hear Miles's laughter echoing through the halls and I'd look up, expecting to see him round the corner into my doorway. He'd grin at me, ready to tell me what he was laughing about. Ready to crawl into my side and cuddle against me.

Miles wasn't an omega but so much of his behaviors and instincts were the same. It made our longing for one all the stronger and yet, that pining was partially satisfied as we loved on Miles.

Sometimes, I'd hear the rich laughter of Foster from his room as he watched a movie. He was addicted to comedies. The dumber the better. But when I'd go to investigate, the room was empty. The laughter was only a phantom sound.

I'd turn at the deep laugh of Emery's. He was a big man, and his laughter was just as big. It was such that when he laughed, everyone else was smiling, too. Whether we thought it was funny or amusing or not.

But I'd never find the source of their laughter except in the echoes of my memory. I wandered through my empty house, waiting to find Ronan on the couch with a book, or Zack in the kitchen making something.

Their laughter, their presence, it was only the ghosts of them left. I squeezed my eyes closed as the pain coursed through me.

I couldn't bring myself to put my pack in a crypt. Or even in traditional graves. They were too cold and lonely.

My pack was very close. Had been. We had been very close. We enjoyed our time together more than our time apart. Four of us worked in the same complex and we rode to work together. We ate lunch together. We'd do the shopping after work together.

Date nights were always the six of us. We cooked together, hobbied together. More often than not, we slept piled into the same bed.

Sure, we took some time for ourselves on occasion. We each had likes that were all our own more than a shared one and we indulged in those interests solitarily.

But what my pack had was a strong, solid relationship in which we preferred each other to anything else.

Separate graves were not an option. For my pack, it meant we all needed to rest together.

They needed to rest together. Because they left me behind.

I dropped to my knees in front of the grave and rested my hand on the hard, cold surface. I hadn't cried in days. A combination of exhaustion, misery, and probably a big dose of dehydration meant I was pretty dried up.

But I dropped and sobbed again, bowing my head as I tried to catch my breath. My body wracked with sobs, the pain of it making my head ache.

I should have been in the SUV with them. We were supposed to go together. But I wanted to finish some last-minute details at work so I could take the week off carefree. I'd told them to go without me. I told them I'd be right behind them.

And now they're gone. They're gone without me, leaving me alone and empty as I choked on my tears.

———

ONE OF THE best things about our house was the nest. It was in the loft space, having once been storage before we gutted the house down to its studs. The ceilings peaked into the roofline; each gable end filled with tinted windows. We controlled the amount of sunlight with technology we splurged on, giving us the ability to crank up the tint so much that it could appear night in the middle of a bright summer day.

Nothing was beyond the satisfaction of spoiling our omega. When we got one, anyway. For now, it was prep.

We kept the walls a light gray but covered them and the vaulted ceiling with panels of warm fabric and string lights that we had on a dimmer. The floor had plush carpeting, but you couldn't see it. Covering it nearly wall to wall were cushions of all sizes. Pillows, blankets, throws.

It was cozy and made to feel smaller than it was. We kept it a decent size because we were already a pack of six without an omega. It would be difficult to fit six big guys in this room without making it a good size.

But we filled it with warmth and texture, closing it in with the feel of a nest. It was a great nest. One of the best I'd seen. Yes, I might have been biased but still, it was a great nest.

One that we never used. Sometimes one of us would peek in at it. We'd have it cleaned regularly, getting rid of the dust and making sure the fabrics stayed fresh and aired out. But it was never used. We never got the call that an omega was interested in us.

And now, it sat emptier still. The one room in the house that held no scent at all. I sat in it for a while, thinking maybe I needed to break from the assaulting scents of my pack, but that made the pain worse. Because the room was a symbol of our future. Of a deep hope and faith that one day we'd get a call from the Omega Registry that one was interested in our pack.

But the call never came. And the room sits emptier still, despite being filled with our broken dreams.

I COULDN'T REMEMBER the last time I cried before the officer's call. Was I six? Maybe seven?

I suppose the sobbing of a child is different from that of an adult. A child was fragile. Their emotions were new and unfamiliar. It was easy to make a child cry because they didn't understand how to regulate and understand what they felt.

It wasn't the same thing for an adult. And it was even more uncommon for an alpha.

But I think I've cried more in the past two weeks than I had my entire childhood combined. My jaw ached from it. My head throbbed. My throat hurt. My body ached from the constant tension. I could hardly breath from congestion and coughing to try and clear my chest.

Crying sucked. Feeling eyes on you with sympathy sucked. I wanted to turn around and rip them apart. I don't want apologies. I don't want compassion or empathy. Unless you can bring my pack back, I want nothing at all. No kindness. No company. No pity.

I rested my forehead on the cold stone by my hand, imagining that I could feel them on the other side with their hands pressed against it, too. Reaching for me like I was them. I held my breath as a new wave of sobs tried to break free. I forced myself to keep them in, to not give in to the uncontrollable bawling that I now spent all my miserable waking life doing.

"I'm sorry," I whispered. "I love you so much."

———

I STARED at the empty suitcases on my bed. I had three. There was nothing in any of them. I had a duffel bag on a chair and another bag on my dresser. But when I opened my closet, I just stared.

Wasn't that Ronan's favorite shirt?

That one was missing a button from when Zack ripped it off me.

When did Miles return that hoodie? He always wore it. Ah, yes. He returned it so it would become covered in my scent again.

I wore that one the last time I hugged Ronan. And that one when Foster and I went to the movies, holding hands like teenagers.

I shut the closet again. The question was, could I bear to take them? Or could I stand not to? Did I need that reminder? Would the reminder be of them or of their absence?

I wandered their rooms, opening their closets and running my hands along their clothing. Silent tears dripped down my cheeks. Throw them out or keep them? Bring them with me or leave them here? Which was harder? Which was the right thing to do?

My phone ringing made me jump. The house was so quiet now. Every little sound, every footstep of mine, every breath or sniffle, was magnified by its emptiness.

I left Emery's room to find my phone, catching it before the call ended.

"Mr. Andersen?"

It took a lot not to snap at the voice. It was my fucking cell phone. Who else would be answering it when my entire pack was dead?

"Yes."

"This is Rudy Stillwater. How are you?"

I gritted my teeth. If I was asked that one more time!

"Never been better," I growled.

It wasn't her fault. Knowing that didn't appease my irritation.

"I understand," she said, her voice quieter. "I'm sorry. I didn't mean to ask."

"Fine. What do you need?"

"There's an offer on your house, Mr. Andersen."

"Accept it."

"You don't want to hear what-"

"No. Just accept it. Rudy, I need someone to pack this place up and. And." And do what? Do what with it? Bury it with them?

I closed my eyes, my face crumpling as I tried to hold it together.

"I'll have it packed and stored until I hear otherwise, Mr. Andersen," Rudy said gently. "Is there anything else you need?"

Nothing she could give me.

"A real estate agent on the east coast," I answered.

There was a pause before she answered. "Any particular

state?"

"*No. I don't care where. I just need to leave.*"

"*I understand. I'll text you a couple names in a few minutes.*"

"*Just give me your best recommendation, Rudy. I don't want choices.*"

"*Okay, Mr. Andersen. I'll text you his name when we hang up.*"

"*Thank you.*" *I ended the call and Rudy Stillwater did just as she promised. My phone pinged a minute later with a text message from her. Drake Blain. And a phone number followed. Mid east coast.*

I stared at my empty suitcases again.

———

I MANAGED to pull myself together as the sun started to set. It was more likely that I simply ran out of tears. I couldn't remember the last time I drank anything. Or ate anything.

I ran my fingers along the curvature of their names. Zack Andersen. Ronan Andersen. Miles Andersen. Foster Andersen. Emery Andersen. Various dates of birth. All with the same date of death.

I didn't add any poetry or quotes. There weren't even any other carvings. Miles and I loved the carvings on graves. We'd spent a lot of time admiring them. Commenting on them. Making a list of our favorites.

But when it came time to fashion the grave of my pack, I was a blank slate. As if I'd never thought of death. As if graves and the cemetery were a sudden, surprising step in life.

I was thankful now that I'd been present enough to state where I wanted their tomb and that I wanted them all together. I was pretty sure I spent a fortune with the whole get up. But since I'd been too distraught to think of the finer details elsewhere, this was the least I could do.

Maybe Miles would be disappointed.

I pulled myself to my feet, keeping my hand on the top, next to where the angel's arm hung over. I wasn't an angel, but I agreed with the grave designer who gave me this option. Because it was me. Not the angel, but the presence that would forever mourn over the bodies of the pack he lost.

Words wouldn't come to my lips. I tried. I wasn't sure what I wanted to say but I found I couldn't say anything. How do I tell them that I'm leaving? That I can't bear to stay in our empty house without them? That without them, I can't live at all?

I took a deep, burning breath, holding it in my lungs until it was forced out. My head throbbed. My eyes hurt from the constant onslaught of tears.

The only thing that I could say, I said again. Over and over. Meanwhile, my mind was filled with promises, broken and new.

"I love you," I said again. "I will never stop loving you."

I don't know where I found the strength. Or maybe it was a weakness. But I pulled my hand from their tomb and turned. I walked, letting my feet carry me back to the car I rented.

I LEFT *the open suitcases on my bed. I packed the barest necessities in the duffel. Clothing that I never wore. I selected one item of each of theirs. One of their favorites. Or maybe they were my favorites.*

I carefully tucked those items into sealed plastic bags and tucked them safely into my duffel before zipping it up. Still, I stood frozen.

The packers and movers would be here in the next day or so. Their orders were that everything outside of food gets packed. Everything. I didn't want their judgment to decide if something should stay or go. Right down to their fucking underwear. It gets packed.

It might have been kinder to myself to have them go through it and choose just some items to keep. But they didn't know my pack. How would they know what to choose? What if they chose wrong and I would forever be without something?

No. It all had to be packed and stored until I was strong enough to know what to do with it.

And in the meantime, I was moving to Ocean City, Maryland. I liquidated most of our west coast assets, selling the majority of our shares of anything that felt like it was remotely holding me here, and stuffed it all into several insured bank accounts. I kept a few of Zack's businesses.

But the primary one I held onto happened to be in the city I was moving to. A juice bar, Juice Me. Conveniently, above it, was an empty studio apartment. I had Drake Blain hire a contractor and gut the place before remodeling it. Since I hadn't needed his services in any other capacity, this felt like a fair trade. I'd still pay him a commission.

It should only take me a week to drive, but I was making short days of driving to assure that my apartment was done by the time I arrived.

I walked from room to room, running my hand along surfaces for the last time. I gathered as many memories as I could, storing them away. I buried my face in pillows and leaned my forehead against doors and walls. I stared out the window, looking down at our perfect yard. The perfect home we'd built.

With my duffel in hand, I walked out of our house for the last time.

CHAPTER TWO

Terence
Present

I tightened the belt around my waist, making sure I had the support, so I'd not hurt myself. I was graduating to the largest tire the gym had today. I'd been working up to it for months. I started with the 450-pound tire, but I grew out of that one quickly.

Over the last week, I'd found the 650-pound tire getting easier, too. That meant it was time for the 800-pound. This beast was massive.

I checked my earbuds, making sure they were secure. My playlist was loud and angry, though still never penetrated the bubble of numbness around me.

With a deep breath, I squatted to grip the treads and braced myself. I stared straight ahead, seeing nothing at all, as I took deep breaths and released them through my mouth. With a mental strength more than physical, I pushed against the ground with my legs as I heaved it with my arms.

I wouldn't have thought 150 pounds could feel so different but damn it was heavy. The muscles in my arms burned. The ache of it was satisfying so I continued to pull until it was time to turn my hands around and push it up further with the palms of my hands.

I shoved it up the rest of the way, nearly straightening my body before I got it upright and let it fall backwards. I sighed as I looked at it. Yep, this was the new ache I needed.

Stepping up on it, I walked over the tire before readying myself to do the same process again. And again. For five reps, I flipped the tire until my hands were slick with sweat.

Nodding in approval as I caught my breath, I moved to the side to take a few pulls on my water bottle. This was my third one, half empty. That meant my day at the gym was nearly over. I set it down again and looked around. What next?

I didn't have a true routine. I'd tried to get into a few but I found that my interest waned after a few weeks of the repetition. I was better when I could roam throughout the large building, choosing whatever piqued my interest that day. Sometimes, something would truly catch me, and I'd find myself working up to a goal.

That's how I found the tires. For the last handful of months, I'd been working up to the 800-pound tire. It was a small but satisfying victory that I was able to perform five reps.

Maybe I'd go for the battle ropes and shake them for a bit. My arms already stung from the effort of the tire. The ropes would give me more delicious pain. I started for them when one of the smaller tractor tires caught my attention instead. It had been a while since I'd worked on my abs. I'd been too focused on my legs and arms to work on the strength I needed for the massive tire.

Okay, then. Time to make my abs burn, too. I left the room for one of the large fifty-pound stacking weights and brought it in. This might be overdoing it. When was the last time I'd done a crunch?

I sat on the smaller tire with my feet inside the perimeter. Sliding down so that the edge of the tire cradled the lower part of my lumbar, I used my core muscles to lift my feet and hooked them under the opposite lip of the inner tire.

With the weight in my hands, holding it over my chest, I began doing suspended crunches, alternating them with slight twists to make sure I hit the obliques as well.

The song changed to something dark and demanding, the tempo and rhythm was such that I could shut out the world and disappear within the anger of the song. The words didn't reach me. They didn't penetrate the fog in my mind as I continued to let gravity and the weight I held over me pull me backwards before I used my abdominals to sit up further.

Over and over until I could barely hold the weight over me. Finally, I let it slide as I rolled off the tire to land on my hands and knees. My body shook with the effort to even hold myself up. The perfect amount of exhaustion I need. Enough that my mind was too tired to even think.

It took me a few minutes to gather the remaining strength in me to pull myself to my feet. I bought some time and returned to my water bottle. It was clear that I was barely this side of overworking myself when even that light mass made me twinge.

It was easy enough to hide my fatigue when I returned the round weight back to its holder. Hide it inside my tiredness. I'd expended my energy for the day.

I dropped the water bottles back into my bag before dragging a towel over my face and through my hair. I was soaked. The air outside would do me some good, help me to cool down and dry in the sun. Draping the towel around my neck, I left the gym not seeing anyone or anything except the path I wove between machines to the front door.

There was a two mile walk back to my apartment. I made it shorter some days by cutting through the park instead of going around it. It was a beautiful park filled with lush greenery, an abundance of large trees, flower gardens, and a couple small ponds. Those were the sections I could see from the path I cut through it.

The park expanded in either direction. The map on my phone said it was a large park, having both playing fields and child play gyms littered throughout. But I kept to my path, having no interest in exploring it.

I had no interest in anything.

Choosing to cut through the park today, I breathed in the scent of freshly mown grass. I appreciated that the city was well kept. In the distance, when the breeze blew just right, I caught a whiff of sea water. The ocean was only a few miles from my apartment, but I'd never been there. I went to very few places. Gym. Juice bar. Grocery store. Home. And even the grocery store was only when I found I was out of something that I didn't want to wait for. Otherwise, I had my groceries delivered by a few different services.

There were people around me everywhere I went. It took a solid three months to make sure everyone knew I wasn't interested. Not in them. Not in conversation. Not in giving directions. Not in their sympathy. I wanted no one and nothing. I'd carefully constructed the air of unapproachability around me, and it was pretty well impenetrable now.

My juice bar was on the opposite side of the street when I exited the park. It was recently expanded before I moved to Ocean City. On occasion I'd wondered if Zack had told us he was doing that. There was certainly a feel of him here in the clean lines and warm touches. So, I was pretty convinced he'd been involved. But I didn't remember.

There was a lot I didn't remember.

I stepped in the front door, the quiet chime ringing over my head. It was busy, which I was glad to see. Zack had always liked to juice things. He'd been in on the first machines that were decent for residential. So, I wasn't the slightest bit surprised when he'd made the investment.

The wall the door was on had a bank of windows on either side and a bar set up with stools that ran the length of it for customers to enjoy their drinks and talk. The left side of the shop was where the juice counter was. It took up half the length and turned the corner. The back wall was lined with blenders and refrigerators.

The front half of the left wall was filled with hanging bins of fruit and vegetables. Basically, if you could imagine it in a drink, it was there. There was an order where you could completely customize your drink. It told you how many of which types of fruits, vegetables, berries, blends, etc. you needed, and the customer chose them. Kids especially loved this.

Along the back wall was another bank of refrigerators with our bottled blends that were easily accessible for someone in a hurry. They could grab one, scan it in the kiosk next to the bank of refrigerators, pay and be on their way. It was filled with our most popular blends and occasionally a few specialty blends.

The wall opposite the counter had a long table with glass juice drips. You'd purchase a cup from another kiosk and choose which juice you wanted. You were able to mix them or have an entire cup of just a single juice. This allowed you to customize your drink without waiting in line.

There were half a dozen customers in front of me when I stopped in and four betas tending the counter. I knew there were likely another three on the other side of the door behind the counter, keeping the refrigerators stocked and the juice jugs filled.

I made it a point to only employ betas. The city was bursting with them, as was common everywhere. I paid generously and treated them well. My turnover wasn't high because of it. I was pleased to find Jakob running a blender. He was the best juice artist – a title they chose. I wasn't sure what he did to the drinks since I'd made it a point to watch him closely, but everything I chose when he made it was divine.

To boot, he was quick, efficient, friendly, and a pro at multitasking. Already, he had three blenders running as he started chopping items for another blender.

The other three employees I could see were Carly, Gina, and Megasin. Carly was a lot like Jakob. Quick and efficient while being super friendly. Megasin was still rather new and learning the ropes. I'd found she was shy and hesitant, even if friendly. And Gina was a whiz with the juicer, making it a show for the customers.

"Hi Mr. Andersen," Carly chirped, causing the other three employees to look up at me.

I pulled my earbuds out and dropped them in the small pocket of my bag that had my phone in it.

Jakob grinned brightly before turning back to his machines, two of which had stopped. Megasin smiled but it was shy, and her face heated immediately. Gina only offered me a grin as she continued with her juicing.

My employees were well trained in handling all designations. Juice Me was a popular and successful juice bar in Ocean City, so we had a whole lot of alphas come through the doors as well as the influx of betas. I'd carried along in Zack's legacy and made sure that anyone who entered the doors knew that my betas were in charge in this store. And they were to be treated with respect and kindness. Otherwise, they'd be banned.

Once, I was a strong alpha. Now, I was an absent one, though I stopped in daily for a juice.

I nodded at Carly's greeting, offering them a vague smile. Behind me, the door continued to open as other patrons entered the establishment. It was a good feeling to know that it was successful.

Zack would be happy to know that I could keep it that way.

Though, to be fair, I did nothing. Jakob was an assistant manager. Between him and the two managers I employed, I simply signed checks on Fridays and was a tie breaker and approver to anything they felt should be run by me. On the whole, I let them do their thing. They knew I came in every day. So it's not like they could hide something from me if they wanted to.

When I finally stepped up to the counter, Carly was grinning her happy, eager smile. Her cheeks were slightly pink. I was pretty sure she looked at all alphas this way.

"What will it be today, Mr. Andersen?" she asked.

But before I could truly think about the dilemma, Jakob turned and handed me a prepared smoothie. He smiled, flirty and sensual. I was well aware that this beta was interested. He'd said so on several occasions. I'd also made it clear that I was a lone wolf. No packs. No company. Nothing.

"Banana berry chai," Jakob said. "I've been messing with the mixture ratios, and I think this one is really good."

I nodded. "Thanks. Put it on my tab."

Jakob's smile widened as he turned to face me fully. He was a good-looking man with dark curls and bright blue eyes. He was tall and lean, though I was pretty sure that was his natural physique more than any effort on his part.

Once, he would have been exactly what I'd looked for.

Exactly the beta that would catch my eye. He had the same
basic structure, features, and personality as Miles and Ronan.

Once.

I turned, meeting Carly's eyes again before leaving. I
waited to take a sip of the smoothie until I was out of sight. Not
because I thought it would be bad. But because I thought any
reaction to it at all might encourage Jakob more. I wasn't
interested in hurting anyone. I just wanted to be left alone.

It was fucking good. That boy needed a raise. Hell, the
shop should be his. It was so good that I had half of it in me
before I'd even reached my door around the side of the
building.

The door led into a stairwell. And the second door, the one
that led into my apartment, was at the landing on top. There
was a short bench there with another couple pairs of sneakers. I
kicked the ones I wore now off and nudged them with the
others before unlocking my door.

I walked into the studio between the small kitchen and
small living area. The kitchen ran along two thirds of the length
of the left side of the apartment. It was the length of the wall,
starting with a decent sized refrigerator, a gas stove and oven,
sink, and a short counter. Across from the counter was a short
peninsula with two stools opposite the kitchen.

On the other side of the kitchen was a bathroom that took
up the rest of the left side of the studio. There was a large
shower and a large vanity sink and, of course, a toilet. It was a
good size considering the size of the apartment.

The right side of the apartment was open space. It was
separated a third to two thirds with the bedroom at the back
being the bigger of the two. There was a half partition between
the two areas with a flat screen television that swiveled so that I
could see it in both places.

There was no closet. No storage. I lived out of a dresser and the few cabinets in the kitchen and under the sink in the bathroom. It was fine since I didn't own much. I'd ordered a new wardrobe, furniture, and furnishings online, all of which were delivered my first week here. I wasn't even sure where a store was outside of the grocery store around the corner across from a large cemetery.

I wasn't sure if the cemetery being so close was a comfort or a sore spot. Ten months later, I was no closer to deciding. In any case, I ignored it entirely.

I stripped as soon as I shut my door. I set the cup of what little remained of my juice smoothie on the table, dropped my gym bag on the floor and walked towards the back of the space, tossing the sweaty mess of clothing into the hamper on the far side of the room. The studio was too small for a washer and dryer. Even a combination washer dryer. Too small for a dishwasher. I paid for laundry services, so I'd not have to find a laundromat and spend time doing that.

I stepped into the shower as I turned on the water. It sprayed over me in cold sheets for several moments before it heated up. It wasn't slow about it, but it was a shock to my sweaty body for that initial blast of cold water.

For a long while, I stood with my face tipped into the spray of water, letting it wash over me and pelt against my sore body. Hopefully I'll sleep. Hopefully, I won't be plagued with dreams. I washed without noticing I did so.

I was out of the shower before long and drying. I didn't dress again. I'd never been a huge fan of clothing anyway. I was pretty sure that my lack of being dressed inside the house kept me able to live out of the few drawers that held my clothes.

The window in my bedroom overlooked the park across the street. It was a nice view, but I never spent too much time admiring it. Although it didn't look anything like the backyard at my pack house, it was a lush green space and the view made me ache.

I turned into the living area, grabbing the remote on the way. I flicked the television on as I dropped to the couch, finally giving in to the exhaustion in my body. If I could get a massage without being touched, I'd probably do that. But there was no satisfaction in the vibrating chairs. They didn't hit my deep muscles.

Resting my hand with the remote on the cushion, I leaned my head back and closed my eyes.

Almost as soon as I did, I heard the echoes of Ronan and Miles's laughter, the sounds making my heart jump. Then the image of the mangled mess of our SUV that had collided head first into the front of a Mack dump truck rotting in the junkyard. The memory made me hold my breath as it faded into the angel forever weeping over the tomb of my packmates.

Gasping for breath, I opened my eyes again.

I wasn't tired enough. I would still have nightmares when I closed my eyes.

CHAPTER THREE

Terence

After my morning stretches to get myself warmed up, I went straight to the tires. I started with the 650-pound tire, going through the tumbling reps quickly. Then I went into sledge chops – using a heavy sledgehammer and swinging it around like I was chopping wood. It was repetitive, easy labor that allowed me to get lost in it for a long period of time.

There was a lot you could do with a tire, especially since there were several different sizes and weights available. There were even more if you were willing to interact with somebody. I was not.

I went through the motions of a variety of arm routines using the tires. I started with what one might think pretty easy, planting my feet on the floor and my hands at the edge of the tall tire and began the steady rhythm of pushups.

When I got bored with that position, I inverted it. Planting my feet above my head on the edge of the tire and my hands flat on the floor, I went back into pushups. I continued in this position until I was red in the face and slightly lightheaded.

After a water break, I used the weight of the 650-pound tire as a means to add to the difficulty of lunges. Keeping it balanced on an edge, I rested the weight of the tire in my palms and began my lunges until I was almost grunting with the effort. It felt good to let the tire fall, slamming into the mat when I was done.

This seemed like a decent warm up and I went to the 800-pound tire to start some flips. Since it was early, I scattered these reps throughout the rest of the day, enjoying the way my body protested with each revisit to the tire.

I didn't care which muscle group I focused on. I didn't go to the gym for any purpose other than that I found it was a great place to lose myself and waste the day. I generally focused on goals rather than muscle groups and strength building.

I'd wanted to master the 800-pound tire. I wanted to be able to use it like a damn toy. That meant I needed my legs and arms to primarily carry the brunt of the muscle work, but I also needed my core and back ready to hold myself how I needed to be.

Sometimes, I played with random things. The battle ropes, for instance. They were tied to the back of the room and the thick bands were seven or eight feet in length. I'd watched others use them and found the most common use of them were in bouts of four sets. Work really hard at a particular move for twenty seconds, rest for ten, change up the exercise for another ball-breaking twenty seconds, rest for ten, and this pattern repeats for four different exercises. And that is one rep.

The first time I tried it, I thought my arms were going to fall off. I'd been nearly obsessed with it for weeks. And then I spotted the tires in use and my focus had shifted. But for now, I went back to the ropes. Picking them up, I started with twenty seconds of alternating waves. My hands moved opposite each other, up and down as fast as I could. I watched the clock that was conveniently located at the base of the wall where the ropes were anchored tick by.

I released a breath when I hit twenty seconds, watching as the second hand ticked by. Even more difficult was the double wave. Moving your arms in the same up and down fashion simultaneously. You'd think this would be easier, but it burned far worse. Then a ten second break.

I moved on to shoulder circles, rotating my arms in front of me, both of them inwards. Ten seconds. And then the last exercise of snake rotations. Moving my arms from side to side in the same motion together.

That was one rep. I did four reps before I needed a water break.

I spent the day in the same room, using the different ropes, tires, bands, and whatever else caught my attention before I ran out of water. That's when I packed up.

This gym was a decent size. There were three floors, the bottom having an Olympic sized swimming pool, saunas, steam rooms, and tanning booths. The second floor had a lot of open rooms where classes and exercise groups were held.

I tended to keep to the main floor where the primary bulk of the equipment was.

I liked this gym because there was a healthy mix of alphas and betas and there wasn't any segregation between them. I'd always chosen places I worked, lived, and shopped to have this kind of healthy designation mix. There would always be a whole lot more betas in any given place because they made up nearly 80% of the world. But I'd found the more pleasant places to be were where betas were comfortable among the alphas in any given environment.

Everyone naturally craved a pack, and a true pack could

only be built with at least a single alpha involved. It was an alpha's bite that created the pack bonds. Betas were often thought of as common and unimportant because they were so predominant. That made alphas special because they were rare.

And omegas were the treasure that everyone sought.

But because everyone craved a pack, you had betas willing to trip over themselves to get the attention of an alpha. Any alpha. So many weren't picky at all. And then you had alphas who would flaunt what they were, tease and torment betas without any real interest or intention of biting them.

So, I hunted out places where betas and alphas co-existed in peace. No drooling or begging. No pompous arrogance. Just moving about, minding their business in a friendly, casual place. This gym was exactly that.

I was used to the strong scents of the other alphas and the more background, floral scents of the betas. They were plentiful, despite the advanced air filters that the gym boasted, and I'd gladly admit any day that they were good. It was only when I happened to be within a five-foot radius of someone that I caught their scent.

What I never found at this gym, or in most of my normal daily travels, was the sweet, gripping perfume of an omega. And yet, the pine and cinnamon scent stopped me in my tracks as I started my way towards the door. I closed my eyes, letting it wash over me. Through me, around me. It seeped into my skin and bones, making my entire body wake up as if it hadn't been alive before this moment.

I took a deep breath through my mouth, trying to clear the haze of the sudden onslaught. Around me, weights slammed together as alphas groaned at the sudden perfume filtering through the air.

"What sweet madness is this?" I heard someone growl.

I nearly smiled. That's exactly what this was. Using the hand that wasn't holding the strap of my bag, I washed it over my face, trying to clear my mind and rid my lungs of the smell.

You could be attracted to anyone. An individual's scent could wrap you like Velcro regardless of their designation. But an omega grabbed you by your balls, your heart, and your mind in one fell swoop. It was the sweetness that hit you first. The promise of the omega heart that made an alpha stand up and look.

But when their particular perfume spoke to you, it was a whole-body experience. And sweet fuck, I was ready to jump out of my skin right now.

I needed to get out of here.

But when I opened my eyes, the omega was standing in front of me. Watching me with wide steel blue eyes as he stood frozen before me. Yes, he.

All omegas were rare. At the last census, they made up just over 3% of the world population. Of that 3%, males were less than half a percent. It made sense. The female alpha was just as rare among alphas.

I tried to swallow the lump in my throat as I stood trapped in his gaze. He was shorter than me, leaner as omegas tend to be. His hair was short, dark with golden streaks. His skin was tanned but it looked natural, blending with his hair tone rather than separated by a faint line.

His perfume filled the room further and I groaned, taking a step back from him. Fuck, I couldn't do this right now. I was far too tired to keep my head. Far too broken to even look at an omega.

"Hi," he said, a smile touching his lips.

A sudden purr broke from me before I could stop it. I swallowed it as quickly as I could, forcing myself back another two steps. "Hello," I answered, my voice low and tense.

"I've never been to this gym," he said, tilting his head. "I'm Kaiser." He held out his hand to me and I was seriously trying to convince my body not to just take off running. Or jump on him. Whichever came first.

"I'm sweaty," I told him, keeping my hand firmly at my side.

His smile turned into a beaming grin, making everything in me gasp for breath. Fuck, the pull of an omega was real. As it was, I was trying ridiculously hard not to breathe through my nose. But even then, swallowing mouthfuls of air ladened with his perfume was just as torturous.

"That's a cute name," he said, dropping his hand. "This is Marley." He reached behind him and pulled a woman to his side, wrapping his arm around her.

This time it felt like I was punched in the chest as my body lit up. She smiled up at me shyly, her sapphire eyes glinting. She was small, slight, with long smooth brown hair and soft skin.

The pair of them together was a threat to undo me.

"Terence," I answered through my teeth. "I'm sorry, I was just leaving."

Kaiser nodded, his smile fading a little. But I felt both of their eyes tracking me as I rounded the machine next to them in a hurry to leave. I stopped outside the door and sucked in a large lungful of air to clear his scent from my head.

I'd always known omega perfumes were potent. I'd been around a few in my lifetime. But I'd never felt it quite so thoroughly. As if it touched my soul with claws. Branded me with a hot iron.

I shivered, taking another cleansing breath as I stared across the street at the park. Shortcut today. Through the park so I could get home. Nothing else. No more.

Waiting for the traffic to slow, I pulled my earbuds out and dropped them into the pocket of my bag with my phone before heading across the street. I glanced behind me and fuck if I couldn't see Kaiser in the window watching. He smiled when I met his gaze, and I blew out a harsh breath as his phantom perfume filled me again.

I shook my head and turned away. No. I'm sorry, omega, but no. I'm not looking for a pack. I'm not looking for an omega. I just want to lose myself in this city and let life pass me by.

I noted nothing as I walked through the park and jogged across the street to the juice bar. It was busier today than other days. There was hardly any room to stand inside. But there was primarily the quiet, relaxing scent that only a crowd of betas provided. I closed my eyes again and let it wash away any lingering hints of the omega.

His perfume had been too strong for me to have caught any hint of Marley. But I wasn't blind or ignorant. I could feel a reaction to her just as strongly as there'd been one to Kaiser. And I knew she wasn't an omega.

"Good afternoon, Mr. Andersen."

I looked up at Nora's greeting. She was one of my two managers. I waved at her, holding a hand up before letting it fall back to the strap of my bag. I think I managed to smile. Hard to say right now.

"What will it be?" Nora asked.

I shook my head. "Tend to the customers. I'm in no hurry."

Except that I was in a hurry. I needed to shower. To wash off any remnants of scents that hung around. How could one omega penetrate the wall around me? As if I'd built it with sponge instead of steel. A thin membrane instead of stone. I needed to wash it off. Wash it away. Make the entirety of it go away.

They better not be at the gym tomorrow. Or I'd have to find a new gym.

I was pulled from my thoughts when Jakob stood in front of me, offering me a tall juice smoothie cup. "Sweet tea blend," he said. "You look a little stressed so I thought this might be best today. Not too much sugar."

"Thanks," I said.

His smile climbed back into the flirty suggestion that was typically there. "Anything for you, boss."

I nodded sagely and turned towards the door, telling him to put it on my tab. I heard one of the crowd ask, "We can open tabs?" as I opened the door. Carly answered with a laugh. "No. He owns the shop."

Maybe I should allow the long-time patrons to open tabs. I was sure that was probably a poor business model. The kiosks had been a suggestion of Nora's, designed to allow more people to move through who didn't have time for the lines. The acquisition of them had nearly doubled revenue. I'd given all of my employees raises because of it.

Though the frozen tea was cold, it soothed and calmed me as a warm one might. I stopped inside my door and leaned against it, closing my eyes as I continued to sip the frozen tea. I didn't think frozen teas were on the menu, but perhaps they should be.

After another minute went by in which I was sure that nothing pine or cinnamon was in my house, I dropped my bag on the floor and set my tea on the table. I stripped on the way to the bathroom, tossing my sweat-soggy clothing into the hamper on the way.

Per usual, I stepped into the shower as I turned it on. The blast of icy water made me flinch and I closed my eyes as it steadily warmed up. I relaxed under the heating spray, imagining that any remnants of Kaiser were sliding down the drain.

But it wasn't enough. My body responded despite the

coldness of my heart. Actually, even my heart was misbehaving, beating faster than it should be. Not racing, but the rhythm had picked up to an uncomfortable pace that made my breathing harsher.

I couldn't remember the last time my body felt like anything but an exhausted shell. For the first time in nearly a year, I felt wired. My skin was hot. My cock twitching.

I swallowed it all down. *Just going to have to suffer, body.* I scowled and washed, ignoring any other urge that sparked within me. *Suffer. I don't give a fuck what you want. You don't get anything.*

I stepped out of the shower and dried before leaving the bathroom. I grabbed my frozen tea and the remote so I could drop onto the couch and flick the television on. I closed my eyes, slowly sipping the tea and letting it relax me.

But as what always happened when I closed my eyes, memories of my past crept up. At least this time, it didn't start out painful. Not in the typically painful way.

Miles and I were curled in the hammock outside with Zack in a chair. His feet were on the hammock as he rocked us gently.

"We should get a bigger hammock," Miles said. "It would be nice if we could all be in it together."

"We'd be sardines," Zack said, a smile in his voice.

"That's not so bad," Miles told him, turning his bright eyes to Zack. "I like being too close to breathe."

Zack's phone rang.

But the memory faded. It wasn't Zack that answered the phone. It was me.

"This is Officer Marks with the Roanak County Police Department. There's been an accident, Mr. Andersen."

My heart sped up, beating harshly in my chest as the words repeated in my mind.

"Your pack is in critical condition at Melview Hospital in Roanak. I need you to get here as soon as you are able."

But I didn't go to the hospital. I walked into the empty nest. The nest we'd built for our omega. The omega that we'd never get. It was large but felt so small. Cozy, but it felt suffocating. Bright, but I couldn't see anything in the darkness. There were no hard edges or surfaces, but everything felt sharp and harsh.

The emptiness of the nest spread its broken dreams throughout the rest of the house, causing echoes of my once happy, perfect life to shatter around me.

I opened my eyes but saw nothing but a blur as I tried to breathe. "You came too late, omega," I murmured, squeezing my eyes to force the tears to run out and down my cheeks.

I have no pack. No nest. No desire at all for anything or anyone. I've got nothing to give you. I'd never be able to take care of you when I can't take care of myself.

CHAPTER FOUR

Terence

Days went by and the memory of the omega faded. I didn't catch his scent at the gym when I returned the next day, for which I was grateful. I wasn't sure if it was because of the ventilation or if he hadn't stayed long. It wasn't often that you'd find an omega at a gym.

Only when I could think clearly did it occur to me that an unattached omega wouldn't be at a gym at all. A bonded one might, but not without his alpha. Maybe with a beta but not one such as Marley. She was... beautiful. The kind of beta a pack would readily take in just because she appeared as fragile and coveted as an omega.

That was the only reason I reacted to her at all. It was her appearance. The image I'd always dreamed our omega would be. The girl that would fill our home with love, with warmth, with children. The omega we'd been missing.

The omega was a male though, which didn't bother me. It was almost more surreal to find that. Male omegas were a fairy tale. When you find one, you can't help but react since there are so few. The proverbial surprise princess story. Needle in a haystack. Whatever other cliché metaphor you could find.

I'd had them both in front of me. Everything I'd ever wanted. Too late to have it.

I concentrated on the battle ropes again before moving on to the tires. But for the first time since I'd started spending my days at the gym, my heart wasn't in it. I couldn't keep myself focused or interested. I wandered through the main floor, sampling machines but ultimately moving on.

I'd only made it through a bottle and a half of water, and I was done. Maybe I should try the basement level. Swim? I had trunks in my bag, always prepared for the pool but I never used it.

I stood in the door and watched. There were three lanes in use with people doing laps. I watched, waiting for an urge to join that never came. Sighing, I turned towards the saunas and steam rooms, but I walked by them, too.

Okay, maybe I'd just go home. Maybe I could take a nap and lose myself in that instead.

I took the long walk home, staying on the sidewalks instead of cutting through the park. I skipped the juice bar and headed inside, straight into the shower. The water ran over me longer than usual as I attempted to search within myself for something that I might do. There was still more than half the day to get through. There was no way I was going to sleep.

I found myself on my back on my bed, staring at the ceiling. A year ago, I was happy. Nothing was missing from my life. Not even an omega. We wanted one. Waited for one. But an omega would only add to our happiness, not make it.

I was less than a shell now. With no will or desire to change that. Part of me thought I'd just stay in this room and never leave again. My will said that wherever I die, I was to be buried with my pack. So, I could let that end come and join them.

And yet, I couldn't do that. They wouldn't be happy to see me. They'd be mad I'd thrown my life away. But how do you convince someone you have no life without them?

Sitting up, I stared around the room. There wasn't even a book here. No magazines. Not even an empty notebook. I had zero hobbies. The only form of entertainment was my television. And my phone, I supposed, though I hadn't touched more than the dial pad since I left my old life.

Drumming my fingers on my leg, I decided that maybe I'd go to the store. See if I can find something that I'd like to cook. My meals typically came in the form of ready to heat so I didn't have to so much as turn on my stove. I used to enjoy cooking, but it was time we'd spent together as a pack. I haven't cooked since. I hadn't used more than the microwave since I'd been here.

I slipped back into clothes and left. I'd purchased a car when I arrived in Ocean City, but I barely took it out. Usually, I let Nora use it to run errands for the shop. Otherwise, I sent it in for maintenance and ignored it. Even now, the grocery store was only two blocks away, so I opted to walk.

It was a short stretch to the end of the street before I turned left. The block of storefronts was short before I crossed another road. And then the cemetery spanned for quite a way on my left. It crossed many blocks on that side of the road and swept well beyond and through the city.

I turned my back on it and crossed the road to the grocery store. The store smelled fresh and clean, filled with the subtle scents of produce and the shoppers. I didn't mind the grocery store for it, too, had very good ventilation. These are the things you don't think about when you're happy. But when you're trying to drown out the world, too many strong scents can make you crazy.

I wandered through the meat aisle for a while, waiting for something to give me inspiration. When nothing did, I headed for produce. I'd always enjoyed roasted vegetables. They weren't the same when they were pre-roasted and then you had to reheat them.

The stalks of broccoli were beautiful, and I paused to look at them. But what would I make with broccoli? Hell, did I even remember how to cook it?

I sighed as I picked one up. With it came the clean scent of rosemary and sage and I groaned, feeling it rush through me like a current. Is that what broccoli smells like? It can't have been *that* long since I'd smelled fresh broccoli.

"Terence?"

I froze at the quiet voice. I knew, *I knew*, that this delicious scent that made me spark wasn't broccoli. It was Marley. Kaiser's perfume had been too overwhelming to actually register it before, but my body knew it.

Tense, I shifted until I found her. She was holding onto a cart as she looked at me with concern. "Would you like me to speak to the broccoli for you?" she asked, a hint of a smile on her lips.

The question was so absurd that I laughed, startling myself since I hadn't heard the sound in so long. Her smile grew and my heart raced.

"Sorry," I said, shaking my head as I dropped the broccoli into my basket. "I was wondering if I remembered how to cook it."

"Well, I suggest you clean it and then blanch it first. That first shock helps to retain whatever else you want to do with it."

I nodded, feeling a smile plant itself on my face. "Thanks. And what do you suggest I make with it?"

"Mm," she said, the sound racing through me like she'd run her delicate fingers over my body. I stifled another shiver. "Are you interested in healthy or savory?"

I shook my head. "I have no preference at this point." I released a breath, letting the reality of my life settle back on my shoulders. "I think whatever you suggest would be fine. It would save me from having to decide on my own."

"Well," Marley said as she rounded her cart to get closer to me. I stilled as I stared at her. The gentle brush of her scent grazed me, and my eyes fluttered shut before I could stop them. Marley chose three large heads of broccoli for herself and placed them in the cart. "I'm gathering ingredients for three broccoli dishes. Kaiser lost a bet and now he gets broccoli for the night. If you'd like to join me, I can give you some ideas."

I found the smile still touching my lips as I thought about Marley punishing Kaiser by feeding him broccoli. "Yea. Tell me about the punishment."

"Technically it's a chastisement, but I'm sure he considers it punishment, too," Marley said, smirking.

I loved her lips. Soft and delicate roses. Perfectly shaped, and when she smiled, I had the sudden urge to brush my fingers against them. When she spoke, I wanted to bite them, just to see what other sounds I could coax from her perfect mouth.

No. Focus. Broccoli. We're talking about broccoli.

I followed Marley through the produce section as she loaded her car with cranberries, carrots, cauliflower, onion, tomatoes, and lemons. I followed her further still as she hunted down fresh cheeses, almonds, bacon from the butcher counter, and cream. We stopped at the fruit and picked up some mandarin oranges.

"What about dessert?" Marley asked, pausing at an intersection to peer down the aisle.

I didn't think she was talking to me, but I asked, "Do you plan to make it with broccoli?"

She flashed me a smile and my stomach fluttered in appreciation. "No. That sounds dreadful. But I could make it green, so Kaiser thinks it is! He'll be mortified."

I found myself smiling with her, as if I were in on her scheme. It sounded delightful, a whole lot of fun and pouting and teasing. The same kinds of things that Emery would do to Miles.

The thought didn't sober me like it typically would have. Probably because Marley turned her cart and headed down the aisle. We were looking at pudding mixes and pie crusts. "I can't go with lime or mint," she said, taping her chin. "They're too easily discernible by scent." She looked at me. "What do you think?"

Her eyes were gorgeous. Bright, shining like they were backlit. I blinked a couple times to clear out the cobwebs. "I think you don't focus on flavor at all. Use food dye to turn it green."

She lit up and I swear, my soul soared. I only barely caught the purr from bursting from me as she gave me an approving smile. "Oh, he's going to be horrified!" She turned back to the aisle to reconsider her options.

I was too busy fighting my own internal struggles to note what she'd decided on. I stared at her between forcing myself to look away and telling myself to behave. It was at this moment that I spotted the bite on her shoulder, just barely peeking out from under her shirt.

My stomach dropped. My heart stuttered. Of course, she had an alpha. No omega would be wandering around with a beta like this if they didn't have an alpha. I swallowed the sudden lump in my throat and started to turn away.

"Terence?"

I paused at my name on her lips. Fuck that felt good and like a knife at the same time. I looked her way. Again, there was concern in her gaze.

"Are you okay?"

I nodded but I couldn't get words out.

"Do you need anything else?"

I didn't remember if I did. So, I shook my head.

Marley smiled and steered us both to the front by taking the side of the basket in my hand. She didn't speak anymore as she pushed me into line in front of her. I would have let her go first but I think she trapped me there so I couldn't run away.

Though I still could have. The cashier handed me my single bag and I stepped out of line. But I found that I'd paused as I waited for Marley to cash out. I admired the way she spoke to the young cashier. How she smiled and put the young woman at ease. How she thanked her as she loaded up her cart.

Then she turned that quiet, beautiful smile to me. "Thanks for waiting," she said, a tinge of pink in her cheeks.

Again, no words formed as I nodded and walked beside her to the automatic doors. They opened and I let her go ahead of me. Instead of turning for the sidewalk, I walked Marley to her car.

"Now, don't give away my torture plan," she said, glancing up at me with a teasing smile.

I started to ask her what she meant but then the driver door of the car in front of us opened and out stepped her omega. My feet dug into the pavement for a moment before I regained my composure.

Kaiser stared at me with big eyes, a barely contained smile on his mouth. A mouth I wanted to suck on.

No. Jesus fuck, no!

"Hi," Kaiser said as he moved forward, grabbing the cart from Marley, and pushing it around the back of the car.

Marley grinned at him as he started to load the bags into the trunk, his attention more on me than what he was doing. He finished quickly and closed the trunk before turning to look at me. He bit his lip and a whole slew of images flashed through my mind concerning his teeth and lips.

I forced a breath out, relieved that the wind was not blowing at me but away.

"Hi," I finally answered.

My single word made him smile wider. "Do you always shop here?"

I washed a hand over my face and looked across the road at the cemetery. It had the effect I'd hoped for. Dampening. Chilling. "No," I told him quietly. "I usually have my groceries delivered."

"He needed to talk to some broccoli," Marley said.

I tried to fight the smile as I looked at her. And the sweet little thing winked at me. Again, I cut off my purr before it was more than a hint. "It needs to be shredded," I said, my lame attempt at... what? Please tell me this wasn't flirting.

Marley grinned, turning to look at Kaiser again.

Kaiser was looking between us, smiling with giddiness and excitement. "I hate broccoli, so that sounds like a cathartic thing to do with it."

"He'll like it when I'm done," Marley said as she pulled the cart towards her and turned to push it into the nearby corral.

"I won't," Kaiser muttered, shaking his head after her.

I didn't miss the way his gaze scanned the area. Almost as if he were watching over his own omega. Making sure she wasn't going to be bothered. His focus remained on Marley until she was back.

"Thanks for keeping me company," Marley said to me, a soft smile on her features again.

"Thank you for the recipes," I countered, lifting my bag in

response. I waved as I turned and started towards the road to cross it. I knew they were watching. I could feel their eyes on me, tracking me as I crossed the road.

Following me as I started walking down the street. And then the wind changed, and I received a face full of washed-out Kaiser perfume. Pine and cinnamon. Mixed in with it was the hint of rosemary and sage.

I groaned, my footsteps faltering, as my body heated up in a way it hasn't in far too long. I looked into the cemetery to remind myself why it was inappropriate.

CHAPTER FIVE

Kaiser

I watched him walk away, frustrated and irritated at the same time. I could see his reaction to me. Never mind that, I could smell it. His pheromones filled the air as soon as he got close. A delicious grounding flavor of toasted almonds and... mineral oil? Whatever it was, it reminded me of a spa. Putting my body on high alert.

Marley walked into my side, and I met her gaze. I'd always wanted a pack with a girl. I'd imagined a female alpha, but this was better. There was enough alpha with Phynn and Adrian. I liked the calming soothing presence of the little beta better. She wasn't as big and intense as our alphas.

"Let's go home," Marley said. "I have cooking to do."

I scowled at her before urging her to the side of the car and opening the door. She smiled at me, reaching up on her toes to kiss me before dropping gracefully into the seat.

I let out a breath and shut the door, turning towards the opposite side of the street. Terence was just crossing the street beyond the cemetery. He wasn't far enough away that I lost him completely in the crowd milling about but it was getting close. So, I watched until he disappeared before turning to the driver seat.

"What did you really talk about?" I asked her, hoping she'd say they were talking about me.

"Broccoli dishes," she said, grinning at me. "He apparently wanted broccoli but didn't know what to make with it. He's got the ingredients to make one of the recipes I'm making tonight."

I appreciated her pride in the statement, even as I internally pouted a little. I thought that maybe it had been a fluke thing at the gym. Maybe there were too many unfamiliar alphas around and the combination of them had triggered my overly horny omega self. I'd heard their reactions. It was the same I got everywhere I went, especially since my bites were somewhat hidden.

I didn't hide them intentionally. But Adrian's bite was on my shoulder which was under my shirt. And Phynn's was on my ribs. Neither were in places that were readily visible when I dressed normally. Marley's were more visible. Adrian's was on the fleshy part of her neck and shoulder and Phynn's mirrored it on the back side. As long as her hair wasn't covering it and she wasn't wearing a scarf, usually they were seen.

We went out together often. I've been with my pack for seven years now. A pack that consisted of the two alphas and this lovely beta. They were one in a whole slew of pack cards that I ordered. I hadn't even smelled them until my Guardian and I were driving there. And damn, I wanted to bathe in them as soon as I smelled them. And that was it. They were my pack. And they were even better in person.

My first heat was what I'd always dreamed about. You know, mind-numbingly good sex with people who wanted me. Who took care of me and spoiled me. They'd only gotten better with time. I wasn't forced to stay home and hide. I wasn't a decoration for their mantel. I was a proper member of the pack.

Having said that, I didn't work. And they brought me gifts all the time. Still. Even though courting ended years ago. And the three of us spoiled our little beta, as well. Marley was sweet and quiet and soft. I loved to just wrap around her and hold her while she sighed into me.

I also loved to bury myself in her while I loaded her with my release.

Growing up omega, you're always told that your orgasms were plentiful. No one really emphasized that that meant messy with a whole lot of excess cum. It was kind of gross and messy. My pack didn't care. In fact, I was pretty sure they enjoyed it.

On the other hand, I was mortified. Horrified. Embarrassed enough that I wanted to hide for a week after my first time with my pack.

I pulled into our garage and turned the car off. The garage door lowered as the door to the house opened and our alphas stepped through. Adrian looked like the alter ego of a superhero. He had long dark hair, a strong, lean jaw with a shadow of his day's growth. His eyes were a warm brown. And his body was swoon worthy.

Phynn was just as beautiful with lighter golden hair and a rough scruff of facial hair to go with it. His eyes were bright blue. And his body was just as hard, though leaner than Adrian's.

They were fucking gorgeous. It was no wonder I was in a constant state of arousal. I mean, that came with being an omega anyway, but it was on higher alert when my alphas were around.

Except I was still somewhat pouting when I climbed out of the car as my alphas and beta retrieved the bags from the trunk.

I followed them in, hanging the key on the hook as I stepped inside. I lingered in the doorway to the kitchen as they started to unload all the broccoli and things Marley was going to make with the broccoli.

"Was there any trouble?" Adrian asked.

Marley shook her head, smiling in his direction. He leaned down to kiss her, a soft purr meeting my ears. Marley made me want to purr most days and I hadn't figured out how to make that happen.

"Come here, Kaiser," Phynn said.

I sighed heavily as I came into the room and sat on a stool to watch Marley make a green dinner.

"What's wrong, floof?" Phynn asked, pressing his lips to my temple. He liked to say that I laid with my 'supple' ass on display and my legs out like a husky does their floofy butt. And so, Phynn calls me floof. I didn't even care. I secretly loved it. I have a nice ass.

Marley met my eyes before turning to bring the vegetables to the sink. We hadn't mentioned Terence from the gym even though we'd talked about him while we were there, following his scent into the room that was heaviest with it and imagining him moving through it. We'd discussed him on the way home, reasoning out that it was just the strong alpha pheromones at the gym that I'd reacted to.

I'd let her get out of saying she enjoyed it, too. I didn't have any issues taking that on myself.

But I know differently now. I could feel her through the bonds we shared with our alphas. I could smell that her scent spiked in his presence in the same way it did with our alphas. And I knew her looks. I knew, *I saw*, that she was into this man as much as I was.

"Kaiser," Phynn pushed, the slightest hint of a bark in his tone.

I dropped my chin into my hands, resting my elbows on the counter. "The other day when Marley and I went to the gym, we ran into an alpha there." Adrian and Phynn stilled as I spoke. Generally speaking, an omega bringing up an alpha outside his own couldn't lead to a good conversation. "We reasoned away our reaction – my reaction – that there was a bunch of alphas around and, you know, my stupid omega nature."

Phynn kissed me. I didn't actually mind being an omega. It didn't bother me. Not the little bouts of jealousy or that I was prone to pouting. Not even wanting to be the center of attention and affection. I liked that they wanted to wrap me up and take care of me. I loved little surprises and gifts and being spoiled. I didn't even mind the unnecessary excess of cum or how easily I orgasmed anymore. I didn't mind that I was constantly aroused and ready.

That didn't change that I was a man and could act as such outside of my designation. I wasn't an omega named Kaiser. I was Kaiser. And I happen to be an omega.

But sometimes, in instances where my reaction comes faster than I can reason through it, I get frustrated with being an omega and the biology that comes with it. Hence my subtle dig at myself and Phynn kissing me to soothe it away.

"I'd be lying if I said I hadn't thought of him since, but it wasn't enough that I constantly looked for him or anything," I said, shifting as Phynn pulled me closer to his side. I sighed and let him snuggle me into him. "But Marley came out of the store with him and... it's like he was you. Not *you* you but one of my alphas. The way my whole body responded. The way I perfumed. The way I nearly jumped for him."

"Why would you-?"

"Because I *wanted to*. He didn't bark at either of us. Despite his hugeness, it almost feels like he doesn't have a bark.

But, Phynn, he smiled, and I almost creamed myself just looking at him."

Phynn laughed quietly at the scowl in my voice.

"He's huge," Marley said. "Big arms. Big, thick legs. Broad shoulders." She looked at Adrian. "I swear, he's going to burst from his t-shirts if he doesn't buy bigger ones soon. And he's sweet. He smells sooo good."

We were lucky. Our alphas weren't overly jealous. Not of each other and not when we commented on someone else. Even as wrung up as I was right now, I knew how fortunate I was to have this kind of pack.

"Well, what do you want to do?" Phynn asked.

My stomach fluttered. My cock hardened. I groaned, closing my eyes.

"If you feel this strongly about him, let's meet him," Adrian said.

I sat up straight and looked at him. Adrian was the head of our house. He was an alpha of alphas. I'd never heard or met anyone who's bark was louder than his. But he was kind, generous, and thoughtful. Something you'd not expect from the most dominant of men.

"Really?" I asked, almost falling from the stool.

Marley turned and looked at me. But she wasn't smiling. There was a frown pinching her brows together. "Honey, I know you're excited about him, but I don't think that's going to be as easy as you think," she told me.

"Of course, it is. I have biology on my side."

Marley rolled her eyes, even as a smile touched her lips. "I mean it, Kaiser. There's very clearly something going on there."

"What do you mean?" Phynn asked.

"When he saw Kaiser in the gym, he looked terrified. When Kaiser tried to shake his hand, he backed away and basically ran from us. He relaxed with me in the store today, but something happened towards the end. The smiles were gone. The almost light, carefree demeanor was crushed under something dark in his eyes. And as soon as he got close to Kaiser in the parking lot, he was ready to run again, which he did pretty quickly."

"He's not scared of me," I scoffed.

Marley shook her head. "No. But there's something about you that bothers him. I don't actually think it's you personally. It's just exaggerated when you're near."

"Like what?" I asked, frowning at her. "That's like the exact opposite response I've ever seen an omega get from anyone! How can I repulse the alpha I want?!"

Marley's smile turned sympathetic and sweet as Phynn held me tighter to him, as if he could squeeze the idea out of me. But Marley was right. I'd been so caught up in my reaction to him that I'd missed initially noting Terence's reaction to me.

And it had not been the drooly, greedy response. It was very much a run away with your tail between your legs. Very un-alpha like.

"I don't know," Marley said, gently. "I really don't think it has anything to do with you specifically, Kaiser. He shut down on me too in the store and we were simply talking about desserts."

"Oh no," I said, cringing at her. "You're not putting broccoli in dessert, are you?"

Her grin turned smug as she returned to the sink and the vegetables.

I let the thought of food dissipate as I turned my thoughts back to Terence. I twisted so my face was smothered in Phynn's chest and took a deep breath. I shuddered as the clean almond cherry flavor skittered through me, leaving me with the familiar happy, content, horny feeling.

Okay, distress is under control now. What to do about an

errant alpha that runs away from me? Ugh, how did I get dealt this hand? Was I too needy? Too whiny? Is it so much to ask to have my alphas fall at my feet when I wanted them?

I supposed my alphas didn't fall at my feet, but both of them would get on their knees if I asked them to. Sometimes I did, but I was typically too eager for their knots for that kind of patience. During heats I received more head than any other time while they tried to sate my hunger and fever. But then, I was too lost in a heat haze at that point to notice. I knew it happened. I was there. But I had no actual, vivid memories of those moments. Just one long recollection of endless pleasure. And begging for more when they were slowing down if I wasn't ready for a break.

'Break' was putting it rather tamely. I needed to be fucked into exhaustion to give *them* a break. That was all biology. That was a heat. I was glad to have never had to suffer a heat without my pack. I could only imagine how miserable that would be.

My next heat wasn't due to set in for another month or so. My life was easy and filled with luxury and leisure. With my environment stable and stress-free, my heat cycle was every five months or so. Sometimes a little longer. Because I had the longer breaks between, they lasted a solid four days but there was like six days leading up to it that I was constantly spiking. And then another couple following the downward spiral of aftershock spikes.

Yes, being an omega was a blast.

I closed my eyes, melting into Phynn's side as he rubbed his fingers into my hair. His soft purr ran through me, making me sigh in contentment. I turned my attention inward, reaching for Marley's bond.

There was the normal feel to it. Happy. Relaxed. Shy but comfortable. But then there. That little bit of hesitancy. The concern but deep interest. That was in response to Terence.

She wasn't wrong. Terence had run away. But he was an alpha. And an alpha always wants his omega. I was sure that that was me. I'd take care of this. I'd bring this alpha home to our pack. All I had to do was figure out how to find him again. For once, biology was on my side and would work to my advantage.

CHAPTER SIX

Terence

I'd made a habit of checking the air for any hints of Kaiser when I stepped into the gym now. Just in case. He'd been there once so it wasn't completely out of the question that he'd show up again. Other than that simple sweep, I pushed both him and Marley far from my mind.

Exhaustion was hard to come by. I needed it to run so deeply that I could just pass out when I got home. No thought. No memories. No nightmares. Just sleep.

To meet this end, I altered my routine. Too tired too quickly wasn't working anymore. I needed the drop after a long pull of endurance. That meant I started small and continued long reps until I got too bored with it that the music no longer drowned out the dullness of the routine.

I also left the fun stuff for the end. The ropes and tires and free weights. I spent most of the day yesterday just hitting the bag. It was almost entirely upper body and it carried me straight through lunch. I used the afternoon to play with the ropes but at that point, I was completely whipped.

I'd also passed out and slept the entire night without a single dream.

I wouldn't go so far as to say I woke up refreshed. My life was still shit. I was still empty and dead. But I had actually slept and that made a world of difference.

The only thing that had been different yesterday was that I'd stayed at the gym until I was ready to pass out. I'd made the morning stretch two hours longer than normal. Maybe I could make a repeat today. So, after my protein shake, I jogged to the gym, taking the long way around the park.

And now, I focused on something simple. Kettlebell swing. Hold the handle with both hands so it rested in front of my junk. With a little bend at the waist and in my knees and hips, I let gravity pull it lower between my legs. Then I used the strength in my core to burst it forward and up before gravity brought it down again.

There was a lot of hip thrusting involved in this. A voice in the back of my mind said it was a good workout to prepare for marathon sex.

Or a heat.

Since neither had any place in my life, I just went with the idea that it was a good way to work my core, my glutes, and my legs – not to mention, getting my metabolism going. There were no set reps to this. I swung it as long as I could until I needed a break. After a break, I started again.

When I got tired of the kettlebells, I went the no-equipment route and did several rotating rounds of burpees and mountain climbers. They are hated for a reason. Since there's nothing needed to do these exercises outside of your own will and determination, it was pure hatred for them that made people avoid them.

It's simple really. They worked on your entire body. Arm strength as you hold yourself up. Leg strength as you jump into the air or climb the mountain. Core strength to keep your middle from sagging and pulling yourself from the ground into the jump.

I did these in alternating rotations until I rolled onto my back and closed my eyes to catch my breath, feeling how my entire body stung with the effort.

In an effort to continue with the whole body exercises, I moved on to the rower. It was such an effortless, mindless routine that it was easy to lose myself in the repetitive motion until I was jelly. I hooked the handle under the grips and rested with my forehead on my knees for several minutes before taking a water break.

One bottle left and I was losing steam.

That meant I could move on to the fun stuff. Battle ropes. I messed with these in intervals of thirty-ten until I crouched on the floor to catch my breath. My body ached and it was an effort to keep my eyes open.

Similar to yesterday. The proper level of exhaustion to facilitate dreamless sleep. Hopefully. It worked once. I just needed to find the proper routine to repeat it.

I pulled the buds from my ears and dropped them into the pocket with my phone before stuffing the empty bottles into my bag and throwing it over my shoulder. I paused in the door, scanning the area filled with machines that separated me from the door.

No omega. No pretty little beta. Home free.

If I'd have had more stamina for the day, I'd have rounded the park. Instead, I crossed through it. Every step made my muscles ache. My eyelids were heavy. It was such a delicious combination that I was eager to get home. Eager to stand under the cold water until it got hot. Eager to fall into my bed and let sleep take me.

First, a juice.

Once again, it was busy in my juice bar. But it was on the quiet end of busy. There was a gentleman at the refrigerator in the back, deciding on what prepared, prepackaged item he wanted. There was a family at the juice jugs, making custom mixes for themselves. And there were three people in line.

"Oh, good," Nora said as she left the counter. "You're later today, Mr. Andersen."

I smiled at her, shrugging. "New routine."

She smiled though I didn't miss the tisking in her tone. She was a lovely beta in her mid-forties. She had a husband and three kids, all of whom constantly visited her. I'd been in on more than one occasion when the youngest one was sitting in the office on a tablet or coloring as she sang. She was four. Or maybe three?

"I have some ideas I'd like to discuss with you," Nora said as she approached me.

Maybe she couldn't see how tired I was. But I nodded and followed her into the back. I nodded to the employees at their stations as I walked into the manager's office. There was a second office, one that I assumed they kept unused in case I ever wanted to be a part of this place in more than name and the occasional opinion.

Nora shut the door and rounded to the side of the desk. She would never sit behind it while I was there, but she didn't want to force me behind it by sitting in front of it either. So, she always stopped at the side, leaving both options available to me.

She pushed a chart in front of me. A graph that had a steady increase. "This is our growth in the last eight months, Mr. Andersen."

"It looks impressive," I told her.

"Yes," she said, smiling up at me before looking back at it. "Most of our customers are from foot traffic. With the park so close and the gym, plus the high school down the road, we have a continuous stream of clients. However, what I'd like to propose is expanding."

"I don't think we're zoned to expand any further. I think we're already at our capacity. There's nowhere to go." Unless we got rid of my apartment upstairs. But... I was not interested in that.

"No, sir. We are certainly maxed out here." Nora shuffled papers around, lining the table with a few more. The one she pointed to looked like a map. She tapped it and I noted the name under it. "The university employs nearly 700 people. There are nearly 4,000 students."

"They're across town, Nora. We're not in the right location for-"

"I know," Nora said gently, cutting me off. She gave me a placating smile, apologizing for being rude as she held up her hands. "There's a storefront that's going to be available soon. It's 900 square feet with a back half the size of what we have here. But for a secondary location, close enough that we can transport the refrigerated beverages for restocking, I think this is an amazing business opportunity."

"You think I want to expand?" I asked her.

"If you don't, I have a second proposition for you," she said, her voice turning more timid and nervous.

"Okay, shoot."

"Sami and I feel strongly about your company. We love it here. You're a great employer and your product is amazing."

"But?"

"No," Nora said, shaking her head. "No buts. We really want to make Juice Me a household name in Ocean City. We have a great market and I think moving towards the college is a smart next move in expansion to make that happen. I understand if you don't want to take that on. But how would you feel if we franchised? There's even a tertiary location that's likely going to be opening up in the business district and the foot traffic there would make our growth huge, Mr. Andersen. We could sell shirts and hats and stickers, too. Especially in the college location."

"You want to open another store of your ownership but with my product?"

"With your permission, of course. And we'd pay you a percentage of sales, too. We'd continue to run everything by you. You get final decision-making power."

"That's not wise if you own the business."

Nora tilted her head to the side. "Okay, I know that. But-"

"You feel this strongly about a second location that you're willing to offer that in order to do so?"

Nora nodded.

"You have three young children, Nora. Where are you going to find the time to run a juice bar? Being an owner is a big responsibility."

Her smile turned a little indulgent and I knew what she was thinking. I bowed my head in acknowledgement. "You understand that the reason I can be as absent as I am is because of you and Sami, right? If you move to another store, I'm going to be forced to find new managers."

"Jakob is ready," Nora said. "And we would never leave you high and dry, Mr. Andersen. Carly is ready for assistant, and Sami and I would rotate being here as the second manager."

I nodded thoughtfully. "What do you have that I can bring home to think about this?"

Nora grinned and opened one of the drawers. She pulled out a neatly clasped report and handed it to me. Always prepared, this girl. This was why I knew she could pull it off.

My only real decision was whether I wanted to own it or allow her to franchise my business.

"I'll get back to you."

"I don't mean to sound ungrateful, but that location is pretty hot, so..."

"Sooner rather than later. Understood."

Nora nodded, smiling.

"I appreciate that you love my shop as much as you do, Nora. Maybe I don't tell you all enough."

"You tell us plenty and we know that," she said, patting my hand. "It's okay Mr. Andersen. I'm not proposing this because I want to leave you and Juice Me. I think the world of this place. I just want the rest of the world to see you, too."

"Alright. I'll look at it and have an answer to you by Friday."

Nora sighed with relief. She didn't argue the two days. Good. Because I was too tired to make a decision right now and didn't want to regret it later.

Nora followed me out as I made my way back to the storefront. There was a single person at the counter as she spoke to Daniel. Carly was behind him at the mixers and she grinned widely when I looked her way.

"Hi, Mr. Andersen," she said and came to the side of the counter. "What would you like today?"

Another decision. Jakob should be here on days I was too tired to do so. I scanned the menu and shook my head. "Surprise me."

Carly looked like I'd just given her a medal. She turned with a skip in her step, her hair bouncing behind her. I watched as she gathered ingredients and started chopping.

The doorbell tinkled behind me once as I watched her dump a handful of various fruits in before turning to the mixings. It tinkled again as she capped the blender and set it on the base. As soon as she turned it on, the pine and cinnamon perfume enveloped my body and I gasped, spinning around to stare at the door.

Kaiser was standing inside the door, his gaze on the menu. He hadn't spotted me yet. Where could I run? How do I hide in my own shop?

Wait, what the fuck was wrong with me?

And then his steel blue eyes turned in my direction and he looked just as caught in the headlights as I was. We stared as if there was no one else there. His brows knit together as a tentative smile touched his lips.

His lips that I wanted to taste.

I swallowed, fisting my hands together, pressing my back into the counter behind me. Fuck me, how do I move around him without getting closer?

"Mr. Andersen?"

I snapped around. The sudden movement made Carly jerk backwards as she looked at me with wide eyes. The first hint of fear flashed in her expression, and I took a breath to school however it was I was looking at her.

"I'm sorry, Carly."

Her smile was weak as she offered me the drink and backed away.

Okay, I'd let out a little too much of what I'd hidden for so long. Maybe I hadn't hidden it. I'd just let it die inside me. But it had clearly surged to the surface in a rather aggressive way. I reached for her hand, and she let me take it. I squeezed it gently. "Really. I apologize. I didn't mean to startle you."

"It's okay," she said, relaxing. She nodded and I let her go.

Taking a breath, I turned for the door again. Kaiser wasn't there because he was standing almost directly behind me. I held my breath as I stared at him.

"Hi," he said, his voice quiet and timid. "I didn't know you came here."

"Silly omega," Nora chided, and I knew what was coming. There was no way for me to tell her to keep it to herself. "Mr. Andersen owns Juice Me."

Kaiser's lips parted as he stared at me with something that looked all too much like awe. "This place has the best juice smoothies anywhere!" he exclaimed, stepping closer in his excitement. His perfume slammed into me as it filled the room, and I couldn't back away any further than I was. Already, I was going to have the impression of the counter in my back. "I had no idea you owned it. That's amazing."

"I do nothing here," I told him, trying to keep my voice even and breathe through my mouth. "I sign checks. The success belongs solely to my employees."

I'd hoped that would dissuade him from looking at me like he was. But I imagined my truth made me sound humble instead of the deadbeat owner I was.

He took another step forward and it was suddenly far too close. I couldn't catch my breath. And if he touched me, I was liable to spin him around and throw him against the bar so I could taste him while he squirmed under me.

The visual was all too real. The desire to do so was nearly crippling. I slid away from him, still holding my breath. "I'm late," I said lamely and rushed to the door without a further explanation.

I wasn't sure what possessed me, but I glanced in the window. He was watching me with confusion. But brighter than that was the hurt shining from his eyes.

Fuck. That stung. And not the kind of sting I liked.

CHAPTER SEVEN

Adrian

We'd thought we were done expanding our pack. We had two alphas, an omega, and a beta. One out of the four of us could bear children. There was no need to expand. Our relationships and pack dynamics were great. As far as I knew, there were no complaints. We were happy.

But I sat back when the hurt bloomed inside me, screaming down the mate bond of my omega and filling me so completely I closed my eyes. I stilled to really listen to it, offering him love and affection in return. It wasn't a physical pain. If it had been, I'd be up and charging to find him, dismembering anyone who had harmed my omega.

This was different. It was a deep ache filled with longing and confusion. I assumed that meant he found the lone alpha and it hadn't gone well. I'd been feeling the piques of interest and arousal since he met Terence. I felt it in quieter, softer notes from Marley, too. There had been confusion from both Kaiser and Marley as they separately tried to figure out what was wrong with their new alpha.

This pain though, that was a new development.

One I was expecting unfortunately. According to Marley, there was something not sitting well with our errant alpha. Something that made him look at Kaiser like he was a disease, not an omega who wanted him. An omega who was basically offering him a mate.

That was my analogy for what Marley described. Based on the way she said he ran from Kaiser every time, it seemed appropriate. A disease he didn't want to catch.

Kaiser was out with Phynn though, so I assumed that Phynn would have Kaiser in hand. He'd nurse our omega back to good spirits, even if that underlying misery remained. It was a longing, pining ache that I knew only too well.

From the moment Kaiser came into our lives, that ache was persistent until I bit him and made him mine. It was only with his forever presence within our bond that I didn't suffer that feeling anymore. But knowing what it felt like never left me. It wasn't something I'd soon forget.

I was sad that he was feeling it now.

It hurt me that my omega hurt, especially when I couldn't do anything about it. There was nothing I could do to soothe this pain outside of finding this alpha myself and see what was up.

That option wasn't off the table. But we weren't to that point. Not yet.

I looked up as Marley paused outside the door to my office. She peered in at me, looking like the beautiful doll she was. I sat back, offering her my lap. Nearly ten years together and our pretty beta still blushed when she walked through my office door.

Marley was tiny. I was sure that she was supposed to be an omega and her biology just never caught up. She was all the sweet and soft and hungry that was our Kaiser with none of the more spoiled sides of him. Omegas expected to be spoiled. To be taken care of and cuddled and coddled, too.

Kaiser tried to push that part out of him, hating how he acted at times; but it was who he was, and we loved even those parts about him. What he identified as negative traits, we knew were just his omeganess. They might bother the man that suffered through them, but the alpha that I was wanted him just like that.

I wanted to cuddle him and coddle him. I wanted to satisfy him until he was sighing happily as he fell asleep. I wanted to give him everything. I strived to put that happy, giddy smile on his face when I gifted him something. It was made even better when he hadn't realized how much he'd wanted whatever I handed him.

More than anything, our omega wanted to be loved and shown that he was loved. He wanted to be wanted and needed, but not just for his designation. Not for the hand that biology gave him. He wanted an identity outside of that. And we enjoyed making sure he had that.

"I once read a story that when a wolf doesn't get their mate, they become almost sick," Marley told me as she perched on my lap as if she thought she was too heavy. I scooped my arms under her, pulling her against my chest as I looked into her face.

"Fortunately, we're not wolves," I told her, rubbing my nose against hers.

"No," she said. "But the way he's hurting kind of feels like that, doesn't it? Like he's sick to his stomach. Lost and miserable?"

I really tried to find something inaccurate with how she

described Kaiser through our bonds. But she was right. "What about you?" I asked.

She sighed. "I think he's going through something and isn't in the right mental place for us right now."

"Maybe you're right. But I didn't ask about him. I asked about you."

Marley smiled, closing her eyes. "I'm not an omega," she said quietly. "My reaction isn't nearly as drastic and consuming."

"But you like him."

"He feels like a comfortable blanket to wrap around me on an exotic island while the ocean breeze grabs at me. Warm and comfortable and always there. He feels like home, Adrian. I don't know how to describe his presence."

I nodded. In the distance, the garage door opened and the engine to the car hummed quietly before shutting down. A moment later, the garage door sounded again as it closed.

"Should we go see what happened?" I asked.

Marley nodded, concern already bright in her face. She could also be an alpha for how much she craved taking care of Kaiser. Taking care of all of us, really.

I picked her up, carrying her in my arms like a small child against my chest. One of my favorite things was carrying Marley around when she'd let me. I think that Kaiser's misery was resounding loudly within her because she wanted this alpha, too. So, she was going to let me dote on her for a little while. Coddle her, just a little, while she nursed her own quiet longing.

Phynn and Kaiser were in the kitchen with three bags on the counter and two smoothies. But Phynn had a sniffling Kaiser in his arms as he held him tightly. I immediately ached, longing to hold him, too. To make whatever discomfort he was feeling go away by whatever means necessary.

I stayed where I was with our little beta in my arms instead as we watched them.

"Did something happen?" Marley asked.

Kaiser was only four inches shorter than Phynn but right now, it looked like Phynn could wrap around him three times. "He owns the juice bar," Kaiser said, peeking out over Phynn's bicep.

"Really?" Marley asked, perking up. "Juice Me?"

Kaiser nodded, not at all enthusiastic about it. "His last name is Andersen."

Marley nodded, dampened by his apathy.

Phynn met my gaze before gently pushing Kaiser into the living room and down onto the couch. I brought Marley and followed, sitting nearly on top of them so the four of us were all touching in some way.

"Start talking, omega," Marley said gently, brushing her fingers through his hair.

Kaiser somehow managed to curl into all three of us as he sought comfort from his pack. "There isn't anything to tell. He looked at me just like you said he did, Mar. Like he wanted nothing to do with me. He all but climbed behind the counter to get away. He burst forth so quickly when he saw me that he scared one of his employees and had to backtrack and apologize enough to her so she wouldn't be afraid of him again. He acted like a cornered mouse, terrified of me. And then he ran out the door. By the time I gathered enough courage to follow him, he was gone."

Phynn's purr was quiet as he rubbed gently along Kaiser's back. He was looking at me, his lips pressed together, confirming it as Kaiser said.

"But I don't understand," Kaiser continued. "Before he knew I was there, I barely felt his presence. When he saw me, his pheromones filled the room. He leaned *forward* first, before he knew what he was doing. Before he tried to push his way back through the counter to get away. He was trying not to breathe my perfume." He picked his head up to look at me. His brows were knit together in confusion, but it was barely noted as the sorrow covered his face. "We can't fight biology. I know that more than anyone. But he's trying like his life depends on it."

"Marley's right in her reading of the situation, I think. There's something going on that has nothing to do with you, love," I told him.

"But how do I make it go away? How do I get him to talk to me, so I know what he needs me to do so he stops running from me?" he asked, his voice wobbling.

I didn't have an answer for him. Without knowing this man, without knowing what haunted him, I couldn't even begin to guess on how to help either of them.

Cupping the back of Kaiser's head, I pulled him down, so he was snuggled against Marley's chest as I considered the options. But really, there weren't any yet. If the alpha didn't want anything to do with us, we couldn't force it. A cornered alpha was dangerous. A desperate one was more so.

CHAPTER EIGHT

Terence

I paused inside the door to the gym and closed my eyes. Nope. No omega.

I slept decently most of the night last night, until I woke up just before dawn. The sleep that I got between then and seven had been filled with grief. Exhaustion only took me so far.

With that in mind, I headed straight for the tires. I brought myself through a series of random exercises, whatever caught my interest as I went. I watched as one of the betas ran around the room as he carried a tire.

Thinking I'd end the day with that, I stepped inside one of the tires for my last workout. Hooking my hands under the lip of the inner ring, I stood, letting out a puff of breath. Yep, this was enough cardio and strength to end the day with.

I didn't run because I'd been greatly overestimating how fast the beta was going. Not only could you not spread your gait wide enough for a run, but it was pretty impossible to move that quickly and continue to breathe.

Even so, I enjoyed the burn in my chest. The strain in my arms and the ache in my legs and ass muscles. Sweet, delicious pain. I lost myself in the laps, pausing every three for a swallow of water before starting up again.

His perfume hit me in the gut as soon as I laid eyes on him. I froze, dropping the tire and falling to the ground with it. My ass hit the edge and I let out a harsh breath while I sat there. My chest heaved as I tried to breathe any air but that which was laced with Kaiser.

The omega remained in the doorway as he stared at me. I could see the horrified look on his face as he stood rooted to the spot. He needed to remain there while I caught my breath. Another minute. Maybe two.

But then he was in front of me, kneeling on the sweaty mat as he looked at me in concern. The grimy floor. I cringed at the thought that this omega was touching the dirty mat.

"I'm sorry," he said. "I didn't know you were carrying around a giant tire that probably weighs as much as I do."

"Likely more," I told him, glancing up to meet his eyes.

I'd never been quite so close to him. His steel blue eyes were gorgeous. As was his perfect face and features. I'd been right before. His tanned skin was natural, not artificially gotten. I'd wager a guess to say it wasn't even from the sun. He was simply just this perfect.

"Are you okay?" he asked, resting a hand on the tire.

No, no, no. Don't touch the tire. It's disgusting!

I shuddered and nodded. Probably. I had dropped the tire and let myself fall with the weight. I knew how to fall without getting hurt. Even if the movement should have hurt.

"Yea. Tire caught me."

He smiled and I almost choked on my tongue. Goddam.

Sure, they warn you about this growing up, but it's a fucking trip experiencing it. A painful and all-consuming trip at that. I was trying to breathe very little so my head didn't just melt.

"One dinner, Terence," he said, and my eyes went wide. "Please, just one dinner."

I think I probably stared dumbly for an entire minute.

"One dinner," he said again, lowering his voice to softer octaves as he pleaded at me with his eyes. "I know you don't like me, but I promise, I'm not an awful person."

"What?" I asked in confusion.

"Do- do you not like my perfume?" he asked, his voice timid. I swear there was a hint of tears in his eyes as he looked at me with uncertainty.

My mouth hung open like a fool as I continued to stare at him stupidly. "Kaiser," I said, shaking my head. "I like it fine." What else could I possibly say? That he was going to make me come undone by just existing? That seemed a little over the top.

"One dinner, Terence. Please. Just once. Let me show you I can be a good omega," he said quietly.

I groaned. Fuck, I'd been a huge asshole. "Kaiser, I-"

"Please, please don't tell me no. Just one dinner."

I didn't think I could tell him no when he was sitting right in front of me. Touching gross sweaty mats and dirty tires just to get me to take him to dinner.

And yet, I tried desperately to shake my head. I nodded instead. And damn, his face lit up like a child on Christmas. He pulled his phone out and handed it to me, already unlocked and on the dial pad.

"You don't have to do anything but pick me up," Kaiser said. "I'll take care of everything else."

I felt absolutely helpless and utterly pathetic. I took his phone and started tapping in numbers. How much of a shit would I be if I gave him a bogus number? I was going to have to find a new gym if I did that. Hell, I'd have to find a new city.

Even so, I meant to give him Juice Me's number. But when I handed the phone back, it was my cell phone that I'd punched in.

He was beaming at me. Ridiculously pleased by my agreement. How could he ignore the fact that I was an awful alpha for making an omega chase me? For making him beg me to take him out? Why didn't that matter to him? Why was he still looking at me like I was worthy of him?

Kaiser took the phone, being mindful not to touch me since I was being such a damn pansy. "I'll text you later." He got to his feet and nearly skipped out the room, waving to me as he went.

I stared after him, horrified at what I'd just agreed to.

One of my water bottles was dropped into my lap and I looked up to find one of the betas that was often in the room with me grinning down at me. "Looks like you might pass out, alpha."

I groaned, letting myself fall further into the tire with a scowl. "Thanks," I muttered.

Since I didn't have to avoid Kaiser anymore today, I didn't wear myself out so thoroughly. Stopping at the juice bar should be easy and pleasant. You know, if Carly wasn't working and looking at me like I might explode.

I swallowed down the rest of my water and packed up. I walked outside the park this time, not through it. No hurry. Never in a hurry.

It was before the lunch rush when I walked in so there were only a handful of customers milling about. Carly was behind the counter. I swear, that girl worked every day. She smiled brightly at me and greeted me as she always did. At least I hadn't scarred her.

Nora looked up at Carly's greeting, as did Daniel, the third employee on. He bowed his head to me and returned to what he was doing.

"A word, Nora?" I asked as I headed for the back door.

Nora followed a minute later and met me in the office. The desk was cleaned of the loose papers that had been there yesterday. She stopped at the edge, still allowing me to take the seat in front of or behind the desk as my spot.

I took neither but handed her back her bound proposal. I read it over this morning while I drank my breakfast shake. I'd tried to make a concentrated effort of truly studying it. Once, I might have been better at doing so. I didn't have that kind of interest in life these days.

She looked at me with hope shining in her eyes.

I didn't *need* to open a second location. I was by no means hurting for money. After liquidizing my pack's assets and the sale of our house, I spread the money through a handful of bank accounts. I probably didn't need to even keep Juice Me. I did because Zack had loved it.

I wasn't a billionaire. But I could live comfortably if I chose. And since all I wanted to do is barely survive, I was fine with money.

But Nora was a good employee. Between her and Sami, they'd done great things for this store. Zack would have approved. And would have adored them. He would have agreed with enthusiasm, bursting with a ton of ideas that they'd gush over.

She wouldn't get that kind of energy from me.

"We'll open a second store," I told her, and she shrieked with excitement. I smiled, shaking my head. "The only reason I'm not franchising is because I'd rather you spend your efforts on your family. I know I make this look easy but owning a business can be time consuming and challenging. It's not because I have you and Sami. So, here's the deal. You handle it all. Everything. I want to continue my role of signing checks and nixing anything that's going to bankrupt this place. I'll have my accountant and attorney be in touch with you so that you can legally act on my behalf. I'll need to continue to sign payroll checks and anything over $10,000. And if you're looking to knock down walls or set up a haunted cooler, run those ideas by me first. Deal?"

Nora was still jumping up and down, her hands clasped in front of her. "Yes!"

It was nice that I could make one person happy. And this time it was something they deserved to be happy about. Kaiser needed to have his taste checked. I was a fucking disaster on two legs, and I'd never given him any indication to the contrary. But this was a positive move. Something good for Nora.

I really didn't care in the least whether it was a positive for my business. Nora was a damn good manager. She deserved this. That I could give it to her was enough.

"Take care of hiring. Another manager for this store to replace Sami, who will move to the second location. Move Jakob up. Carly as assistant. And work on hiring me a new Carly. Starting pay matches what we pay here. You will move between the two. But first, secure the real estate and get the construction under way. Then we'll talk."

"I will, Mr. Andersen. I won't let you down."

"I know you won't," I told her, resting my hand on the side of her face. She calmed and sighed, looking at me with a continuous beaming smile. "I'm agreeing to this because you've worked your ass off. Not because I care to expand. You understand that, right?"

Nora nodded. Her face softened and for a horrifying second, I thought she was going to bring up my pack. But she didn't. "I appreciate that, Mr. Andersen. I really do love this place and I want to see the world take note. And despite what you think, you're a pretty good boss."

"Mm," I snorted. "I'm going to get my smoothie and head home. You have my number for an emergency."

"I'm going to call Sami and the real estate broker for the shop before I come out."

I nodded and left the office, shutting the door on the way. I didn't think we'd been in there long but when I stepped back into the shop, there were more than a dozen people waiting at the counter with only Carly and Daniel behind it. I thought there were four per shift who worked up front?

Daniel was good at the blender but not nearly as good as Jakob. He ran two at a time and only two. I sighed and stepped behind the short gate.

"What can I do?" I asked.

Carly stopped and stared for a minute before glancing at Daniel. "You know how to run the register, Mr. Andersen?" she asked.

"Nope."

"How about blend smoothies?"

"I can turn on the blender, yes," I told her, flashing her a smile.

Daniel snorted, shaking his head.

Carly sighed, looking at the customers. "How about cutting fruits?"

"Yes, now you've tapped into my skill set."

She laughed and took one of the small bowls from a customer and handed it to him. "Chop these and toss them in a blender. Then let Daniel finish it," she instructed.

"Yes, ma'am," I told her, turning to the bench. I paused long enough to wash my hands. No one needed tire sweat in their smoothie.

I made a serious mess in chopping, something that Daniel

enjoyed ribbing me over, but I found that the whole experience was rather relaxing. Even with the hustle and bustle of the lunch rush. I found a rhythm in chopping whatever was given my way before sliding it along down to Daniel. I didn't know what he did to finish it off but before I knew it, the crowd had calmed and the shop was empty.

I picked up the remaining smoothie and frowned. Had I chopped too many bowls?

"Yours," Carly told me. "You earned it. On the house today."

I laughed, taking a sip of it. Yep, good. Not Jakob good, but fucking good. It tasted all the better now that I knew exactly what went into this. I looked up as Nora came out of the back and stared with wide eyes.

"Oh, no," she said, looking horrified. "I'm so sorry. I didn't mean for that to take so long."

Carly shrugged. "We taught him the ropes."

"It'll never happen again. I swear. Gina's kid is sick, so we were short an employee this shift. I'm so sorry. So, so sorry."

Her apologies were for me. It hadn't taken Carly or Daniel long to figure that out. I retrieved my bag from where I'd tossed it on the floor around the corner and crossed back to the side of the counter I belonged on.

I patted Nora's shoulder. She flinched in embarrassment. "Give them raises. I didn't realize how stressful that can be. I'm going home."

Nora nodded.

"And hire a couple extra bodies for call out purposes. I'm sure you can find plenty for them to do, Nora."

"Yes, Mr. Andersen."

"Good. Have a nice afternoon."

The little bell over the door jingled on my way out. I sipped my smoothie as I headed home. My routine picked up as if I never left it. Through the door. Up the stairs. Kicked off my shoes before I got inside. Drop the bag inside the door and set the smoothie on the table. Strip on the way to shower.

Ice-cold water as my teeth rattled until it had a minute to heat up. And then I sighed, closing my eyes to let the water wash the day off. It wasn't a bad day but a day, nonetheless.

I'd almost forgotten. I lay back on the bed and closed my eyes as the quiet of my small apartment settled in. Quiet and soothing. The peace almost lulled me to sleep until my phone pinged.

Maybe Nora had already run into an obstacle.

Pulling myself from the bed, I headed for my bag and pulled my phone out. It was flashing red. Needed a recharge. Since I never used it outside of music, I forgot to charge it regularly.

But the notification was from an unprogrammed number.

I opened it and my heart stopped.

[6549] Hi, Terence. It's Kaiser. Thursday. Pick me up at 6. Reservations are at 6:30 at Big Italia. Please don't cancel.

It followed with his address.

And suddenly the world went dark all around me except for the screen with his text message. What had I done?

CHAPTER NINE

Terence

The feel of the blade against my neck was a rush. So sharp, a simple nick could run deep. But Foster was an expert at the single blade, close shaves. He'd been using them on himself since he was a teenager.

The cool of it ran over just the curve of my neck and then under my jaw. A single smooth motion. He was both quick and took his time. Efficiency at its finest.

I was sitting on the vanity with my head tipped back, Foster between my legs. One of his hands was on my thigh while he hovered close to assure a clean and close shave.

"This really is a whole lot easier on another person," Foster said. "I can see what I'm doing at all times. And yet, it feels like it takes three times as long since the angle is all new."

I smiled slightly as he took the blade away to wipe it on a towel. I didn't speak. This wasn't a time to speak unless I wanted a new scar.

He finished up and wrapped my face in a warm, damp towel

to soothe my skin as he cleaned the blade. When he took the towel away, I watched as he rubbed aftershave between his hands before rubbing it on me just as expertly as he had done the shaving.

Then he stopped, dropping both hands to my thighs. His smile was proud and gorgeous. "Hot," he said, winking at me.

I chuckled, leaning in to kiss him. He tasted like mints. All the time, as if the flavor coursed through his blood.

————

MONTHLY, Foster would give me a shave. I loved the feel of my skin after the shave. But for years, I'd tried to match his skill on myself, and I'd end up with more tiny lacerations than anything. So, I stuck to an electric razor.

The man I stared at in the mirror did not have that clean, close shave. I couldn't even bring myself to use the same aftershave. I wasn't in that good of a headspace. Sometimes, I get the urge for that close shave. I could go to a barber and have it done, but I was afraid I'd break down in the chair from all the memories that would surge through me. Hell, I wasn't in a good headspace, period.

I had no idea what the hell I was thinking. Agreeing to a date. With an omega. Absolute insanity. This could only end in disaster; end with me hurting him when he didn't deserve it.

He already had alphas. I was sure. Positive. I caught a whiff of their scent each time Kaiser was close. But only a hint since his perfume was so strong.

I rubbed my face and eyes until I was a rosy shade of pink and turned away. I didn't give myself a clean shave. It was close but the lines were messy, and I made no effort to change them. My hair was getting shaggy and nearly unmanageable.

If I were a better alpha, I'd go to the barber to make sure I was presentable for this omega.

But maybe subconsciously, I was trying to self-sabotage. I know, what was the point? He's already seen me dripping with sweat. A couple times. I've made a complete fool of myself as I *ran away* from an omega and beta. A couple times.

Weak. Pathetic. Disgusting. That's what I was.

I turned away from the mirror with a scowl and stepped into the shower, turning it on and being rewarded with the shock of ice-cold water. I closed my eyes as I waited for it to heat up.

I couldn't do this. I needed to cancel.

———

"You can't wear that," Emery teased as he leaned against the doorframe of the closet.

I glanced down at the slacks and polo shirt. I guess the shirt was a little big. I'd stopped spending so much time defining my muscles, preferring to get work done so I could be home with our pack.

As a result, my shirts were getting a little loose. I looked up to meet Emery's green eyes. Such a lovely, deep color.

"What's wrong with this?" I asked, frowning.

What was wrong was that Emery was a men's fashion consultant. He was the epitome of style and grace. He knew just how tight pants should be, framing your dick bulge to perfection and yet, keeping it tasteful. He knew which socks to wear with every ensemble – and yes, they mattered. He knew the proper material to wear to a birth. There was such a thing.

"Take it off," Emery said as he stepped into the room.

"Which part?" I asked.

"All of it, Ter. Whatever underwear you have on, lose them, too."

I rolled my eyes but did as he said. He tossed a pair of socks at me first before he found the boxer briefs he thought suitable. They were soft, almost mesh-like, and so damn comfortable it was like I wore nothing and yet my balls were cupped perfectly.

The pants he threw at me were Ronan's and the shirt was Zack's. Both fit me exactly right. I apparently no longer had my own size but a combination of my pack's. Maybe I needed to put in a little more effort into my physique.

Emery ended with a belt, which he weaved through the loops and buckled, before meeting my gaze. We were the same height, but he was lean, without much definition. His goal when he worked out, and he did daily, was staying slender. He wanted no fat, but he didn't try to gain muscle either.

"Perfect," he breathed, pressing his lips to my jaw.

I smirked against him, wrapping my arms around his waist. "The mechanic will appreciate the effort." I was getting my tires and oil changed. Nothing exciting.

He grinned, shrugging, and turned from the closet, calling behind him, "The black sneakers with the green laces."

———

I STOOD STARING over the contents of my drawers, frowning. I had ten pairs of gym attire to last me between washings. I had a pair of bed pants that still had tags on them. At the bottom of the bottom drawer, I found a pair of jeans that were far too small.

Rubbing at my face, I wondered how it would go over if I canceled because I had nothing to wear. It wasn't even a lie. I had nothing but gym clothes. And I had (probably purposefully) not checked on the state of my wardrobe until two hours before I needed to leave to pick up Kaiser.

But I was haunted by the last thing he wrote. *Please don't cancel.* I don't know why, but I found that, as many times as I picked up my phone to do so, those words screamed at me, and I was too ashamed to be the coward I am and back out.

However, that didn't change the fact that I had nothing appropriate for dinner. Not even at a fast food establishment.

Glancing at the clock, I scowled and turned away. I didn't have a choice. I was going to have to shop. That meant wearing clothing without washing them first, which made me shudder. Emery had always beat into us that we wash clothes first! You don't know where they'd sat, or for how long before they got into your hands.

I threw on some gym clothes and headed for the door, grabbing my keys on the way out. The car I bought when I moved to Ocean City was a Volkswagen SUV. Taos. I rarely used it. So, I wasn't at all surprised when I opened the door and it smelled like the beta that managed the juice bar.

She kept it clean and tended to, letting me know when it was due for any kind of maintenance. So far, it had been very little since it was brand new off the lot. It had needed an oil change last week, which she'd marked on my calendar. I had no idea how she'd managed to connect that to my phone's calendar, but it dinged me a reminder. When I checked with her, Nora just smiled and said it was already taken care of. She'd used the card I'd given her for gas to pay for it.

The girl was more than a store manager. She was a personal keeper, tending to some of the more obscure needs that I often overlooked.

I stopped at the closest clothing establishment I could find and ignored the knowledge that Emery would have cringed that I was buying clothes here. But he wasn't here to dress me, which meant these decisions were put on me alone. Even as a child it had been Miles telling me what made me look frumpy, or that clothing being ten sizes too big, so my pants were hanging around my knees, was not sexy.

A smile touched my lips at the memory before the sting of heartache set in. I took deep breaths to try and keep myself together while I stared at the red light.

The store I parked at was certainly out of my age range. I was already sure when I walked in that it was intended for the younger generation. High school and college. But one of the attendants stopped me as I stepped inside, offering me a friendly smile.

"Hello," he said, tilting his head sideways. "Can I help you?"

Since I was only just inside the door, I realized that I might have been a mistake. I glanced back at the door, searching out the seal that meant it was a beta only establishment.

"It's okay, alpha," the young man said, causing me to turn back. "We're open for all designations. It's our goal to greet everyone who walks in and offer assistance."

I nodded. "I have a date," I told him, frowning. I glanced around the shop and nearly scowled at the idea that I was going to have to go somewhere else. "You're the closest clothing store and all I own is a variation of what I'm wearing."

He grinned wider, nodding. "Come this way, alpha. I have an idea that I think will be appropriate for most places."

I followed the young beta, relaxing as his clove scent brushed me. There was something calming and unassuming about a beta's scent. They weren't overpowering like an alpha's or overwhelmingly arousing like an omega's. They were soft and pleasant.

"What size pants do you wear?" the young man asked.

Sighing, I shook my head. "I don't know. I've been living in gym clothes for ten months."

He glanced my way, his light eyes tracking down my body as he studied me. "I'll take a guess."

I watched as he started pulling out several different pairs of pants and laying them over a center shelf display. He glanced at me several times in a way Emery often did with clients, gauging body structure and appearance to determine style.

After he'd laid out six different options, he turned to me. "Okay, here's what we have. These slacks are versatile at a neutral dark gray. You can pair them with just about anything. I have two shirts, lightweight but different styles and then a sweatshirt you could layer with but also change the feel of it slightly." He moved down to the next option. "Jeans can be worn in a lot of places. If you're going to the movies, there's no need to go beyond the comfort of jeans. But if there's a chance that you might try a semi-casual restaurant after, pairing it with this shirt and jacket gives it just the uplift it needs to escalate from casual to nice."

I watched as the man explained more pairings. One with a tie, one that was close to a four-piece suit. Some that changed when you added or took away an article of clothing. But then he paused as his gaze dropped to my sneakers. He didn't ask. After acquiring my shoe size, he walked away, returning with three different options and explaining what pairing them with different ensembles could afford me.

"What do you think?" he asked. "Anything you like, or should I move in a different direction?"

He was very much like Emery. I bowed my head while I caught my breath at the thought. "I'll take the lot," I told him when I looked up.

His eyes widened. "Really? Please don't feel obliged. If there's something you don't like-"

I glanced at the items again and tried to decide if there was something I was strictly opposed to. "Okay, I don't like the mustard yellow sweater. Swap it with another color, maybe? And the tie is a little... intense. I'm fine with patterns but that one is a bit too much."

He smiled and pulled the items off the pile, tossing them over a rack behind him. He offered me a burnt orange sweater but when I raised a brow, he laughed and took it away. This time he returned with a dark navy sweater that I nodded at. The ties were patterned but they were definitely more my style. I agreed to both the options he brought.

"Good," I told him. "I'll take it all."

"Are you sure?" he asked, brows knit together. "I wasn't laying it out to pressure you to take it all. I just wanted to offer you some options."

"You did hear the part where I said I own ten variations of what I'm wearing now, right?"

He looked down at me and chuckled. "Yes. I'll meet you at the front then."

I nodded and turned as the young man gathered the clothing he had assembled into piles. There was a young beta at the register who looked at me with big, nervous eyes and pink cheeks. I could almost feel her pulse spike in the air.

Growing up alpha, you learn how to dissuade anyone from misinterpreting an expression as interest. When I was very young, my fathers used to tell me that, because a pack isn't truly a pack without alphas, and our biology craves the bonds and family structure a pack affords, that alphas are hunted nearly as much as omegas. The difference was simply biology here, too. An omega did nothing for a beta. But an alpha was the necessary ingredient for a pack and so, betas desperately wanted to catch an alpha's interest.

I hadn't noticed what my parents were talking about when

I was young. It wasn't until I hit my early teens that it became apparent. Miles said it felt like he was constantly fighting the other betas who were trying desperately to catch my eye. I tried to be nice, kind and considerate growing up. And found that that could land you in a lot of misunderstandings with betas. I'd switched to the more aggressive asshole in avoidance, but found that I hated being like that and that it didn't dissuade them at all.

An alpha was an alpha, with a bite and claim regardless of whether he was a good person or not.

It took me a couple years to find the right combination of honesty and kindness – and telling other betas a slight fib. I had my beta, Miles, and I wasn't interested in a second. The first part was the truth. The second part was the lie. I wasn't set on a single beta. I wouldn't reject another beta if one came around that we were interested in. Even then, at fifteen, I knew that Miles would be my pack and we'd grow from there.

But since I couldn't be bothered to find the nicety in me, I did my best to ignore the beta at the register. Avoid eye contact entirely until it becomes a point of manners.

The beta who had helped me brought up my new purchases and piled them on the counter. The girl behind the register started ringing them up as the young man walked away. He returned with the boxes of shoes, the jackets, and a basket. He set the shoes and jackets on the counter next and brought me the basket.

"So, I realize we didn't talk about this, but you need undergarments that work. Dressier socks than those you'd wear to the gym." He dropped his gaze to my sneakers before looking up with a slight smile. He picked a few up and showed them to me. I waved them towards the register, and he placed a dozen pairs on, different material, styles, and colors, but all in the color range of my pants.

Then he pulled out the two different packs of boxer briefs. "The pants you chose are designed to work around very specific types of underwear so that they become nonexistent in appearance. No lines or embarrassing... reveals." He explained which pants each were for before looking at me.

I decided I liked this man. There wasn't a hint of embarrassment. Nor was there any straining for catching my eye or subtle flirting. He was a man doing his job.

"Is clothing something you're interested in?" I asked, taking the two packs from him and placing them on the counter.

He shrugged. "Right now, it's a job. But I internally cringe when someone buys something that clashes while trying to force them to look good together. I don't know that it's a career, but I don't hate working here."

"You're very good," I told him, and it was the first blush I'd seen on him. I'd be skirting the line with my next statement, but if I had to suffer through clothes for any other reason that might come up, he hadn't made it horrible. "Do you have a business card?"

He shook his head. "I'm just a greeter," he said, smiling. But he reached to the counter and plucked a card out of the little display. "We're a franchise with local owners."

"Write your name on the card. If I have to go through the torture of shopping again, I'll be tracking you down."

His blush reappeared as he wrote his name down and I handed my bank card to the cashier. I pocketed my card and the business card when they were handed back to me. Ben, the young man, helped me carry my four bags to my car.

I thanked him and climbed in, glancing at the clock. I had just enough time to get home and change. I'd made all the effort of buying clothes, I couldn't cancel now. I shivered and stared ahead at the light.

CHAPTER TEN

Kaiser

"He's not coming," I whispered as I stared at the clock. He still had fifteen minutes, but I was convinced that he wasn't coming. I could feel it in the pit in my stomach.

Marley glanced at my phone in her hands. "He hasn't canceled."

"But I backed him into a corner. I didn't stop asking him until he said yes."

Both my alphas were sitting on the table in the foyer instead of the chairs on either side of it as they watched me pace. I could feel their eyes on me as if they were caresses. And within me, I could feel their quiet strength and support as if it were their purrs.

"He gave you his number," Marley said.

But did he? I hadn't received an answer. No

acknowledgement. No cancellation. No hello. Nothing. I'd received nothing.

I was seriously trying not to be pathetic. I hadn't gone looking for him since the day I found him in the gym. I hadn't even been to Juice Me. I hadn't left the house, just to insure that I'd not run into him and place more pressure on him. I thought maybe it would help ease him into the idea of going to dinner with me. If I wasn't always there, he'd not see how much of a mess I was.

I jumped when Phynn caught my hand. He pulled me into his arms, and I relaxed a little. How could I not? He was my alpha and he smelled like a heavenly orchard. And he loved me. Just as the ridiculous and neurotic an omega as I was.

"Relax, Kai," he murmured in my ear, rubbing his nose against my cheek. It wasn't quite a scent marking but it was close. "*If*, for whatever reason, he doesn't show up, then we'll all go out together and have a good time and we'll make sure we take your mind off him."

It was meant to soothe me. I knew that. And I suppose to some extent, it did. Because this was my pack. Mine. This was my home, with or without the addition of Terence. I wanted him in the worse fucking way, and I couldn't imagine not having him.

But Phynn was right. I had a pack that I loved and who loved me. I might fall apart for a while, but in the end, I'd be fine.

Probably.

Right?

The doorbell chimed through the open space, making me jump. The pit in my stomach jumped and bile rose in my throat. He was here. Oh my god, I couldn't catch my breath. He was here! He was here?

Marley grinned widely and handed me back my phone.

She kissed me and I clung to her for a minute before accepting the hugs and kisses from my alphas.

"Call if you need anything," Adrian said.

I nodded and sprinted to the door, throwing it open.

And fuck, did he look good. I stared for a solid minute as I tried to swallow the sudden mouthful of drool. Marley was going to be jealous.

"Hi," I said, letting my gaze track down his body. Dark jeans over brown dress boots. The collar of a white button up was tucked within the collar of the dark blue knit sweater. And then there was a short charcoal wool jacket that he wore open.

"Hi," he said. "Ready?"

I nodded, stepping out the door and shutting it behind me. He waited until I moved in line next to him before walking down the steps and towards the dark SUV in the driveway. He opened the door for me, and I got inside. He waited until I got settled before shutting the door.

Maybe I'd been too distracted with him being so close, but as I reached for the seatbelt, I caught the strong presence of another scent and his was barely there at all. Was this a rental? Borrowed?

I buckled as Terence got behind the wheel. I watched him out of the corner of my eye, biting my lip. He smelled so good. And the longer we sat in silence, the stronger his scent became. Which, of course, only made my perfume increase.

"Is this your car?" I asked.

He glanced at me, nodding. "I don't use it much. Nora, the manager of Juice Me, uses it for errands mostly."

I relaxed. Okay, unfamiliar scent explained.

"Are you familiar with Big Italia?" I asked.

Terence shook his head.

"It's close to the university. Not super high-end and the

food isn't strictly authentic, but the atmosphere is nice. Quiet without being isolating."

He nodded and headed towards the university. I remained quiet as I studied him out of the corner of my eye. He determinedly looked straight ahead. His hands were tight on the wheel, his leg bouncing slightly.

But damn, he looked good. He was gorgeous in his tight gym clothes but seeing him like this, smelling so fucking good, I was almost dripping; it was difficult not to just jump on him. Make him pull over so I could ride him in the front seat. Fill this car with our scents so fully that it would never come out of the fabric.

I gripped the handle on the door as tightly as he was gripping the steering wheel, trying to hold myself still. This date was meant to convince him I was a good omega so that he'd want me.

I could be a good omega.

It was a quiet evening as we pulled into the parking lot. Since I wasn't sure if Terence wanted to open the door for me, I moved exaggeratingly slow in unbuckling so that I could determine whether he was moving around the car to me or going to pause at the hood and wait. I was relieved and encouraged when he moved to open my door.

He didn't offer his hand, pushing it firmly into his pocket, but he managed to offer me a smile. I would spend this time tonight trying to read everything without being too enthusiastic. I didn't want to scare him away, which seemed to be the only thing I had managed to do so far.

The hostess led us to a round booth and I slid around until I was close to Terence. Not too close. Not close enough to touch him, though I desperately wanted to. But close enough that it wouldn't be mistaken that this was a date.

It was a date!

After the waitress had taken our drink orders and left us with menus, I found I couldn't read anything in front of me. I was almost too jittery to see straight.

"Have you been here before?" Terence asked, his voice low and smooth.

It made me hard. I gripped the menu tight and wished I'd had my pack fuck me throughout the day just to try and keep myself under control. What was I thinking going out with an alpha I wanted as bad as I did, knowing he was as skittish as a kitten, while still being my horny fucking self?

"Yes," I told him. "I like the environment. And the servers don't look at me like I'm on the menu."

He snorted a quiet laughter as he glanced at me. My heart fluttered in response. "I can imagine that gets old."

"Old. Obnoxious." I shrugged. "It's my understanding that alphas deal with the same thing."

"Yea," he said, nodding as he continued to peruse the menu. "But it's a little different, no? You have to avoid the looks primarily from alphas, which is problematic enough. And though betas hunger after you, it's not quite as drastic, is it?"

I shook my head, setting the menu down. "No. I find that the betas that constantly look at me hungrily are the ones who crave what an omega is as opposed to wanting one. Betas think we're to be worshiped and that everything they want comes easy for us, not realizing that we fight biology at every turn. We're spoiled and stupidly aroused all the time."

Terence looked at me, tilting his head. "Omegas are meant for packs. And betas only think about that when begging the powers that be to make them into an omega."

"Yes!" I said, nodding. "Exactly. Betas don't really want the omega in a pack. They want what an omega brings with it. The pack."

He shook his head and turned back to the menu.

"But I guess you fight the struggle in a different way," I said.

The corner of his lips quirked up slightly in a half smile. Again, my dick twitched, and I almost groaned in annoyance. See?! Fucking miserable biology.

"Yes. It was a very long childhood until I figured out how to not be a dick while still getting the point across that I wasn't interested in every beta that threw themselves at me." He paused and set the menu down. "What's good here? I can't remember the last time I had Italian."

I smiled and leaned a little closer to point to the items that were my favorite. "Their stromboli is amazing. Their stuffed shells are ridiculous. Oh, their gnocchi is just – mm. Actually, any of their pasta is remarkable."

Terence chuckled. "So basically, the whole menu?"

Nodding, I flushed. "Yes. Stick to the entree section and you'll get the good, authentic Italian dishes. They take liberties in the other sections. They're not bad, but I like the real Italian best."

He nodded as he watched me, a hint of a smile on his lips. His eyes were brown, or maybe a hazel. Green even. But they were so light in the middle, distracting from the dark ring. I bit my lip as we held stares.

The moment was broken when the waitress interrupted us. I had to work to hide my scowl as Terence shifted away from me a bit. We ordered and then she left.

We kept the conversation light and I paid close attention to my tone and body language, so I wasn't coming on too strong. I'd never had to pay attention to these things before, but I found that maybe it was paying off. Terence seemed to relax as we talked before the food arrived. Once, he even laughed and my heart soared.

I thought it was going well. I tried hard not to overanalyze what it meant when he asked me if I wanted dessert and if I'd mind sharing a slice of lemon ricotta cake with him.

But then I must have messed up. Maybe I agreed too enthusiastically. Maybe I hadn't controlled my expression enough. Or my perfume. I visibly saw when he tensed and closed up. It was like watching a wall drop between us and I wanted to cry.

"Terence," I said, helplessly floundering for something to fix it. "I'm trying."

Confusion marred his perfect features as he looked at me. "Trying what?"

"To be a good omega so you don't hate me," I whispered.

He groaned and closed his eyes, wiping a hand over his face. He swore under his breath, shaking his head. There was turmoil storming through his eyes as he looked at me. "What makes a good omega?" he asked.

And... I didn't know how to answer. I just stared at him with my lips parted as I waited for words to come to me.

Terence sighed. "Tell me about your pack."

It was probably the last thing I thought he'd asked me, so I stared at him dumbly for several minutes. Which was stupid because he stiffened further.

"They know you're here, right?"

"Oh, yes! Absolutely!" I quickly recovered.

"Then?"

I bit my lip and looked at him before sagging. Somehow, I thought I'd already ruined the date and yet, I couldn't bring myself to answer him. "I can tell you're trying to keep me away," I told him slowly. "This was going really well until I did something or said something, and I think if I talk about my pack, it's only going to be more detrimental."

"You didn't do or say anything wrong, Kaiser," he said, and

I loved the way my name fell from his lips. "I really shouldn't have come here. I shouldn't have agreed to this."

"But you did, and you're here," I said, ignoring the fact that I hadn't exactly given him anywhere to run to when I begged him to take me out.

To my relief, a smile touched his lips again. "Yes, well... I've made worse decisions." I started to smile but then he shook his head, the hint of his smile fading. I'd heard the tease. I desperately wanted him to tease me. I wanted anything he'd give me.

We shared our cake in almost silence and Terence paid. I tried not to let him, considering I hadn't let him get out of this, but he insisted that he wanted to.

"You're not a bad omega," he said quietly as he drove me toward home. "You're a perfect omega."

"Then why don't you want me?" I whispered.

I felt him flinch and he turned away, watching as the houses went by. "I'm an awful alpha," he answered quietly. "I promise, you don't really want me."

I pressed my lips together. I was going to argue. Going to throw a fit. Pout until he took me in his arms. But if I'd learned anything, it was that I wasn't going to get anywhere with him by being what I was. He didn't want an omega. He didn't want me!

The car ride was silent as he pulled into my neighborhood. I searched within me desperately for something to say that might reverse the last half hour. Something that would make him smile at me again. Or laugh at me for being ridiculous.

But I had nothing, even as he pulled into my driveway. He put it in park and waited. I stared at the front door, knowing my pack was inside and that they could already feel that I failed. They were waiting to make me feel better.

How do I tell them that I don't think I'm going to feel better unless someone can convince this alpha that I was already his omega? I just needed him to realize it, too.

Terence unbuckled and opened his door. I took that as my cue to do the same. At this point, I knew it was just a habit and what he determined to be polite by opening my door for me. I couldn't bring myself to look at him as I climbed out.

He walked me to the door and paused. "I'm sorry," I said, trying to hold in my tears. Being me sucked. Why couldn't I have just been a beta? "I didn't mean to mess this up."

"Look at me," he said, and I swear, there was just a little hint of a bark. I brought my eyes to his. His expression was closed but there wasn't anything harsh in his face, either. "You haven't done anything wrong, Kaiser. Stop apologizing. You were a great date. You're an amazingly perfect omega. *I* can't do this."

I don't know how I didn't burst into tears as I stared at him. His words cut like a knife. Buried deep in my chest and twisted until I couldn't breathe.

CHAPTER ELEVEN

Phynn

The three of us nestled in Adrian's bed while Kaiser was out. It wasn't often just the three of us anymore. I forget how comfortable and quiet it can be while we lay together. We used to do this often.

Kaiser was everything we'd ever wanted. He was... just magnetic. Sweet and thoughtful and smart. Those weren't the qualities he saw in himself. Because he rarely had a mental picture of himself outside of being an omega. And so, the only traits he ever saw were the ones common for his designation.

He thought we were doing him a favor by making sure he understood that it was him as a person that we loved, and that being our omega was just a bonus. But it wasn't only kindness on our part. It was the truth. We loved Kaiser for who he was as an individual. Everything else that came with him was just extra.

The first hour he was gone there was a bit of hesitancy and a whole lot of nerves through his bond. It was as if he were walking a tightrope. Waiting to fall one way or the other. And then it turned giddy, filled with excitement as their date must have taken a positive turn.

We all breathed a sigh of relief when the only hesitancy left in him felt like he was trying to hold himself back.

"Maybe this was a good thing," Marley said as she leaned her head on Adrian's shoulder. "I thought it was going to backfire."

I chuckled quietly.

"We did, too," Adrian said. "Trapping him like this seemed like a disaster with our omega's heart on the line."

"It still is," I pointed out. "I can't imagine that this sudden shift is going to be permanent."

"I wish I knew what it was that changed in the store," Marley said with a sigh. "Then we could determine where it came from. It would help Kaiser to avoid such things. But I swear, we were talking about dessert! And it came from nowhere."

"Maybe it's something more obvious than we're making it out to be," I said as I tangled my fingers with Marley's, my bigger hand swallowing hers. "Alphas are pack-driven in the same way omegas are pack-necessary, and betas are pack-craving. And from what you two can tell, he's a lone alpha without a pack."

"Rejected from a pack?" Adrian suggested, frowning.

"His hesitancy to get near us might support that," Marley said. "If you started to get close to a pack before being pushed out, why would you open yourself up to another one?"

"And yet, you don't sound convinced that's what the issue is," I noted.

Marley sighed. "I'm not, but at least if that makes sense, we'd have a better idea of how to proceed."

"Would we?" Adrian asked.

She grinned up at him. "I don't know. I feel like knowing the root of the problem makes finding a solution at least plausible."

And then there was an abrupt change in the bond with Kaiser. At first, it was like he was holding his breath. And then it was something else, something that made Marley choke and squeeze her eyes shut.

I nearly jumped out of bed when I realized what it was. He was deep inside self-deprecation. Despising himself. Miserable and distraught.

The feelings continued to grow and become more riddled with unshed tears as the night continued. We heard the car pull up just before nine.

"I'll take care of him tonight," I said quietly. "Join us in a bit."

A tear trickled down Marley's cheek. Adrian pulled her into his arms, brushing it away as he met my gaze. We should have been a full pack. This was an unnecessary complication.

Kaiser was just stepping inside when I reached the bottom of the stairs. I watched as he let the door shut behind him. He wasn't looking at anything as he stared off, his chest rising and falling, and I knew without examining our bond that he was trying to fight his way through what he determined were weak omega emotions and instincts.

When I moved into the room, his eyes snapped to mine. His face crumpled as tears streamed down his cheeks. I caught him in my arms and held him tightly while he cried.

To my surprise, it was a quick weeping. It wasn't more than a few minutes before he was done and wiping his eyes.

"Come on," I murmured, keeping my arm tight around him and bringing him upstairs. "My room or yours?"

"Yours," he said, his voice weak and filled with defeat.

Although he was sagging, he wasn't leaning into me and

letting me carry his weight. He trudged up the stairs and turned into my room, stripping out of his clothes as soon as we hit the second-floor landing so that there was a trail to my door.

I left them there as I followed him. Kaiser crawled onto my bed and dropped. I watched as he snuggled into the blankets, pulling more around him as he tried to nest himself within my bedding. I pulled my clothes off and tossed them into the hamper within my closet before pulling down more pillows and blankets.

Dropping them on the bed, I helped him make a little nest in the middle of my mattress before joining him in it. He took a deep breath and sighed as he released it.

"I don't know what I did wrong," he whispered as he nuzzled into my chest. I immediately started purring as I curled in closer. "It was good. We talked and laughed even. I know he likes me! I know he does! But he got all weird at the end, closing off completely, and then told me he couldn't do this. But I swear, Phynn, I was careful with what we were talking about. I kept it, you know, stringless and all that. I tried not to get too excited or come on too strong." He paused and wilted. "Maybe I perfumed too much. Maybe I should have gotten some scent canceling-"

"No," I told him, making him jump. I hadn't meant to put such a bark on it. I took a breath, breathing him in as I tried to calm the irritation that sparked. I lifted his chin, gently forcing his gaze to mine. "You are not going to hide what you are, Kaiser. No matter how much you want this man. Do you understand?"

"But maybe-"

"It's not an option," I insisted.

"I'm not saying as a permanent thing," Kaiser whined. "Just... what if it's my perfume that keeps setting him off, Phynn?"

"An hour and a half into your date?" I asked, frowning.

Kaiser didn't answer as frustrated tears filled his eyes. "I don't know," he whined again, wiping furiously at his eyes.

I let go of his chin and pulled him close to me. Kissing him lightly, I waited until he was responding before I rubbed my cheek against his. "I know you're upset, and I can feel how much you're hurting, but I'm not going to let you hide anything about you for this alpha. He wants you the way you are, or he doesn't get to have you."

"What if he doesn't want me at all?" he asked, the sorrow in his voice so deep it made his question quake.

"I don't believe that's the case, or he wouldn't have agreed to take you to dinner," I said, maybe wrongly. Maybe I shouldn't encourage this if every encounter they had was going to end up with my omega in this much emotional despair.

"I didn't give him an option."

"An alpha that wants to say no will do so," I assured him.

"Even to an omega?"

"Yes, even to an omega." That might have been a lie. But in this case, I didn't believe it was. Terence had said no, very clearly, in their previous encounters, even if not saying the word itself. He'd said yes this time, even if it was under a bit of duress and forced proximity. And Kaiser had set a date three days in the future, giving Terence more than ample time to cancel.

He hadn't, so I had to assume that he wanted Kaiser, too. There was just something preventing him from moving in.

Maybe it didn't have anything to do with Kaiser. Maybe smelling his alphas on him already was enough of a deterrence. Marley smelled like us, too. Perhaps he'd suddenly caught a lungful in the store, and it had reminded him that they were already in a pack.

I'd run the idea past Adrian, see what he thought of this theory.

But right now, I was going to please my omega until he fell asleep with a happy sigh.

Kaiser was a beautiful man with clothes on. Without, he was absolute perfection. He didn't have a late awakening. He'd known all along that he was an omega. With the expected body structure of an omega, he'd have been pegged as one even if his designation wasn't known.

Standing at five foot nine, he was lean, trim, and shaped to be the perfect small spoon to any alpha. And since he was an abs man, he spent a lot of time on his own. As such, the rest of him tended to stay taut from the exercise.

Though he wouldn't admit it, he also enjoyed his smooth skin. He'd like us to believe he was naturally soft. He was, but he also kept his skincare routine to himself. He liked hygiene. And he loved soft skin. Lotion was something he had an entire drawer full of. We kept it well stocked. I was sure he knew that, even if he pretended that he didn't.

These were things he thought made him a weak omega. It wasn't that he cared about being clean and having soft skin. It was that he felt like he was compelled to focus on it so much.

I ran my hand down his soft back, feeling how perfect he was under my touch. Smooth. Firm though soft. His height afforded me the luxury of being able to draw my hand down to cup the globe of his ass.

He was still pouting, even as he rocked his hips into me. The whine in his throat wasn't a true omega whine. Just the sound of a man not getting what he wants.

I urged him on top of me and he splayed over my chest, his legs dropping over my hips. Immediately, he began rocking, rubbing his cock against mine. He was already mostly hard as omegas go. But then, so was an alpha when there was an omega around.

His cock was a beautiful specimen. Just over six inches and thick as all hell, it was soft in its thickness. I found I was always curious about how evolution settled with that. If a male omega was designed for a female alpha, how does their lock work better on an omega's thick but soft cock?

Kaiser's groan drew my attention back to him, out of my thoughts regarding omega cock. I didn't care about other omegas. I cared about mine. He was panting, his hot breath moistening the neck of my skin. His hips moved more erratically, the thick, soft dick that I was musing over a wonderful stimulant to my hard one.

Where omega's were thick and soft when hard, an alpha was nearly made of stone when hard. That didn't even include the knot that at times felt like it could expand indefinitely.

I took his head in both my hands, drawing him up so he was looking at me. His eyes were half lidded in arousal, his lips parted with heavy breathing. I leaned up to kiss him, a slow, slicking kiss that drew out a moan. His fingers dug into my chest.

As I kissed him, I rolled us over. My weight on him made him buck against me harder, a whine in his throat that I swallowed.

"You want touch?" I asked.

His whimper was adorable. I slowed his response by taking his lip in my mouth and sucking it. He moaned, his hips jerking against mine again.

"Knot," he said. "Please, alpha. Then touch me."

I nodded, moving my mouth down his chest until I could lick at my bite on his ribs. His fingers tangled in my hair as I did. I kissed it as an erogenous zone, which it was since it was my bite. When I brushed it with my teeth, he arched into me.

Pulling back onto my knees, I looked down at my beautiful man. His steel blue eyes were made darker with the dimness of the room and his arousal. The golden streaks in his hair looked as if they were glowing.

"Present, omega," I told him, a low growl in my voice.

Kaiser shivered as he scrambled up. In his haste, he fell on his side before managing to get on his hands and knees. Then he lowered further, bringing his face to the pillows, twisting as he did so he could look at me.

"Good boy," I cooed.

Kaiser moaned in response, his ass wiggling a little.

"Perfect boy," I said, moving both my hands over his ass. "So pretty. So, so good."

He whimpered. "Please, alpha. I need your knot. Please."

I also love the slight beg in his voice when I take my time. But despite the arousal and heat coming through our bond, the hurt and upset were still there. All I wanted to do was make it go away.

So, I didn't make him wait tonight. I grabbed a squirt of lubricant from the pump bottle on the table at the edge of my bed. Early in our relationship, I used to put it away, so it wasn't readily visible when you walked in. But since two-thirds of my lovers were male who didn't produce their own juices – and thank fuck for that since the idea freaked me out – I kept it handy.

Rubbing it over my cock, I switched hands and continued to rub it in while I used the one most heavily loaded with lube to prep Kaiser's ass. I wasn't going to drag this out, so I slid my fingers over his clenched ass, making sure he was ready for me. I slid a finger in, and he pushed back, moaning.

Most people keep books or pens or something useful in their night table drawers. I kept hand cloths. After I wiped my hands, I leaned over Kaiser and kissed his hot skin. I loved that when my omega was turned on, his skin became feverish. Not nearly so hot as during a heat, but still a whole lot hotter than usual.

It was all the more arousing as I pressed my lips to his shoulder while I lined the head of my cock up. The first stretch as I pushed my head past the tight ring of muscles always made my eyes roll.

"So good," I groaned, moving my hand around to grab his wrist. "Perfect and tight."

Kaiser shivered, wiggling for me to move faster. He was never a patient man. Especially when I started praising him. I couldn't help it. I loved to tell him how wonderful he was.

"More," Kaiser said.

I grinned and quit stalling. Where I liked to savor, Kaiser wanted to get to the good parts. I usually saved my slow for Marley. She didn't mind it being drawn out. Kaiser didn't want to wait. He wanted orgasms. Plural.

I curled my hips, pushing further and further into him. I knew when I reached the point where I really started to stretch him. Kaiser gasped, his hands digging into the bed as he shoved his ass back at me. I shivered every time, this time being no different.

"You feel so good," I whispered, kissing his shoulder again. He moaned and wiggled as I continued to push into him deeply. "You're doing so good, Kaiser. So, so good. My perfect lover."

In these moments, he didn't mind me calling him omega. But I knew that he'd remember after when I called him by his name instead of designation. He appreciated that more.

He pushed back into me, the sounds coming from him nearly driving me mad. I stopped trying to push myself all the way in and started thrusting into him instead.

"Yes," Kaiser said. "Yes, alpha. Please."

"What do you need, love?"

"Orgasm," he whined. "Please. It hurts."

I'd asked many times after the fact whether it truly was painful. But I was convinced that he didn't really remember. Sometimes he told me yes; that it was painful, even while not in heat, when he didn't get an orgasm when he needed one. Other times he'd tell me no. Though he'd never been denied one, he said there was some biological memory that gave him a phantom pain at times, as if he were being denied a knot when he needed one.

I thrust harder, driving deeper and with more urgency. He was close already, so his first orgasm came crying out of his throat in a gasp as his eyes widened.

"That's it. Feel good, love?"

"Yes. Yes. Another."

Leaning back so I was on my knees, I took his hips in my hands for leverage and plunged into him until he was crying out with another orgasm.

"More, alpha. Please."

And another. I was going to have to roll us away from where he was spilling all over the bed. I think part of his obsession with hygiene was that he hated how much he released. He cringed away from it, embarrassed. Meanwhile, I thought it was the hottest thing ever. Who doesn't want to give their lovers so many orgasms that the bed is soaked by the time they're done?

"Knot. I need your knot."

I spread his legs wider with my knees as I started to rock more slowly, working my knot into him. His muscles fluttered around it as I made room inside him. Stretching him more and more until I was buried to my hilt, his body locking tightly around me.

"That's it," I whispered as he trembled. "That's my perfect omega. You feel so good."

"Touch," he whined, a voice that nearly broke me.

I curled back around him, draping over his body so I could wrap my hand over his cock. He was covered in cum. One stroke of my hand as I bowed my hips into him had Kaiser howling through another orgasm.

"You're doing amazing, Kaiser," I murmured before biting into his skin. I didn't break through but the sting of it was enough that he was dripping more. "Need another?"

"Yes," he said breathlessly. "More. Please."

"Anything you need, love."

I didn't need to move a whole lot while my knot was trapped within him. An alpha and an omega were designed for this kind of pleasure. Omegas were programmed for easy orgasms. For unimaginable, prolonged pleasure. And alphas were designed to deliver that. With my hand around his cock, handling him with long hard strokes, and my teeth in his skin, but not quite hard enough to break through, I ground my hips into him.

His howls of pleasure filled the room for a long time as I gave him what he wanted. When he finally started to sag in my arms, I allowed his orgasmic cries to bring me to finish before rolling us to the side where I could curl around him.

"You're amazing," I whispered, kissing his neck and the back of his head. "Perfect and beautiful. And so, so good at pleasing your alpha."

His happy mewl was what I needed to hear. I smiled, hugging him tightly to me as he started to drift off.

I was still tightly locked inside him when he stopped begging for more orgasms. Even outside of heat, Kaiser wasn't satisfied with a single orgasm or even two. He wanted at least four or five. Tonight had been five. I'd have given him a dozen if that was what it took to replace his sorrow with something else.

I curled around him, bringing my leg up to hook under his as I pressed my body weight against him, crushing him under me. Kaiser groaned when it made my cock shift inside him, a shiver sweeping through his body. Sometimes, that was enough to arouse him into wanting another orgasm.

It didn't tonight. He sighed, his grip on my wrist tight as he started to fall asleep. It didn't matter that my knot was still nearly fully inflamed, securing us together until I relaxed a whole lot more. Kaiser was stressed and hurting and just wanted to escape into a peaceful sleep. I let him, not caring if I remained there all night.

Adrian carried Marley in a few minutes after Kaiser had fully fallen asleep. Marley was partially awake, and I thought maybe Adrian had woken her up to carry her in. I actually thought they'd be in here while Kaiser and I fucked. Make it a pack sex pile. But they hadn't, which was fine. Individually, we could all take on each other, bringing pleasure and satisfaction to our partners. We'd made sure to nurture all of our relationships individually as well as within the group.

Adrian shifted the wall of Kaiser's make-shift nest so he and Marley could be inside it. Marley wrapped her arms around Kaiser's head and snuggled in close. Kaiser responded in his sleep, shifting to pull her against him. He moaned quietly, his hips thrusting backwards, when he felt the tug of my knot still wedged inside him.

If he did that too many more times, I wasn't ever going to soften. Just that little bit had my heart stuttering for a minute.

Adrian closed Marley in, confining our beta and our omega between us. It wasn't long before the two were fast asleep and Adrian asked, "What happened?"

I repeated to him what Kaiser had said and then told him

my theory about their scent markings. Adrian nodded slightly, meeting my eyes in the dark.

His long hair was back, and I loved that look on him. When it was down, he looked like a different person. A little wild and hard in all the right places. But when it was back, he was a powerful CEO. A mafia boss. Dangerous as a viper ready to strike.

"I like that theory more than the idea that he'd been rejected before. I feel like a rejection would make him bitter not... terrified," Adrian said. But there was a frown in his voice that I mirrored on my lips.

Okay, that bit didn't fit in. Why run away in terror? Not quite a fear-driven terror. It's not the same thing. I'd seen him when he left the juice bar the other afternoon. He had all but run from Kaiser. I'd seen the exchange through the window. He was panicking about getting away.

Kaiser wasn't a small man. He was five foot nine with lean muscle. He liked the gym but finding one where an omega would be left alone was difficult. And that was why he and Marley were trying the gym where they'd met Terence.

They had been left alone. After the initial shock of Kaiser's perfume, no one had bothered them from what I understood. But even so, he wasn't an overly large man. Omegas weren't. They were meant to be smaller so that an alpha could wrap around them when rutting. Could hold them and protect them and embrace them fully.

So, it wasn't actual fear that had been in Terence's face as he tried to run away. Considering his bulk alone was easily two of Kaiser, it certainly wasn't fear. It was something else.

"You know, maybe Kaiser's right," I noted. "We know how consuming his perfume is. Maybe he's overwhelming the alpha. Maybe Terence hasn't been in close proximity to an omega before now."

"What are you suggesting?"

"He's excitable. And he's desperate to make this alpha want him. That only makes him perfume all the more. Maybe we can convince Kaiser to sit it out for a bit and see if Marley has an easier time of it."

Adrian didn't answer for a minute. "You really think it's his perfume?"

There was doubt in his voice. No, I didn't think that was it. But maybe it was adding to it. "He's going to be a puzzle unless he comes out and tells one of them what's going on with him, and it doesn't sound as if he's open to doing that. Our options are a guessing game until we hit on something that breaks the ice. Marley is less aggressive. And her scent is a whole lot more subtle than Kaiser's."

"Alright," Adrian said. "We'll see if she's up to it tomorrow."

I was kind of hoping that Adrian would decide that they were both done with this alpha and we'd move onto the part where we worked on getting our beta and omega over their longing for him. I could follow that wholeheartedly. I would support that.

But I suspected, like me, he wasn't going to go down that route until we'd exhausted all other avenues. Because our omega wanted this alpha. And there was nothing we wouldn't do for our omega.

CHAPTER TWELVE

Terence

Dinner had been great. I wasn't at all surprised that I liked Kaiser. He was sweet and adorable. His smile was gorgeous in his perfectly tanned face. He was smaller than my betas had been, both in height and bulk, and I found I was craving to see just how well he fit within the curl of my body.

I tried to tell him over and over that this was the only time. I couldn't do this. But every time I tried, his intoxicating scent would fill me, and I was constantly trying to swallow the instant purr that kept trying to erupt. Not okay. That was not acceptable.

It wasn't just Kaiser's perfume. It was also his personality. He was quirky and kept trying to hide it. I was smiling more often than not as he continued to backtrack on what he was saying to sound more kosher and submissive.

He wasn't any of those things. Without being so, his

personality was big and loud. I could almost feel him trying to keep that all inside, physically trying to push it back.

What made me break was realizing my need for him was nearing as great as my need for my own pack. I'd never wanted anyone so badly as Kaiser since Miles and then Zack. That comprehension made me stop short and catch my breath. I couldn't do this. I *couldn't* have this omega. Not without my pack.

And I'd never have my pack again.

I knew how bad I was making Kaiser feel, and try as I may, I wasn't sure how to fix it. I wasn't sure how to ease his mind that this had nothing to do with him. He was the perfect, exact omega I'd always wanted.

But it hadn't just been what I'd always wanted. It was what my pack had always wanted. We'd have enthusiastically agreed that 'fuck, we don't need children' if Kaiser had shown up in our lives. He was exactly right.

But not only did he already have a pack but mine was dead and it was far too late for that. And I was not the kind of alpha that could take care of an omega like they deserved. Not even knowing he already had alphas. And he did. I could smell them on him.

I forced myself to finish dessert with him. Refused to leave him there – because that would be a *shit* thing to do. It's not that I wanted to leave him there; it's just that I needed to get away from him. Between the suffocation of betraying my pack and the hurt I was causing him, I wanted to bury myself in the backyard.

The look on his face when I told him I couldn't do this had my heart shattered all over again. And yet, I forced myself to walk away.

It was dangerous, but I didn't remember the drive home at all. It was a wonder I hadn't crashed into something or someone. I hadn't even noticed that it had started to rain. By the time I stepped out of my car, it was pouring.

I stood there, letting it fall around me and pretending that if there were any tears on my face, it was just rain. By the time I made it inside, I was sopping wet, but my breathing was normal again. My chest hurt, like I'd been punched. But I wasn't crying.

Stripping out of my clothes, I curled up in bed and closed my eyes. Every so often I caught the faint pine scent and then the brush of cinnamon. I fell asleep imagining that Kaiser was wrapped in my arms. It was no wonder I had nightmares of putting my pack in the ground all over again.

———

I CARRIED on with my life the next morning. Dragging myself out of bed, I poked around in my freezer until I gathered which frozen fruits I wanted to mix into my shake this morning. I let it blend while I stared at the contents slowly turn into a muddy shade of red. The color felt appropriate.

The bags of clothing I'd bought yesterday were still strewn all over the couch where I had tried to recreate the pairings that Ben at the shop had made. I thought I'd done well. But then it didn't really matter as I heaped them all into the hamper. They needed to be washed before I did anything with them.

Like sticking them in drawers. Drawers that were already filled. Maybe I needed more drawers. A taller dresser? But then I wouldn't be able to see the television.

Rolling my eyes, I continued to sip at my shake as I pulled gym clothes out. It's not like I ever watched television from my bed. Fuck, I didn't even watch it when I turned it on. It was noise. Meant as a distraction from my dark and suffocating thoughts.

It didn't work but I still tried.

I loaded two bagels up with cream cheese before heading out. I needed the carbs in me to get through whatever misery I was going to lose myself in today. And I hoped it would be deep, all-consuming muscle aches so I could forget anything else.

I paused in the door and let the scents move around me. Nope, no omega. There were two betas that I knew as frequent users of the back room when I walked in. I wasn't sure what their names were. One of them had been the beta who'd dropped my water in my lap after Kaiser had been here the other day. I swear, he looked at me with sympathy now.

Deep breathing through some stretches and a short jog on the treadmill had me ready to go. I gazed around the room and found that nothing truly appealed to me today. Instead of the battle ropes, or tires, or kettlebells, or anything else the room had, I turned and made my way through the jungle of equipment.

The rower seemed mindless, so I set myself up on one of them, turned the music in my earbuds to deafening, and went to town. I remained on the rower until I ached and was somewhat dizzy from my need for water. After I'd rehydrated, I headed for the leg machine where I did a full rotation through the muscles in my legs: hamstrings, glutes, quads, and hips.

When noon rolled around, I found that I just wasn't into the gym today. I still had one water bottle left but I couldn't find any interest in anything else. Slinging my bag on my back, I headed into the park.

There were several paths, one of which I knew was a dedicated running path. Though it was a little far from the university, I knew that the college cross country runners utilized it frequently. They often held rallies and runs with proceeds going to their team. I'd participated in a few on a whim as I was walking through in the past.

The day was nice so there were a lot of people in the park, despite it being a work day. It was a work day, wasn't it? Since my routine never varied regardless of what day of the week it was, I tended to lose track of the days.

I arranged the strap of my gym bag, so it crossed my chest snugly and began to jog the trail. My only complaint was that the sun was bright, and I wished I'd brought sunglasses. Did I have sunglasses? Maybe the clothes store had some. Did I care enough whether they matched my clothing to make the trip there again?

At the moment, since I still had music screaming in my ear and it was drowning out every other thought, I wasn't in a horrible mood. So, yea, I could go get some sunglasses. That might be nice.

I wasn't sure how long I ran the path. My easy jog had eased into a comfortable run, and I'd lost myself in the motions and scenery as I followed the trail around the park. The signs said the path was three-quarters of a mile. I think I ran three laps before I stopped and lay under a tree at the side of the small pond.

It was quiet as I nursed my water from time to time and let my body relax. I'd never been huge on running but I suppose there's a lot of peace to it when you let yourself go and don't concentrate on the effort needed to get through it.

I yawned, thinking I could probably take a nap. It likely wouldn't be the first time someone had fallen asleep by the pond. I studied what was around the pond. There were those who were obviously laughing. I imagined the quiet quacking of ducks on the water and the gentle splashes they made. The clear songs of birds within the trees were probably scattered throughout the park. All of it together would have lulled me into sleep - if it wasn't for the music in my ears loud enough to drown it all out.

Until a shadow stood over me and I opened my eyes.

She was the most beautiful woman I'd ever seen and the way the sun haloed her head, I thought she might be an angel. My fingers itched to touch her, to feel her shine and fill myself with it through a kiss. I stared up at her inanely as she smiled down at me.

"Terence." Her lips formed my name, but I didn't hear her voice through the loud music in my ears.

A shiver raced through me as I sat up, pulling the earbuds out. "Marley," I greeted, disturbed about my initial reaction to seeing her.

She sat at my side, and I tried not to act like as much of an ass as I had last night. Making one of them feel like shit was bad enough.

I hadn't always been such an awful alpha. Once, I was attentive, strong, and did well taking care of my pack. My betas, especially, but my alphas too when they needed it.

Now, I couldn't get out of my own way most days. I'd lost the ability to talk to anyone without the horrors that lived inside me beginning to seep out. Shining through the cracks that broke me.

"I didn't know you ran here," Marley said.

I shook my head. "I don't regularly. But I was bored at the gym, and this seemed... less annoying today."

She smiled, nodding. It was then that I saw she was in a tracksuit.

"You run here?"

Marley turned that beautiful smile on me. "Yes, most days. If I work, I stop here after work. On days I don't work, I drop in whenever."

"Alone?" I asked, narrowing my eyes.

Her grin got bigger. "No one bothers a beta usually. I've never been harassed or followed. Besides there being a whole bunch of people around, I'm a quick runner. It wouldn't take much for me to run into a crowd or into one of the establishments close by."

"Hm," I grunted, glancing around for said crowds. There weren't any today.

"Sometimes I can convince Kaiser to run with me. He hates running so it's not often. He'd much rather use an elliptical or mess around on the weight machines where he can focus on his abs." She rolled her eyes. "He's obsessed with having a solid stomach."

I found myself smiling with that knowledge, despite trying to convince myself that it just didn't matter. Irrelevant information.

Time to move away from the omega subject.

"Where do you work?" I asked.

She waved down the road. "I work for a software developer down the road. Mostly office management but I get in on the brainstorming meetings. I shine when it comes to ideas and suck when it comes to making them happen." She grinned at me again.

"I'm sure you don't suck at it," I said before biting my tongue. Not my job to make her feel good or reassure her!

"No, I really do. I've taken so many classes in several fields pertaining to the skills needed in the industry, specifically the company I work for. I do decent in the classes but I'm following models. When it comes time to put the principles I learned into action, I flounder, and it comes out like a three-year-old did it." Marley shook her head.

"Why do you stay?"

"I love my job and the company. The directors are constantly finding new things for me to do to continue to use my talents, and compensate me how they think I should be without having to worry about the other employees feeling like they're playing favorites with me. It's a lot of fun and constantly shifting."

"Bloodcore Industries?" I asked. I was pretty sure that was the office right down the road.

Marley grinned. "Yes. They have different outlets and branches all over the place; smaller branches in different industries, but their primary bread and butter is software development."

I nodded as she shifted to face me a little more. "What about you? You own Juice Me?"

"Yes," I said, shrugging. "And I'm apparently expanding into a second location."

"Oh?" she asked, raising a brow. But my gaze was caught on her lips. So small and perfect. The right size and shape that begged to be bitten, to be kissed.

"Yea," I said distractedly. "My store manager is enthusiastic. I'm letting her open a second location as long as I don't have to be involved."

"That's nice of you," she said, smiling.

Was it my imagination or was she getting closer? Oh, she was for sure. I could suddenly smell her soft rosemary and sage scent. I took a deeper breath, letting it fill my lungs and head. She smelled so good. So soothing and tasty. I appreciated that she was on the herbal side of a beta scent opposed to the floral end.

And then I stopped breathing when her lips pressed against mine. My thoughts came to a stop. Flailingly, I wondered how I'd missed her getting that close. How had I missed that she was pressed against me with her mouth on mine, her soft hand on my shoulder as she leaned in?

My reaction was too quick and immediate as I leaned in

and kissed her hard. Nipping at her lips as I'd imagined doing just a few short minutes ago. Sucking on it a minute later, feeling the way she sank against me. I made one sweeping pass through her mouth with my tongue, feeling how my entire body suddenly burst to life, before pulling myself free and to my feet.

Marley stared at me with pink cheeks as she fell backwards onto her ass and looked up at me.

"I'm sorry," I said, shaking my head and holding my hands out to her as if to convince her to stay right where she was. No moving or I might come undone. "I really, really can't do this, Marley. I'm sorry."

I turned and walked away before she could answer.

CHAPTER THIRTEEN

Terence

I fell asleep dreaming about kissing Marley for the next two nights. But I woke up as I buried my pack in the ground, heaving for breath as my stomach tried to turn inside out.

Typically, I didn't take a shower until after I came back from the gym. What did I need to shower from when I never did anything but sit around once I got home? But when I woke up choking on my pain, my first reaction was to shock it out of my system with the icy water.

The second morning, I sat on the tile floor with my face turned into the water as I shook. Their faces danced behind my eyes. Smiling. Laughing. A hand brushing my cheek. I kept my eyes closed until it became too much, and I had to open them or drown.

I wasn't sure if it was strong or weak to have not taken my life to join them at this point. I had nothing left. Why was I still here when everything that mattered to me was encased in stone? But then, my pack wouldn't have wanted me to take my life. And I didn't seriously think about it. If I died, either of natural causes, in an accident, or someone killed me, I'd not be unhappy about it. I'd not be mad as I joined my pack again.

But I couldn't even think in a solid line of thought to take me down a path that would deliver me to that point.

I sighed. A therapist would probably tell me that was a good thing. Right? Or would they tell me I was pathetic and didn't love them enough to have those thoughts?

My phone buzzed in the other room. I knew the sound. Calendar notification. I rubbed at my eyes before getting to my feet and turning off the water.

Grabbing a towel on the way out, I halfheartedly dried myself as I fished my phone from the floor next to my bed. I raised a brow at the two appointments. Lease signing. Bank signing. Nora was on the ball.

Sighing, I started to pull out gym clothes and decided that maybe it wasn't appropriate for these types of meetings. I'd dropped a small fortune on clothes, and they were back from the cleaners. I should wear them.

Because I had no closets, the items that came back on hangers and I thought probably needed to remain on hangers if the launders had delivered them that way, were hanging off Command hooks on my wall as if they were art.

I noted that I should have taken pictures of the outfits that clothing specialist Ben had laid out for me. Especially since the only mirror I had only showed my chest and above.

Using the reflection on my television, I dressed in something that I thought might be presentable, and headed out.

This was my routine for the next week. No gym first thing in the morning. Now it was early meetings and sometimes an afternoon meeting. My gym hours were being cut short and sporadic. And yet, somehow, I found that I was constantly running into Kaiser all over town.

The first time was right out front of the new store. I was studying the surrounding area, admitting that Nora was right. This location was basically in the middle of campus. There were campus buildings surrounding this little strip mall location.

And then Kaiser was standing in front of me. His smile was hesitant and sheepish as he looked up at me. I was such an ass to have made him feel so uncertain.

"I haven't seen you down here before," Kaiser said, his voice quiet.

I pointed to the shop behind me. "New Juice Me location," I told him.

His face lit up in excitement. "Really? That's great, Terence."

"That's what I hear," I said.

He tilted his head. "You're not sure?"

I shrugged. "I'm sure that Nora is right. This is a phenomenal location as far as traffic goes."

"I'm going to be first in line when it opens!" he said, grinning at me. I watched as he glanced away. There were too many people milling about, so I had no idea who or what he was looking for. But his smile had turned demure again when he turned back to me. "I just wanted to say hi," he said. "So... hi."

I smiled, once more kicking myself internally for making him feel like this. Feel so unsure and like he was the horrible person in this situation, despite my assuring him it had nothing to do with him.

"Hi," I returned.

He smiled softly and bowed his head. "I'll see you around?"

I nodded. Nothing I could say was going to take away his

reserved tone and sagging shoulders. He gave me a weak smile, turning steel blue eyes to me filled with a quiet plea.

"Okay," he said quietly. He lifted his hand to wave and walked away.

I watched as he disappeared into the crowd and waited for Nora.

The next day I ran into him twice. The first was when I had to sign a check for $53,000 for the beginning stages of remodeling. I was now waiting for Nora to finish what she was doing.

This time, Kaiser didn't look quite so down when he stopped at my side. "Okay, I'm trying to guess why you're here."

I chuckled and tapped the wall I leaned against. "Remodeling company has an office here. Just signed a check that I might get sick over later."

He scrunched his face and I wanted to lick the wrinkles it produced at the bridge of his nose. "Eww."

"What about you?" I asked, trying to get that look from his face.

He nodded to one of the buildings across the street. "I broke a vase," he said, his eyelids hooding. "Marley is inside trying to find a replacement."

"And you're waiting out here because...?"

Kaiser grinned, a glint of amusement in his eyes. I enjoyed it when he acted more natural like this. "If it was a beta-only place, I'd have gone in with her. But I'm just not in the mood to deal with unwanted attention right now." He sighed. "I'd like to just turn it off sometimes, you know?"

I nodded. Yes, I knew that all too well. What would it be like to live in a society that wasn't so filled with scents and maddening biology that made you react to them? Peaceful, I would imagine.

A couple hours later, I found Kaiser sitting on a bench outside the building next to the one where I may or may not be needed as Nora picked out aesthetics and equipment. It depended on whether or not she would need to put a deposit down today.

I walked the few dozen feet to him and sat. Kaiser grinned at me before returning his attention to watching pedestrians.

"There are three alphas inside watching me," he said, shrugging.

I glanced back and he wasn't wrong. Instantly, a growl settled in my chest that I wasn't quite quick enough to silence before it escaped. Kaiser didn't acknowledge it. Not even with a change in his expression.

"I'm usually left alone," he told me as we sat there, my shoulders tense as I stared at the alphas inside. "I mean, there's an assumption that my alpha is around. How many unaccompanied omegas do you see wandering the streets?"

"All it takes is one psycho," I started.

"Yes. And I know a good few kicks and gouges to get myself loose, all the while making a pathetic omega scene," he said, and I noted the slightly bitter tone of his voice.

I didn't address it but sighed. "Waiting on Marley again?"

"Yep. This time, it's a work errand for her. Then we're going to an early dinner before a show. Have you seen 'Rapunzel in the Wastelands?'"

I shook my head, not having any idea what that could possibly be about.

"It's a weird dystopian thing that Marley's interested in." He looked at me with a teasing roll of his eyes. "She's obsessed with dystopian books and movies. I swear, it's her fantasy to be stuck in one."

My phone interrupted my chuckle as Nora messaged that she needed my signature. I raised my phone to him. "My bank account is about to get another hard gouge. I'll see you later, I'm sure."

Kaiser smiled and this time, it was flirty as he nodded and batted his lashes at me.

I smiled in return and walked away.

There was a day reprieve before I ran into Kaiser again, this time outside my juice bar. He was more hesitant today as I approached. He'd been sitting outside on one of the picnic tables as he sipped at his juice. He paused when he saw me, his eyes widening, and he shot to his feet.

Yesterday, he was at ease and playful. I wondered what was different today.

"Hi," I greeted.

"Hi," he answered, his voice a little higher than normal with nerves.

"You okay?"

He nodded, his shoulders relaxing a little. "Yes. Sorry. I thought-" His words cut off as he shook his head. "Never mind. Yea, I'm good. You?" His eyes tracked down my body, taking in my attire. "It's late for the gym, isn't it?"

I rolled my eyes. "As it turns out, spending money is primarily a morning activity. I'm stuck going to the gym after."

"Ah. What did you buy today?"

"Refrigerators," I said, shaking my head. "Damn things are expensive."

Kaiser grinned. "Want to sit?"

"No Marley today?"

He shook his head and I had to guess that meant his alpha was here somewhere. My guess was inside. "She's working. Meeting her after for a run." He didn't quite hide his scowl. "She makes me do things I hate."

There was a whine in his voice, and I chuckled, making him smile at me instead. I sat with him for a few minutes, and we continued our easy conversations. When his watch chimed, he sighed dramatically. "My torture sentence begins now," he said, getting to his feet. I stood as well, and he looked at me.

For a moment, neither of us said anything. "Terence," he started and then pressed his lips together. I shouldn't have let him continue but I waited. He sighed in defeat before I even had a chance to tell him no, but he looked at me with shy eyes anyway. "Please?" he asked and nothing else.

"Kaiser," I said, sighing.

"This time, I'll come to you. And I'll bring food. I'm a shit cook but I think I can manage this."

Omegas weren't meant to cook. They were meant to be fed. Taken care of in all of life's menial tasks. I was at least pleased that he was living that life.

He didn't press this time. He just stared at me.

I nodded and his smile went full on beaming. "Really?"

Holding my breath, I nodded. "Yes."

His smile softened as he swayed a little, trying to lean in closer but not letting himself give in to that reaction. I reached my hand out for his cup and he handed it to me. "I'll text you my address."

Kaiser's smile beamed again as he nodded. "Okay. I'm going to run until I die at Marley's cruel hands. Whatever night you want."

I grinned, nodding.

I watched as he walked away. A man met him at the crosswalk, though I only saw him from the back. Long hair tied at the base of his neck. I could tell from here that he was an alpha. Kaiser hadn't come alone. I sighed in relief.

I threw his cup out as I went into Juice Me for my drink. Jakob already had it waiting, having likely seen me outside. He winked at me, giving me a flirty smile. I smiled back and headed home.

The afternoon fell into evening as I prepared one of the meals that came with all the ingredients. I ate with the background noise of the television as I stared absently at it, not seeing anything as the pictures moved.

As I lay in bed that evening, I did as I said I'd do. I texted Kaiser my address. A moment later, he responded.

[Kaiser] That's the address for Juice Me.

I smirked.

[Me] I live above the shop.

[Kaiser] That makes a whole lot of sense in hindsight. What date?

I closed my eyes, trying to push down the way my stomach started to roll. Just dinner. That's all this was.

[Me] Saturday?

[Kaiser] Yes, okay! Goodnight.

[Me] Goodnight, corpse of Kaiser.

He responded with a whole lot of laughing emojis. But I didn't miss the one he snuck in with heart eyes.

———

RONAN WAS A BEAUTIFUL BLOND. He was elegantly proportioned and prone to trying trends on social apps. Especially ones where his junk was nearly on display as he bounced or thrust his hips towards the camera.

Once, he managed to get the six of us to go at it with him. Shirts off. Thin gray pants with nothing underneath. He made sure the house was nearly too hot to breathe in so that we were not hiding but certainly on display underneath our pants.

He'd even gone so far to give us a sensual show and make us all a little hard before he turned the camera.

I wasn't surprised when the short video went viral. It was put to the background of characters in books, blind reactions, mixes and stitches and comments. Ronan was ecstatic with the results and happily plastered everywhere he could that the video was featuring his pack. And yes, they were even sexier in person.

Ronan sat on the couch with me a few weeks after the video went viral, leaning into my chest and closing his eyes. "I know it's just a little thing and doesn't translate into anything of importance, but it means everything to me that you guys did that video with me."

I smiled, kissing his head and holding him to me. My betas weren't soft or craving too much spoiling. They were strong and independent. But sometimes, they let us hold them as if they were our omegas. Let us wrap around them and take care of them. Even if in just these short, quiet moments.

"We'd do anything to make you happy, Ronan. Anything at all."

———

I AWOKE as bile rose in my throat. Tearing my sheet off me, I skirted into the bathroom before I could make a mess all over the apartment. My eyes burned as I heaved for breath, spitting the acidic flavor from my mouth.

What was I doing? I had a pack. I wasn't on the market for another one.

My skin was sticky with sweat as I let myself fall to the tile and lean against the cool wall. Closing my eyes, I tried to ignore the way my stomach churned inside me.

I'll never stop loving you, I told them silently. *I swear.*

CHAPTER FOURTEEN

Kaiser

I was nearly hyperventilating as I stared at Phynn preparing the ingredients for dinner. I'd been ecstatic when Terence had agreed to another dinner with me. I was probably annoyingly carrying on about it when Adrian dropped me off with Marley to run. He was heading out for groceries and would pick us up in an hour and a half.

By the time we got home, I could feel Marley's jealousy through the bonds, and I tried desperately to stop myself from gloating about it. I wasn't trying to make her feel bad, nor rub it in or anything like that. I was just so damn excited that he'd agreed.

I managed to carry on with the rest of the day until he texted me that evening with his address and a date. And then I turned obnoxious once more. But I tried to make up for my behavior by concentrating solely on her pleasure that night.

The days following had me becoming more and more nervous as the impending date of our dinner approached. I'd screwed up last time. What if I did that again? I didn't think I'd get another chance after this.

"Calm down," Phynn said, nearly cooing to me.

Easy for him to say. An entire new alpha for our pack was resting on my totally incapable shoulders! I was completely inept at this type of thing. Being courted was easy. I just accepted gifts and purrs and strokes of needy affection.

Being the one who tried to reel someone in, *that* was a whole different kind of pressure that made me want to curl up and cry like a pansyass.

"Look at me."

I turned at his words, feeling the panic slowly start to spiral forward until I burst.

Phynn's expression softened as he sighed. He wiped his hands and pulled me to him. With a hand at the back of my head, he buried my face in his neck, forcing me to become surrounded by his calm scent until I wasn't shaking so badly.

"I know you're not going to accept this, but love, he's going to be the one missing out if he pushes you away, Kaiser. I know how you think of yourself, but I promise you, you're the only one who thinks that."

I squeezed my eyes shut as I tried to accept his words. But I knew what I was. I knew that I was a whiny, needy, spoiled omega with a constantly half hard dick and gallons of cum ready to unload in my pants at even the slightest of touches.

Forcing a deep breath out, I nodded. I didn't agree, but I wasn't going to argue with my alpha. That usually ended with me being pinned somewhere while he forced me to repeat my virtues as he saw them. It was uncomfortable at best.

"Adrian said he looked a whole lot more relaxed at the juice bar the other day. And you confirmed your encounters with him all last week had been pleasant. Right?"

I nodded again.

"Then maybe whatever he's been going through is subsiding. You're going to his house, Kaiser. That's a big step in the right direction."

It's not that I didn't believe him this time. He was right. It was one thing having an in-person date. It was another thing entirely to be invited to another man's house.

Although, once again, I'd kind of forced that. Just as I had the first dinner.

Before I could start to berate myself again, Phynn bit my shoulder and I winced. It wasn't gentle. It was definitely a reprimand. He'd likely felt the dark place creep up again in our bond. I really needed to do better about hiding that stuff.

"I love you," he said, rubbing his cheek against mine as he purred gently against me.

I sighed, letting myself fall into him so he had to hold me up. "Love you, too, alpha."

"Nothing will ever change how much love there is in this house for you, Kai. Regardless of what you think of yourself, there's not a damn thing we'd change about you. And if you're not going to go to dinner with that attitude, I'm keeping you here. Understand?"

"What attitude?" I asked, frowning.

His hand tangled in my hair, telling me it was time for a trim. I rarely let it get long enough where one of my alphas could get a grip. I wasn't about the hair pulling.

"That you're fucking phenomenal. And fuck him if he doesn't see that," he said, his bright blue eyes flashing with the threat in his voice.

I shivered at the tone and leaned in to kiss him. I knew I wasn't really distracting him, but he accepted the kiss and let go of my hair. Tomorrow was a haircut. Tomorrow might need to be a pampering all the way around if I fucked up again.

"Okay?" he asked. "Attitude realigned?"

I smiled, rolling my eyes. "Yea, alright."

"Good, now get that sexy floofy ass over here and pay attention to what I'm doing so you know how to finish this," he commanded.

Phynn put me to work in the least hazardous way possible while he finished dinner as he recited exactly what I needed to do to finish each item. Basically, I was going to Terence's house with a plethora of Tupperware and a very long list of steps to finish the meal.

I was nervous as fuck.

But finally, it was all packed up with a very long text message from Phynn with step by step, detailed instructions while I worked myself into the next panic as I tried to decide what to wear. I was not good at picking out clothing. I left that task to Marley or Adrian, which was enormously inconvenient since neither of them were home.

Marley was a little sad and jealous that I was getting another dinner date. Despite the fact that I pouted for an hour in my nest when she came home after kissing him. Sure, it had ended in a disaster, but she'd still kissed him. He wouldn't let me touch him and she'd had her lips on Terence!

It wasn't a competition. We knew that. And when we got to the point where it felt like we were competing against each other, we'd curl up together and focus on our relationship for a while. Marley and I were incredibly close. We had a lot of common interests and we indulged in each other's hobbies in a way our alphas didn't. Sure, they would, but our likes are more closely aligned than they did with our alphas.

We acknowledged when our feelings for Terence were becoming detrimental to our bond and took a time out to focus on putting our priorities back in order. It wasn't about one of us winning over the other. It was about working together to get the alpha we wanted integrated into our pack. And it didn't matter which of us accomplished that.

Anyway, she was a little sad, even as she tried to hide it, so Adrian took her out to an art gallery and expensive hors d'oeuvres that were not at all filling. Phynn was left to take care of me if I pulled on our bond in a panic.

Phynn settled me on jeans and a shirt, dressing it up slightly with a nice thin sweater but letting me wear sneakers. They were new, never having been out of the box. So at least they were clean.

I hadn't known there was an apartment above the juice shop, and it took us a couple tries to locate the door. Phynn helped me lug the bags of packaged food up the stairs and left me with a kiss as I stood staring at the door, trying once again to catch my breath.

Finally, I knocked on the door.

Terence opened it a few moments later and I stared for a minute as his toasted coconut and mineral oil scent filled me. I almost whined, wanting to climb into it.

"Hi," he said, a smile touching his lips. And yet, I could see a closely guarded, haunted expression behind his eyes.

"Hi," I answered. "I brought food." I waved my hand over the two enormous reusable bags filled to the brim with storage containers.

Terence raised a brow and chuckled. "I'm not hiding more people here, Kaiser. It's just the two of us."

I know that was directed at how much food was here but still, I was elated at the words. We were alone. Just the two of us.

He reached forward to bring both bags inside and I swooned nearer. He was dressed in nice slacks and a button-down, rolled half way up his forearms. His chest through the shirt had me almost drooling.

Terence started taking containers out and setting them on the counter as I stepped inside, the door shutting behind me. The apartment was... tiny. There was a pocket-sized living area to my immediate right and a small kitchen along the wall on my left. I could see the bed beyond the television on the right and that left me presuming that the bathroom was behind the slightly ajar door.

It was little and cozy, and reminded me strongly of a nest. So much so that I felt the sudden urge to just... bring things a little closer and hunker down with him. Especially since it was warm, filled with earthy colors and his scent alone.

"Small, huh?" Terence asked.

I turned to look at him as he finished folding the second bag and placing it on one of the chairs with the first, all the storage containers on the counter.

"I love it," I told him, smiling a little. "It's very..." Was it inappropriate to say nest-like? Would that be off-putting to an alpha?

He chuckled. "It's just me. I don't need a lot of space."

His voice didn't sound sad and yet, I could almost feel the grief in his words. Alphas don't want to be alone. Hell, no one wants to be alone. We crave the family of a pack.

"What do you need me to do?" he asked, looking at the containers.

I shook my head. "Nothing. I got it. Just... keep me company?"

Terence smiled, rounding to the other side of the counter – which I now realized was a table – and sat as he watched me step into the kitchen nervously. I have no idea what I'm doing!

The fact made me swallow. I closed my eyes for a moment and pulled out my phone to pull up Phynn's instructions.

"Okay, just point me in the direction of baking sheets, a

casserole dish, and a small frying pan." I was most nervous about the frying pan.

He pointed to cabinets, and I took my time working my way through each step, reading it thoroughly (twice) before actually doing it. I could feel Terence's gaze on me, and I was almost bouncing on my feet because he watched me with a constant small smile.

When I almost panicked from missing a step, he touched me. For the first time ever, he touched me. His hand landed on mine, stilling me from shaking as I gripped the correct bowl in my hand. I couldn't screw up this dinner!

"Hey," he said, his voice quiet and gentle as he lightly squeezed my hand. My heart stopped from his skin on mine. "No pressure, Kaiser. I'd have been just as happy ordering pizza. You didn't need to go through all this trouble."

"I wanted to," I told him, biting my lip. I winced a little before admitting, "I didn't actually prepare this. I'm just supposed to finish it." I nodded towards my phone. "When I say those instructions are detailed, I'm pretty sure a preschooler could finish them. I'm just... nervous."

"Don't be. Whatever you're making is going to be amazing. It already smells fantastic, Kaiser."

I sighed, bowing my head a little. "Thanks."

"Let me help you," he said, getting to his feet and letting go of my hand. I'd have rather he hung onto it.

I wanted to tell him no. I wanted to make this dinner for him. I wanted to prove that I could be better than an omega and cook something delicious – even if I hadn't fully made it. I'd have been better off serving cereal and toast.

"Okay," I conceded. I handed him the bowl and moved further into his small kitchen. I read the line of instructions and Terence went straight to work. He was already anticipating the next step, reaching for the right container and popping the lid off.

"You know what this is?" I asked.

"Close enough," he said, grinning at me.

I nearly fell over. When he fully smiles like that, it felt like I was coming undone at the seams.

It wasn't long before the two of us had whatever concoction Phynn had put together into the casserole. I had pre-seasoned vegetables on a baking sheet and freshly risen dough balls on a second baking sheet.

Meanwhile, in the small pan on the stove, was where I was going to toss the freshly roasted vegetables when they were done. What did Phynn call it - a glaze? And lastly, we put together a salad with the remaining couple containers. Phynn hadn't mixed all the vegetables with the greens in case there were some Terence didn't like. But Terence had me dump them all. I set the buzzer and turned around to watch the mixture on the stove with a sigh. Almost done. And it wasn't a disaster yet. It could still burn. I could still bake it too long. But right now, it was on track. And it smelled good.

Terence reached over the stove and flicked one of the dials. I flushed, realizing I hadn't actually turned the stove on. I squinted at it, my shoulders raising. "Guess it helps to do that, huh?" I asked, timidly.

He chuckled. "It certainly cooks a little quicker, yes."

"Sorry. I'm not usually the one cooking."

"Good. You shouldn't be."

I looked at him, my brows furrowed together. "I shouldn't?"

His smile turned a little wider as he shook his head. "Absolutely not. You should be fed, Kaiser. Not waiting on anyone else."

"I wanted to make you dinner, though," I told him. "To prove to you-"

"That you're a good omega?" he asked, cutting off my words.

I flushed and nodded.

Terence sighed. "I'm really, really sorry for making you feel like you're not. You're a great omega. I'm just a shit alpha."

CHAPTER FIFTEEN

Terence

His eyes widened and he shook his head.

"Trust me, if I've made you feel like you were a bad omega by the way I've acted since the day we met is in any way your fault, I'm a shit alpha, Kaiser," I assured him.

The way he looked at me made me want to pull him against my chest until he stopped doubting himself. I hated myself a little more the longer he looked at me like that. *I'd* made him feel like that. Zack would have kicked my ass until I was unconscious.

I reached in front of him to shake the pan a little, moving the butter and herbs together so they mixed evenly as I tried not to let the thought of Zack interfere. I couldn't. If I did, if I thought about my pack too long, I was going to send Kaiser home with that broken look again. And fuck, I couldn't live with myself if I did that.

I'd agreed to this. I'd invited him here. The least I could do was act how a damn alpha should act.

"Let me finish this," I told him. "There's a remote by the television. See if there's something you're interested in watching while we eat."

He bit his lip as he glanced at the stove and then the timer. "But I'm supposed to-"

"You're supposed to be taken care of. Let me finish."

"I don't always need to be taken care of," he said.

I heard the pout in his voice, even as he tried to hide it. There was also a bit of defiance there, too. It made me smile, and my smile only spread when he looked up at me with a flush.

"Alright," I agreed. "I let you prepare dinner. And I think we can both agree that that wasn't in an effort to take care of you, right?"

"Yes," he said carefully.

"I even let you bring dinner, with a dozen containers to boot, meaning, if anything, you were taking care of me. Right?"

His eyes narrowed slightly as he agreed again.

"That means, you've already proven to me that you are perfectly capable of shouldering the weight of some responsibilities, even when they're not to your strength. Now you can let me finish this while you find us something to watch."

I watched as he studied me, trying to determine what to make of the conversation and my reasoning. Once more, he glanced at the stove before looking back at me. "Okay," he said with a sigh of defeat. I didn't miss the way some of the tension left his shoulders as he backed out of the small kitchen.

"Good," I said, smiling as I watched him turn for the small living space across from the kitchen. He didn't have far to walk, so I only had thirty seconds of watching that fine ass perfectly framed in his dark pants. How have I not noticed how impeccably shaped his backside is?

Too busy running away and acting like a jackass. He glanced at me, his cheeks flushing when he caught me watching him. I smirked and turned away. I spent the next minute tending to the butter sauce and determining that it needed more butter. I had no idea if I had any.

I rummaged through my fridge for a minute before I found half a stick of butter. And then I frowned further when I saw that I had almost nothing in there to drink. Wow, I'm a shit alpha and a shit host. This is going great so far.

After adding the butter to the pan, I returned to my freezer to determine if there was anything in there worth having. Oh! I had wine. I closed the fridge and opened the cabinet above it, pulling out the bottle of white wine. I glanced at the meal and determined that it would have to work.

"Wine?" I asked, turning to show Kaiser the bottle.

He smiled and nodded.

Great. Now, do I have wine glasses??

I'd paid to have this place fully stocked. The wine had been a housewarming gift from the realtor. Hopefully that meant he'd thought to gift glasses or at least stock them.

I was momentarily distracted when the buzzer went off. I pulled the biscuits out of the oven and set them on the counter while I rearranged the vegetables and whatever delicious concoction Kaiser had brought. The cheese hadn't melted quite yet, and the vegetables weren't quite brown or somewhat shriveled either. Few more minutes.

Another quick toss of the butter sauce and I went back to searching for wine glasses. I found them, tucked behind all the water bottles. I had a problem. Why exactly did I have eight water bottles?

Hopefully the wine was good. I pulled the cork and poured

two glasses. I'd never been into wine. Miles had been developing a taste for it, but-

Nope. I can drown in that sorrow later. Right now, we are getting ready for dinner. I brought Kaiser a glass and sat next to him. I hadn't realized how small the couch was until that moment. If I wasn't careful, I'd be right on top of him. And after the touch of his hand in mine, I was burning for another feel.

Kaiser took his glass with a soft smile as he looked at me with those gorgeous steel blue eyes. I held my glass up and he softly tapped his to mine. We were holding the other's gaze as we brought the glasses to our lips, not dropping the hold as we each sipped.

"Mm," Kaiser said, looking at the glass. "This is good."

I grinned. "I admittedly am not too versed in wine so you could completely be lying, and I'd believe you."

Kaiser grinned. "Not lying. I like it."

I nodded, getting to my feet to return to the kitchen for another check in the oven. Vegetables were done. I pulled the tray out and immediately dumped them into the pan. I'm glad Kaiser had pulled one of the larger pans out. I spent the next minute tossing them to coat them in the butter sauce before turning the burner off. By the time I pulled plates out and dished out these first few items, the casserole-something should be complete.

This was one of those times that I wished I'd thought through a table for the living space. The room was small and a table would completely fill the room, but how were we going to eat in there when we had nothing to set plates and glasses on?

Okay, the tiny table that served as a counter was going to have to work. I cleared off all the empty storage containers and piled them in the sink. I'd opted not to have a dishwasher since it was just me. It hadn't seemed practical. But now I was rethinking that.

By the time I had wiped the counter and went back to arranging plates, the cheese on top of the casserole was nice and brown so I pulled it out. I waited a few minutes while it rested and cooled a bit, cleaning some of the storage containers as the time passed. After I loaded the plates, I pushed them to be in front of the chairs before rounding the side.

Kaiser was already watching me. "I realized I didn't have any kind of furniture that would make eating on the couch efficient. Table instead?"

He nodded and stood. I pulled the chair out for him and pushed him in as he sat. They were tall chairs at the tall counter. I moved to the other chair, pulling it away from him just a little so we wouldn't be on top of each other while we ate.

We ate the first few bites in silence while we both sampled what was in front of us. Whoever prepared it was a damned good cook. This was excellent.

"Thank you for having me over," Kaiser said.

I sighed, turning slightly in my chair to face him. "I can't promise I won't freak out again in the future," I warned him. "I'm... not good at some things and life catches up sometimes."

"I trigger that in you."

I shook my head but shrugged. "Kind of, but it's truly nothing you're doing, Kaiser. You've never done anything wrong."

I was sure he didn't believe me, even as he nodded. I wanted to touch him. To pull his face around to look at me and assure him until he trusted my words. But I was too afraid. Touching him was a step I wasn't prepared for. I wasn't there yet. I wasn't- I just wasn't. This was already bordering on too much.

We ate quietly, commenting on the food from time to time.

It seemed that he really did like the wine. I thought maybe he was nervous drinking, but his praise of it seemed genuine at least. I'd have to find out where this was purchased.

I finished washing his storage containers after dinner and started dishing the leftovers into it. Kaiser tried to make me keep them, but after some convincing, he relented that it was just me in the house. I didn't need leftovers. Even so, I kept one more meal of all the fixings. The rest were going home with him.

Sitting together on the couch felt a little too close for me. But I didn't want to kick him out yet. I didn't want to kick him out at all. When he left, I wanted it to be in a better place than the departure of almost every other meeting we'd had.

As much as he wanted to prove something to me, something that was entirely unnecessary, I needed to prove to both of us that I wasn't a complete disaster. Internally, I was. But he didn't need to know that. He didn't need to carry my burden with me.

So, we moved to the couch. It really was the only size option for the wall. A large one wouldn't have fit in the room without blocking the door. But damn, it didn't feel like it was made for two people. Certainly not two people who weren't touching. I was nearly curled around the arm rest, so I'd not be on his lap.

Our night remained quiet and conversation easy over the next couple hours. We settled on a movie that he said was one of Marley's favorites. Long minutes would go by without either of us talking but I didn't think it was as uncomfortable as it could have been.

I didn't watch much of the movie. My attention was wholly on the omega next to me as his perfume saturated the air. I was sure he was working hard not to fill the place with his scent. I could tell that he became uncomfortable every time a fresh wave burst forth.

But he didn't apologize anymore. Even if he looked at me a little sheepishly.

Finally, I thought the best way to put him at ease was not to try and sit on the armrest. I got up to refill his wine. When I sat back next to him, I let myself fill the cushion as I naturally would. That put my shoulder against his.

Kaiser inhaled as he stilled, his hand not holding the wine glass fished around his pant leg before relaxing. His perfume bloomed as it gushed through the room, and I was sure my pheromones exploded in response. They weren't something I recognized often anymore since they were my own, but based on my physical reaction, I was sure it had happened.

He was settling after some time when I didn't pull away. He sighed, smiling at me as we watched the rest of the movie. And then he received a text message.

"My ride's here," he said.

I nodded and stood, offering him my hand. His eyes met mine as he placed his hand in mine. It was almost electric, and I worked hard not to let my purr out. Gently, I pulled him to his feet and took his empty wine glass.

With both of his bags in hand, I walked him to the door. He watched me with curiosity as I slipped into my shoes and followed him down the stairs.

"Never let an omega out alone at night," I said as we reached the bottom door.

He smiled, bowing his head as I reached beyond him to open the door. We stopped at the edge of the building where a car was parked on the opposite side of the street. It was dark enough that I couldn't make out who was inside.

Kaiser turned to me and waited. But I couldn't bring myself to kiss him.

"Thank you for dinner," I said. He smiled shyly and I was sure he was going to comment. "You did a damn good job."

His smile widened. I offered him the bags, letting my fingers brush his as he took them from me. "See you later," I said, thinking how incredibly lame that was.

Kaiser nodded, his smile fading some, as he turned away. I watched him walk across the street. When the driver side door opened, I turned for my door.

I stopped just inside my apartment, letting his perfume fill me with a longing I hadn't felt in a long time and never for an omega. Maybe one more glimpse. Flicking the lights off, I crossed to the back of the apartment to look out the window.

Whoever had been in the driver's seat wasn't Marley. Definitely a man and certainly bigger than Kaiser. He had Kaiser in his arms, and I was sure they were talking about something as he comforted the omega.

Maybe I hadn't done better this time. Maybe Kaiser was still leaving upset. He wasn't doing anything wrong. I was.

The alpha walked him around to the other side of the car, opening the door for Kaiser to get in. I sank to the bed as I watched, and I swear, the alpha even went so far as to buckle Kaiser in. The thought made me smile. See? That's how an omega should be taken care of.

He closed the door and rounded the car, pausing when he was facing my building. I couldn't make out his face in the dark night, but there was no doubt in my mind he was watching my window.

I hoped he'd be angry enough at me if I'd sent Kaiser home upset again that he'd not let his omega near me. Or his pretty beta with the delicious lips. The thought made me ache and once that feeling set in, everything I'd been pushing away over the evening came crashing down.

I gasped for breath as I watched the alpha get into the car.

A moment later they drove away. And I let myself fall back, curling up as the onslaught of memories fell around me.

They weren't bad memories. Not a single one. But they were memories of a time I'd never get back, of a love I'd lost and never have again. Of a future that was filled with promises I'd never get to live.

On top of all that, there was an omega who wanted me, and I wasn't sure I was strong enough to allow it to happen.

CHAPTER SIXTEEN

Terence

I woke up groggy, as if I hadn't slept all night. That meant it hadn't been a peaceful dreamless night. Thankfully, I'd never actually seen the accident that took my pack. And though I'd identified their bodies later, those weren't images that stuck with me.

If I truly thought about them mangled and dead, I could see their broken bodies in my mind. But for whatever reason, and I was willing to bet it was just the trauma of it all, those weren't the memories that plagued me.

It was their sudden loss. Losing any packmate would be hard. But losing them all, in one fell swoop, was devastating. I was a very broken man, and I wasn't sure I'd ever fully heal. Not from this.

I'd constantly reflected that if I'd just been unhappy, if there was even the slightest bit of suffocation or resentment or jealousy – anything at all – maybe this wouldn't be so bad. Maybe it wouldn't have hit so hard.

It was a lie, of course.

The emptiness I felt at their bonds suddenly going silent hadn't hit me right away. A week went by before my grief settled into a constant blanket around me. Only then did I find myself reaching. Reaching blindly to grasp onto anything.

But there was nothing there.

That's when the debilitating sorrow took over my life, when I realized what I'd been reaching for were my packmates' bonds. And those bonds were empty. There was an echo of where they'd once been. A hollow part of me that had once been filled that was now barren.

Even now, I unconsciously reach for one of their bonds from time to time. Last night, I had reached for Zack and Miles' respectively when I'd thought about them. And, per usual, I came up empty.

It was probably those moments that caused my panic and meltdowns. It was so natural for me to relate everything back to those I loved. And in doing so, I'd innately reach for their bond. When there was nothing there, the reality of my life came crashing down, leaving me breathless and filled with pain all over again.

And so, I ran from Kaiser. Ran from Marley. Everything about them pushed me towards emotions that had only ever been solely reserved for my packmates. And now, I was a walking disaster.

I stretched before I sat up. My foot hit my phone where I'd dropped it on the floor. Glancing down, I watched as a little light blinked up at me. Sighing, I picked it up. What had Nora scheduled this morning?

But it wasn't from Nora. It was from Kaiser.

[Kaiser] Please see me again. Wherever you want. I'll even go to the gym.

I chuckled, shaking my head and flicking the phone off. I

was feeling a little stiff this morning. Probably because my gym routine was off. My muscles were getting sloppy and lazy from the lack of physical strain.

I stepped into the shower and let the icy water turn hot. I didn't wash. Even in the bathroom where Kaiser hadn't been last night, I could still get the occasional hint of pine and cinnamon. It made me pause as I breathed it in. It made me ache as I emotionally and physically reacted. It made my dick harden and throb, which I also ignored.

Dressing in gym clothes, I headed for my shake first, drinking it down before I stuck a couple bagels in the toaster. I looked around the kitchen as I waited. Wine glasses. Plates in the sink. The dirty casserole dish and pan that had the vegetables on it.

Glancing towards the couch, I knew Kaiser's scent would be clinging to the right side. Part of me wanted to get closer, bury my face in the cushion to gather it all up.

I would not. He was not my omega.

Maybe I ought to open the window and air the place out while I was gone for the day.

The bagels popped up and I smeared them with cream cheese. I paused as I stared at the couch. Yes, open the window. Crossing into my room, I pushed all three windows that overlooked the park open and took a deep inhale of the crisp morning air.

Good. Better.

After I finished my shake and tossed it into the sink with the rest of the dirty dishes, I threw my gym bag over my shoulder and grabbed my bagels. Time to get back on track. Gym. Smoothie. Home. In that order. And with nothing else.

I walked the perimeter of the park as I ate my bagels, watching as early risers were already jogging around the park. Even though I started to shake my head, I was now lumped into the group of early risers who did stupid ridiculous extenuating exercises as a means to... okay for me, it was a means to lose myself in the pain and monotony. Other people probably saw it as healthy and shit.

I didn't pause in the door to search out the scents this morning. Kaiser had been at my house. I'd slept with his perfume in my lungs. I could deal with it if he was here. Hopefully, he didn't just appear. He needed a bell or some shit to alert me before he stepped into the room.

I tucked my earbuds in and flipped open my screen. The text messages were up still, and I stared at it as the little dots in the corner said Kaiser was typing. I watched, waiting to see what he was going to say.

After a minute and nothing, I flipped to the music app and loaded the playlist. I turned back to the text message quickly, but the little dots had stopped.

Or I had been imagining it. That was it.

I watched one of the betas using the stretch elastics for a while before grabbing a set for myself. Yes, I was pretty impressionable when it came to gym activities. Whatever looked interesting was where I was going to go next. He smirked at me as I walked by with them, nodding towards the bars.

There were bars that were designed for these bands specifically, where we could attach them to the ends and then adjust the resistance and length. I hooked the handles around my feet before squatting to drop my head under the bar, so it rested along the back of my shoulders.

It was like lifting weights on your shoulders but using the elastics. I did this in rounds of twenty reps and fifteen second breaks between. I switched it up after, setting the bar on the ground and standing on it. Alternating arms, I used the elastics to work on my biceps in reps of twenty with fifteen second rests.

My music cut off as soon as I was done with the reps. Since it seemed like a good time for a water break, I headed for my bag and pulled out my phone.

The text message with Kaiser was still up and I watched once again as little dots danced while he typed. I watched it for several minutes as I sipped my water. The dots would bounce for several seconds before stopping for longer. Until finally, they stopped all together.

He was trying to type more. I sighed and closed the text message to turn the music back on. I returned to the bands for an hour before deciding that I was done at the gym for the day. Instead, I ran around the path at the park until I ran out of water.

Marley wasn't there. I looked. Then, denied I had looked on my way to the juice bar.

Since I don't pay much attention to the days of the week, I only determined it was the weekend by the quiet, slower pace of the customers within Juice Me. I liked that there were always four employees, regardless of whether or not we had customers enough to warrant that many. Nora had conceded that I'd have a fourth on weekends as long as that fourth could be cross trained with the back juicers. Those who made the prepackaged and pre juiced features. I may own the place, but Nora ran it. I conceded to her decisions.

"Appointments this week," Nora reminded me on the way out. "Tuesday and Wednesday, Mr. Andersen."

"Yes, ma'am," I answered, nodding at her.

She grinned and turned back to work.

With smoothie in hand, one that had to be my newest favorite flavor, I headed upstairs and continued with my daily routine of showering after the gym. I finished my smoothie on the couch, the lingering notes of Kaiser reaching me as I sat there in the silence of my small apartment.

I busied myself cleaning the rest of the dishes before dressing in clothes that didn't belong at the gym and left for my car. After a quick search, I found a liquor store and perused up and down the aisles until I found another bottle of the wine Kaiser had enjoyed. And then I suffered through a forty-five-minute lesson on wines while the woman explained the difference between regions and the finer notes. All I'd wanted was another couple wines that were as good as this one. It wasn't such a difficult question.

With two more whites and a red in addition to the bottle of the one Kaiser had liked, I headed back to my car and drove to the grocery store. I had no idea what I was buying as I strolled through the aisles filling my cart, making sure that I picked up more options to drink as well as basics, like butter and flour. I spent $290 on food. It had been a while since I'd purchased that much food!

But I wasn't going to think about it. I drove around the part of town I lived in for a while, just to see what else I could find. I stopped at a flower shop and perused what they had. This one was filled with an entire wall of buckets of flowers that one could pull out to have a bouquet made.

On a whim, I started picking a few things. Dark greenery, a couple lines of ficus. A couple branches of boxwood and dark grasses that were almost feathery. I added a few succulents that ended in a deep burgundy before turning back to the grasses and finding a few different fillers with those deep notes. A couple that curled at the tip like fiddleheads were particularly fascinating. And then a few that looked like they were dark little green beads at the end of a stem. I added a few flowers at the end, all in deep burgundy or blush shades.

With my handful of flowers in hand, I brought them to the florist at the counter.

"Would you like them wrapped or a vase?" she asked.

"Suggestion?" I countered.

She smiled. "Vase."

I nodded in agreement and watched as she turned and placed my pickings in a deep sink before turning to the glassware behind her. She didn't choose a rounded, feminine vase but something with crisp lines, tall and round. She filled it with water before dumping in a small scoop of what I assumed to be plant food. She mixed it with a long stick and then wiped the outside of the glass dry.

She wrapped it with a clean, canvas ribbon and brought it to the side. I watched, almost mesmerized as she snipped one piece at a time and stuck it in the vase, arranging as she went. By the time she was done, I was thoroughly impressed and pleased with the pieces I chose. They went together rather well.

I paid her and left, setting the vase of flowers between my many bags of food. One more stop. How do you watch television and eat without something to eat on? A furniture store was last on my list.

But this proved to be more challenging than I anticipated. The television in the living room was already nearly right in your face when you sat on the couch. Maybe I needed a bit of a reworking of furniture. A bed with drawers under it for more clothing storage. And then maybe a television stand that could somehow come apart, so a table popped out. Was that a thing? More importantly, if it wasn't, could it be?

The only thing I couldn't quite fix was the lack of hanging space in my apartment. I'd have to come back to that. Since I was going to need more time to determine how to make my space more functionable, I was handed a couple product and style catalogs and left the store with two TV trays.

There was produce and meat in my car though and the day was shaping up to be quite warm. I couldn't dally anymore.

It took me several trips to empty my car from my errands. I managed to fit the two TV trays under the couch and decided that maybe I was going to need to replace that as well. The size was fine, in hindsight. If I have company over and we sit on the couch, it was just going to need to be someone I was happy to touch and be close with. Seemed reasonable.

My fridge and cabinets had never been so full, and I stood back to look at my kitchen. If I added a couple extra overhead cabinets and got rid of the excess water bottles, I could get a dishwasher. But was that necessary? Did I *need* a dishwasher?

If I was going to cook, I thought it would likely come in handy. And I'd just bought almost $300 worth of food. Clearly, I was going to cook.

The easier explanation was that it was time to move into a bigger apartment. I was outgrowing this one.

After I'd taken one of the slabs of meat (which would be amazing on a grill – I was going to have to find a place to put a grill!), I tenderized it a little before rubbing it with seasoning and sealing it in a storage bag. It was two in the afternoon. If I let it marinade for a few hours, that meant I could let it sit out and rest, coming close to room temperature before I cook it. Plenty of time.

Now that everything was set with ingredients strewn all over the place, I picked up my phone. I watched, once again, as the little dots in my chat with Kaiser bounced. I must have caught him at the end of an attempt to say more. It stopped quickly.

After waiting another minute or so to see if he'd actually send something, I texted him instead. It was almost instantaneous that he responded, and I swear, I could hear the relief in his voice.

Yes, I was a shit alpha. I should have texted him this morning. I shook my head and turned to the stack of clothing on top of the dresser with a frown. Time to see if I could stuff more things in the drawers.

CHAPTER SEVENTEEN

Marley

The shift of the bed woke me. And then the blinding white light of Kaiser's cell phone. I shifted, pulling myself up so I could pluck it from his hands and turn it off.

"Marley," he whined.

"Go to sleep," I demanded. "Leave the man alone. You can harass him in the morning."

I felt his pout through the bond we shared with our alphas, neither of which were in his room with us. I sighed and pulled him against me, burying his face in my chest and humming to him so he'd release his tension.

My understanding, though I didn't listen to the whole explanation, was that his date with Terence had gone well. And yet, Kaiser still came home defeated and pouting.

Our alphas sent me to bed with him in their strategic way so that Kaiser and I would reconnect. It's not that I didn't want him to have a good time with Terence. It's that I wanted to spend time with Terence, and for Terence to not run away after I kiss him.

He'd kissed me. When I pressed my lips to his, he'd kissed me, too. And then he ran away. Almost literally, he ran out of the park. I was horrified.

When I'd gotten home, Kaiser had cooed all over me while also sincerely commiserating with me. It had been what I needed and yet, we were both left feeling defeated.

It was a strange feeling. Wanting a man who, by all appearances, wanted us in return and yet, acted like he was being taunted with fire. It was disheartening. The thing that caught me by surprise the most was how much it had hurt.

I had a very long conversation about Terence with Adrian. He and Phynn agreed that Kaiser and I could pursue this alpha, but the ultimate goal was that, if we wanted something permanent with him, Terence needed to join our pack.

Kaiser had readily agreed. And it's not that I disagreed that Terence should join our pack. It's that I wasn't convinced that Terence was going to be up for that any time soon. How patient were our alphas going to be? How lenient were they going to be with letting their omega and beta date another alpha?

And what if it led to courting?

Betas weren't courted by tradition. We were just the extra in society. We were the plentiful. The ordinary. There was nothing special about us since we made up 80% of society. It was the alpha bite that we craved. The belonging and wholeness of a bond that only an alpha can provide. It was the high, and heat that an omega promised a pack.

I'd heard of some nasty underground organizations that saw an opportunity with both limited designations and exploited them for money. Trafficking and black-market sales. Of omegas and alpha bites. It made me shudder.

Kaiser finally fell back asleep, but now I was wide awake.

Though I was feeling a little jealous about my omega's progress with Terence where mine had been left dead in the water, I sighed in contentment, nonetheless.

I live an amazing life. I have what every beta dreams about. A real pack with real bonds. I was loved and taken care of and yet, still had my freedom to be me. I had a job I loved but not that I needed since my alphas provided for Kaiser and I. I also had the occasional gift from my alphas. They didn't just spoil their omega. They indulged me as well.

The family I came from was what society referred to as mock packs. A group of betas living together in family pack units without the binding of an alpha. Only an alpha could form a true pack. Anything else was a mock pack.

My family was one such. One of my fathers and mother had gone so far as to bite each other and pretend that they had a bond. I'd asked another of my fathers once if it was real and he shook his head with a sigh.

"No, there's no real bond but it makes them feel better to pretend that there is," he told me.

I learned a lot about betas in that one statement. Our craving for a pack ran so deep, ingrained into us by biology and evolution, that we were desperate for a pack.

My family was likewise thrilled to find that I managed to gather the pack that they never could. Not just a single alpha, but two. And that the alphas treated me with respect, with love and kindness.

I also learned a lot about alphas during that first visit with my family and new pack. Not all alphas were good people. I was incredibly lucky.

So, although I craved this new alpha that Kaiser was having more luck with than I was, I wouldn't be discontent. I swore to myself as I lay there, running my fingers through my sleeping omega's hair, that I would support him however he needed me to so that he could progress with this new alpha. With Terence.

Because I was sure, if he won, that meant that I had a better shot with Terence, too. And I was sure that our alphas would like Terence. When he wasn't actively looking at Kaiser like he was a living embodiment of a disease and trying to run from us, he was kind and interesting. He was beautiful, with the body of a god.

I dozed until the room was filled with the first notes of breakfast sausage. Kaiser woke at almost the same moment, groaning as he turned his face into the air.

"I didn't think I'd be hungry again," he mumbled. "I ate so much last night."

I grinned. And then I was startled as he jolted upright and dove for his phone.

"Oh no," he groaned as he flopped back onto the bed.

Raising a brow, I pried his phone from his hand to look at the screen. At four a.m. when he woke me up with his phone light, he'd texted Terence. I nearly giggled.

"He's going to think I'm a psycho," Kaiser whined. It wasn't a true whine. Not that deep, sad sound that made our alphas come running. It was a child's whine when he knew that he'd fucked up a little bit.

I handed him back the phone and crawled from the bed. Without having any true advice on this subject, I wasn't going to suggest something that might make the situation worse. It's not like he'd said anything awful or cringeworthy. Maybe just a little desperate.

When he was still lying in bed after I dressed, I sighed and rounded the bed to stand over him. He was staring at the screen. He'd typed something more, to the effect of 'I'm sorry. Please ignore me.' I watched as he shook his head and erased it.

"I want him to ignore my desperate middle of the night

text, but I still want to see him again," he muttered and started typing something else.

'I'm sorry. You were probably asleep. I swear, I'm not pathetic all the time.'

Then he erased that and closed his eyes on a miserable groan.

I took the phone from him again and shut it off. He opened his eyes to watch me. "Our alphas are making breakfast. Get out of bed so they can feed you."

A smile drifted onto his lips. He sat up, using nothing but his stomach muscles in a way that made me green with envy, and pressed his lips to mine. "Yes, beta," he murmured against my lips.

Kaiser was a swoon-worthy man. Designation aside, he was gorgeous. All the proportions of an alpha in a more compact body. Slightly shorter, slightly leaner, but still hard, taut, and defined. His features were smoother, without the constant shadow of stubble. And his cock was slightly different.

Alphas were big in all senses of the word. Growing up, anatomy class said that it wasn't just their knot that made them different. It was their size, length and girth, too. I'd only been with Phynn and Adrian as far as alphas were concerned, but I could certainly agree to that in relation to the betas I'd been with before them.

Betas were rumored that, on the whole, they were smaller, averaging out at five to six inches. Alphas were approximately three to five inches longer. We weren't going to talk about their thickness.

And then there were male omegas. They fell somewhere between. An average six and a half inches and their thickness, though visibly looking on the thicker side, was softer. Not quite so rock hard. They were more pliable.

Although I obviously couldn't speak for other male omegas,

not only because they were incredibly rare, but also because I'd only been with Kaiser of the male omegas.

Anyway... I managed to get my horny omega from the bed with little groping, and dressed in at least some shorts. Just shorts. Since he was a pinup model, I didn't mind in the least when that's how he decided he wanted to traipse through the house.

Both Phynn and Adrian cooked on the regular. Phynn was a slightly better cook because he came from a pack of foodies. They were obsessed over good food. Adrian learned to cook out of necessity. An alpha provides for his pack. They were both preparing breakfast this morning. Adrian was on waffle duty while Phynn took care of eggs, sausage, and I was pretty sure the scent of blueberry muffins filled the air.

"Morning," Adrian said, his warm brown eyes trained on Kaiser as he dropped into a stool at the counter.

"Hi," Kaiser said, smiling at him.

Adrian continued to study him for a minute while he poured Kaiser and me juice. We were big juice drinkers in this house. Which was how we'd found Juice Me. We bought several gallons of their pre-packaged juices every week.

"Sleep well?" Phynn asked.

Kaiser pouted a little as he accepted the glass. "I texted him in the middle of the night."

Phynn turned around to raise a brow. Adrian chuckled.

"Kai," Adrian said, shaking his head. "Maybe you need to give him a little breathing room, love."

"I know," Kaiser whined like a child again and dropped his head onto his arms. "I didn't mean to. Maybe I- I don't know, had a dream and thought it was a brilliant idea while I was half asleep."

Adrian grinned, turning back to the waffle maker and taking the finished one out.

"I tried to text something this morning to excuse away my crazy, but it all sounded even more pathetic so now it's just sitting there waiting for him to notice it."

Chances were, Terence had already noticed it and hadn't responded. I wasn't sure if that was a good thing or not.

———

I FOUND Kaiser in his nest later that morning, curled up on the floor of cushions and staring at his phone. My heart ached for him, and I didn't know how to help.

Instead, I dropped onto the floor behind him and curled around him. His sorrow was deep. The bond we shared said he was close to tears. That explained why the alphas were lingering close to the nest this morning.

"I know you feel this," Kaiser said quietly.

"I feel you," I told him.

He shook his head. "Yes, but you're lying if you say you don't feel about him like I do. He is pack. I know he is. Why doesn't he know that?"

I didn't answer. He was right, of course. And I was choosing to ignore the red flags that said I shouldn't feel this way about a virtual stranger. At least I wasn't alone in feeling a craving for a man that wasn't one of my pack.

We remained in the nest throughout the morning. I caught Kaiser periodically attempting to text Terence. But each time, he deleted it. Eventually he'd turn off the phone and close his eyes. Some time would pass and then he'd start the whole thing over again.

Periodically, I suggested we go do something outside of the nest. But Kaiser was so miserable that he'd just shake his head. I could feel his anxiety building as the day went on. Adrian brought us lunch and hand fed our omega to make sure the man ate. And then finally, Adrian's patience came to an end.

He took Kaiser's face in his fingers and forced our omega's gaze to his. "I'm giving you one day, Kaiser. But then we're done with this. If he doesn't respond and you continue to be miserable like this, no more attempts with him. I will not let you chase him. Understand me?"

Kaiser's anxiety spiked as he stared at Adrian. "Two days," he countered.

"No. One day. He has until tomorrow morning to answer you. That's it. No one gets to treat you this way, regardless of what he's going through."

"But-"

"One day," Adrian said, the force of his tone making Kaiser flinch.

Kaiser didn't argue again. He watched Adrian leave the room before looking at me with wide, desperate eyes.

Since I wasn't sure what I could do to mollify this situation either, I just pulled Kaiser back down into the warm cushions and spooned him.

Maybe I needed to sneak out and impress upon Terence that he was on his last chance with Kaiser. If he wanted our omega at all, he needed to step up.

I was dozing, biting on my lip, when Kaiser suddenly jumped to his feet. He was staring at his phone with wide eyes. His bond burst so brightly that Phynn threw the door open to make sure he was alright.

But Kaiser said nothing as he stared. Then his wide eyes looked up, meeting mine. "He's making dinner. For me. I can come over."

Phynn raised a brow and turned to leave.

"Love you, alpha," Kaiser said quietly, his voice making Phynn stop.

I caught the smile on Phynn's lips on his profile. "I know, Kai. Love you, too. Let me know what time you need to be there, and I'll drop you off."

Kaiser nodded as Phynn left the nest, shutting the door quietly behind him. He remained where he was, completely overwhelmed as he stared at the phone, his chest barely rising and falling as he struggled to breathe.

"Did you answer him?"

He shook his head.

"You probably should," I suggested.

By the short answer, I assumed he typed something like 'yes' and nothing else. Then he looked up at me with panic. "You're going to need to fuck me silly so I can keep myself together tonight," he told me.

I laughed and held my hands out to him. Kaiser dropped his phone and lunged for me, his mouth hitting mine as he shoved me down into the cushions again.

It didn't start out as me fucking him silly. Kaiser liked to try and take the lead with me from time to time. I let him, knowing it didn't generally last long. He was good to carry on until he hit his first orgasm. But those orgasms were like a drug. When the first one hit, he needed more. And so, he begged me for another.

Our clothes were off almost as soon as he fell into the cushions. I wasn't sure if they were still in one piece. Kaiser wasn't big on warm up for foreplay. But with an omega, it was rarely a problem for him or his partner. He was already dripping when he brought his cock to me. Rubbing his head through my folds and over my clit a couple times, my body jerked as he started to push into me.

The difference between taking Kaiser's cock and one of my alphas' was all about how hard they were. Dildos for example. You had your soft silicone ones that you could squeeze, and they had some give. They were hard but also flexible. This was what Kaiser felt like. Then there were the hard plastic ones that may as well be a hard stone cylinder. That was an alpha except with the loose skin moving over that hard core.

I love both feelings. It was good that Kaiser was a bit softer since he wasn't keen to take his time or start his thrusting slowly. He pushed his way in and began slamming into me as hard as he could. I was pretty sure this was an omega thing. The drive for an orgasm consumed everything else in him.

He hovered over me, his eyes glossy as he stared down. His hips thrust hard and quick.

I bit my lip, trying to keep the spikes of pleasure in. Kaiser smiled. "You're beautiful, Marley," he said.

He melted my heart when he said something like that. I knew, especially when we were in the middle of fucking, that he was fully present when he spoke like that. I reached for him, and he let me pull him down. I wrapped my arms and legs around him as he continued to thrust.

"Love you," he whispered.

I squeezed him tighter. "Love you, too. So much. I'm so glad you're in my life."

Kaiser gasped and stilled for a minute as he filled me. And there lies another difference between an omega and other designations. There was so. Much. Cum. Even with just this first orgasm, I could feel it seep out.

He whined quietly, nuzzling in my ear. "Mar," he whimpered, and I knew he was trying to stay with me instead of being lost in a sex haze. "Please. I- I can't- I need more."

I grinned as I locked my ankles behind him. I'd learned real quick that I needed a whole lot of core muscle strength to be able to please Kaiser on my own. It had taken me a while to get there. With an insatiable omega, a beta needed to learn how to compensate for what they naturally lacked. It was the that was alpha built to please an omega until they were passed out. A beta was mearly a fill in if an alpha was still hungry after.

But I made sure I could keep up with Kaiser. It hadn't been my sexual appetite that was the problem. It was my lack of muscles. I no longer had that issue. I grinned at my success as I brought my omega to orgasm again, his body shuddering in my arms as I continued to use my legs to thrust my hips up.

"Another," he said before this one had fully passed. "Please."

"As many as you need, Kaiser," I whispered. "I'll always give you what you need."

In a window of clarity, Kaiser answered. "I know. You're the best thing in our lives, Marley."

I nuzzled my cheek against him as I bit my lip and closed my eyes. I was pretty sure he was the best thing in our lives, not me.

CHAPTER EIGHTEEN

Terence

I might have gone overboard. I stood back to look at the mess I had strewn all over the kitchen. To be fair, the kitchen was a postage stamp, so it wasn't hard to fill it. I already had dessert soaking – Merlot poached pears with cinnamon and vanilla. It's true that wine wasn't something I was familiar with, but I'd had this particular dessert before, and it was good. The trick was trying to alter recipes for two people.

My colorful carrots were marinating on the counter. My peppers were stuffed and ready to be put in the oven. My appetizer of bruschetta with seared tomatoes, roasted garlic, ricotta, and some pretty leaves for decorations was nearly ready to assemble when Kaiser arrived. And then there was the seared roast that would be drizzled in a mushroom wine sauce.

Everything was ready to start cooking. I was just waiting for the later hour to arrive. I pulled out the roast to warm up twenty minutes ago. And now, the nerves set in as I stared at the timer over the stove.

RONAN CAME FROM A STRONG PACK. *Imagine their surprise when the youngest of four children turned out to be a beta when the rest were alphas, including their daughter. One would think that this meant Ronan would be raised as an alpha. Instead, he was raised like an omega.*

He had very little skills as his siblings took care of him. I'd thought that part of it was biology – the alphas always take care of others in their packs and thus, his siblings' natural inclination was to take care of their brother. There was also the fact that Ronan was the baby and so, he was spoiled as such.

But when we'd taken him into our pack, the poor man was at a low point mentally. He couldn't do anything that a beta should. He didn't even have his driver's license. His siblings had only been too eager to bring him where he needed to go.

And so, we started with the basics. Holding down a job. Managing money. Doing laundry. All things we, as alphas, would have been happy to take care of, but skills that Ronan lacked, making him feel inadequate and worthless. So, we nourished them.

Since we were typically busy over the week and focused on spending every minute that we weren't working together, we hired out the menial tasks that took too much time and energy. That meant laundry, once Ronan understood the process and could make it happen on his own. Cleaning was done by an agency once a week. And cooking – meals were prepared and prepackaged by a new eco-homemade company that we were only too happy to support.

But once a month, we took a long weekend and cooked a plethora of dishes for each meal, incorporating leftovers for the following week.

Ronan had been overwhelmed and horrified in the

beginning, the whole process making him feel even worse, but we'd spent a lot of time working on basic skills like using a knife and cleaning vegetables. And now, he was preparing lunch for us. A recipe that he'd found and was handling all his own.

It was from one of those social media channels that showed you food hacks, and he was ecstatic to try them himself. So, the five of us gathered around the peninsula to watch.

Tortilla with a single cut half way through. Buttered pan. Cheese in one quarter. Sliced meats in another quarter. Aioli in a third, topped with some greens. And then tomatoes in the last. Then we watched as he folded the corners over until he was left with a triangle of goodness.

Ronan tended to it with quiet focus, flipping it and checking it every so often. When he was satisfied that it was done, he pulled it out with a spatula with expert skill and set it on a plate. We watched as he stared at it for a minute and then looked at us with fear in his eyes.

It was the first thing he'd ever made solely on his own.

Emery reached for it and Ronan hesitantly handed it over. The alpha wasted no time biting into it. There was a satisfying crunch and we watched as he closed his eyes to savor the mouthful. Ronan stared, paralyzed, while Emery chewed and swallowed that bite.

"You know what the best part is?" Emery asked.

Ronan shook his head.

"That you made this," Emery said. "And it's fantastic. There's a taste of everything in a single bite. It's perfect."

"Really?" Ronan asked, narrowing his eyes. "You aren't just saying that?"

"I would never intentionally hurt your feelings, Ro," Emery said. "But I would tell you if it needed some work. This is amazing, beta."

Ronan relaxed, sighing. He nodded as a smile touched his lips and he turned around to make another.

———

THE KNOCKING on my door made me jump, pulling me out of the memory. It felt like a door slammed shut, locking it away as I caught my breath.

Yes, lock it away. I couldn't concentrate on my pack right now. I had an omega to pamper.

I wasn't sure why I was doing it. This couldn't go anywhere. Maybe it was guilt because I knew he'd constantly felt like he was a horrible omega after being near me each and every time. I couldn't let that stand. It was me who was defective. Not him.

Stopping in front of the door, I took a deep breath to clear away the remnants of memory and opened the door.

Once again, the man standing in front of me was stunning. Everything in me reacted. Not just because he was a beautiful man, but also because the alpha in me was desperate to reach out to this omega. His perfume was divine. He was sweet and witty when I wasn't making him nearly whimper because I'm an asshole.

"Hi," Kaiser said, his smile small and demure. I could almost feel the way he was trying to hold back.

I held my hand out to him in a moment of weakness. I needed to touch him again. Feel his skin against mine. Kaiser's smile ticked up a little. A touch of excitement flickered in his eyes as he reached his hand for mine.

And yes, there was the shock. A warm tingle that made me crave him in my arms all the more. I guided him inside, gently pulling him closer to me until we were nearly chest to chest. "Hi," I greeted, my voice low and quiet.

His lips parted as he looked up at me. This close, I found that he was a handful of inches shorter. Perfect. Just the right size to wrap myself around, locking him in my embrace.

Wait, no thinking about locking anyone.

I stepped back, shutting the door behind him and, with his hand still in mine, brought him to the chair at the table. Kaiser sat; his steel blue eyes glued to me.

Where did those flowers go? I looked around until I spotted them by the television. That's right, I hadn't wanted flower petals or leaves in the food. Good enough reason to get them off the counter.

Kaiser lit up when I handed him the vase. He stared at them for several seconds before looking at me. "You got me flowers?" he asked.

I smiled, nodding. "I should have texted you this morning when I saw your message," I told him, hooding my eyes. "But I was..." I didn't have words for what I was. Avoiding reality. Per usual. "I'm sorry. They're an apology."

Kaiser nodded, a slow bob of his head as he watched me.

"And a gift," I added, turning into the kitchen. I didn't miss his face light up. He didn't care about the apology. He wanted the gift.

"What would you like to drink?" I asked, stopping at the fridge. When I glanced back, it was to see Kaiser with his face in the flowers. He opened his eyes as he looked at me through them and I had a sudden urge to throw them on the floor and then Kaiser on top of them.

Were my pants too tight?

"Um, anything?"

"Mm," I hummed before rattling off what I had stocked my fridge with and then the four bottles of wine I'd walked away with.

"You went shopping," he noted as he looked around my overly stuffed kitchen and fridge.

"Yes, well. I've been living in a shell. You cooking me dinner proved how sloppy at life I had become."

He bowed his head and sighed. "Whatever goes with dinner."

"And there's the problem. Remember when I said I'm not well versed in wine?"

Kaiser grinned now. "The red wine. But I also love juice."

"Do you?" I asked, glancing at him as he smelled the flowers again.

"Mhm," he answered, looking up again to watch me. "That's how we found Juice Me. I'm pretty sure I spend a small fortune in your juice shop every week."

"Pretty sure?" I asked as I handed him a glass of wine, bringing mine close so he could tap his against it if he chose. I was pleased when he did with a slight flush in his cheeks.

He sipped the wine, shutting his eyes as he smiled. "It's good," he told me. "And yes, I'm pretty sure. I don't pay attention to money." He pressed his lips together before giving me a sheepish look.

"Good," I told him, setting my glass down and sticking the bread slices in the oven before turning on the stove. "Wanting to be independent aside, there are things you shouldn't worry about."

"Like money," he noted.

"And food. Yes."

"What are you making?" he asked.

"Bruschetta for you to snack on while I prepare the main course."

I could feel his grin without turning. I suddenly wished I could face him while I cooked. He was worth looking at. And I enjoyed watching his face when he spoke.

It didn't take long for the bread to crisp in the oven. I pulled it out while the tomatoes and garlic warmed through. I'd sauteed them earlier so I just needed them hot, now.

On one side of the bread, I spooned some ricotta. The other side got a spoonful of my tomatoes and garlic. I rolled a piece of thinly sliced prosciutto into a flower and added a leaf of basil. After half a dozen of them were made up, I turned with them on a wooden board and placed them in front of Kaiser.

His eyes widened as he looked at them. "They're so pretty," he said.

I hadn't realized he was still holding the vase of flowers in his hands until he set them on the table to slide the board closer. "Pretty, yes. But tell me if they're good."

He grinned and picked one up. After looking at it like he was a diamond, he chose a spot to bite into. His 'mm' that followed made me heat up. A shiver raced down my back as I watched his lips. There was a bit of ricotta in the corner of his mouth, which his tongue poked out to lick, that made my dick twitch uncomfortably.

I was going to get myself in trouble.

"This is delicious," he gushed, looking at me with a bright smile. "Really, really good. I swear, I'm not just saying that."

I chuckled and grabbed one to bite into. His eyes tracked it to my mouth and then stopped there as I chewed. I was so distracted by his watching that I almost missed that he wasn't wrong. It was good. The prosciutto added a nice salty note to the creamy ricotta and warm tomatoes. I swallowed and his eyebrows knit together, his tongue tracing his lips as he shifted in the chair.

Fuck.

"Eat," I told him, turning away to prepare the rest of the meal. The actual meal. I shivered, still feeling his gaze on me.

The covered tray of stuffed peppers went into the oven but

since they'd take a little bit to cook, I couldn't start the meat yet. Instead, I heated up another pan to work on my medley of colorful carrots.

I appreciated that I could hear the crunch of the bread as Kaiser continued to munch on the appetizer. I turned to gauge how he was doing and found that he was slowly making his way through the second. To keep myself occupied while the peppers cooked, I took a second and ate this one more slowly.

"So," Kaiser said. "How is your new shop?"

I shrugged. "I have asked to be involved as little as possible. I sign checks. But I can tell you, my bank account isn't appreciating this business venture."

Kaiser grinned. "It really sounds exciting. Did you have to do much work to the inside?"

I shrugged again. "I have no idea. But I can take you by next week and we can check it out. Pretty sure I have a key anyway."

The way his smile climbed made me nearly euphoric. That was the look an alpha was supposed to give an omega. That, right there.

"I'd love to see," he said. "Juice Me is truly one of my all-time favorite places."

I nodded. It had been Zack's too. That's why I kept it.

I turned at the sobering thought and tossed the carrots around, so they'd fry evenly. The peppers were about halfway so I turned on the skillet that I'd been making the tomatoes and garlic in so that it was screaming hot. Needed a nice sear on my meat before I could let it cook a bit. Not too much.

"How well do you like your meat?" I asked.

"I'm not too picky. Though, I prefer it if it's not actively bleeding."

I chuckled. Same.

"But if you like-"

I shook my head and he stopped. "Nope. I don't like blood for my sauce."

His sigh of relief was quiet. And then a soft crunch followed, making me smile.

"I swear, if I eat too much more of this, I'm not going to be hungry for the rest," Kaiser said.

"You'll be plenty hungry," I told him. "But don't feel you have to eat them all. Just wanted to make sure you weren't starving while I was finishing dinner."

"I think I'm always hungry," Kaiser said.

My body stilled as if his words hadn't been about food. I swear, I heard, 'I think I'm always horny.' That was a lesson on omegas in school. They were damn near insatiable. Always ready. Always slightly on.

Just like an alpha.

Okay, okay. Back to carrots. Nope. Back to burning this meat.

I clenched my jaw together to ignore the rest of the errant thoughts and the way my body responded to them. The loud hiss of the meat that filled the front of me with steam was a nice hot shock back into food land.

It didn't take long to sear all sides until they had a nice crisp skin. Then I let it cook a bit with the cover on and over a lower temperature while I tossed around the carrots, adding a bit more spices and butter. Could never have too much butter. I didn't care if physicians disagreed.

Even with as thick as the roast was, I didn't let it cook too long over heat. I took it off and set it on a cutting board to rest while I deglazed the pan and tossed in the mushrooms to cook through. And then came the cream for the sauce. Yep, delightful aroma.

Something was looking down on me with favor. Just as the sauce was done, the peppers were finished, and I pulled them out. And the meal had come together. As I stared at a prepared dish, I wondered if the pepper was what should have been paired with the roast and carrots. Probably should have gone with a starch, like gnocchi or roasted potatoes.

But I made a mean stuffed pepper. I chose to play to my strengths. So, I turned with two plates and set them down. Then filled both wine glasses before I took a seat next to Kaiser.

He kept the flowers close enough that he could just turn his head and his face would be in the bouquet. I wondered if he actually liked flowers or if he was more focused on me gifting them to him.

The sounds that came out of his mouth as he ate were nearly erotic, making the meal a very hot and sensual experience for me. I stared at him as he ate. Kaiser didn't speak until his plate was clear but the reverence in his eyes was plain when he finally turned.

"That was probably one of the best meals ever," he told me.

I smiled. "Hungry still?"

He shook his head. "I mean, I could probably eat a bunch more because it was amazing, but I'm actually full."

"Then we can save dessert for a bit," I told him.

"You bought dessert?"

I shook my head as I took our plates to the skink. Yep, I needed to reconsider the dishwasher. There were a whole lot of dishes strewn around the kitchen now.

"Nope. I made dessert."

His silence made me turn and I found him watching me with that same awed look. I found that I closed the distance between us so that I was hovering over him. I wasn't touching him. Not quite. But I was close enough that I could feel his body heat and his breath.

"Don't look at me like that," I told him. "I don't deserve your admiration."

"Why don't you?" he asked.

"Because I've been a complete piece of shit since we met. And the worst of it wasn't how I acted, but that you were blaming yourself for my behavior. The least I could do was cook you a decent dinner."

He swallowed as he stood. Since I couldn't convince myself to take a step back, he was pressed against me now. "Does this mean you're not going to see me again?"

I should have agreed. He deserved someone a whole hell of a lot better than me. But I shook my head. "No, Kaiser. I'm only starting to make it up to you."

"But... But by that, do you mean-"

Okay, I knew I'd only had one glass of wine. Not nearly enough for me to blame alcohol on my poor decision making skills, but the next thing I knew, I had my hand at the back of his head as I kissed him, cutting his words off.

Kaiser immediately wrapped around me, pressing his body to mine in a way that said he was always meant to be there. The shape, the feel, the heat. Fuck, he was burning up through his clothes. That was normal, right?

I didn't break the kiss, too afraid I was going to say or do something stupid if I did. I couldn't mess this up. Not again. I didn't deserve an omega. Not a perfect omega like Kaiser. But I couldn't bring myself to hurt him again either.

He tasted like cinnamon candy. The kind that has a bite but turns sweet in the end. I chased the flavor, trying to catch it and make it my own. Kaiser tried to climb up my body, I wrapped my hands under his ass and hoisted him.

This changed the angle of our kissing. No longer was I slightly bent down. Now my neck was craned back as he tangled his fingers into tight fists in my hair and tried to suck my breath from my lungs. Or maybe my soul from my body.

My groan turned into a growl when I found I'd pressed him

against the wall. It was just a little lip of a wall, but I pressed Kaiser's spine down it. He moaned, his hips rolling against mine. I broke the kiss on a gasp as my cock throbbed.

Holy. Fucking. Hell.

This is what it feels like to be sexually absent for ten months and suddenly turned all the way on. Fucking. Painful.

"Terence?" Kaiser asked, a note of concern in his voice.

When I opened my eyes, there was a hint of tension and fear in his eyes. That's what I caused him. If I was strong enough, I'd stop this now. Because it was only going to end in pain for both of us. But knowing I was the one responsible for continuously putting that look on his face broke me.

"It's just been a while," I whispered, taking his bottom lip between my teeth. "I forgot how good it feels," I said around his lip.

His hips jerked against me again as he whimpered. "Terence," he said, my name garbled because his lip was still between my teeth as I sucked on it. But my name in that tone made me growl and I jerked my hips against his hard.

Kaiser shuddered, groaning as his hands tightened in my hair.

"Please," he whimpered.

That was my undoing. I pulled him from the wall and turned us to the bed a few feet away. I laid him back, crushing him under my weight. With him beneath me like this, I swear he was only half my size, maybe less. My body swallowed him.

I covered his mouth with mine, kissing him with hard determination to commit his taste to memory. He was shaking as his hips continued to shove up into me, rubbing his cock against mine.

The pain was real. My balls ached in a way I couldn't explain. There was almost a roaring in my head from the ache that was creeping up my entire body. All I wanted to do was bury myself deep inside this man until my name was the only thing on his lips.

"Please," he whimpered again when I dropped my mouth to his neck.

I bit softly before I rubbed the spot with my tongue and sucked on it gently. The choked, garbled sound as his hips rocked against mine wildly was only another log on the fire. I was burning up.

"What do you want, omega?" I asked, my voice a low rumbling purr.

The whine that escaped him made me want to tear cities down and lay them at his feet. Fuck that sound shouldn't come out of him. It was going to drive me insane.

I'd never felt a need so great. The smell of him was making me delirious. Making me want to shove my cock into him up to my knot and rut him into the bed until all he saw was stars.

Could I do that? Would he let me?

The need to knot someone was always there but it hadn't ever felt quite so consuming. Generally speaking, there were so few omegas around, alphas had become used to that constant ache in them that was never quite fulfilled.

But with an omega under me, whimpering and saying 'please,' everything in me shattered until the only thing I could focus on was giving him whatever he wanted in hopes that he'd want my knot. That he'd want me to give him pleasure. That he'd allow me that honor.

"Touch me," he breathed. "I need to feel you."

My hindbrain interpreted that as 'take my clothes off.' So, I pulled from him enough to rip at his clothing. Somehow, I'd managed to declothe him without tearing any of it. Before I could touch him, he was pulling at my shirt.

"You too," he said, his voice almost a whisper.

I felt clumsy and foolish as quickly as I stripped for him.

But then I was hovering over him between his legs looking down at the perfection that was Kaiser. He was... everything. He smelled like heaven. I could already tell he would fit exactly in my arms when I curled around him. His eyes were an enchanting shade of blue.

"You're so big," Kaiser said, and I realized I was staring into his blue eyes because they were wide as he looked at me.

I glanced down to where my throbbing dick was pressed against my stomach, a bead of precum dripping down the side. My knot was already swollen and an angry red. My balls were tight with their newly screaming ache in the back of my head.

My gaze moved to his dick. I'd been well acquainted with a knotless cock, but I'd forgotten. My hand covered him before I thought better of it. It was different from what I remembered. Softer. Squishier. But still hard.

He was weeping, a long line of precum stretched between his stomach and the slit of his cock. I curled my hand around his cock, bringing my fingers up over the head and capturing it. I brought it to my mouth, raising my eyes to his as I licked him off me.

His eyes were wide still, staring at me with dread. His cheeks bright pink with embarrassment. His lips parted as he panted.

But when that cinnamon roll flavor exploded against my tongue, my eyes rolled as I growled in pleasure. "You're fucking dessert," I said through my teeth as I dropped to take his cock in my mouth.

Kaiser gasped as I sucked him in, his hands finding my hair again as his hips thrust up. I let him, bracing my hands on the bed on either side of his hips.

"I'm coming," Kaiser cried as his hips thrust up again.

Okay, I think I was good at sucking dick, but I hadn't even had a chance yet. When he brought his hips up again, I dropped my head to meet him, taking him to the back of my mouth. Kaiser choked on a gasp, the sounds coming out of him as his body went rigid under me and his spicy sweet flavor coated my throat was everything that eroticism was made of.

"More," Kaiser whimpered when his hips hit the bed again. "Please, alpha."

I stilled for just a second, my eyes widening like saucers. Everything inside me that had been dead for months suddenly reared to life with those words on his lips. My eyes rolled as I closed them, taking the length of him in my mouth and sucking him down.

His legs boxed in my head as he howled and spilled into me again a moment later. I greedily swallowed it all. Fucking pheromones making cum taste this good was a sick twist of nature. I was so enamored with his flavor that I continued to suck him until I was almost choking on his next release.

His hands tightened in my hair as he pulled my mouth from him. I was going to apologize. Maybe I'd taken it too far. But the words that fell from his mouth had an animal waking up inside me.

"Please," he said, his eyes alight with need. "I need your knot, alpha, or I'm going to cry."

I released a harsh breath and pulled up. "Turn over."

Kaiser quickly turned, shoving his ass in the air and his face in the pillow. I stared at him as a need in me so great made my vision blur. Hyper focused so all I saw was Kaiser and nothing else. He wiggled his ass as another whine escaped him.

He would be my undoing.

I rose up, shuffling closer so I could press the length of my cock along his ass. I licked my hand, rubbing it over my dick. I dragged it over him, pressing it between his cheeks as I brought my head to his tiny hole. I pressed in, using my hand to guide me and being especially gentle as I was going in dry. His muscles gave way and I watched as my head disappeared inside him.

I released a breath as I paused, feeling how he strangled the head of my dick. Biting my lip, I pushed in further. Kaiser gasped, his muscles tightening as he shivered through another orgasm. It was heady, watching your lover come undone so many times. Knowing you were giving them that satisfaction.

Letting my dick go, I gripped his ass cheeks as I pushed further inside him, watching as his ass swallowed my dick. It wasn't long before my hands slid up his back and I bent over him while I buried myself to my knot.

Fuck, it was so good. Everything about him. His heat. His shape. His strangle hold grip on me. The way he was panting beneath me, his hips gently bucking backwards as I slowly rocked in and out of him.

It became too much, I stilled when I was fully sheathed before my knot. I licked his skin, tasting the salty sweat mixed with his heavenly cinnamon roll perfume.

"Do I feel good?" Kaiser asked through a whimper.

"Yes," I said, digging my teeth into his skin hard enough to mark him but not enough to break his skin. "No one has ever felt this good."

Kaiser whined quietly and something in me said I needed to keep talking to him. He was nervous.

"You're perfect, Kaiser. So sweet. So beautiful. So kind. So thoughtful." Kaiser moaned under me as he pushed his ass back and I finally sunk my knot into him. I wasn't sure I would fit. And then my mind went blank as pleasure like I'd never known before filled me.

"Fuck," I muttered, dropping my forehead to the back of his head. It felt like he stole my breath as his body trapped me inside. Wrapping around my knot and holding me there. "Fuck Kaiser," I said through gritted teeth.

"Are you okay?" he asked, his voice high and filled with anxiety.

Maybe I should have shared that I'd never knotted someone before. Was that information that would have been beneficial for him to know? My mind was spinning as pleasure swept through every cell, threatening to make me implode.

"Terence?" he asked, reaching over him to grip my hair. His hand was shaking.

"Sorry," I whispered. "Yes. So good. I've never felt anything like this."

"You haven't?"

I shook my head. Only after the admission was out did I feel the vulnerability sweep through me.

"Tell me what you need," I said because I needed direction, or I was going to jump out of my skin.

"Rut," Kaiser told me.

Okay, so the first time I'd felt the need to rut was when I was a teenager with Miles. When we were messing around. He said he enjoyed it, though I was sure it was really fucking overwhelming for him. Later he admitted that he wasn't a fan, so I'd tried to avoid doing it with him when I could. I was relieved when we brought Zack in, because another alpha understood the need to rut, and we could work each other through it though never with knots involved. While not ideal, Betas were set up for accepting knots. And Alphas sure as fuck weren't. We were designed to knot; not be knotted.

Never had someone told me to rut. And now that he'd said so, it was all I could think about. "I don't want to hurt you," I said, my body tensing with the need to rut now.

Kaiser grinned. "Silly alpha. I'm made for your rut."

His words were the last piece of straw that broke my resolve. I slammed into him deeper, eliciting a cry from his throat as he arched. As much as I tried to ease myself into it, my mind was gone as my hips turned to pistons and I rocked furiously into him with my trapped dick.

It was only because I'd been so focused on Kaiser that I hadn't come undone yet. Now that I was chasing pleasure, it was like being a wolf sprinting after a rabbit. It was so close. I could taste it. Dark cinnamon custard. Lights flashed in my eyes. Kaiser's cries of pleasure filled my head.

Almost had the rabbit's tail. Almost touching its ears.

"More," Kaiser rabbit said. "Please. Another."

Then he was flat on the bed below me as I thrust wildly inside him, trapped as I was with my knot locked. "You're a god," I growled, digging my hands into his arms to hold him still.

"Cum," he demanded. "Fill me, alpha."

As if his words were law, I roared with my release as he whined and convulsed under me in pleasure. The grip on my balls finally loosened to where I could breathe again as I dropped heavilty on Kaiser.

Coated in sweat and panting, I squeezed my eyes shut, waiting for the surge of guilt and pain to sweep over me. But with my nose buried in Kaiser's hair, the only thing I felt was bliss as my purr filled the room.

"You okay?" I asked through gasps.

"Mmm," was his answer as he settled under me. "You have a big, hard knot. It's incredible."

My cock twitched at his words, ready for another go around if he kept talking like that.

"You're just..." Words wouldn't come to me. I couldn't find anything to express what I was feeling. "Damn, Kaiser."

He appreciated my speechlessness, his smile climbing as his eyes drifted shut.

Once I'd managed to relax enough that my knot shrunk, I gently pulled out of him. He sighed in contentment. I kissed the back of his shoulder, catching the smile that rose on his lips. It was a similar look to how Miles always appeared after we'd done this.

Nope. Memories needed to stay away. I wasn't going to think about anything else than this right here. Not while Kaiser was here. I couldn't. Or I'd fall apart.

I pulled the blanket up and tucked a pillow at his back.

"Where are you going?" Kaiser asked, and I could hear the caution in his voice.

"Dessert. I think we worked off enough calories to make room now."

He grinned at me and snuggled further into the blankets as he watched me move through my tiny apartment.

CHAPTER NINETEEN

Adrian

In a lot of ways, watching Kaiser date was like having a teenager in the house. But feeling his pain through the bond was like having a knife shoved through my chest.

This situation was out of my control. I needed to be able to make my omega happy. I needed to give him that security, to make him smile, to provide for him a happy nest that he'd never want to leave.

Kaiser didn't want to leave us. I knew that for certain. But if he felt so strongly about another alpha, it was my duty as his alpha and mate, to put forth every effort to make sure that he got what he wanted.

That being said, I couldn't take the way this fucking dick was toying with Kaiser. I had no doubt that he was going through some shit. Marley was a whole lot more level headed than Kaiser and Phynn had seen this alpha's reaction first hand. And recently, so had I.

Kaiser was caught up in his hormones. And when they ran

high, his emotions were a mess. It made it hard for him to react logically. To analyze what was going on around him. To read the state of mind of this alpha and not become so attached to someone quite as damaged as this man appeared to be.

I was caught between wanting to protect my omega and making sure he got exactly what he wanted. So, my choice was forbidding him from this miserable alpha and nurse his pain until it passed, or go strangle this fucker who was hurting my omega.

And that was just my omega. Marley was working hard to shield her feelings, but she couldn't hide them from me.

So, all that being said, I couldn't decide if I was pleased or irritated that Terence had gotten his head out of his ass and texted my omega back. Half the fucking day was gone but he finally grew a pair and messaged Kaiser. And now we were listening to Marley and Kaiser fuck, celebrating in the nest.

"You're a little all over the place," Phynn said.

I'd bitten Phynn the last year. It was a very strange thing to be bonded to another alpha. It was both exactly the same and incredibly different as being bonded to my omega and beta. Still, more than a year later, I couldn't figure out how.

"I'm debating on whether I'm still okay with this. I don't like him toying with my omega's emotions," I answered.

Phynn smirked, nodding. "As devil's advocate, I don't think he's doing it on purpose."

"Doesn't change the fact that he is."

"Based on what we know, I think he keeps trying to tell Kaiser no, but he doesn't want to and he's giving in to his instincts to spend time with Kaiser."

"Still doesn't change my statement," I said, frowning at Phynn.

Phynn chuckled. "I know. And for the record, I agree.

Caught between wanting Kaiser happy and keeping him away from this alpha until he has his shit together."

"And so?"

Phynn shook his head. "He's too excited to keep home. We've encouraged them thus far. We can't just change our minds."

"Sure, we can," I said, sitting back and crossing my arms.

He grinned at me, tossing a pillow that I made no effort to stop from hitting me in the face. We were parked in Phynn's room since it shared a wall with the nest. When our omega was miserable, he tended to lock himself inside. It wasn't often that Kaiser was ever upset. He was generally an upbeat man.

It also wasn't often that he took a step back and let his designation control so much of his personality. But he'd been doing just that for the last couple weeks. More and more, he was falling into the role of omega, with all the quirks and traits that he generally hated.

That alone was enough to keep giving this fucking alpha a chance to get his act in gear. If Kaiser was relying on his biology as a means to reel this alpha in, he was desperate to have him.

Alpha and omega biology was a double ended hook. The omega is designed to appeal to a bigger predator as someone soft and special. A heartbeat that could only come from an omega. He wanted protection, to be indulged, held in an unyielding embrace. And also, being given pleasure that can only come from a knot.

And an alpha's hunger was to do all that. Protect until the very last breath and by whatever means necessary. Provide love, happiness, home, and spoils so that their omega wants for nothing. To hold them until the world falls away, so it's just the two of them as everything around them burns. And being given a body that can take their knot, delivering both pleasure that was unmatched anywhere else.

Betas and alphas weren't designed to take a knot. They could, physically, but it wasn't nearly as pleasant as it was for an omega. Only an omega could do that comfortably, readily, and longingly.

There were other things, too. Alphas needed control and were given a bark that made their command law. That bark was louder on some alphas than others. And an omega was given a whine that could bring an alpha to their knees, doing whatever it took to make the omega happy.

But perhaps more than anything was the magic that was inside an alpha's bite. The ability to create a bond so strong and secure that there was nothing in existence that could break it apart. Except death. And that was unthinkable. It was an instant home, a door that allowed you to know your partner like no other. It afforded you the ability to respond in any given situation how your partner needed you to. It was trust and love and family.

So, if Kaiser was giving way to his instincts in order to reel this alpha in, he was dead set and desperate to have him. I didn't mind sharing. I wasn't against expanding our pack. We always knew we were considered a very small pack, so I'd been prepared to grow even if I'd always been perfectly happy how we were.

"I think our involvement would hinder any progress Kaiser has made," Phynn said into the quiet.

I was sure it would without a doubt, or I'd have inserted myself a long time ago.

"If anything's going to get him hooked, it's going to be Kaiser being what he is," I conceded. "He's already figured that out, even if he's done so subconsciously."

Phynn chuckled. "You've noticed, huh?"

"Hard to miss at this point," I said, shaking my head but smiling nonetheless.

"Is it wrong that I'm really enjoying that he's let the needier side of him out a bit?" Phynn asked, tilting his head to the side as Kaiser's voice filtered through the wall. Phynn smiled, his gaze turning glassy.

Marley wasn't an alpha, but she'd been taking notes on how to give our omega extended amounts of pleasure. I was sure she'd be able to take care of him all on her own. And it would be something she'd be quietly proud of later.

And then she'd pass out for a solid eight hours at least.

"No. I love when he lets us treat him like a pregnant woman," I agreed.

Phynn chuckled.

———

KAISER WAS PACING by the front door at five that evening. Marley sat on the banquet table in the foyer watching him with a quiet, indulgent smile. Again, as if she were a parent watching her teenage son get ready for a first date. I stood next to her, leaning against the table with a hand over her legs.

And Phynn was getting the oil changed.

We had another car and if Phynn said he'd be too late, I'd take Kaiser myself. But he'd be on time. He left a couple hours ago, during Marley and Kaiser's first break in their sex marathon. I suspected that Kaiser's heat was going to be coming early. His begging changes in the weeks prior as does his appetite – both for food and for pleasure.

He was a lot like the aforementioned pregnant woman in the weeks prior to his heat. He craved food. And usually, it was carbs so he could store the energy he needed to get through it. He'd been on a pasta kick for the last three nights.

"I think Phynn's going to be late," Kaiser said, looking at us with panic in his eyes.

"It's 5:13, Kai. You still have twenty minutes before you need to leave," Marley said gently.

Kaiser cringed and turned away, his hands opening and closing fists as he continued to pace.

"Come here," I said after another three minutes had gone by and he'd looked at his phone a solid dozen times.

Kaiser let out a breath and came towards me. I didn't touch him right away, waiting to see what he'd do. His eyes were steady on mine as he waited for my next command.

"It was less than a day," he said, a soft shyness in his voice.

I chuckled and pulled him against me. When he relaxed and leaned his body weight on me, the alpha beast inside me settled down and started to purr. Kaiser nuzzled his face into my chest.

"I'm sorry," Kaiser said quietly. "I know I'm acting..."

"You're fine," I assured him. "I'm not at all concerned or bothered by your conduct."

After another minute of quiet, he said, "I didn't think he was going to message me back." His voice was almost a whisper, but the hurt that rang loudly in it made me clench my jaw.

"I know you want him to go away," Kaiser said a little louder. "I'm sorry I'm not strong enough to give you that."

I hugged him tighter. "I don't want him to go away," I told him, pausing so he could hear the truth in my words. "All I've ever wanted since you stepped into my life is your happiness; I swore to you that you'd have that, no matter what it took. That includes adding another alpha to our pack. I just want him to get his head out of his ass and stop hurting you."

Kaiser didn't respond. Then he laughed. "Sorry," he said. "It's the image of someone's head in an ass."

"You like things in your ass," Marley said.

I felt Kaiser's wide grin. "Yes. Yes, I do. And you do, too."

Marley's smile was shy as her cheeks flushed.

"But I don't want a head in my ass."

"Of course, you do. It just depends on what kind of head," I said.

A beat of silence and then Kaiser laughed again. "Fine. And I also heard what you said before I started laughing like a child."

"Good. Your happiness is my sole goal in life. Yours and Marley's."

Kaiser stood back and looked at me, an easy smile on his lips. He'd relaxed and I was glad I could give him that peace. Especially since he wouldn't recognize his irrationality and sensitivity as his heat was coming on a little sooner than normal. It would likely be a couple days before he made that connection. And he was not going to be happy about it, either.

But it wouldn't be a surprise, either. When an omega's environment was stable and peaceful, their heats were further apart. But when they were stressed, they came on more often. It was somewhat counterintuitive but that was the way an omega worked.

Phynn walked in the front door and immediately, the bonds were filled with a burst of anxiety as Kaiser turned.

"Ready?" Phynn asked, holding his hand out to our not-truly-a-teenager omega.

Kaiser kissed me quickly and afforded Marley a slower one before almost sprinting to the door. He took Phynn's hand and looked back at us with a nervous smile. Yep, first date jitters were back. And it was what, the third date?

When the door closed, Marley sighed and leaned back against the wall. "He feels my envy and responds without realizing he's doing so."

I chuckled and swept her off the table. She grinned, wrapping her arms around my neck. The longer kiss he'd given Marley was exactly what that was about.

"When he lets himself truly become wrapped in his omega makeup, his instincts are dictating a lot of how he's reading and reacting to a situation, Mar. He feels your sorrow. He's acknowledging it and reacting to it even if he can't get himself to fully attend to your needs."

Marley shook her head. "I don't need him to. I just wish that I could be of help in the situation, but I think I made it worse."

"As both you and Phynn point out regularly, his entire state of mind has nothing to do with either of you. I'm guessing he doesn't know what to do with himself and just as much as Kaiser has turned around and is embracing his biology to get what he wants, I think this alpha is doing the opposite."

"Or trying to anyway," Marley added.

I carried her upstairs and it wasn't more than forty minutes before Phynn joined us and the three of us sat back to monitor Kaiser through the bond.

He was anxious, nervous and then suddenly, there was admiration that was creeping into awe. I knew when he was enjoying the food because his emotions died down to something that was warm and filled with joy. Given the situation and how his heat was sneaking up, I was positive that it had to do with food.

And then it became interesting. Little spikes of arousal had been shooting off like firecrackers before being drowned with something else. But now, they were bursting faster. I could almost feel the echo of it in my body.

It was a thing. When your omega, or someone else you've bonded, is in a deep place of arousal, you feel the reverberation of it within yourself. Generally speaking, when you have an omega involved, you get used to the constant state of semi-aroused. You learn to move around it and live outside of having sex all day.

But that meant it was clear when that status quo arousal spiked.

Phynn shuddered at the onslaught as he rolled at my side and buried his face into my ribs. I raised an arm to let him get closer, his hand circling my thigh in a tight grip. Marley had dozed off almost an hour ago. As I predicted, the poor girl was exhausted.

The spike hit a peak, stalled for a minute, and then took off like a rocket. I felt the ricochet as my cock hardened.

"Well, I wasn't expecting that twist," I admitted.

Phynn grunted. I glanced down at him, finding that he was rubbing his dick through his pants. I grinned as I sat back and closed my eyes to continue monitoring my omega through our bonds.

CHAPTER TWENTY

Marley

I was a little jealous. Maybe more than a little. I was happy to see that Kaiser had finally made legitimate progress with Terence and more than a little relieved to find him happy again. But I was seriously coming down with some massive envy now.

Every day, Kaiser would get together with Terence, even if it was for a short period of time. Once, he even spent the morning at the gym with Terence. He came back in an almost worshiping state, telling us about how Terence goes through some ridiculous routine.

"Did you exercise?" Adrian asked.

Kaiser rolled his eyes. "No. I was too busy watching him and handing him his water."

Adrian grinned, kissing his cheek and moving back to make lunch.

Then Terence had picked him up to go check out the new store. Kaiser had come back beaming that he'd met Nora, and that Nora had liked the idea Kaiser had about a student program. And that they had both liked the color palate that Kaiser had suggested.

It wasn't just the little outings. It was that every time they went out, or rather, when Kaiser went over for dinner, it felt like I was hearing and feeling the effects of a porno without actually being involved.

And, if that wasn't bad enough, I was pretty sure Terence was courting Kaiser without either of them having the intentional conversation about it. Sure, the procedure was a little wonky since they were already sleeping together – something Kaiser was more than happy to give a play by play of – but he kept coming home with little gifts.

First, it was the bouquet. Then there was a dark forest leather braided bracelet that Kaiser only took off to shower. There was a beanie and a blanket, and he'd very excitedly told us that Terence bought another towel for the bathroom.

But when he came home with a toiletry bag while he told us about the new furniture they picked out for Terence's apartment, I was trying very, very hard to hide my jealousy.

"We even picked out a wine rack for the wall," Kaiser said as he drew us a diagram and explained all the changes.

I was almost thankful when the first real spike of his heat came on. Kaiser had been so wrapped up with Terence that he hadn't been paying attention to the signs that it was approaching. I was angry with myself when I found that I was pleased that he'd been caught off guard and was irritated about it.

"But it's not fair," Kaiser whined as he stripped from his clothes. His body was a mini heater right now, burning up as he began to sweat.

Heats were a little counterintuitive as far as his body's reaction went. A fever overtook him but instead of shaking from the chill it caused him, he was a ball of fire that needed to be put out. And the way to break the heat was by giving him enough orgasms until he was too exhausted to pick his head up.

These pre-heats typically happened once or twice a day, hitting him for an hour or two, and then he could carry on as usual.

I watched as he undressed with a feeling that made me ashamed. Glad that it came early. Glad that he had to put off his plans with Terence while he tended to it with us – his pack. Glad that he was disgruntled about it.

And then completely horrified with myself for feeling that way. It made me want to turn away and cry. Repent like I'd just committed the gravest sin, and to me, I think I did. These aren't feelings you should have towards a loved one. Ever.

I let Phynn and Adrian work Kaiser through this preheat spike and shimmied my way out of reach whenever Kaiser tried to grab for me. Since he wasn't truly in a heat, he was a whole lot more lucid right now. And I didn't miss the hurt on his face when I pulled away.

Fortunately for me, I was spared having to explain myself directly after. It had only taken our alphas fifty minutes to break this spike, but they'd delivered Kaiser enough orgasms that our omega had already passed out before Adrian's knot had withdrawn enough that he could pull himself out.

Kaiser might have fallen asleep, but both alphas were watching me.

Phynn had had dick duty this round, meaning he concentrated on Kaiser's cock. So, he was wiping himself off from the cupfuls of cum. His bright blue eyes bore into me as if they were a spotlight.

My chest heaved as if I'd been involved in their activities as I tried to catch my breath. I knew it was coming before he said anything. But I didn't miss the little bit of bark in his voice, leaving me no room for argument, when Phynn said, "Come here, Marley."

I wasn't an omega. I didn't have a whine. But I knew how to whimper, and one escaped my mouth as I crawled closer to him.

My alphas were never rough and rarely ever angry. I could count on a single hand every time I've seen either of them angry. But it felt as if he slapped me with the gentle touch of his hand when he pulled me into his naked lap.

His naked lap with his still hard cock, knot red and angry for attention.

His fingers on my face forced me to look at him. Tears blurred my vision. He might not have read my thoughts, but he could feel my emotions. I wasn't sure how much he'd felt with Kaiser's heat screaming through the bond, but I was sure they'd both felt some, even if Kaiser had missed it.

I really hoped he had.

"What happened, Marley?" he asked, his voice gentle and low.

I swallowed, tears dripping down my face. "I'm sorry," I whispered. "I didn't mean it."

"Didn't mean what?" he asked. Though his voice was quiet and gentle, I felt it like he was yelling, which was doing nothing to help me catch my breath.

"Mean thoughts," I said, snot starting to drip down my nose. Great. Now I feel gross, too.

Phynn chuckled and pulled me into him. I wiped at my face as he hugged me tightly. I wasn't one of those betas who always wished to be an omega. Sure, I had that craving for a pack that everyone does, but I never wanted to be something I wasn't. I didn't care that I could never truly enjoy a knot. I didn't care if I didn't have a whine. And I didn't care if my scent didn't make alphas hunger after me.

But sometimes, I wished I could get lost in the oblivion of an omega. I could act irrationally and needy and no one would think differently of me. 'Oh, she's just an omega being an omega. We love her all the more for it.'

I scowled at myself again, knowing that that was also a mean thought. And it wasn't even a true one. I didn't want to get lost in my emotions. "I'm sorry," I said again through a hiccup.

"Hush, sweetness," Phynn chided, and I felt just the slightest hint of a bark in his tone again. It was in the reprimand that he countered with the affectionate term. I flinched anyway.

"Let's hear what's wrong," Adrian said as he gently pulled himself out of a sleeping omega.

Kaiser sighed dreamily, not waking or stirring more than the simple release of breath. Adrian covered him up and wiped at his forehead. He nodded as he sat back. Kaiser's spike was over. His temperature was back to normal.

I sighed in relief and then felt stupid for it. I'd just been a little bitch, excited for his misery and now I was relieved for his relief? What was wrong with me?

I wasn't excited about his misery. Not really. I was jealous that everything was falling in line for him, and I was being left out.

"Hm," Adrian said, and I flushed, realizing that their quiet as they gave me time to think was also allowing them time to analyze the feelings they were getting from me through our bonds.

"Jealousy is a poisonous beast," Phynn said quietly as he stroked my hair.

"I know," I whispered, squeezing my eyes shut.

Once, before Phynn and Adrian registered with the Pack Listing, we'd had a very long conversation about whether or not we wanted to allow an omega into our pack. Adrian and I had been kind of seeing each other for a year. When Phynn, his childhood friend, moved back into town, there had been almost an instant connection between him and I. And that first encounter of the three of us being together had led to a very long and exhausting hot night.

We'd become almost an instant pack. Adrian had bit me within the following week. Phynn was a little slower, but it was expected since I'd already had an established relationship, even if not official, with Adrian.

It was after seeing one of their other childhood friends within a pack with an omega that the conversation had come up. Did we want to register and be made available for an omega?

The Pack Listing was the mirror organization of the Omega Registry. And either designation could peruse the other. An omega who was intrigued by a pack on the list could request a scent card and/or a meeting. Likewise, a pack who found an omega in the registry appealing could put in an 'interested' ping, alerting the omega that a pack would like another consideration.

I hadn't been concerned. Especially when my alphas assured me that they were happy with me and didn't *need* an omega to make our pack complete. I thought they were wrong because an alpha will always need an omega. So, I only had a single stipulation: it had to be a male omega. I wasn't generally a jealous girl, but I could only imagine becoming a monster with jealousy if there was a female omega in my house with my alphas fawning over her.

They agreed, the gender of the omega meaning nothing to them. They assured me that there would never be an instant that I should ever feel jealous. They'd treat me no different than an omega.

And they hadn't. This new alpha... maybe he was. Maybe that's what I was jealous about. He preferred the omega to me.

The thought made tears sting my eyes. I turned away, not wanting either of them to see me. Neither alpha pushed me any further. I was sure they could feel my own shame and probably thought that was enough punishment.

———

I DECIDED I deserved a time out. While Kaiser slept off his spikes over the next few days, I kept to myself in my room. I didn't exactly avoid him or my alphas, but I didn't participate in anything that I would normally do.

So far, my alphas let me stew in my self-deprecation. I was sure that was likely to end soon, but for now, I was left to my own devices. And Kaiser had been too consumed with his heat spikes and Terence to take note of my absence.

Or so I thought.

I looked up at the gentle knock on my door. I assumed it would be an alpha, but it wasn't. When I called for them to enter, Kaiser opened the door. I could tell another spike was coming. He looked feverish and miserable. But right now, he was looking at me guiltily.

"Can I come in?"

I nodded and Kaiser crossed the room to sit on the window seat with me. But he didn't touch me, which led me to believe that maybe he felt my horrible emotions, too.

"Are you mad at me?" he asked.

I shook my head.

"Are you sure?"

I dropped my eyes to my book and nodded. "I'm not mad at you."

"Then why don't you come near me anymore? Do you not want to be a part of my heat?"

As much as he tried to keep the hurt from his tone, I could hear it like a wrecking ball that tore its way through my chest. I swallowed, closing my eyes for a minute. I set my book down and moved to him, so he'd take me in his arms.

I should have pulled him into mine. As my omega, I should comfort him. But Kaiser was just as good at being the comforter as the one being comforted. He didn't have a purr, but he tried sometimes. Just like I did.

"I'm sorry," I whispered.

He sighed. "Did I do something?"

I shook my head. "It's me. I'm just being an awful person."

Kaiser frowned into my hair as he rubbed my back. I could feel how hot he was through his clothing. That he was sitting in here and not trying to get fucked told me how upset I had made him by staying away during his spikes.

"I don't understand," he said, exasperation in his voice.

I smiled, despite the situation. He was always frustrated during heat spikes when the only thing he could truly rationalize was getting a knot.

I pulled away and put both my hands on his face, his skin burning under me. "I love you," I told him. "So, so much, Kai. Please, don't ever doubt that. I'm sorry I've hurt you."

Kaiser smiled. "It's okay if you need a sex break. I do too but my body doesn't agree."

I giggled and rested my forehead on his. "I'm a little jealous," I admitted.

"Don't be. Heats are fun and all but the way they dictate your life is maddening."

I smiled, nuzzling my face against his. He returned the scent exchange, pulling me into a tight hug. "No," I said. "Believe it or not, I've never envied you a heat."

He snorted. "Good."

"I meant, I'm jealous of you and Terence," I whispered. "And I'm not doing well at being a good person about it."

He didn't answer for a minute and then his arms tightened until I couldn't breathe. At first, I thought the heat spike had hit a critical level. It was a thing. Kaiser said it was a point where he was going to explode. And then it became painful if he didn't get the release he needed, and even worse when he had to handle it on his own.

"I'm so sorry, Mar," he said, his voice filled with tears. "I didn't mean to make you feel that way."

This was exactly why our omega was an amazing man. He tried to take my shortcomings as something he'd done. And this was exactly why he didn't just fall into the traits of an omega that he hated most. He was too good a person for that. It wasn't an act. He really believed this was his fault.

"Don't. You didn't do anything wrong. I'm just upset that you managed to get somewhere with him, and he ran from me when I kissed him. Talk about a blow to my ego."

He tried to laugh at my lame attempt at a joke. And then he pulled away so he could lock my face in his hands this time. "I promise you, Marley. As soon as I'm not high on this heat, I'm working you in. I haven't forgotten that this is *our* alpha. But you know I'm useless in a heat. I'll be lucky if I'm making coherent words in a few days. I'm as likely to start bawling as I am to have a spontaneous orgasm."

I laughed and yet, he wasn't wrong. We've seen both.

"Speaking of," he said with a scowl. "I'm getting close to combustion. Do you want to come?"

"Pun intended?" I asked, winking at him.

Kaiser laughed.

"Not this time. But next time. I promise."

He nodded. "I love you, my beta. You know that, right? So much I can't stand it most days."

I nodded in return, tears blurring my eyes for an entirely different reason now. "I love you, too."

Kaiser left me and I leaned back. It felt like a weight had been lifted from my shoulders and I relaxed, closing my eyes.

I awoke as the sun went down to gentle hands on my face. I expected Kaiser but it was Adrian. "Hey, sunshine. Want to join us for a movie?"

Smiling, I nodded, and Adrian picked me up. He didn't bring me downstairs but to his room where Phynn was already curled in bed.

"Is Kaiser still asleep?" I asked as Adrian set me down against Phynn's side and then wedged me in with his big body on my other.

"Nope. He's going to be out for the night," Adrian answered.

I pretended that a sleepover with the alpha we both wanted didn't bother me at all.

"We thought it was an even trade, really," Phynn said.

"Oh?" I asked, trying to figure out what he was talking about.

"Mm. You see, our beta has been pouting in her room. And we thought a night alone where we could lavish her with a dozen orgasms in exchange for our omega's other alpha dealing with a heat spike was an even trade."

I stared at him with wide eyes.

"You let him spend the night?" I asked, incredulous.

Adrian chuckled. "We'll see. He seems to be doing okay right now." He paused as we all turned reflective as we felt for

Kaiser's bond. It was there, blazing with happiness and the constant background of arousal, now filled with needy heat that was ready to boil over at any given moment. His bond was always like a pot of boiling water during heats and the lead up. A gentle simmer with the bubbles of a promised boil starting to hint. It could very easily boil over at the blink of an eye.

"Besides," Phynn said, pulling me from examining Kaiser's bond by pulling my face to his. "Seems to me like you took a big step and confided in Kaiser what was wrong. I think that needs rewarding."

"And it's been a while since we've showered you with our undivided attention," Adrian said.

"Years, at least," Phynn agreed.

My pulse spiked as they converged on me. Both mouths hit mine and I giggled. Before Kaiser joined us, we'd been trying to master the three-way kiss. It provided more entertainment than success most days. We'd moved away from perfecting it when a four-way kiss was just silly and impossible. We were an even number. There was always someone to kiss.

But as their tongues lapped at my lips and I stuck mine out to join theirs, we all broke into laughter. It felt good to laugh again. The weight of my jealousy, even after admitting it to Kaiser, left me feeling heavy and breathless. The pure fun of trying to kiss two men at once was just the adjustment I needed.

I'd get over my jealousy. It was stupid and selfish and unfounded. I knew Kaiser wouldn't do that on purpose. He may be an omega, but he wasn't by any means selfish. He loved attention but he also loved to share affection.

"Stop thinking," Adrian demanded, a tone without a bark but still commanding enough that I grinned. "You're not allowed to think about other men right now. Not even our omega."

"Talk about a blow to our ego," Phynn muttered as he moved his lips to my neck, dragging his teeth along my skin.

You want to know what instantly gets this beta wet? Their teeth on me. I squirmed with how uncomfortably moist I was getting.

"I suppose that means we've been challenged, Phynn," Adrian said. "Think we can push all other thoughts but us from her mind?"

I shivered at the implications.

"Fuck yes. I'll hold her. You eat her."

My clothes came off before I could counter. I loved when they licked me, but I liked a cock in my mouth while they were busy with me. I didn't get an opinion right now as Phynn came at me like a predator. They'd both lost their clothes as they stripped mine from me. They were glorious. The most beautiful alphas ever made. Perfection, big, and mine.

Phynn pulled me into his arms, dropping his mouth to my neck as he curled his knees up. I was small enough that I felt like a doll most days. Adrian hooked my legs on the outside of Phynn's, pinning them wide open. His grin was wicked as he licked his lips.

Phynn took my hands, holding them straight at my sides, trapped between his hands on my hips.

"While I work her up, maybe you should get yourself situated, too," Adrian suggested, looking at Phynn over my shoulder.

I felt Phynn's answering grin as his lips touched my ear. "What do you think, Marley? Want a dick in your ass while Adrian works your pussy?"

I shivered. I swear, I was dripping like an omega in heat at this point. Being filled by both of them was a trip. Both painful and stupidly arousing. Every time, my mind turned to mush.

"Yes, alpha," I whispered.

He grinned. "Wet me up, Ad," Phynn said.

Adrian smiled up at me before spreading out on his stomach. His fine ass was like a small mountain that I kind of wanted to bite right now. But the squishy wet sound of his mouth over Phynn's cock made me look down.

Well, if I wasn't dripping before, watching Adrian take Phynn's dick in his mouth between my legs was something else entirely. I whined, my hips moving on their own as desperate arousal filled me.

Adrian moved his eyes to look up at me, a smile across his face as he brought his mouth up. Wide open, he dropped his tongue to tease Phynn's slit with his gaze locked with mine. I shuddered, the rumble of Phynn's purr moving through me like a vibrator.

"Ready, princess?" Adrian asked.

Phynn lifted me by my hips, my hands still pinned. I nodded. Adrian moved Phynn's hard cock, dragging his head across my opening as he settled his head at my ass. His mouth closed over my clit at the same time he started working Phynn in.

My mind was a tug of war as I volleyed back and forth between the nearing uncomfortable pressure in my ass and the near explosive pleasure coming from Adrian's tongue on my clit. I whimpered as I tried to wiggle.

"You're doing great," Phynn whispered huskily in my ear. "I know you can take me."

I did know, because I have before. Many times. Though, it's been a while.

"That's it. Relax. Good girl. So good, my precious."

There was something to be said about the praise talk that alphas instinctively did and omega's instinctively craved. I wasn't sure what a beta's instinct was supposed to be in terms of praise talk, but it fed me like fuel on a flame.

My orgasm bled out of me as soon as Adrian pushed a finger inside me, rubbing at my G-spot.

I gasped, making a whole bunch of high-pitched noises as my hips moved on their own. Trying to encourage the orgasm, my jerks brought Phynn in deeper. The pleasure was a delicious mixture of pain, sending spikes of heat through my veins.

Little explosions went off like fireworks as I watched Adrian lick me slowly and carefully. His fingers were hovering outside me as the palm of his hand worked Phynn's sac. I moaned watching him handle Phynn. There was nothing hotter than the two alphas going at it. Even this little bit.

Another orgasm was hanging around the edge, waiting for that last invitation to come undone. Adrian always knew right before I was going to lose it. Like the previous, he shoved his fingers inside me, pressing against every pleasure button he could, as I cried out.

My body went rigid as I came, throwing my head back as little convulsive twitches covered me.

"That's it," Phynn purred. "Feel so good."

His words made my foggy mind focus on his cock. I knew he was fully seated. Not just because I swear, I could choke on it right now, but because I wasn't truly sitting in his lap anymore. I was sitting on his knot, the only part of his dick left outside my body.

I shuddered as he started to rock. I whimpered, my fists balling at my hips. Adrian stopped his slow teasing and clamped his mouth around my clit, sucking on me as he flicked with his tongue.

Light burst before my eyes as I cried out, Phynn's quiet praise never letting up as Adrian milked my orgasm as long as he could.

And then he was there, pushing his dick into my dripping

pussy, rubbing it against Phynn's with only the thin membrane inside me separating it. They groaned together, their mouths meeting over my shoulder.

And then their attention was on me as they moved simultaneously. It started slow before moving to a quick hard thrust that had me in a constant mewling state. My orgasm built again before it suddenly rushed like a volcano. This time, their mouths locked on either side of my neck as they bit their scarred claims and the pleasure heightened until it was the only thing that existed.

Them and maddening pleasure.

CHAPTER TWENTY-ONE

Terence

I t had been a long time since I'd felt anything more than the numbness I surrounded myself with. My existence was walking a tightrope, either side had me falling and I wasn't sure it mattered which way I slipped – both would be disastrous.

But as I let Kaiser in my apartment for the first full night, I was having serious second thoughts. Keeping myself together while he was here so I could break down when he left was one thing. I wasn't sure if I had the strength to keep it together for the entire night, too.

I'd found a rhythm that allowed me the best possible chance at being human again. And all of it involved this omega who refused to give up on me. Refused to let me push him away.

He was everything. And somehow, I found myself waking up vomiting every morning. Because I was betraying my pack by being with this omega. An omega who already had a pack.

"Hi, alpha," Kaiser said with his sugary sweet smile that I wanted to lick.

Only now, I didn't hold that urge back. I pulled the man into my arms and covered his mouth with mine. He groaned, immediately rocking his hips against me. I shivered against him, wrapping my hand around to grab that tight ass and haul him harder to my body.

And then I realized how he was burning up, even as I licked his lips as I pulled away.

"Why are you so hot?" I asked through a near growl.

He tilted his head, a teasing smile coming to his lips, and I was waiting for the snarky remark. He didn't disappoint.

"It's how my mommy and daddy made me," he said, batting his lashes at me.

I growled again, nipping at his jaw and pulling him inside. He was hanging onto the little toiletry bag I'd given him days ago, only this time, I knew there'd be items in it. Items that facilitated an overnight.

"No, really," I said. "You're burning up. Do you need a hospital?"

He laughed quietly, a blush tinting his cheeks as I pulled the bag from his hands and tossed it to the couch. "No, alpha. I'm an omega. Why do you think I have a fever?"

I tensed as I stared at him in horror.

Kaiser laughed again. "Calm down, Terence. It's not the full heat. For almost a week prior, I go through spikes of pre-heat. I do need, you know, orgasms and all that. But the spikes usually only last an hour or two at a time." He paused and a glimpse of the timid omega who I'd run out of my house a couple times with his tail between his legs peeked at me. "I can go home if you want. And not come back until it's over."

"Mm," I said, pushing him against the wall that the door opened against. He whined, a quiet sound that lit me on fire.

"You're telling me I need to fuck you for a couple hours to break a fever, right?"

Kaiser nodded. "You know, foreplay and stuff work, too, but not as quickly. Nor as thoroughly."

"Noted," I said, covering his mouth with my own.

I loved the way he immediately jerked into me, even as I had him pinned against the wall. I knew they were reactions, not something that he was doing consciously. But I loved it all the same.

Loved the way his body fit against mine as I used my weight to immobilize him. He was only a handful of inches shorter than me, but when I pressed him like this, his feet practically left the floor.

I loved the way his heat, not normally *this* hot but heat all the same, seeped into me through our clothing.

I loved the way he moaned in my mouth, taking fistfuls of my hair. His hands always went to my hair for the first few minutes of being together. As if he were making sure I was real. That I'd not get away. So he could keep me there, kissing him.

I loved the way his hips rocked against me, even when I held him flush. The way his ever-hard cock filled further. The way it rubbed against mine, sending bursts of fire through my body.

With my hands fisted in the front of his shirt, I pulled him from the wall and walked him backwards through the small space until I could drop us onto the bed. Kaiser grunted, his body tensing as he tried to roll.

Our kiss broke as he grimaced. "Are you playing with blocks in your bed?"

I looked at him in confusion before I flinched. "You tell me to fuck you and I forget everything else," I muttered, reaching under him for the little box.

Kaiser grinned. "Well, I try to keep my needs simple. Heat

spikes mean I need plenty of orgasms." He was teasing and I fucking loved it. The tone, the playful smile, whatever words came out of his perfect mouth.

But his eyes were glued to the box I'd pulled from under him.

"Want this now or later?" I asked, waving it slightly in front of him.

Kaiser bit his lip, and it was a true testament to how strongly heats have a grip on an omega. He wanted the gift. But his need for the spike relief was real.

"Tell you what," I said, setting the box down and running my hands up his body until he was groaning and wiggling under me. "How about during?"

He groaned, his hips pushing up. "Yes, alpha."

"You want to get right to the goods or play around for a while?"

"We can play later. I *neeed* a knot right now." His whine was almost to the point where I was going to have to break something.

I dropped my mouth to his chest as I worked his clothes from him. Kissing along the smooth flesh covering dancing muscles. He helped me undress him, struggling out of each layer as I went. And then he was pulling at my clothing even more impatiently.

He licked up my abdominals as soon as I started to pull my shirt over my head. I sucked in a breath as a memory of Zack doing just the same thing flashed in my mind. I pointedly looked at the omega nipping at my stomach, digging his teeth in as if he could take a bite.

Kaiser. Not Zack. Kaiser.

Kaiser!

His hands went to my pants and undid the button before struggling with the zipper. It was only made so difficult since my pants were stretched so tightly over my throbbing dick. Finally, he pulled his hands back.

"While I know you wear underwear, I don't want to catch your cock in the zipper. I kind of need it in one piece right now," he said, looking up at me with a mixture of hunger and mirth in his stunning face.

I pushed him back again, so he sprawled in front of me on his back, laughing as he went down. His hand immediately wrapped around his dick as he watched me undo the offending zipper and push the material down. I couldn't help but think 'and this is why gym clothes are easier.' No zippers to snag an unsuspecting cock in. Also, I'd already be undressed and buried in his sweet little ass.

I kicked my pants off and then my briefs before coming down and taking his cock in my mouth. There was an instant burst of cum shooting into the back of my throat as he groaned, his back arching.

I grinned around him, sucking him down until he loosed another load into my mouth, filling me with sweet cinnamon rolls.

"Sorry," he hissed as he writhed in frustration. I didn't miss the pink on his cheeks. "I'm even more of a mess during spikes and heats."

"You're fucking glorious, Kaiser," I growled as I lapped at him.

He moaned as he reached for me, dragging my face from his dick so he could kiss me. "In," he demanded as he licked at me sloppily. "Knot me."

Kaiser wasn't lying when he said he was more impatient during spikes. I chuckled, moving up the bed and pushing his legs back and wide. I wanted to look at him as he sprayed all over himself. I wanted to see the bursts of ecstasy across his face.

He was ready for me, his ass accepting me with ease as I pushed slowly into him. He grunted, moaning, squirming under me as he gripped the bedding.

"So good," I murmured, purring into the room. "You are like a perfectly tailored glove. Made just for me."

"Knot," he whimpered. "Oh god, please. I need it so bad."

His words sent chills through me. There was a longing in him I'd never heard before. He always asked for my knot, but that tone. The underlying ache in it. The desperation and plea. The pain.

I was still for just a second as I let that tone seep into me. Fill me with a raging need to give him the world to fill that need. The stars. The elixir of life.

But he didn't need the world. He needed my knot.

I hiked his legs up so the crook of his knees hooked at my elbows and leaned in to give myself more leverage as I worked my knot into him. Gentle rocks as his body made room to accommodate me.

"Yes," he panted. "Please. I need it."

His desperation made me crazy. With a snap of my hips that I definitely didn't mean to do, I slammed myself home. A deep satisfying groan left Kaiser's chest as his body settled around my knot, securing me in place.

On the end of his groan was an orgasm that had a stream of cum shooting out of his throbbing red dick and across his chest. I leaned in to lick it. His arms wrapped around my head as I cleaned him. When I couldn't reach anymore, I nipped at his chest, his nipples, his neck until he was begging for an orgasm again.

He was so sensitive right now that it only took a few rough rutting jerks of my hips to get him off. I spread my hands, knocking into something hard. I glanced around the circle of his arms to find the box I'd thrown him on earlier.

I grabbed for it, opening it with one hand and pulling out the string of rock lava beads. We'd half heartedly watched a documentary on volcanoes once and he was fascinated with the dried lava.

Getting it around his neck in this position was a challenge, one that every little movement I made, had Kaiser mewling in pleasure. Sounds that made me insane.

"More," Kaiser whined. "Please. Please, Terence."

I wrapped my arms around him tightly and started grinding my dick in his ass until the sounds coming out of him were nothing but a long series of blissful howls as he filled the space between us with his cum.

———

My purr was loud even in my own ears as Kaiser snuggled against my side. I'd only just managed to pull myself from him.

Growing up, they tell you that there would never be a better feeling than having an omega strangle your knot. I'd initially called bullshit on that when I'd taken Miles. And then the other members of my pack.

I'd never had my knot involved until Kaiser and let me just say, it's an entirely different kind of orgasm. One that feels like you're dying and flying, and it might be the end of you for how tightly his body grips your knot.

I couldn't bring myself to say it was better. Because I'd give anything to have my pack back. Anything at all. But this was different. And it was good.

Taking a breath, I rolled so I could turn into Kaiser. He wasn't quite asleep, though he warned me that he'd likely pass out for a while after. I believed it. I was ready to pass out, too. But first, I needed to stuff all the thoughts of my pack tightly away where they couldn't surge up and tear me apart when I let my walls down to sleep.

"Terence?" Kaiser asked and I shifted further to look at him.

His gorgeous blue eyes were open though filled with sleep.

"Are you going to sleep with me?" he asked.

I kissed his nose before running my skin over his cheek. He was cool again, his fever broken. I feathered kisses along his jaw as I pulled him tight.

"In a minute," I told him. But I didn't move. I just held him.

He mumbled something and I smiled, gathering myself to pull away. Now his eyes were wide open as he watched me move from the bed. I stopped in the kitchen, retrieving two bottles of water from the fridge and returning to the bed. I opened one and handed it to him. "Drink," I told him.

Kaiser grinned as he sat up and accepted the bottle. I drank the other one. I was pleased to see that he downed it all. I threw them in the recycle bin under the sink before I started tossing blankets and pillows at Kaiser that I'd lined between the wall and the bed.

He laughed as he caught them. Some of them. Most of them hit him as he tried to look at the ones he caught.

"What is this?" he asked as he looked around, nearly buried in the plethora of bedding I'd piled on him.

"I didn't know about the heat spikes nor that your heat was coming," I told him. "Maybe there were signs I missed but it's been a long time since I was in school."

He grinned. "I ignored all the signs, so it was just as much a shock to me."

"I couldn't remember if you needed a nest outside of heat so I thought I'd caution on the idea that maybe you did and, well, I don't have a designated room, but I thought you could build a makeshift nest out of bedding if you wanted one."

The smile he gave me made my heart stop before racing. "You bought me a nest," he said.

Over the last week or so, I found I kept buying Kaiser things. Everywhere I went. And I was going out of my way to stop somewhere that might have something that caught my eye for Kaiser. I was thoroughly, stubbornly ignoring the idea that maybe I was doing some backwards courting gesture and leaned more on the side that I was satisfying my urge to shower him with gifts. He was an omega. And they should be stupidly spoiled.

And I'd finally stopped trying to excuse it away. "Yes," I said, smiling. "Make a nest. I'm going to cook up some carbs and you're going to eat before you nap."

I hadn't just bought him a nest. A fake nest. I'd bought other little things, too. But the nest was first since the occasion called for it.

Okay, not first. That had been the lava rock necklace that shone beautifully against his bronzed skin. Like a dark halo around his neck. He hadn't noticed it yet since he was pretty deep into his pre-heat induced sex haze.

I pulled a bag of frozen sweet potato fries out of the freezer and turned the oven on. I think I'd even bought some melba sauce to go with them. You couldn't have decent sweet potato fries without melba sauce.

While the oven preheated, I watched as Kaiser arranged pillows and blankets. When I'd first started sleeping with him, he'd been embarrassed about the excess cum he left all over the place. Then he watched me lick it off him until the only thing he was sticky with was my spit.

I was pretty sure it still bothered him since I often caught him covering the area he sprayed his load in. I might have believed he just didn't want to lay in it. But now I was sure, since his cheeks were always flushed when he did so, that he was trying to hide it.

I've since bought several changes of sheets. Those were also between the wall and the bed. I'd ordered a bed with drawers under it for this kind of storage, but it hadn't arrived yet.

He finished arranging the bedding when there was a very distinct round nest in the middle of my bed by the time the fries were done. He looked up at me as I set the plate at the table.

"Come on. Time to eat up," I told him, and he hurried from the bed.

He didn't sit but stood at the side as he leaned over and took a fry, dipping it into the melba sauce. I'd made many observations about this particular omega over the last week or so, too. One being that he was a big foodie. He loved to eat and appreciated good food.

Mostly, I cooked for him. I'd like to say it was because I didn't want eyes on us. But really, it was because I knew this was going to lead to him begging for my knot and then curling up on my chest after. We'd talk for a long time and then I'd feed him dessert and he'd go home – after a long, lingering kiss that left me tasting cinnamon until morning.

I pulled him around the counter until he was standing in front of me, and I could press into his back. He smiled as he continued to munch on the fries. He wasn't feverish, but he was still an omega. So, he rolled his ass against my cock as he leaned against me, chewing on a fry.

I growled, baring my teeth as I nipped at his ear. Kaiser grinned, rubbing against me again.

"You can knot me while I eat the fries," he said, shifting in my hold to look at me with mischief in his eyes.

"Eat the fries," I commanded.

"Yes, alpha," he said, the submissive obeying tone made my whole body turn to fire as if I were the one in heat.

I held myself together as he continued to shimmy against my dick until he'd swallowed the last of the fries. I handed him another bottle of water and he drank half of it without me needing to tell him to.

And then I picked him up and bent him over the counter so I could thrust myself inside him.

He whimpered before groaning. His hands flailed until they found purchase on the counter. I should have thought to put a towel at the edge under his hips so I wouldn't hurt him. He'd be a little mad now if I stopped to do that, so I took my chances.

I didn't give him my knot right away. Instead, I gave him a proper fucking as he sprayed my floor with his cum. My hands on his back, I kept him steady while I railed his ass, all the while he begged for more.

The second he said he needed my knot, I gave it to him. It wasn't hard to know how far to thrust before your knot was in the way. Since there was only a small handful of the population who could easily take a knot, an alpha was well practiced at knowing just how far to push until that threshold was met.

But when he insisted he needed my knot, that barrier left and I shoved in until I was knot buried inside him at the tail end of a thrust. Kaiser cried out as he gasped, another orgasm painting my floor.

There was a sickeningly deep satisfaction in knowing that Kaiser was leaving his mark all over my kitchen. It drove me further, harder. Determined to wring every last orgasm from him that I could.

I curled my hands around the table under his arms and rutted into him until I was delirious with his scent and climax. The world was a series of lights and his voice telling me, 'more.'

Not knowing how long I barreled into him, we finally went limp over the counter.

I leaned over him, both of us coated in sweat. I could feel his heart beat wildly where I rested my forehead on his back.

"You okay, Kaiser?" I asked.

His words were nonsensical as he answered, his entire body slack where he hung over the counter.

Grinning, I slipped my arm under his chest and pulled him up. We both moaned at the way my knot shifted inside him. And then he tensed, gasping as he grabbed my arm.

"Less okay?" I asked.

His laugh was strangled, and his breathing was harsh. "Little less," he agreed.

"Grab the water," I told him.

He whimpered and I decided that I would now have bottled water everywhere within reach throughout my apartment.

"Never mind. Just hang on. Going to bed where you can be more comfortable."

He nodded and I snagged the water before trying to carefully bring him to the bed. Kitchen had been a great idea until it came time to actually treat this omega like he needed to be. Fucked like an omega in heat, sure. But coddled like an omega needed to follow. Therefore, knotting had to happen in a better place than this.

Lesson learned. Hopefully he'd be okay enough to forgive me.

Kaiser whimpered one more time as I tried to carefully crawl us into his nest. The most I could do was lay him face down and follow with my weight on top of him for a minute. But he sighed in relief and relaxed completely under me.

"If I wasn't so tired, I'd tell you to fuck me again," Kaiser said sleepily.

I grinned and buried my face in his hair, tangling my fingers with his. "Sleep, omega. We have all night."

———

I DIDN'T ACTUALLY MEAN to fall asleep, but I awoke with a touch that felt like someone had burned me with a branding iron.

"Holy fuck," I said, jerking upright.

"Sorry," Kaiser whispered.

I pulled him to me after I oriented myself to what was going on, bringing his mouth to mine. He latched onto me with a fierce grip, trying to curl himself around me so I could push myself inside him. But I thought maybe my heated omega needed a change.

Okay, he probably didn't. I was sure omegas in heat wanted a knot more than anything. But I kissed him as I pushed him to his back. He went willingly, shifting under me so he could bring his legs up.

"Uh uh," I murmured as I started kissing down his body. "You haven't let me taste you since you got here. Got all hot and right to the point as soon as you walked in."

His whine went straight to my dick, making it throb. His words made me growl as I dragged my teeth over his skin. "Please, alpha," he begged.

I shivered at his words and continued down his body as he grabbed fistfuls of my hair.

"Please," he whimpered, and I bit my tongue.

Not my omega. No biting. No biting.

"Bite me, Terence. Make me yours forever."

Miles's words echoed through me, and I nearly jerked away from Kaiser. His hands loosened in my hair as I squeezed my eyes shut, burying my face in his thigh so all I was smelling was him. His perfume was consuming and sweet, with a rush of exotic spices mixed in with the cinnamon.

But the sweetness dropped off as anxiety surfaced.

"Terence?" he whispered.

I released the breath I was holding and looked up at him. His eyes were filled with concern, bordering fear. His body was tensing under me.

Forgoing my mission to take him down my throat, I returned up his body and reclaimed his mouth. His arms wrapped around me, and then his legs around my waist. But he wasn't bucking into me. His hold on me was different.

He was holding me, comforting me. And I clung to him all the more for it. We lay like that for a long time with his body burning up under me, the heat alone making me sweat, as I clung to him, and he held me through my moment of panic.

I hadn't realized I'd stopped kissing him until I pulled my head up from where it was buried in his neck.

"Tell me what you want," I told him. "Anything. Name it."

"Make love to me," he whispered.

I shivered again, but I kissed him softly, letting him feel how much I needed him at that moment.

I pulled his arms from around my neck and pushed my hands along them until we could twine our fingers together as I kissed him slowly. Softly.

He still wasn't moving against me as he normally would. His legs clung to me instead, securely wrapped around my waist as if I might disappear.

Or run away.

He'd experienced that several times.

But right now, as much as he needed the reassurance that I was here, not going to leave, going to pleasure him through this heat spike, I needed to feel him under me. To taste him. To lose myself in this omega who wanted me badly enough that he was looking past all my transgressions towards him.

I continued to kiss him as I shifted. Trying to line myself up with his ass and not let go of his hands, and with his legs still deadlocked around me, was a comedic episode in which we were both laughing breathlessly.

But we weren't so hurried that either of us were willing to let go of the hold we shared. I needed him under me. I needed him wrapped around me. And I could still taste the underlying acerbic hint of fear in his perfume.

Fear that I was going to kick him out when he needed me.

I gripped his hands tightly as I layered sloppy, slow kisses on his lips. Without breaking from the hold his legs had on me, I rocked my hips up and somehow managed to snag the head of my dick on the entrance to his ass.

He grinned into my mouth, and we both froze so as not to lose this mini success.

"I didn't realize my aim was so awful," I muttered.

Kaiser grinned again, spreading sweet kisses along my jaw as I slowly, carefully tried to shimmy my way into him without the use of my hands. I slipped up, jabbing my dick into his balls. He jumped and yelped, then laughed.

I buried my face in his hot neck, sweat coating my body, as I tried to finesse my body movements into where they needed to go. It was a masterful dance that I failed miserably at for a while. But then, fate took pity on me, and I was able to push inside.

I remained slow and steady until I was sure I wasn't going to pop back out and stab his sac again. When I was finally moving as a proper man should, I moved my mouth back to his and resumed our slow, deep kisses that somehow matched the intimate motion of my dick moving in and out of him.

His orgasms came just as readily as they did when I fucked

him mindless. But they were slower, drawn out. I tasted them through our kisses as his body stretched beneath me. His moans were erotic stimulants that drugged me. His fingers flexed in mine before holding me tightly.

I didn't wait for him to ask me for my knot. After a few slow orgasms, I pushed inside him, welcoming the harsh latch and lock that trapped me there. Holding me for what my body thought was eternity. And my soul welcomed it, I could die here and not be mad about it.

His first knotted orgasm like this had him crying out, jerking under my weight until he could catch his breath. Then I shifted, wrapping my arms under and around him, holding him tightly to me as I buried my face in his neck.

Kaiser's arms circled my neck, a hand tangling in my hair. "I love this," he breathed. "It feels like heaven."

I nodded as I rocked into him. Still slower than my normal rut, but quicker than I'd been moving. It seemed that was the lowest speed I could do this.

"Incredible," I agreed.

"Can we do this again?" Kaiser moaned.

I grinned. "We're not even done yet."

"Let's not ever be done. We can just stay like thhiiissss." His word trailed into a string of incoherent syllables as he was swept away in another sweet orgasm. The sounds of his release were different like this. Still unmistakable pleasure, but it was deeper; far more intimate than other times.

It should have hurt something deep inside me. Instead, I swear every time he said my name, it healed a bit of my broken soul, one suture at a time.

I continued to make love to him far after his fever died away. Because I couldn't stop. I didn't want to stop. I needed him in a way I couldn't understand. By the way he clung to me, I thought he understood it even when I didn't.

CHAPTER TWENTY-TWO

Terence

I awoke with Kaiser sprawled over my stomach. He was sleeping peacefully, and I smiled. As soon as I closed my eyes, the world came crashing down around me and my breath caught. I forced my eyes open again as I caught my breath.

Okay, I was awake. No closing my eyes again. Kaiser was still here. I couldn't fall apart yet. There'd be time for that later.

His skin was still cool, so he'd lasted the rest of the night without another spike. I was beginning to think that maybe the alpha courses had missed some key aspects about being with an omega. The spikes for one. I hadn't known about them.

And how painful a knot can be when locked inside an omega and you needed to move them, so they weren't hanging over a counter while your knot slowly relaxed. Emphasis on slowly. There was no quick release for that.

Speaking of the counter, I probably needed to clean that

before I tended to breakfast. And the floor. Pretty sure there was a pile of cum on the floor. I smirked at the idea.

Kaiser mumbled and turned his head before squinting and turning back.

"Curtains," I murmured. "Sorry. I'll add them to my list."

I felt his smile as he squirmed up my body so he could bury his face in my neck. "S'kay," he whispered.

I hugged him to me and chanced closing my eyes again. This time, I wasn't assaulted by memories of my pack that left me with the bitter taste of betrayal in my mouth. It was just peaceful, sweet, omega.

"Want to lounge around a while longer or are you hungry?"

"Both," he answered, his fingers moving into my hair and making me purr.

I nuzzled my cheek against his, marking him with my scent despite telling myself I wasn't going to do that. He wasn't my omega. Even if I was somehow making a backwards and inside out effort at courting him, he wasn't mine.

And yet, I wanted him to be.

The idea was both elevating and painful.

"How about you stay here and relax a bit while I start breakfast," I suggested.

"You don't like to lounge, do you?" he asked, a pout thick in his voice.

"I do, but I become a monster when I'm hungry. It's not pretty and not something you want to see."

He grinned. "Okay, fine."

"Sorry about the curtains. I forget about the bright lights."

Kaiser shook his head. "No biggie."

"It is and I'll pick some up today. Dark ones. So, no light gets in and you can sleep all day if you want to."

Kaiser shifted so he was leaning on his arm looking down at me. His hair was short, irritatingly too short to take a handful of, but even so, it was rumpled, and he looked all the sexier for it. But the expression on his face was hopeful.

"Does that mean I can sleep over again?" he asked.

I grinned, nodding. "Yea. Whenever you want."

He kissed me hard, stealing my breath and making me groan as my purr basically turned into the roar of an engine.

I sat up, taking him with me and getting out of bed with Kaiser's lips still locked on mine. I smiled against him as I gently pried him off. "Seriously. Nasty monster," I told him.

Really, I was just overwhelmed with his emotions and needed to catch my breath for a minute. Then I'd be happy to kiss him again. All day.

Kaiser nodded, his smile still bright and beaming.

I grabbed one of the blankets off the floor and threw it around his shoulders. Then I picked up a little stuffed bear and handed it to him before scooting him out of the bedroom.

"What's this?" he asked, looking at the bear as I steered his perfect ass towards the couch.

"Something for you to cuddle while I'm making breakfast."

His grin was beaming again as he hugged it to him. Kaiser curled on the couch facing towards the kitchen. I walked in and grinned, enjoying that I was right about his cum all over the place. I grabbed one of the kitchen towels and soaked it with water while I began wiping the counter, the side of the counter, and then the chairs. It wasn't just in a nice, neat puddle on the floor. The man had sprayed all over.

"That's horrifying," Kaiser said, appalled. "I'm so sorry. Let me clean it."

"Don't," I barked, and he froze as he started to get up. "Sit your cute little ass right there," I told him, looking at him from where I was crouched at the floor. Kaiser eased back into the couch as he stared at me with wide eyes. "Believe me, I'm not at all bothered by cleaning this up, Kaiser. Giving you a multitude of orgasms is one of the biggest joys in my life. I'll be happy to paint my entire apartment with your release. And you will never lift a finger to clean it up. Understand?"

It was the first time that I'd really put an alpha bark to him. And part of what I said was a lie. He wasn't one of the biggest joys in my life. He was *the only* joy in my life right now.

His cheeks flamed red, but he nodded, burying himself in the blanket so he could barely see me. I smirked, and then found myself grinning even more as I had to pull out some green cleaner to really get the cum off the wall. Well worth every effort.

And I was pretty sure I was going to need to hire a cleaning service to truly find all the splatters. Nope. Still well worth it.

Finally satisfied, I turned to wash my hands and pulled out the blender. I loaded it with fruits and protein before mixing it. Out of the cabinet, I pulled two bottles, one green and one blue. Splitting the shake between the two, I capped them off and brought the green bottle to Kaiser, turning it so he could see his name.

He paused as he stared, a smile spreading across my face. He'd noted at the gym the other day while he watched me work out that all my bottles had my name decaled on them. I explained that if I ever left one behind, there would be no question as to who it belonged to. Kaiser had enjoyed holding onto the bottles.

So, I'd gotten him his own.

Little gifts. Not expensive – well, maybe the fortune I spent on blankets and pillows might have been a little excessive. Again, still worth every cent, but maybe I went a little extra on them since I wasn't satisfied with boring, rough cotton.

His thanks was quiet as he pulled it to him and watched me head back to the kitchen. "Drink it all," I told him. "Protein is good for your energy."

Kaiser snorted. "I think you should add some melatonin so maybe I could sleep through my heat instead." His voice wasn't bitter, but I heard the frustration in it.

"Not a chance, omega. Pretty sure your heats are a biological necessity."

"No. At one time, they assured conception by as many opposite sex omega-alpha pairs as possible. As if our species was going to die out." He paused and though I wasn't looking at him, I was sure he'd rolled his eyes. "Now, they're just unnecessary torture. We're a race that is suffocating the world. And honestly, who am I impregnating?"

"Marley?" I suggested.

Kaiser grinned. "Someday, yea, Marley. She's going to be a rockin' momma, too. It's like she's all three designations rolled into one. Absolutely perfect."

I smiled at him, nodding. Yes, the girl was pretty damn perfect. Even if I hadn't seen her since I ran away after she kissed me. I swear, if anyone was reading my story from the outside, they'd think I was a terrified thirteen-year-old the way I run scared. Not a thirty-eight-year-old, damaged alpha who's made himself look like a royal ass.

We spoke quietly as I cooked.

"It's no wonder you have a juice bar," Kaiser said after a while. "This smoothie is just as good as what you sell."

I smirked, refusing to allow my mind to lean towards Zack. "Not quite. And I've had nothing to do with those recipes. Besides, that's a protein shake."

"Then you should add a protein shake line," he said.

I paused, wondering why that had never occurred to me. "Next time you see Nora, suggest it. Tell her I endorse it, but she's the boss."

Kaiser grinned.

When he'd finished his smoothie and breakfast wasn't done

yet, he meandered into the kitchen and set his bottle into the sink with mine. I watched him closely as he turned on the hot water, ready to scold him back into the living room. But he filled the bottle like I had and turned it off before turning to me and leaning his hip on the counter.

We were both still naked and so the look of him standing there with a slightly hard dick had me licking my lips.

"Are you making a feast?" he asked as he examined the spread of food. I had each burner going and that didn't account for the spread of fruit in the fridge.

Maybe I'd gone all out knowing Kaiser was spending the night. But I'd do it all over again in an instant. Next time with curtains.

"Yes and no. Just multiple components and I added an extra carb dish to give you more energy stores for your heat." I nodded at the crisping home fries mixed with onions, mushrooms, and sausage. Damn good combination, especially when you get the spices just right.

I was making a version of eggs Benedict that didn't require me to poach the egg. I hated runny egg whites so I needed a way that would afford that the yolks cooked just slightly so that they were runny but that the whites were thoroughly cooked. No, I didn't care if I was missing the point of eggs Benedict. Runny whites were disgusting. End of story.

"Did your parents teach you to cook?" Kaiser asked.

I nodded. "Yep. In a family filled with alphas and an omega mother, food was a big thing in my house. As was feeding our omega."

I grinned at him, and Kaiser beamed. "That's why you're so good at this."

"Cooking?"

"And everything else," he agreed.

My hand stilled as I stirred the hollandaise for just a

moment before I continued. Can't screw that up. Then the whole thing will be shot. "I'm glad you think so," I said quietly. Because I wasn't so sure. Kaiser's wounded looks as I ran away will forever be burned in my mind.

Between the memories of my pack, anyway.

None of which was I allowing to surface right now. The only thing I was concentrating on was making a perfect hollandaise, and Kaiser.

"You are," he said, his voice gentling. "I know why you don't think so, but maybe I came on too strong. Too insistent."

I didn't answer as I whisked the sauce until I was satisfied that it was done. I turned that burner off and moved it away from the heat before I turned to Kaiser and pulled him against me, pressing my lips to his forehead.

"How about we don't discuss that right now, okay?"

He nodded.

"I acknowledge that at some point, it'll probably be a good idea to. But right now, let's just talk about breakfast and how your fever is coming back."

Kaiser sighed in irritation. "I swear, sometimes I just want a good breakfast without a hard-on."

I laughed, hugging him to me. "We can take care of both. But I need to finish the food first."

He nodded and backed away, but didn't leave the kitchen as he watched.

"Alright. Choose some drinks from the fridge," I told him. I watched in the corner of my eye as I tended to the eggs while he shifted everything around until he'd seen all the options. He came away with a couple different prepackaged juice options from the shop downstairs and set them on the counter.

"Under the couch are two TV trays. Want to set them up?"

Kaiser nodded and left the kitchen to do so. I pulled plates and started piling the toasted brioche slices on the plates. Two each. They got eggs next, the yolk perfectly jiggly. Then I doused both with hollandaise sauce.

I piled on a load of home fries before grabbing the fruit from the fridge and bowls. Fruit was mandatory, regardless of the fact that I'd loaded the smoothies. Good sugars to balance out the starch and fats.

I handed the bowls of fruit to Kaiser when he returned and tucked the drinks under my arm and took the plates with two forks in my hand.

He'd set the trays up in front of each cushion and I placed the plates on them. But I looked around, trying to determine how I could make this work like I imagined it.

Ah, fuck it. We might end up with cum on our plates, but I didn't care. I pushed both the trays carefully to the side and sat in the middle of the couch, looking up at Kaiser with a sly smile.

"So, about that hard-on." His face heated and before my eyes, his dick stiffened. "Let's tackle both hungers at the same time, hm?"

Kaiser's eyes widened as he swallowed.

"Sit on my lap, omega," I purred.

He shivered and came towards me, turning so that perfect tight ass was in my face before he was lowering it into my lap.

I didn't need to be fully hard to start to push inside him when he lowered himself onto me. I would harden quickly enough. In fact, I didn't really plan to truly fuck him. I wanted to bury myself in his ass, knot deep and let him ride through the spike as I fed him.

Maybe I should have gotten a towel. Thankfully, there was a blanket close.

Kaiser lowered himself onto me until I was stuffed inside him. I spread his legs open, so they hung over mine before wrapping an arm around his chest.

He groaned low and guttural, dropping back against me as his back arched. His head fell on my shoulder.

Let me just say, growing hard while I was already so deep inside him had my mind reeling. Fire racing. My heart pounding against my ears.

"Feel me hardening inside you?" I murmured.

Kaiser gripped his cock at my words and spurted all over his chest as he gasped. His eyes went wide as his body jerked. I pulled his hips down hard, making sure I was as deep as I could be as I continued to lengthen and stiffen inside him.

And then my knot started expanding and his body reacted as if I was injecting him with an orgasm inducer. He whined, a sound that started low in his chest, until he started thrashing against me as he came. Over and over while my knot continued to build inside him, and his body flexed around it.

"Terence," he whimpered. Begged. "Alpha." He couldn't get any more out. He tried as he continued to succumb to the onslaught.

"What do you need?" I asked.

"Hold- Hold me. Tight."

I wrapped my arms around his chest, holding him in a vice. His hand was still gripping his dick, a hold that matched mine around him.

"I'm coming," he gasped. "I'm coming. Coming."

Yes. Yes, he was. I licked the side of his face where he'd sprayed himself. My dick twitched inside him as his sweet cinnamon flavor went down my throat.

"Alpha," he whimpered.

"You're doing amazing," I crooned.

He relaxed a little and I realized I was slacking again. Too lost in the sensation of him that I was forgetting what he needed.

"Such a tight fit." I gripped him hard, the position assuring that I couldn't possibly get any deeper. "You were made exactly for me. Feel how good my knot is in you."

"Yes," he whispered. His muscles started to relax.

"Was it too much?" I asked.

"No."

"Hurt?"

He shook his head. "Orgasm," he muttered.

I had no idea what he was trying to say at this point. Throwing out words in a way that I wasn't sure what he was telling me.

"You need more?"

Kaiser nodded. "Yes, alpha."

I kept one arm wrapped tightly around him as I dropped my hand to cover his on his dick. He had the thing in a fucking rigid hold. So, I dropped my hands to his balls. As soon as I started massaging them, he burst up his chest again.

"There you go. You're doing amazing, sweetie."

He moaned as his head lolled to the side. I guess eating while I was trapped inside him wasn't going to happen. I'd feed him after. Hand feed him.

"Give me another good spill, Kaiser. One more. Spray up your chest."

He whined, his nose wrinkling as I toyed with his sac in my hand. His body shook before he gasped and let loose again.

"That's it. Look how well you listen," I crooned. "You're perfect. And you taste amazing. Beautiful. Your voice is a toxic symphony."

"Teeth," he muttered. "Please."

I stilled as panic started to sweep through me. Closing my eyes, I turned my face into his neck and bit him. Not hard. Hard enough that he spasmed in my hold, his ass clamping down on me and he cried out loudly as he coated his chin in cum.

And then he went limp.

I shivered, hugging him to me as I licked at the spot I'd bitten. I could feel the teeth marks. But there was no blood. Just the impression of my teeth. I swallowed the sensation of panic as best I could.

Letting go of his balls, I pulled one of the trays close. I plucked a strawberry from the bowl and brought it to Kaiser's mouth.

"Eat, my precious omega," I murmured as I traced his lip with it. "Eat so we can do this again."

———

KAISER TOOK a shower while I cleaned up. And then I kissed him against the door until someone in his pack came for him. He rushed out with a smile, and I watched through the window as Marley got out and hugged him.

Aware that I was covered in cum and smelling heavily like Kaiser, I dressed in gym clothes and headed out to work through the memories that were trying to surface. They were all good memories. But they hurt like claws in my chest.

I needed them to stop, but I didn't know how to make them. I loved my pack. I will always love my pack. And I would give the world to have them back.

But they weren't here, and I wanted their memories to be sweet without all the crippling pain. How did I get to that point?

CHAPTER TWENTY-THREE

Terence

I didn't see Kaiser for the rest of the day, but I picked him up late the next morning to shop with me. Nora had a bunch of things on her list that she needed to do, but the day was turning out incredibly busy at Juice Me and she couldn't get away. I heard the stress in her voice when she called me, begging for me to pick some things up for the second location.

Shopping didn't interest me a whole lot outside of the occasional boredom and intrigue of seeing what's out there. What had I missed in the last handful of months that I'd shut out the world?

Since Nora and I agreed that I'd not be any help in the juice bar since my skills covered chopping fruits and vegetables, I stopped by to grab her list and then called Kaiser.

He was thrilled to come. The excitement in his voice made me smile. And that's how I found myself in his driveway thirty minutes later. He opened the door before I was halfway up the walk and ran out to me.

I hadn't been expecting him to run into me, but I caught him in a hug in which he buried his face in my neck. Sighing, I rested my chin on him and closed my eyes.

"I missed you," he said quietly.

His words made me smile in that way one does when they're falling for someone but also made a chasm of pain split in my chest. I swallowed it down and held him tighter. Maybe I could squeeze the feeling away.

"Missed you, too," I told him.

After another minute, he pulled back to look at me with a small smile on his face. He looked harder today. More masculine, though I wasn't sure what was different. Jeans that still outlined his perfect ass. A simple t-shirt that fit him in just the right way that said he had a gorgeously trim body without actually showing off the lines of it. And sneakers.

"Ready?"

He nodded, smiling, and turned back to the house. Marley was in the door and my heart jumped at the look of her in a short sundress. Kaiser waved, blowing her a kiss, and turned to the car. I didn't follow him for a minute as I looked at her.

Marley brushed strands of silken brown hair behind an ear and looked at me with an unassuming smile. I thought Kaiser should have been enough. He should have satisfied every alpha need in me. As an omega, it should have been the only connection my alpha craved like this.

But there was no mistaking the way I reared up with a passion to possess her, too. Like fireworks ready to explode. Like a wolf's bite, ready to claim. And like a man who had spotted someone they knew instinctively would complete them.

I inclined my head to her and raised my hand in a pathetic

wave. Her smile widened slightly and I turned away before I could do something stupid.

Like running away after she kisses me.

Fucking stupid.

Kaiser was leaning against my car looking at me with a knowing smirk and hooded eyes. "Marley isn't busy today," he said. "She enjoys shopping."

I sighed, stopping in front of him and pressing my lips to his to keep him quiet. And because I needed to taste him.

He groaned immediately, pulling his body from the car, and pressing it into me instead. I was surprised when he suddenly took his lips from mine. "I swear, if you keep kissing me, we're not going shopping. And I even made it a point to feed the stupid fevers this morning until I was delirious just so I could get through the day sane. You're going to undo me with a damn kiss."

I grinned, pressing another quick kiss to his lips, and opening the door for him to slide in. "Buckle," I told him, and he gave me a heated look in return.

When he'd situated himself, I shut the door and moved to round the car. Marley was still in the door, and I paused to meet her eyes. She held my gaze until I turned away, opening my door, and dropping inside.

It wasn't until I started the car and put it in reverse that I saw the murky outline of someone else in a window on the second floor watching. I couldn't make out any details. The reflection of the outside was too prominent on the glass. I could only discern the shape of a man in the window watching.

"You're sure your pack is okay with you and I?" I asked as I started to back out.

"Yes," Kaiser said, shifting in his seat to look at me. "Why?"

"It's an unusual situation," I paused and glanced at the

house again. Marley had gone inside. But the man in the window was still there. No, now there were two.

"It is. But packs grow and change over time. It's not like I went out looking for you because I was unsatisfied with where I am. I'm not. I love my pack with everything in me. They're amazing. Every one of them. And they let me be me outside of being their omega."

I wasn't sure which part of that I wanted to question. 'Every one of them' had me nervous as to how many were actually in his pack. And then there was the 'packs grow and change' thing that nearly had me running again. I could feel the itch and nausea under my skin and my stomach rolling.

But the safest part that had me curious enough to override the rest, was him able to be himself outside of their omega. So, I asked about that instead. "Explain."

Kaiser already knew what I was asking. He turned away, his cheeks flushing as he didn't meet my eyes. "I don't always act like a spoiled omega," he whispered. "Not needy and whiny and expecting to be taken care of. I'm a man and I can handle myself."

"But you shouldn't have to."

"That's what biology states, yes. I do as you say with your bark, and you lay the world at my feet to make me happy."

There was a tone of bitterness in his voice. This was not a conversation to have while driving since I didn't have the luxury of studying his expression. Since I wasn't willing to let this go quite yet, I pulled into a little diner and put the car in park before shifting in my seat to face him.

He was flush still and now looking rather miserable. "Come here," I said quietly.

Kaiser unbuckled and shifted as close to me as he could get with the console between us. I took his face in my hand and leaned my forehead against his. "Tell me why it bothers you."

I could hear the faintest of whines in his throat as he squirmed a little. His hand wrapped around my wrist as he closed his eyes.

"If I could have swapped being an omega for either designation, I would have. From a young age I've hated the expectations of me. I'm weak and needy and horny and get so much stupid attention just for being an omega. Just for my perfume. There are criminal circles dedicated to abducting and selling omegas just because we're rare. And a male omega is worth a lot because we're the rarest. I've lived with that fear forever. Even being tied to a pack wouldn't fully protect me. I'm still an omega. Still with a strong perfume. That means I'm still a body that can take a knot like no other. And I'll fucking beg for it in heat because I'm a mindless animal. I hate being a commodity in high demand. It's like I'm an object. I'm a person!"

I let him go and pushed my door open. Kaiser's eyes widened at my sudden release of him but his entire body was shaking by the time he got to the part about taking a knot. I rounded the car and pulled his door open, nearly dragging him out of the car so I could wrap him in my arms. I was growling low in my chest as anger swept through me.

There were a lot of criminal trafficking rings. Foster had told us about one that was selling an alpha's bite. I'd been too disgusted to get details. And I was too afraid to look into it.

The world knew about the abducting and selling of omegas. Yes, it was a black-market business. Yes, this was basically trafficking. But some packs were so desperate for an omega, they didn't want to wait for the unlikely chance that one would choose them from the Pack Listing. So, otherwise upstanding packs would lower themselves to purchase an omega.

Our neighbors had been one. Their omega was a beautiful and happy woman. If they'd have not told Miles the truth, we'd never have known. But I could only imagine that not all omegas got lucky and were bought into a decent pack.

But my growling was not stopping as I held my shaking omega. I slid down to the ground, pulling him into my lap so I could tuck him more firmly within my arms and surround him with my body.

"Sorry," he whispered.

My growl got louder, making him jump, before I could swallow it again. "Don't apologize, Kaiser. No one will touch you that you don't want. Ever."

He smiled into my neck. "I know," he whispered. "An omega develops a deep fear when the realities of the world are revealed to them. I'm a lucky one. I know that. My pack and I both know that I'm putting myself at risk by going out without one of my alphas. But I hate living in fear. I hate being branded for my designation. I hate that my best option for going unnoticed would be to suppress my perfume. But it's not just the world. I hate the hand biology dealt omegas. And yet, I let myself become the epitome of one, so I had a better chance with you."

His voice was so quiet that I barely heard his last few words. His shaking had stopped but now he was still in my arms. Tense. His fear made his normal pine and cinnamon turn acerbic.

"It's probably the only way you'd have gotten me to react positively to you," I admitted on a sigh. "Kaiser, I moved to Ocean City to disappear. Not to find a pack or an omega."

"That's why you kept running from me? Why you looked at me like I was a monster?"

I flinched. "Yes."

"I thought you didn't like my perfume," he whispered.

I groaned and bit his shoulder. It was hard enough that he flinched this time, but he laughed, too. "I told you. My reaction had nothing to do with you at all. And really, you shouldn't forgive me for treating you like that. You shouldn't have chased me, omega."

"Because I'm an omega," Kaiser said with a heavy sigh.

I chuckled, nodding into him. "Yes, but also no. Because I was a jerk to you and Marley. Your designations aside, an alpha should never treat anyone else like that."

"There are a lot of ways alphas treat people that they shouldn't."

"Yes, and you don't pursue them. They're not worthy of you."

"I don't know if you're trying to talk me out of being with you, but too bad. I'm here and I'm not leaving. If you need me to play my biological card for a while longer, I will. Just to assure that you stay."

Fuck this man. His hair was too short to grab onto but I still pulled his head back so I could kiss him. Kaiser's hands went straight to my hair as heat swept over his body. His kiss was deep and consuming, filling me with licking flames and making me hard all over.

Once again, he pulled his mouth from me. "Now you've done it," he said, his voice barely not a whine. "I told you. You can't kiss me like that when I'm so close to heat. Those biological things that I hate so much? Heats are one of them."

"Heats?" I asked, dragging my lips across his neck as he leaned his head back. "But you enjoy sex just fine."

He laughed breathlessly. "Terence, everything is completely out of my control. I've been fortunate not to have had to experience one without my pack. But if I was taken and came into heat, I might whine and beg for my pack, but I would still beg whoever was there for a knot. It's disgusting and terrifying knowing that for an entire four days, I'm mindless and willing to do anything to make the fever break."

I'd paused in teasing him when he turned it serious again. I never realized how stressed an omega lived. How much fear ran through them. I released a heavy breath and hugged him tight again.

"Look at me," I whispered. No bark. No moving him to do so.

Kaiser shifted so he could put some space between us, giving us room to look into each other's eyes. There was anxiety in his expression. A deep fear peeking out of his steel blue eyes. But there was more than that, too. He needed my acceptance. There was an open plea on his face that I don't need him to be that constant soft omega.

"Someday, I'll let you in," I said quietly, brushing my fingers through his short hair. He leaned into my touch but kept his gaze locked with mine. "It will probably explain a lot of why I ran from you. And I know I've kept it together decently for a while now, I can't promise you I'm not going to shut down again. I can't even promise that I'll be able to get myself out of it. I need you to know that it has nothing to do with you. Not you, omega, and not you, Kaiser. Your instincts were right to let biology work for you because I was never going to come around otherwise. Again, it has nothing to do with you and I realize that's hard to accept. And I maintain that you shouldn't have continued to pursue me. There are thousands of better alphas out there."

"Maybe, but I want you."

The stubbornness in his voice made me smile. I took a deep breath, trying to build the courage to lay out some honesty. Because, fuck, I wanted him, too. And I couldn't trust myself to not fuck this up.

"I'm not in a good place," I said, letting him see the pain in me. His breath caught and he let out a shaking breath. "I want you, too, Kaiser," I whispered. "But I can't promise you anything. And though I don't want you to be a slave to biology because I know what kind of a bitch that can be, you're going to have to be the alpha in our relationship for a while and read the situation. Know when to let your biology reel me back in. Know when I'm in a relatively stable place and you can be you completely. And understand that I might freak out and push you away but if you want back in, it needs to be you who demands it. I don't have the mental strength to do this. It doesn't mean I don't want to. It just means that I'm too broken to be what you need. Okay?"

Tears rimmed Kaiser's eyes. I tried not to listen to my own tone because I was sure it was broken when I spoke. I had never meant to let him in even that far.

CHAPTER TWENTY-FOUR

Kaiser

I knew he hadn't meant anything to make me feel bad in any way. But the pain in his voice and the grief reflected in his eyes made me realize that all my fears and anxiety were nothing. Whatever Terence was going through was the real thing. Mine were hypothetical. His were reality.

"Okay," I whispered. "I'll be your alpha."

He breathed quiet laughter and closed his eyes for a minute. I expected him to close it down all the way. But the torment was still there when he looked at me again. "Good," he whispered.

Terence pulled me against him and buried his face in my neck. Only now that he couldn't see my face did I let my tears fall. I wasn't sure if they were just for his pain or maybe some residual from my own fears that I'd laid out for him.

"Want to go back to your apartment?" I asked. "We can try and curl up on the small couch and watch TV."

He chuckled. "Yes. But I promised Nora some shopping."

"Am I allowed to demand to know what's best for you and that we should go home?" I asked.

Terence laughed this time. His stubble ran across my cheek until his lips covered mine. I could even taste his pain. There was a salty note to it. The same as what tinged his scent.

I kissed him hungrily. Being this close to heat, there was no other way to kiss him, even knowing he didn't need sex. He needed someone to be here for him. He needed an alpha to take care of him.

"Part of being an alpha is sometimes knowing you need to get work done before you can give in to any kind of stressors," he said against my lips. "But we can make this quick and then go home."

"And you'll let me take care of you?" I asked, rubbing my hand across his stubble. It was long enough that it should be coarse, but it was soft, like the fine bristles of a newborn's brush.

"I'll let you take care of me."

"Then let's go. I can drive."

Terence grinned and stood, picking me up with him as if I weighed nothing. The way his body remained hard under my touch at all times with his stupidly sexy muscles didn't surprise me in the least.

As soon as he let me go, I opened the passenger door for him to get in. This big man looking at me with the smile he was, had my cock weeping. I could feel a heat spike coming on. I was sure it was partially induced because of the kissing.

Hopefully I could push it off for a while. And when we got back to his apartment, I think I could work in taking his knot as part of taking care of him.

I shut the door and narrowed my eyes on myself. No. That was an omega-in-heat need. Not an alpha need. Not the kind of need he had right now.

I wasn't sure I was going to be a good alpha.

I climbed in the driver's seat and buckled. Terence held his phone out. On the screen was the text history with Nora. And a list of things he needed to purchase today.

Normally, I enjoyed shopping. But with my heat right around the corner and my alpha needing something that had nothing to do with shopping, I wasn't in the mood at all. Maybe I could call in a favor to Marley.

"Oh!" I said, looking at him with a grin. "What if I could promise you this shopping gets done and we can go home so I can take care of you."

His smile grew up over his lips and I watched, fascinated, as his tongue traced his bottom lip. "What do you have in mind?"

"Marley," I told him, dragging my eyes back to his. It was harder than I thought it should be. "The woman has many superpowers, and this is one she excels at."

There was hesitation in his expression. And I pressed a little when I thought maybe we'd had enough deep and dark for the day.

"Do you not like her?" I asked.

Terence groaned, leaning his head back. I swallowed a grin as his pheromones filled the small space. Oh, he liked her.

He sighed and opened his eyes, looking at the ceiling. "I can only handle one of you right now, Kaiser. I think you've seen that I'm not doing real good at that, even."

I nodded. "Understood. I just wanted to make sure. But this has nothing to do with that. She'll shop for us." At least, I was pretty sure. I wondered if she would. Maybe I shouldn't volunteer her.

"Alright," he said.

His agreement made me grin stupidly. "Okay. I'm going to step outside the car and call her."

He nodded, his gaze locked on me again. "If she isn't up for it, don't push. I think we can knock this list out in a couple hours making minimal stops."

I smiled and got out of the car, shutting the door, and leaning against it. This might fall into line of taking advantage of a situation, knowing how she feels. And maybe I'm absolute shit for doing this. I dialed Marley anyway.

"Are you okay?" she asked as soon as she answered.

I smiled brightly. "Absolutely fine, Mar. But I have a favor and I've only just now realized that maybe I'm shit for asking it of you."

"What is it?"

Sighing, I told her. "I kinda got us into some dreary shit and now I just kinda want to curl up and not do anything, but Terence has a list of things Nora needs him to shop for so they can keep on track with their timeline."

"You want me to shop," she said. Her voice was quiet, and I was trying to determine her tone. But those five words weren't long enough of a sentence for me to read it fully.

"You can tell me no," I assured her. "I know I'm a bit of a bitch for asking."

Her laughter was quiet. "It's fine. I'll have Adrian drive me around like a chauffeur. He'll keep me entertained as I spend someone else's money."

I sighed in relief. "Thank you. I swear, I'll make it up to you. I'll forward you the list and let you know how to access his accounts."

"You're okay?" she asked.

"Yea," I said, letting my voice drop. "I think I accidentally hit on something dark for both of us in different ways. And you know how I get."

"Text me. Love you, Kai."

"I love you, too."

She hung up and I wondered if she was hiding it well

over the phone, how much of an ass I was. I climbed back into the car and reached for his phone. In a roundabout way, I was giving Marley Terence's number by taking myself out as the middleman and sending her the text directly from his phone.

Terence was watching me when I looked up. "How does she pay?" I asked. "Do the stores have accounts?"

"The ones for these items Nora set up an account with. We'll stop at Juice Me and I'll have Nora add Marley as a purchaser before we go upstairs."

"Ohh, fun!" I grinned. Someday, I did want to shop with him.

I gave Marley a quick 'I'll forward you more details in a bit' text and handed him back his phone.

There was only one car I drove regularly, but this one was fun. And it had the subtle scent of his beta who used it for work. I bet, despite what he thought of himself, they really loved Terence at Juice Me.

Now that he'd let me in a little, even if I didn't know the real wounds, I could see how hard getting through some days were. I hadn't been making it any easier.

But he'd let me see! He trusted me and wanted me enough to let me see! That feeling of floating didn't leave me as I drove us to the juice bar. Terence directed me around back to the garage and then brought me into the juice bar from a back door. It was another almost giddy feeling. Like I was a VIP being shown the behind-the-scenes tour.

We walked into a storage room and then through an enormous kitchen where there were three workers managing industrial sized juicers. I stared wide-eyed as Terence pulled me along. I hadn't realized he had my hand until then and smiled stupidly as we went.

The shop wasn't too busy. There were half a dozen people

waiting. Nora looked up and grinned, winking at me when she saw me.

"You done, Mr. Andersen?"

"Actually, I hit a snag, but we've secured ourselves a personal shopper. I just need you to add her to the purchasing accounts," he told her.

Nora raised a brow but nodded. She wiped her hands on a towel before stepping out.

"Do we have this under control out here or do I need to do some chopping while Kaiser gives you her information?" Terence asked and I stared with wide eyes.

"Oh, definitely help us chop," the man at the blenders said, giving Terence a grin.

Immediately, my hackles rose and my grip on his hand tightened.

Ohhh... possessive omega. That was new.

Terence looked at me with a wickedly pleased smile and planted his lips on mine. I shivered, letting his taste and his tongue placate my reaction. "Go with Nora. I'll be right here."

I nodded, another shiver sweeping down my body.

"Come on, darling," Nora said, winking at me. "Just wait till you see him in an apron."

"I've seen it," I told her, glancing back as Terence stepped behind the counter. My hands fisted. It was surprisingly difficult to continue following Nora when there was a beta wanting my alpha. His flirting hadn't even been subtle. I saw the want in his gaze.

"Relax, Kaiser," Nora said as she led me into an office and shut the door. "Jakob has flirted with Mr. Andersen since he was hired eight months ago, and he's not paid Jakob a single lick of attention in more than complimenting his success with a blender."

I shivered and took a breath. "Sorry," I said. "Not used to that reaction."

She grinned.

"Also, I think you ought to work on a protein shake line. Terence says he endorses the idea but you're the boss."

Nora laughed and pushed a piece of paper at me. "Who are we adding?" she asked.

"My beta, Marley." I added her name and phone number down, adding her birthday when Nora prompted. I waited until she made several calls and wrote down the names of stores and the account number, letting me know that Marley would have to show ID before she could access the accounts for charging.

Then she led me back and I watched as Terence was handed a small bowl of fruits. He washed them and chopped them and dumped them into a blender. Then he slid them down the line for Jakob to add whatever else it needed.

There were little colored sticks, an entire rainbow of shades. One side was pointed while the other side was rounded. Based on what was left sticking up in the bowl, it's clear that Jakob knows the rest of the add-ins. Certain kinds of juice, milks, caffeine, etc.

Everything was truly personalized, and I loved experimenting with flavors here. Nora replaced Terence and he joined me again, bringing me against him and kissing me hard. I groaned at the touch, threading my fingers into his hair, and bringing my knee up along the side of his leg. This man could undo me.

"Ready?" he asked into my mouth.

My skin heated and I swallowed. "Yes," I breathed.

"Take care of our alpha," Nora called as Terence pulled me to the door.

I grinned at her through the window as he pulled me around the corner to the door.

"You have everything taken care of with Marley?" he asked as he let me in.

I nodded. "Just need to text this stuff to her. Want her to drop it off here when she's done?"

"I'll give her Nora's number." I watched as he pulled out his phone and opened the text up that I had used to forward Nora's list. He typed in Nora's information, explaining that any questions would be best asked of her. And if there was anything that needed delivering, she would be the one to ask.

Then I took his phone and typed in the numbers for the accounts at which shops, reminding her that she needed to bring her ID. With that done, I set our phones on the table and urged him to the couch.

It really wasn't big enough for the two of us but with him lying on his back, his legs hanging over the opposite armrest, I climbed on top of him and curled up.

A spike was surfacing. I could feel it. Hopefully, Terence could ignore it for a while before he felt the need to respond. "Do you need anything?" I asked. "Hungry? Thirsty? Cold?"

"Impossible to get cold when you're a heater," he said, his voice teasing.

I sighed and looked up at him. "It's not bad right now. We can ignore it for a while."

"Hm," he answered, curling an arm around my back, and shifting us on the couch so that I was pressed between him and the back.

I tried not to let him see how much I enjoyed that. The tight warm space filled with his scent. I buried my face in his chest, rubbing my nose against him and sighed contentedly. "Really, I want to take care of you right now."

"You are," he said, twisting his fingers with mine. "This is exactly what I need. Your body pressed against mine and the feeling of your breath on me."

I grinned. Alphas' needs were different from omegas. This is what I need, too. But for different reasons. He needs to be the one wrapped around me, and I need to be the one buried so deeply in him that I almost disappear.

I fell asleep and woke up when the sun was setting. I was whining, my body burning so hot that I was dripping with sweat. My hips rocked against Terence as heat clouded my mind. The press of mindless need to be satisfied gripped me tightly and I bit my lip so I wouldn't demand sex.

He said something but all I heard was the tenor of his voice. I'd apparently slept deeply enough that I was already lost within the haze of painful need when I awoke.

"Please," I whimpered, cringing inwardly at the way my voice begged. Pleaded. Pathetic. "Please, alpha. Knot."

I hated this part of me. I hated the desperation that rang loudly inside me. I hated how my body ached in a pain unimaginable until it got what it wanted.

How degrading. How humiliating.

The pain was real.

"I got you," Terence said, and I felt his hands on my skin. Cold touches that made me shake. "There you go. A little more."

I didn't know what he was saying. I was so lost in a fog that was becoming painful that I was struggling to keep in the whine.

The first explosion of an orgasm came, and I breathed in a breath of release. No knot. My body quaked as the orgasm subsided. There was no knot. I needed a knot, or I was going to die. I was sure I was going to die without one.

How do I say so when I could barely make a coherent thought?

"Good omega," Terence purred. "That's my good omega."

Fuck. I shuddered against him, his words soothing something deep inside me.

And then another orgasm reared to life, spraying all over and making me whimper at the feel of it. There was nothing I hated more than being covered in my own cum. Fucking disgusting. I hated it enough that it was a clear thought in my mind, even through the haze of painfully intense need.

"Ready?" Terence asked.

I managed not to beg him as I nodded.

And then he was pushing his way inside me, and I moaned as I tried to shove my ass back at him. Quicker. Deeper. I needed him to reach the end of me. I needed his knot to stretch me wide enough that my body clamps down on him and forces the orgasms from me until I pass out. I needed so much.

He didn't knot me right away. He fucked me into the bed first, wringing two more delicious orgasms out of me before I was begging again for his knot. And I did beg. It was horrifying. And so fucking pleasing when he purred in response.

Terence kicked my legs apart. I was apparently lying flat on the bed with his weight on top of me. Being spread eagle like this made it impossible to move at all. As he started coaxing his knot inside me, little landmines detonated inside of me until I was howling like a banshee.

My body locked him inside me until I was completely delirious with pleasure. It swept through me in hot waves as my ass fluttered around his knot, every nerve ending delivering another pulse within my orgasm. It was so good it was almost painful. The best kind of pain.

The kind that you get lost in as your mind turns off and all you can do is feel.

———

I ALWAYS KNEW the minute the fever broke. It was like a bucket of cold water was thrown over me, putting out a fire that was burning from the inside.

Terence's arms were wrapped around my chest, holding me firmly to his chest. His heart was a drum against my back, his breath a hot furnace on my skin as he brushed kisses over my shoulder.

"Feel better?" he asked, his voice still low and growly.

I nodded, bringing one of my legs up so he'd fully curl around me. The movement pulled on his knot locked inside me and I moaned, my body shaking with a spasm of pleasure. Terence curled his legs up against mine, letting out a hot breath.

Full out heat was still a couple days away I thought. I didn't pay that close attention. I never had to. It just happened when it happened and my pack took care of me. It was different trying to maneuver around someone outside my pack.

A deep longing in me knew that I was going to be asking for him in heat. In that mindless state filled with nothing but want for pleasure. For knots and locks. I'd never felt a lock. We had toys to simulate one, but I wasn't sure how well it measured up.

They delivered ridiculous orgasms that made me feel like my balls were going to explode from the force of my orgasm. Especially when they were paired with a knot.

There was a time growing up when I remember talking to another omega, a female, and she sighed in envy of my gender. "You're the perfect omega, Kaiser. You're equipped for both a male and a female alpha. We're only really set for one. That's why males are sought for even more so than females."

I'd told her she was wrong. What good was a male omega in a group of male alphas? We couldn't carry children. It was a whole bunch of dead lines if a male omega found himself in a pack with a group of male alphas.

She disagreed. And I'd found over the years that there was no one who agreed with my stance on it. A male omega was the epitome of perfection.

Pfft.

I brought my hand over me to grip Terence's hair, just so I could hold onto him. His purr filled my ears, rumbling softly against my chest.

We lay in bed for a long time, the remnants of my makeshift nest still strewn about on his bed. He slipped out of me eventually but didn't shift us in any other way until his phone rang.

I think we both assumed it would be Nora. Terence kissed the back of my head and then my shoulder before pulling away. When he stood to go for his phone, I arranged the blankets to hide my mess. There was little I hated more than that.

"Hello?" Terence answered.

I glanced up in time to see his shoulders tense. The way he stood, I could only see his profile but it was filled with something I couldn't read. His voice lowered when he spoke again.

"Remove us. They're dead." He hung up the phone and held it gripped tightly in his hand.

My heart stopped as I stared at him with wide eyes. Chills swept my body, making all the little hairs stand on end. Long silent minutes passed that became heavier by the second. I stayed perfectly still as I waited for him to say something.

"I need you to leave."

Those weren't the words I wanted him to say. Tears filled my eyes. A pit filled my stomach as bile rose. I pulled desperately on my bonds in a frantic panic, unable to move. Fear and hurt and anxiety filled me as I shot up from the bed to pull on my clothes.

I grabbed my phone and ran out of the apartment. I ran into

the downstairs door, almost bouncing off it into a hard body that made me yelp.

Terence was behind me, his hands on my arms to steady me. The pain I'd glimpsed earlier was bright in his eyes and I knew he was only barely holding himself together. Still, I looked at him in confusion. Why had he followed me?

"You don't send an omega into the streets alone," he whispered.

His voice was thick with grief, low and dark. I ached for him.

He reached beyond me, pressing his chest into my back as he reached for the door handle to open it. As soon as it was open, I ran into the night as tears slipped down my cheeks.

He'd kicked me out. And with the onset of heat, my irrationality was at its peak.

CHAPTER TWENTY-FIVE

Phynn

I jerked off the couch as soon as the burst of panic swept through me. I was already through the house with my keys in my hand when Adrian and Marley stepped downstairs.

"I got him," I said as I nearly raced to the car.

The panic didn't let up. It simmered and spiked and rolled with fear and the sting of pain. And tightly laced through it all was the surge of arousal. I had no idea what had happened. He'd been fine. He'd been on cloud nine for the last two hours. And then he burst apart.

If I had to take a guess, his sudden stress just pushed his heat into the forefront. We no longer had two more days to lead up to it. By the time I got to him, he was going to be falling into a deep fever and wouldn't come out of it for days. I might not know what had happened until then.

I pulled up, slamming my breaks into squealing when I stopped at the juice bar. As soon as I stepped out, Kaiser came sprinting through the dark and into my arms. He was rambling nonsense, his face filled with tears as he clung to me.

His skin was on fire. I'd been right. He'd forced himself into heat with this new stress.

I glared into the dark alley where the door to Terence's apartment was. If my omega didn't need me right now, I'd have gone in there and torn him apart. What the fuck did he do to put Kaiser in this state?

This was it. No more. No one was allowed to hurt my omega like this.

Dreading having to let him go, I urged Kaiser into the car. He'd already pushed up the middle console and was pressed at my side as soon as I climbed in. Tears were still streaking down his face as he shivered, bringing his knees to his chest.

"What happened?" I asked, my growl filling the car.

"Phone call," he said. "Remove them because they're dead."

My heart stopped as I tried to piece together what that could mean.

"It's okay," Kaiser said through tears. "My heat is making me irrational."

I shook my head, wrapping an arm around him. "If you're hurt by what he did-"

"No," Kaiser whined. His whine was enough that everything in me wanted to stop this car and bite him until he felt nothing but good. "You don't understand."

"Tell me what I don't understand, baby."

This time his whine came from deep within his chest as he wriggled at my side in distress. My body was caught between a purr to relax him and a growl at the cause.

"I don't know. Someone is dead. He's upset at that phone call. Not me."

I relaxed, but just slightly. If Kaiser knew that he wasn't the cause of it, then that meant that there were conversations happening. Conversations outside of menial pleasantries. But why was he kicking my omega out when he had clearly just been in bed with him? I could smell Terence all over Kaiser. And not just his scent. He was very clearly dripping with Terence's semen.

I'd come to realize over the last couple days that I didn't hate the smell of this alpha on him. I could tell that Terence had been making an effort not to scent mark Kaiser. Kaiser's need to rub against us when he got home further solidified that assumption. He *wanted* the scent and had been denied it to some level. But not enough that he was emotionally distressed by the denial. Which meant he was fully aware that it wasn't time for that.

Kaiser didn't appear upset about it. Either they'd talked about that, too, or he understood without needing the conversation. He was a smart man and he'd done a whole lot of reading on his biology as a child. Mainly, I think he'd secretly been trying to find a way to change his designation. It wasn't possible, but it didn't stop him from looking.

"I didn't do anything wrong," he said. "I'm a good omega."

I looked at him sharply, another growl in my chest. His hands were balled at the side of his head as he repeated the words. I stopped growling abruptly when I realized he wasn't reassuring himself. He was repeating words.

Not our words. Terence's.

He said them again and again. And when the words changed to, 'I'm a perfect omega,' I knew damn well that those weren't his thoughts. He was trying to reassure himself. But he was reassuring himself of their relationship by reminding him of a conversation they'd had.

At this point, I wasn't sure whether to be pissed or not. I was, because my omega was hurting. But as we've suspected all along, there was something going on here. I was convinced that they'd talked about it. Kaiser knew that whatever Terence was going through had nothing to do with him. And he was right that, at least in this moment, a lot of his panic was due to the sudden onset of heat.

I pulled us into the garage. Adrian was already moving to the passenger door before I'd even stopped the car. I hit the locks so he could open the door. He reached in and pulled Kaiser across the seat and into his arms.

His growl was already low on the air but when he heard Kaiser's mantra, he paused to study Kaiser before looking at me. I shook my head. I had no better insight than him.

Adrian took a breath and changed his growl into a purr as he started to coo to Kaiser. Our omega whined again. He turned big sad eyes up to Adrian. "Fuck me, alpha."

Our alpha didn't move as he rested his forehead against Kaiser's with a soft smile. "I will. All night. But first I need you to tell me what's wrong."

"Heat," he said, pulling at his shirt. He was soaked with sweat.

"I'll tell you after we get him through this, but I'm completely at a loss. Stuck between rage and confusion."

Marley was already in the nest, arranging everything around so that it was perfect when we came upstairs. Kaiser reached for her immediately and started pulling at her dress. Marley let him, petting his face, and nuzzling against him. She'd have been a damn good alpha.

She cooed and praised Kaiser as he pushed her clothing away. On some level, Kaiser understood that Marley wasn't going to be able to fill the primal need in him. But he loved her deeply enough that he sure as fuck tried to make it happen.

He pushed her back and licked all over her skin as he tried desperately to get out of his own clothes. He licked at her pussy, the taste making him pause and concentrating there for a solid minute before he was too wound up to continue further.

Kaiser whined when he pulled away, a sound that tore at my heart.

"Take him," I told Adrian.

Most of the time, we tagged in. When Kaiser's heat was full on, it was easier not to wear ourselves into exhaustion when we could take turns pleasing him until he was ready for a break. We learned early on that as fun and exhilarating as it was to go full on as a group, we lost the battle with endurance far before Kaiser was fully satisfied.

It was a hard lesson. One we never repeated because Kaiser's whimpers when we couldn't quite deliver what he needed had been a torture I'd never forget.

From then on, we took turns knotting him. Marley rode him until she was too tired to move. And if he was still too deeply begging for more, we'd wrap him with a vibrator to ease some of his hunger. If he was close to a breaking point in which he'd sleep for a few hours, whoever wasn't knotting was sucking his cock while Marley took a nap.

I gathered a few bottles of water and lined them up out of the way as I undressed.

Kaiser was already begging for a knot as he thrust madly into Marley, filling her over and over again with his seed. It was a heady sight. I couldn't help but wish her birth control failed and his bucket loads of cum would fill her with a baby.

I didn't care which of us impregnated her. Honestly, it was a toss up as to who I'd be more excited about.

Not that I truly wished her contraception would fail. I wasn't a psycho. I was perfectly content to wait until she was ready, well aware that she'd be doing all the work and therefore could call the shots.

Kaiser only stilled long enough for Adrian to mount him.

Since Kaiser was so stressed and still muttering about being a 'perfect omega,' we weren't going to mess around right now. Our boy needed a knot, and he was going to get one.

As soon as Adrian was locked inside, he dropped his weight and held Kaiser still while he started to rut. Marley's legs were tangled around theirs as she held on, moaning, and still running her fingers through Kaiser's hair to comfort him.

"I'm- I'm p-p-perrfect ommegaaa," Kaiser panted before he came again, dropping his head onto Marley's chest.

"You *are* a perfect omega," Adrian growled, shifting so he could continue to fuck our omega into a blissful state. "The best omega."

Kaiser whimpered. He reached blindly beyond Marley. I watched, unsure what he was looking for until he asked for Terence.

I sighed, moving next to them to lay down. When his hand landed on me, he turned his head. There was no recognition in his eyes this deep into his heat, but he recognized me all the same.

"My alpha," he said with a sigh, relaxing into Marley. That one blissful moment was heightened when Adrian's rutting achieved another orgasm and Kaiser cried out.

I brushed his face, my heart breaking every time he reached and came up empty handed. Every time he called out for an alpha that wasn't there. Every time he muttered that he was a 'perfect omega.'

When I couldn't take any more of the pain, I pulled his face to mine and kissed him until Adrian satisfied him so deeply that he fell asleep between us.

IT WAS WELL past midnight when Kaiser had been worn out enough to collapse into true sleep. He was still whimpering. It had been rough as he kept reaching for or asking for Terence with a whine in his voice. Sometimes he'd even assure himself with another 'I'm a perfect omega' before being lost in his haze of heat again.

When he was passed out, Adrian took a breath and closed his eyes before looking at me. I reported what had happened during the car ride and all the while, a deeper frown pulled at his mouth. I left out all my conjecture. I only told him what Kaiser had said and how he'd acted.

"We've never convinced him to say that in a time of stress," Adrian said.

"We've never convinced him to say it, period," Marley said. "He doesn't believe he is a good omega, never mind a perfect one."

"That suggests they're talking about their relationship," Adrian said. His voice was still tense, but I knew it had to do with Kaiser's stress more than anything. "Yet, he kicked Kaiser out in such a traumatic way that it drove him into heat early. What the fuck am I missing?"

"I think we're not going to know until he's out of heat and can talk sensibly," I answered.

"I don't know if I have the strength for that," Adrian said.

"You need to," Marley said, shifting so she could glare at Adrian. "Our omega needs you here and that's the most important thing right now."

I smirked at her before pinching her ass. She squeaked and swatted at me.

"Yes, beta," Adrian said, a growl in his voice as he looked at Marley with heat in his gaze.

It was a weakness we shared. When Marley commanded us in any way, we got instant hard.

Kaiser groaned in his sleep, his hips jerking back in reflex. I chuckled, knowing that Adrian's knot had just hardened again. He growled as he buried his face at the back of Kaiser's head.

Marley grinned at her success, but her smile faded. "You should have seen Nora," she told me. "The woman has nothing but praise for Terence. It's almost worship, but not in the way betas normally get. And she said they were all over each other in the shop when they stopped."

"Someone is dead," I told her. "That was the crux of the phone call as Kaiser understood it."

"I feel like my reaction would be to lose myself in my pack to try and manage my sorrow," Marley said. "Terence's had been the opposite. Deal with it alone. Make Kaiser leave. Why?"

I shook my head.

We were all pack oriented. All designations craved a pack. It was almost unheard of that an alpha or an omega especially wanted a solitary life. An alpha could demand it. An omega was never allowed it.

Kaiser whined in his sleep, his eyes fluttering opened as he looked straight at Marley. I wasn't convinced he was seeing her though. "Perfect omega," he murmured. "I didn't."

"You are a perfect omega," Marley cooed to him, petting his face. "You're a perfect omega and a perfect Kaiser."

His face crumpled like he was going to cry, but his eyes closed. Slowly, the creases in his face receded and he fell back into a deeper sleep.

"This is going to be a very hard heat," Marley said with a heavy sigh.

It was.

CHAPTER TWENTY-SIX

Terence

The process for making scent cards was almost gross. You rubbed these specially designed pieces of plastic that were coated in some sticky stuff all over the most potent parts of your body.

My pack had done a lot of research about scent cards when we began talking about an omega. By far, the best way to get your scent to stick to something for the longest time was washing it in your cum.

I held mine in front of me, barely touching the sides, as I glared at it. It was almost offensive. I couldn't imagine someone actually touching it and smelling it.

"Mmm," Miles said as he came into the room. His eyelids were hooded as a sensual expression started to curl up his face. "I love that scent."

I shook my head. Okay, so perhaps there was something to it. I'd done as the articles said. Loaded it with my cum and basically let it dry. Absolutely disgusting.

Miles stopped at my side and stared at the card with me. "How did you get it to smell like you?" he asked, leaning forward and closing his eyes as he took a deeper smell.

"I jizzed all over it."

Miles choked and looked at me with wide eyes. "No you didn't."

I laughed. "The internet said that's how we're keeping our scent on it longest. So yea, that's what we agreed to."

"Zack is going to shoot his load on a card?" Miles laughed. "He doesn't like to do that outside of one of us. Not even in a mouth or my hand!"

He wasn't wrong. I still wasn't sure where that came from. He wanted to be in an ass when he let loose and he wasn't in the least bit particular to whose.

"Go ask. Let me know if he chases you out."

Miles left my room, grinning like a Cheshire cat. He was going to get spanked. I was all here for that.

I turned and slipped the card into the plastic case specially designed to keep the scent locked in. My name and pack details were already on it. When the other three alphas were done, we'd pack them in the box and ship them to the Pack Listing headquarters. That would officially put us on the market for an omega.

It was one thing to list our pack. We'd been listed for years and gladly added whoever we invited into our pack. And though we'd checked the box that said we were open for omegas, we hadn't sent in our scent samples that would really put us in the running. We just hadn't cared that much. We were together and happy. We didn't need an omega to make us complete. We had that without one.

But an omega had the possibility of adding to it.

Emery and Foster had been all for it when Zack brought it up. They jumped all over it to the point where Ronan began to look a little queasy at the idea. It took some reassurance that an omega would never replace our betas but maybe we wanted to open our pack up to the possibility of one.

"It's fine, Ro," Emery said, pulling him in. "The chances that we'll actually catch an omega's interest are slim. Besides, we have you and Miles. We don't need an omega. We have everything we need right here."

"But an omega is the perfect complement to an alpha," he countered.

"No. The five of us are a perfect complement to each other. I don't care if you're a beta, an omega, or some weird sigma shit."

Ronan laughed. "That's not a thing."

"There are weirder things in the world. It could be," Foster said.

"An omega isn't necessary," Zack agreed, pulling us all in a little closer together. "We don't need to do this. We're not missing anything without one. But it would be nice to have one."

"So, they can take your knot," Miles said.

Miles had been trying for years to take my knot. But he'd never been able to bring himself to get through it. Once, we'd thought to try starting somewhat soft and buried deeply inside him. The pain of it as I started to swell meant I didn't get very far, and we stopped trying after that.

Ronan never tried. He'd shook his head when it was brought up. Not interested in a knot.

We'd never brought it up to either of them again. It was one of those things left undiscussed because it wasn't going to happen.

"No," Foster said. "Well, I suppose maybe. But no. I'm thinking about a womb. A mother. Someone that we can worship together. Our very own goddess."

Ronan smiled wistfully. Miles hadn't cared one way or another. With or without an omega, he was secure in our relationship. Ronan wasn't quite as convinced, even though he knew we loved him. He finally eased into the idea with the understanding that no one is allowed to join our pack unless all members agree. That goes for an omega.

Miles's yelp and laughter as he ran down the hall had me grinning and pulling from my memory of what brought on the fact that four alphas were painting their cum on a card instead of on our betas. I watched as he streaked down the hall with Zack following after him. He was a predator the way he moved. Not fast, but big and deadly.

Emery stopped at my door as he watched Miles run down the stairs with laughter. He was grinning as he turned to me. "Miles could be chasing an omega soon," he said.

Emery was always optimistic. I wasn't convinced we'd ever get an omega. There just weren't that many. And who were we?

"I think he'd rather be chased by the omega," I said.

He laughed. "Yea, probably." There was a pause as we listened to Miles' laughter turn into a loud moan. I grinned as the moan turned into a yelp. Zack was probably biting him all over. And Miles was caught between the arousal of it and continuing to be his prey. He enjoyed being chased as much as he enjoyed being caught.

"You think we'll attract one?" Emery asked quietly.

I shrugged.

"Honestly. Tell me."

"No," I said. "Omegas make up only like 3% of any given population. Three! We're one in thousands of packs."

"Alphas aren't that common either. It can't be that unlikely."

"That's where your statistics need a little work," I said, grinning. "It takes one alpha to make a pack out of any given number of designations. But if you look around, alphas tend to pack up with other alphas. Sometimes a beta or two. But their real hope is for that far out of reach omega. So, alphas already small numbers are made smaller by packing together but then there are those who like to collect their menagerie. No alphas. A whole lot of betas. And those packs are technically packs and can register in the listing. More and more menagerie packs are popping up. We have three on our street alone. But the real clincher of this is that there just aren't that many omegas. Yes, there aren't many alphas but there are nearly six times as many alphas as there are omegas. And we know that omegas are hunted. I think the last news report said that there'd been 183 omega abductions since the beginning of the year alone. That makes our chances even smaller since there are less free omegas looking for packs and not being purchased by one."

"You're dismal when you get into real stuff, Terence," Emery said.

I chuckled. "Look. I think if we want a pack with kids, we're going to need to look for a beta female. Or consider surrogacy. That's the reality of it."

"And the kicker is that if we give in and take in a female beta, we're basically out of the running for a female omega."

The irony wasn't lost on me.

Miles screeched into laughter downstairs and we both looked in the direction.

"Terence!" Miles yelled. "He's trying to kill me." His words ended on a loud moan, and I followed the sound with a smile.

I didn't need an omega. What could one possibly bring to my life that I didn't already have?

———

I WOKE with a gasp and launched myself to the bathroom where I dry heaved over the toilet for several minutes as tears stung my eyes.

The dreams weren't lies. That was a memory of when we'd finally gone through with sending in our scents to the Pack Listing. And their call was almost a year too late.

It had been like a knife in my chest when the voice came over the phone two nights ago.

"Mr. Terence? This is Lauren with Pack Listing. There's an omega interested in your pack. Would you like to agree to a meeting?"

The words had cut me in a way I couldn't explain. Every dream. Every future we'd planned. Every promise we made to each other. Everything came to a head in that call that came months too late. It wasn't just salt to a wound that wasn't healing. It was someone sticking a serrated knife in and shaking it around to make sure it was good and bleeding.

I hadn't known what to do. My control was slipping, and it didn't feel like I would be able to hold onto it. So, I'd told Kaiser to leave. Feeling and seeing his distress had only made the wound hurt more.

As soon as he ran into the night, tears fell. I closed the door and fell to my knees as I finally let myself fall apart.

It hadn't just been the call and the too-late omega. It had been that another omega had been interested in my pack. A pack that was dead.

In school, the omega-alpha bond was somewhat mystic. It's a magical connection. And when you find your perfect match, there will never be another that feels the same way. You'll know right away that they're yours. That's your mate. Your true complement. No one will smell as good to you.

I was convinced that my perfect omega was Kaiser.

So why was my scent attractive to another omega?

But then, maybe it wasn't mine. Maybe it was Zack's. Or Foster's or Emery's. There was science that said that even alpha's scents compliment each other when they find those they're meant to pack with. It's what assures that an omega finds a pack and not a single alpha out of a pack. The pack alpha scents are similar and complementary.

So why was my scent attractive to another omega? Kaiser was my omega. Not even a female omega but a male one.

I closed my eyes as I slid down to the cold tile and rested my face against it. I cringed a little, knowing I was laying on the bathroom floor. Yet, I couldn't bring myself to care yet. I'd shower and scrub it off later.

Seeing Kaiser run out as upset as he was, had stung. It had made it harder to catch my breath and drag myself upstairs. Harder still that my entire apartment smelled of Kaiser. There was no escaping it. Even so, I didn't leave my apartment for two days.

As if the world knew I needed to be left alone, no one bothered me. No phone calls. No knocks. Nothing.

I forced myself up and stripped my clothes. Dropping into the shower, I twisted the knob and let the freezing water run over me. My teeth chattered before it heated up. I scrubbed my face first, paying close attention to where it had touched the floor by the toilet. And then I just sat there.

I stayed in the shower until the water turned cold again. And then I pulled myself out to crawl back in bed. It was still dark. The bed was still stacked with Kaiser's nestings. Still had dried cum all over the sheets and blankets.

I burrowed down and buried my face in the pillows, surrounding myself with Kaiser's perfume. Sweet and filled with sex. His smile and his laughter and his touch.

Sleep came again but this time it was peaceful. No more memories turned into nightmares from loss. I didn't wake up with my stomach trying to empty itself.

But I did wake up to the sun blinding me. I scowled at it as I rolled away. Curtains. I needed to get curtains today.

And then I was going to fill this place with gifts for my hurt omega.

My stomach was a mess imagining that he was upset. I knew he was. He was in tears when he left, and he ran from my apartment. From me. I hadn't heard from him, but I was sure that his heat was keeping him busy, so I didn't press.

I forced myself from bed and into the shower again. This time it was quick, and I was out in no time. I made my shake, using Kaiser's bottle and leaning against the table as if he were in front of me. I closed my eyes, letting the memory of him mix with the memory of my pack. It was overwhelming and somehow, it settled me at the same time.

Maybe I needed to stop trying to keep the two things separate. My relationship with Kaiser wasn't in competition to my love for my pack. It never was and he wasn't trying to be. It was all me.

I rinsed the bottle and dressed in gym clothes. Full water bottles in my bag with two bagels in hand, I headed for the gym, taking the long way around the park. The gym didn't have any omega perfumes and I sighed.

Not in relief this time. In disappointment. I knew he wouldn't be here. He was in the middle of his heat. He'd be home with his pack being taken care of. Not in a sweaty gym.

With my earbuds in, I lost myself in the gym for hours, letting the strain of my muscles ease me into physical fatigue so I could go home and pass out.

After I went shopping for curtains.

CHAPTER TWENTY-SEVEN

Terence

M ost of my new furniture was backordered. I wasn't surprised since I'd custom designed some items for this small space. The easier solution would be to find a bigger apartment. But I kind of liked the intimate space.

Especially since it was still filled with Kaiser's scent several days later. It had been almost four days since I'd asked him to leave. I planned to text him in the morning but for right now, I had a new couch in my living room that I wasn't sure I liked. More room, sure but now it almost reached the TV console.

It wasn't a true sectional but the way it was shaped made it feel longer. Still the traditional loveseat size but in sectional fashion, there was an extended side against the wall that made that end feel like a chaise. The TV stand I had coming served multiple functions. Not just for the TV but with a table that popped out so we could set drinks on it. There were other fun things about it, too, but I didn't remember what they were.

Since I'd pulled my new curtains shut, I was staring at the

couch in the lights of the apartment. When it had been remodeled, I made sure to have the cool white LED lights throughout. Not the weird yellow lights that made everyone look jaundiced.

My couch was a dark charcoal gray, and I was definitely digging the color. I was also looking forward to cuddling on it with Kaiser to watch a movie or something. Maybe I could feed him strawberries. Was that too corny?

The knock on the door made me turn. Pizza. Right on time.

But when I opened the door, it wasn't pizza, but Kaiser. Actually, it was both. Kaiser had my pizza in hand. Not the delivery I was expecting.

"Please don't make me leave," he said, his brows knit together in misery. "They need a break from me. Pretty sure I've been unbearable."

I frowned as I pulled the pizza from his hands. "You were in heat, no?"

He remained in the door as I moved inside to set the pizza on the table. I turned back to see Kaiser flushed. "Look. I don't know what happened, but I've been absolutely distraught since you kicked me out. Please, can we talk about it?"

I closed my eyes as I silently kicked myself. And then I reached for him, pulling him into me and hugging him tightly. Kaiser sagged against me in relief as he clung to me and once again, I felt like complete shit.

Kicking the door shut, I pushed him against it and trapped him there so that he was pressed tightly between my chest and the door. I nuzzled against his neck, kissing him, running my hands over his arms until I could twist our fingers together.

His grip on me was tight. Desperate.

I hated myself a little more for making him feel this way.

Again.

"I'm sorry," I whispered. "I didn't mean to hurt you. Again. Tell me how to make it up to you."

"Just... hold me?"

"That I can do."

I pulled him further inside and brought him to my new couch. Sitting in the far corner, I dragged him into my lap and wrapped around him, pulling the blanket from the back of the couch, and bringing it over his shoulders.

He sighed into me, his tension relaxing as the minutes ticked by.

"This couch wasn't here last time," he said.

I grinned. "It was delivered an hour ago. I think it's darker than the one we chose but I don't hate the color."

"It's a nice color." His voice was quiet. Subdued. "It's soft."

I nodded. "This is the first time I've sat on it. I was waiting for you."

Kaiser shifted so he could look at me and I saw just how badly I had hurt him. "I heard what you said earlier that day," he whispered. "I thought I could do the alpha thing, but I clearly don't know how."

I pressed my forehead to his and sighed. "I'm sorry."

"I know. I believe you."

"Kaiser, this is exactly why I said I couldn't do this. I'm not in a good place."

"But I want to," he whispered. "You said you do, too."

"I do." I pulled him to me, covering his mouth with mine. He even tasted sad. I licked at his lips until he smiled, trying to grab my tongue between his teeth. "Kai, I've never wanted someone quite like this."

The admission tore at me, but I didn't take it back. I could chalk it up to biology and I was sure that some part of it was just that. The alpha in me found the omega that we wanted more than anything. But I was sure it was more than that.

"Try as I may, I'm just not there yet. I promise you, I'm trying to be, but it's going to take me some time."

"I can wait," he said, pressing a kiss to my cheek.

"You shouldn't have to wait."

"I don't want to be your omega," Kaiser said with a bit of a bite in his tone that made me grin. "I want to be your- your-" He scowled. "Can't I just be yours? Does it have to be an omega thing?"

"No. I didn't mean you shouldn't have to wait because you're an omega. I meant you shouldn't have to wait because you deserve to be happy right now. And I'm not doing all that well at making you happy."

"You make me happy," he argued.

"When I'm not making you cry, sure."

Kaiser bowed his head, leaning in to cuddle against me again. "I want you to want me."

"If I've ever given you any impression-"

"You don't. I know you do," he said quickly. "I mean, I want you to want *me*. My heat is mostly over. I'll still get spikes for three days or so but it's not as bad as the pre-heat spikes. But I can be normal now. I can try to be an alpha again for you. It doesn't work so well when my heat makes me insane."

"I don't deserve you," I whispered, wrapping him tightly in my arms and breathing him in. The salty tang that was mixed into his perfume had faded now. He smelled like heaven. "But I want you until I take my last breath."

His fingers dug into my hair. The gentle sting of pain made me smile.

"I'll try harder, but Kaiser, I meant what I said. I never know what's going to set me off until I'm already falling apart. And I need to be alone when that happens."

"It wasn't me, right?" he asked. "When you asked me to leave, it wasn't my fault."

"No, of course, not. You did nothing wrong."

He sighed, relaxing into me fully. "Okay. Can you maybe lead with that when you kick me out?"

It stung because he knew it was going to happen again. I nodded. If that was what he needed, I was going to make damn sure I remembered to do that.

With any luck, it wasn't information I'd need to recall again. Maybe that would be my last breakdown.

I could hope, right?

"Want some pizza?" I asked.

Kaiser grunted. "Yes. I'm starving. Not sure when I ate last."

I frowned and disentangled myself from him. His smile was shy as he watched me get up. He pulled his knees up to watch me.

"I really do think they need a break from me," he said, resting his chin on his knees. I grabbed some paper towels and a couple bottles of juice from the fridge and returned with the pizza box. Kaiser took the juice from me as I sat next to him. "The bits I can recall outside of sex was me being miserable."

"I'm sorry. I shouldn't have made you leave like that."

He shook his head. "Realistically, I knew something had happened on the phone. I could feel how upset you were. But I was already coming into heat and that little bit set it off. Omegas in heat are not exactly bursting with logical responses."

I pulled a slice of pizza from the box and folded it, so it remained straight. Kaiser watched me as I brought it to his mouth. He grinned, a twinkle in his eyes, as he opened for a bite. It wasn't strawberries, though I think I had some in the fridge. However, I was going to feed my omega and spoil the shit out of him.

"Nora loved everything Marley chose," I told him, making

him smile. I waited until he had swallowed before I brought it to his lips again. Only after he'd taken the second bite did I take one. "She hasn't stopped singing Marley's praises. Pretty sure she'd love to hire her."

Kaiser grinned. "She'll love that compliment. You should text her and tell her."

"Hm," I answered, bringing the pizza to his mouth again. "Maybe tomorrow. Right now is all about you."

The smile on his face was all I needed to convince me that he required my full attention to be on him. I wasn't going to split it between anything.

We shared five slices of pizza before I pulled out the little fondue pot and stuck some chocolate in to melt. I had a plethora of fruits and berries. I was going to feed him chocolate dipped fruit in a bit. But for now, I was going to hold him against me on the couch.

I pulled him up when I returned and coaxed his shirt off him. It didn't take much convincing. "Not about sex," I told him as I dropped his pants. Then again, I supposed it could be as he hardened in his boxer briefs before me. I stripped down to match before pulling him onto the couch with me.

Curling the blanket around us, I held him close, tangling our legs together. His face was flushed, and his skin was only barely not feverish. I pressed my nose to his and smiled softly.

"I know I've said this, but I promise, you've never done anything wrong. You're a perfect omega. An amazing man. All of my running away has nothing to do with you at all. And if you can bear with me, I'll go to the ends of the earth to make it up to you when I get my head back on straight."

Kaiser nodded. "Marley said I kept chanting that."

"What?" I asked.

His face heated. He buried it in my chest before he answered. "That I didn't do anything wrong and that I'm a perfect omega. They're not things I ever say or believe so I think that's how they knew that you weren't just being an ass."

"I'm glad you listen to me, then. And honestly, I can only imagine the impression I'm leaving." The thought made me cringe. And then wonder what was possessing them to let their omega near me again. After all the shit I've put him through.

"They're good to me," he whispered. "And they know how badly I want you. It's enough to convince them that you're not a sadistic asshole."

I kissed his head and closed my eyes. Feeling his breath on my skin and the gentle brush of his fingertips over my ribs made me relax into him.

This was one of my favorite pastimes with Miles. Just lying around mostly naked. Feeling his skin against mine. Feeling his heartbeat and his gentle breathing. I was convinced that the reason we were as close as we were was because of these moments more than anything else.

The thought of Miles made me ache. But it wasn't quite as awful this time. I pushed that ache into the happiness and affection I had for Kaiser. Let the two meet. Mingle. Become acquainted. Because they were going to be close for a long, long time. At least, I hoped so. My love for Miles would never go away and therefore, I was sure the ache of his absence wouldn't either. So, it needed to become familiar with my growing fondness for Kaiser.

"You're getting hot again," I noted.

"I don't care. As much as my body demands fucking, I need a mental break from it." A moment later, he snorted. "For the time being, anyway. It does become unbearable when it reaches a point."

"What's it feel like?"

"Heat?"

"When the need is too much to ignore."

Kaiser was quiet while he thought about it. "That moment, just before orgasm when you're desperate for release? But add to it a denial. How badly that aches. How you want to just... thrash out of your skin and scream-cry in frustration." He paused for a minute. "I've heard that for omegas who have to experience a heat alone, it is painful beyond what I could imagine. It's physical and mental and emotional pain. Exhaustion. Trauma. Added on to it, I've never had to go through a heat without my alphas' knot. An omega who receives release without a knot while in heat is like a starving animal who's only tempted with food by licking the last bit of maple syrup off a plate. I can't imagine what that feels like."

"It's the goal to find a pack before your first heat, then?" I asked, my grip on him tightening.

Kaiser shrugged. "Yes, in general. My heat happened a little late, so I had some extra time. I knew I was an omega from childhood, so I had plenty of time to get accustomed to all the stupid idiosyncrasies of being one. I was obsessively careful of where I went and with who, terrified of being kidnapped and sold. That was my true driving force for combing through the Pack Listing at sixteen."

"Sixteen?" I asked, surprised. "You've been with them that long?"

Kaiser laughed. "No way. I looked early because I refused to face a heat without a pack. We're told horror stories about heats, especially when we don't have a pack. And then there's the terror of being stolen and sold, not knowing what kind of pack bought you. Again, lots of horror stories. So, I started looking through the thousands of packs as soon as I was old enough. I can't tell you how many scent packs I ordered."

I felt his nose cringe against me. "I swear, after years of choosing awful scents, I thought I was going to lose my sense of smell. Which seemed almost welcome at that point. But I found my pack when I was twenty-two. I ran from my room and waved the cards in my parents' faces. 'This is my pack' I shouted at them, waving the cards in the air like a banner before bringing them back to my face and inhaling them like a drug." His words stopped. After a minute he sighed. "Anyway. I set up a meeting. I was with them for almost a year before my first heat. Already bonded. There was no guessing or awkwardness. You know, outside of the heat itself and how incredibly ridiculous I felt in hindsight."

I knew he only had two alphas. I made it a point to know his body from one end to the other. And I'd found two bites. One hidden under his shirt on his shoulder. The other on his ribs. But he tended to talk about his pack in ambiguous terms. He only ever referred to Marley by name. The two alphas I didn't know details about.

I also didn't ask. Someday, I'd need to. Especially if I wanted to keep him. And I fucking did.

CHAPTER TWENTY-EIGHT

Terence

I'd made a lot of extra effort in showering Kaiser with attention and little things. I bought him a belt two days ago and then showed him how to use it like cuffs. The way his eyes lit up with both excitement and heat assured me we'd be using that trick at some point. But he mentioned Marley and I was positive Marley was going to be cuffed soon.

I grinned thinking about it. And then really thought about it and my blood heated through my body like electricity. Everywhere it pumped, I was alight with need.

His next favorite thing was a pair of socks. The bottom of one foot said, 'I'm perfect.' The other said, 'a perfect omega.' He didn't even let me take them off him when I stripped us naked for some knotty good time.

I found these little underwear that you could personalize with a picture of you and your arms wrapped around the bulge. I was positive that he'd wear them with excitement, but I thought that needed to be a gift for later. I wasn't sure how the rest of his alphas would feel about it. I was sure they weren't my biggest fans since I wasn't the best at treating Kaiser the way he should be.

I was when I wasn't tripping over my misery. Slowly, that part of me came back and settled in. I relished seeing Kaiser both enjoy it and press his lips together when he thought I was treating him too much like an omega.

We hadn't gotten to the point where he was comfortable being him without the omega parts. Sometimes, I caught a slip in him, but he'd quickly backtrack and redo his expression or reaction as a 'good omega' would.

For now, I let it pass. In the shadows of my most recent breakdown after we'd *just* talked about me needing biology to pull my head out of my ass some days, I didn't think Kaiser was willing to chance me running again.

I wasn't going to run. Not permanently. It wasn't a declaration I'd made to anyone but myself. Out of fear, I kept that in. Not fear of the truth in it. Fear that I'd break that promise. I might run a short distance, but I'd come back.

Kaiser went home this morning after another breakfast fuck and kissing against my door until his alpha arrived. I noticed that it was typically the alpha with short, light golden hair. Not the one with long hair I'd seen the back of at Juice Me that one day.

I still hadn't asked about them.

With Kaiser gone, I showered and stripped the sheets, so he'd have fresh ones when he came over next. He still cringed away from the places he spilled. So, I made sure to change the sheets as soon as he was out.

I wasn't very good about reshaping his portable nest. I could tell when he spotted it each visit. He'd look on in amusement and before we climbed in bed, he'd arrange it how he wanted it. One day, I'd remember to take a picture before I broke it down so maybe I could get it right.

I headed for the gym and stayed for a couple hours. There was something about Kaiser's presence in my life that was settling my need to lose myself in half a day's workout. I pushed myself all the same, but it wasn't in the same exhausting way. Now I focused on the workout high and concentrating on different muscle groups each day.

The day was nice with a cool breeze under a warm sun. I still had half a bottle of water left so I thought I'd take a jog around the park before heading home. I had no plans, so I wasn't in a hurry.

I'd made a lap before pausing, swearing I caught a whiff of Kaiser. His scent wasn't unusual as far as scents go. There were plentiful pine trees in the area. And cinnamon was a common spice. But there was something strictly Kaiser about the combination and I knew when it was him opposed to natural fragrances in the air.

I paused, glancing around the park as I pulled my earbuds out. I didn't find Kaiser, but I recognized Marley right away. I knew before I got close enough that it was Kaiser's scent on her that I was smelling. He'd just finished a heat, so I was sure she was saturated with him.

My hackles rose as I got closer. There were three men circling her, closing her in. She was standing defensively but aware that she was very outnumbered.

"If you had half a brain cell you'd know that I'm not an omega," Marley snapped. "You'd also take note of my bond marks that I'm not at all hiding."

"You can't be that well treated if your alphas let you out alone, sweetness," one of them said, trying to fake a purr.

They were betas. Betas couldn't purr.

But an alpha can growl. Mine filled my ears. It should have

been warning enough but somehow, they hadn't seen me coming.

I reached them as one of the betas extended a hand up to touch Marley's hair. She flinched away, taking a step back and almost right into a second beta. I caught the hand that tried to touch her, twisting it around until he was brought to his knees. The man behind her who had the audacity to touch her hip when she backed up, I grabbed a fistful of hair and yanked his neck back with a snap until he screamed. That laid him outright.

The third man thought he was enough to challenge me. I let him close the distance as he spewed some nonsense before I landed my fist in his gut. His eyes widened as he collapsed, tears in his red eyes as he fell.

I didn't speak as I held my hand out to Marley. She smirked at the betas, stepping on the hand of the first one I downed on the way by. I brought her into my side, wrapping my arm over her shoulders, as I steered her out of the park.

One thing was certain. She smelled heavily like an omega.

"I probably should have scrubbed his scent from me," she whispered when we were twenty paces away.

"Don't excuse their behavior by trying to change something about you," I told her. "They chose to be dicks. You can smell however you want to."

Marley laughed quietly, bowing her head. She was upset though. Her arms were crossed over her chest in that defensive hiding way women do. I pulled her in tighter as I led us down the path.

"Are you okay? Do you need anything specific?"

She looked up at me with those sapphire blue eyes. My stomach flipped as she shook her head. "I'm fine. Just those little touches that you prevented was all they landed on me. Nothing to be alarmed at."

I sighed, dropping my hand to her hip, and covering the place where the man had touched her before bringing my hand into her hair. Marley grinned as she peeked up at me. "Thanks."

Betas also didn't leave strong scents. Even when they tried to mark. Neither of those gestures had meant to be scent transfers but for most people, any touch was loaded because we were a species so heavily influenced by scents. Replacing a bad one, even if imagined, was almost the best, most immediate response requested by someone who'd been in a traumatic situation.

Or one that could have ended up traumatic.

I hadn't realized I was bringing her to Juice Me until we were walking in the door. I set Marley in a chair and told Megasin I wanted two drinks today. "Make them your best and strong."

"Strong with what?" she asked.

I shrugged and waved a hand. "You're the Juice Artist."

Megasin grinned and shook her head. Her gaze landed on Marley for a minute before turning to the blenders and dumping ingredients in.

Taking the stool next to her, I sat. "I can take you home. Or to your car?"

Marley smiled and shook her head. "I really am fine."

"I think you ought to carry around a taser."

She grinned, biting her lip as she turned to look out the window.

I hadn't noticed her phone in her hand until it made a noise. She turned her attention to it and tapped on the screen for a few short seconds. Then she met my eyes. "I didn't even alarm them more than to check in," she said.

"And did you tell them the truth?" I asked, wondering how

she managed to keep alphas from storming through the park to protect what's theirs.

"That some nasty betas were harassing me, and you downed them all in three seconds? Yes, I did."

I chuckled.

"They also know I'm here and fine. Because I *am* fine."

"Alright, alright." I glanced out the window. "I should have taken their pictures, so my girls know to be wary of them."

"We are adept at knowing who to be wary of," Megasin said as she paused next to us and handed us drinks. "We also have the cops on speed dial."

I nodded, bowing my head. "Alright, Megasin. Point taken. You don't need my protection."

"No. But we appreciate you worrying about us," she said, smiling. She turned and headed back to the counter.

"Maybe I should invest in security cameras," I mused. "Not a lot. Just three or so. Maybe more so I can have one on the back door."

"That's a good idea," Marley said. "And this is wonderful. What did she make us?"

I took a sip and shook my head. "They tend to make me random combinations. I think I'm their test goat." I narrowed my eyes as I looked at my employees.

Marley giggled.

Nora walked out of the back and grinned as she came over. "You're just the two I wanted to see!" she exclaimed. "How convenient that you're together."

"Convenient," I said, raising a brow.

"It is. I need your credit card if Marley will let me beg her into a bit of shopping? I can't get over the colors you chose."

Marley laughed quietly and nodded. "Sure. What do you need?"

"Wonderful," Nora said, clapping her hands together. "I'll text you what I'm shopping for today."

"I feel used," I teased, playfully glaring at Nora. "You just want my money."

Nora laughed. "My husband is more than I can handle most days, Mr. Andersen. I don't want an alpha. Not even a prince like you."

"Oof," I said, shaking my head, making both girls laugh.

It was good to hear Marley's laughter. I believed her when she said she was okay. But there was still a voice in my head raging at the nerve of those men. They'd barely touched her, and I wanted to rip their hands off and shove them down their throats.

"Alright. You two kids shop. I'll be here to collect the goodies when you're done." Nora winked and headed for the counter.

"Hmm. I feel like I'm being set up," I said, glaring at Nora's back.

Marley laughed. "I can go alone. It's alright."

"Not a chance," I told her. "You smell like an omega in heat, Marley. I'd be happy to drive you where you'd like but understand if you prefer one of your alphas."

"Not my omega?" she asked, raising a brow.

I wasn't sure if it was in challenge as to who Kaiser belonged to or not. "No. Kaiser also smells like an omega in heat. I can only imagine the two of you out alone together."

I wasn't even going to ask why her alphas let her out. How could they not smell Kaiser on her so strongly?

"No, it's fine. I'd be happy to have you as my escort."

"Good. Let's go." I stood, waiting for Marley to follow. With drinks in hand, we left the shop. "Mind if we stop upstairs real quick? I feel sweaty. A shower and change would be nice."

Marley nodded. "Sure. I kind of wish I brought clothes. I didn't realize how much like Kaiser I smelled. I guess when you're so used to the scent around you, you don't always notice how strong it is."

I led her around the corner and to the door. She followed me up and slipped out of her sneakers when I did as I unlocked the door.

"I think there's some of Kaiser's clothes around here somewhere," I told her. "I've sent them through the wash, so they don't have his perfume so heavily on them."

"You don't mind?" she asked.

I shook my head. "Not at all. You want the shower first?"

Marley shook her head as she eyed my apartment. There was a touch of a smile on her lips as she studied the area. When she saw the nest on my bed, her smile turned into a beaming grin. "I'm really glad you're making him so happy. He comes home practically bouncing off the walls."

I chuckled as I headed for the dresser. The casual clothes were still in folded piles on top. I grabbed a pair of pants and a shirt that I thought the man said went together before heading towards the door. "I am too. I fuck up enough that I'm glad I can make him happy when I'm on an off season of having my head in my ass. Make yourself comfortable. I won't be long."

I wasn't long. Even knowing I had that gorgeous beta in my house, I managed to put myself through a short shower by not thinking of her or Kaiser. Too good. Too beautiful.

The combination of Kaiser's perfume all over her and her own subtle scent had my skin on fire. It was only because I was so enraged at the nerve of the assholes that I'd been able to hold her so close as we walked out of the park. Otherwise, I might have tried to throw her against a wall and see where it led.

I came out dressed and started rummaging through my drawers until I found one of Kaiser's shirts and a pair of his sweatpants. He liked to lounge around and had brought comfortable clothes. Until he realized that I preferred just to be naked. Clothes were an unwanted obstacle that I was only too eager to get out of at the earliest possible moment.

"At least they're drawstring. And they don't horribly mismatch." The last statement was a guess. Matching clothes was never something that I understood beyond a more basic level of you don't match orange with green type of thing.

She smiled at me as she took them from my hand and headed for the bathroom. "Kaiser's towel is clean. The green one. I'm afraid I don't have any more than that. I think he's got shampoo in there, too but you're welcome to use whatever you want."

Marley grinned at me, the same perceptive look as when she'd seen the nest on my bed. "Thanks," she said and disappeared behind the door.

Her phone went off as soon as the water turned on. And then mine followed. I didn't look at her phone but mine was from Kaiser.

[Kaiser] Have fun with my beta. She knows how to present, too.

My eyes widened as I stared at his message. His bubble was still dancing, and a teasing text came after.

[Kaiser] I meant, she likes presents, too.

I snorted. That's not at all what he meant.

CHAPTER TWENTY-NINE

Terence

Over the next week I started spending more and more time with Marley. It was primarily during the day that I'd spend with her and usually out of the house. And in the evenings, Kaiser would come over. Sometimes he spent the night. Three times last week. I was feeling spoiled.

And also, a bit of an imposter. These two were from the same pack and it was almost as if I were moving in on another alpha's pack. I wasn't. Not really. I wasn't trying to take them. Or join them.

But I kept all those thoughts to myself. Anything too serious in which I needed to really think about what I was doing. Anything in relation to my pack that made me feel like a bad alpha for betraying them in death.

I concentrated on keeping it light, fun, and still meaningful. Light and fun with Marley. Kaiser was a little different just because, despite that he wanted to be thought of outside of his designation, I couldn't ignore that he was a perfect omega for me. And he still erred on the side of caution and predominantly gave me his omega traits. Ones I was learning that he didn't particularly like.

But this morning was about Marley. When I drove up to their house, I first found both of their alphas in the window. It was a bright hot day, so I barely saw their shapes within the glass. But the two of them were there, one with his arms crossed over his chest.

As I stepped out of the car, the front door opened, and Kaiser came streaming out. He was in thin pants that he liked to lounge about in. And nothing else. I was sure he wasn't wearing anything under the pants since he bounced and swayed as he walked towards me.

Marley had once said that Kaiser liked to work on his abs. And he was certainly showing them off right now. He had a light dusting of hair over his chest and down his stomach that he frequently had removed, but as he got close, I ran my hands through the hint of hair.

He scrunched his face as I did, walking into me so I had to move my hand around his waist. "My appointment is next week," he said. "I apparently missed one because I noted the wrong date on my phone." There was a pout heavy in his voice as I brought him into my chest.

"It's really sexy, Kaiser," I said low in his ear.

Kaiser shivered and sighed. "I love that you're going out with Marley, but I wish we could all just be together."

I knew that meant with his alphas, too. He was careful not to include them by name or designation, but I was aware that he meant them, too, when he mentioned 'all.'

"Let's start smaller than that," I told him as I raised my eyes to find Marley standing in the door to the house. Giving us a moment before she joined. "How about you and Marley come over after lunch tomorrow. If that's okay with your alphas."

He pulled back to look at me with a wide smile. "Really?"

I nodded. "Can we begin with that?"

His answer came in a hot kiss, wrapping his arms around my neck and holding me tightly to him. When something pleased him, he reacted with his whole body. It wasn't just a kiss. He pressed against me, wrapping one of his legs around mine as he did.

I'd never get tired of his taste. The bite of a cinnamon candy with the deep, soul-satisfying tang of pine chasing it. And when he was happy, it was filled with a shock of sugar.

When he was aroused, it was cinnamon bursts with syrup and honey.

"Tomorrow," he agreed as he pulled away. "I'll talk to my alphas and work it out."

"I think we should follow it up with a day and night that you two just remain with your alphas," I told him. "I've been taking a lot of your time."

His smile suggested something he didn't voice. "Okay," he agreed and turned away, meeting Marley halfway down the walk. He kissed her lips in a slow kiss before moving towards the house.

Marley met me and I bent to kiss her cheek. Her smile was sweet with a hint of shyness behind it. I took the bag from her shoulder and led her to the car, opening her door so she could climb in. When she was settled, I shut her in and placed her bag in the seat behind her before getting in the car.

Kaiser was in the window with his alphas now, pressed against the one who'd had his arms crossed over his chest.

"They really are fine with this," Marley said, her voice quiet.

I put us in reverse and backed out before I glanced at her. "I keep wondering if I would be and I haven't come to the conclusion that I would."

"We're a small pack and though we've never actively looked for others, I think we all kind of knew that expanding was a possibility."

I pressed my lips together without responding. She wasn't wrong. I couldn't just be with two members out of their pack house and refuse to even meet their alphas forever. Besides, it wasn't like I had to be with their alphas to be a part of their pack.

It wasn't even their alphas or the idea of them that made me hesitate so hard. It was the idea of a pack. There was a dead drop zone in my head for that word. No other packs were possible when I'd lost mine. How could I? How could I join or even start another pack and not be betraying the one I lost? How could that not be seen as replacing them?

"So, all you told me was dress for the beach," Marley said, pulling me out of my thoughts. Maybe I was scowling.

"I probably should have asked if you get seasick," I noted.

She shook her head. Her hair was pulled back and it showed off her beautiful neck that was just screaming for another bite. The neck had never been my preferred place to bite but with hers, I was constantly drawn to it. Long and beautiful.

I reached for her hand, and she laced her fingers with mine. "Sorry," I said quietly. The apology wasn't for not mentioning we'd be taking a boat. It was about the sudden silence I fell into. But like Kaiser, Marley knew that. She smiled, squeezing my hand.

I was taking Marley to the OC Bay Hopper for their Liquid Lunch tour. The boat takes us to pick up lunch and drinks at The Original Greene Turtle and the captain drives us around through canals as we eat and enjoy the sun.

It wasn't private, which was somewhat my goal with Marley. Being alone with Kaiser was a necessity for both of us. We were new together and since we'd already had this whole courtship screwed up thanks to my awkwardness, we'd combined the courting stage, the getting to know you stage, and the irresistible fuck stage into one. I spoiled the shit out of him every chance I could get. We talked for hours. But we also fucked like bunnies at the drop of a hat. I wasn't sure being in public would stop us, so we stayed inside.

But as I was driving, I thought maybe I ought to treat him to something. Perhaps he was thinking I was showing favoritism in treating them differently. Bringing Marley all over the place while I kept him home.

Wow, I was shit at this.

The reason I kept Marley and I out was because it had been almost two decades since I'd been anywhere near a girl in more than a professional manner. It was all new to me. There were five others in my pack - three alphas and two betas. All males. I couldn't even remember the last time I'd touched a girl.

The idea of Marley was great. Exciting. Fucking fire throughout my entire body. But actually, touching her more than the soft, tentative hints was almost terrifying.

I knew what to do with a man. I had no idea what to do with a woman.

The biology of it wasn't hard. I knew where to stick it. But I needed more time to get to know Marley before I could bring myself to make a fool of me.

"You're quiet again," she said.

I glanced at her and smiled. "Sorry. Was just deciding if I was doing this right?"

"You're a good driver."

Her smile said she was teasing but that she wasn't quite

sure what I was referring to. "Last time I bring up Kaiser. Promise."

She grinned and shrugged. "It's fine. We talk about each other a lot."

She wasn't wrong. Kaiser was always talking about Marley.

"I was just debating whether I was being stupid by the different kinds of activities I bring you to and never take him out," I admitted.

Marley's smile was amused. "I think he prefers to stay home with you. He'll want outings later, but right now, he's perfectly content to hang out at your place. He loves to hear me tell him every detail of what we did but I think he's just fishing for something juicy."

I chuckled. "Despite the situation with him, I'm pretty slow at this."

She shrugged again, her smile turning shy. "That's okay. I'm not in a hurry."

"And your alphas? They're truly not bothered by me taking both of you out?" And knotting their omega?

"No." She hesitated before she continued. "They understandably get upset when Kaiser is upset, even knowing that it's something on your end and not between the two of you. So, there are times when I can tell they're ready to put an end to it. But every time you successfully gain Kaiser's forgiveness, he's glowing with happiness."

I rubbed my thumb over her hand. I hadn't mentioned the things to Marley that I had to Kaiser. And I'd been blessedly calm the last week or so. I've been able to manage the little bursts and push them away. Aware that that probably wasn't healthy and may or may not be contributing to the more outrageous bursts of hiding in a hole for a couple days, but it was helping me deal. With everything.

But maybe she needed just a bit. "I need you to know that

if for some reason I need to be alone, it has nothing to do with you. It's nothing you've done. I'm a mess inside and I don't always manage to keep it under control. When it surges up before I can handle it, I run. I need to work it out before I can be rational with you."

"I know," she said as I pulled into the parking lot. "Kai doesn't tell me details and I respect that. But the bits that I know or have seen are all signs of some internal trauma. I have no idea what it could be, but you know that you don't always have to deal alone, right? We won't speak or ask questions but if you need someone with you to help you through, Kai or I will be happy to stay with you."

After I'd turned the engine off, I brought her hand up to my lips and kissed the back of it. "At some point, I might be at that stage. But right now, I find it easier to deal alone. But thank you, I'm honored by the offer."

She smiled and I released her before getting out of the car. I appreciated that she waited like Kaiser did. Neither needed me to open their door but they allowed it since it made me happy. But I didn't let her carry her bag. I draped it over my shoulder and led her by her small hand in mine to the docks.

The pontoon had a long table down the center. There were two other couples joining us, one already there. Marley and I took the seats where we shared a bench.

With my arm around her shoulders, we leaned back to enjoy the cool breeze off the ocean. She leaned into me, and I rested my face on the top of her hair. She carried notes of all her pack on her. Sweet cherries, crisp ice, and sharp cinnamon mixed with her natural rosemary and sage.

The combination of scents was beautiful. Like a wonderful bouquet that I could smell all day. We ate lunch as a group before we broke apart. Marley and I sat together at the bow of the boat with her tucked into my arms.

I loved the way she fell right into me. How her body was small enough that I could wrap her completely with mine. And I especially loved to kiss her.

I wasn't at all surprised that we'd found ourselves acting like a couple of teenagers at the bow of the boat. She tasted divine. I loved to nip at her lips and suck on her tongue until she was breathless. I loved to tangle my hands in her hair, pull her further into my lap by her hips.

I loved her hands on my shoulders, down my arms where she gripped my biceps tightly. I loved feeling and smelling her arousal, knowing that I brought that on, even if she didn't act on it. She didn't try to move us deeper or progress us faster, for which I was thankful.

I also loved that our kisses alternated between sweet, slow, and soft and hard, hungry, and possessive. There was nothing about kissing her and holding her that I didn't like. Nothing that I could find that I thought might be a con.

There'd always been something that one of us wasn't a fan of when we'd considered a girl. Emery and Foster were all about wanting kids. A girl had never been far from our conversations when they spiraled back to family. It wasn't the girl they cared about. A surrogate would have been fine. They wanted the babies.

We'd never made it that far. Just as we'd never seriously looked for a girl.

But this girl, this woman, she was fucking perfect. Small, beautiful, soft. But fierce, feisty, teasing. She tasted like heaven and when she bit me, she was filled with sin. I growled at her touch as she moved her mouth to my neck and playfully sank her teeth into my skin. Not hard. Not enough pressure to even leave a mark. But enough that I forcefully had to restrain myself not to roll her over and pin her beneath me.

She pulled back to look at me with a wicked grin and

challenge. I growled, covering her mouth with mine again, but the little beta with an alpha bite pushed me back against the bench and took command of our kiss.

She was perfect. My pack would have devoured her like the goddess she is.

CHAPTER THIRTY

Terence

Marley drove them over, arriving at two exactly. I waited at the corner of the building as they pulled in, blocking the garage door where my car was. There was a small parking lot out back of the building that I dedicated to my employees. They were careful not to block the garage, but I knew where they worked if I needed to get my car.

Kaiser was out of the car and in my arms before Marley had shut it off. "They agreed that we can stay as long as we want and tomorrow, all day and night, we stay home with them," he said, nuzzling his face into my neck.

My purr released before I thought about it, making Kaiser melt into me further. I smiled contentedly as he settled into my arms. He was a handful of inches shorter than me and maybe half my bulk. Still firm and sculpted in all the right ways, but I loved him being smaller. He wasn't small but smaller than me.

Omegas tended to be on the smaller side anyway. Alphas, when we took care of ourselves and focused on our physique, bulked up easily. We were a designation meant to protect and defend. Omegas, male and female, were small. Easy to hide and shield. Betas fell somewhere in the middle.

Marley joined us and I pulled her in as well. Kaiser made room, wrapping an arm around her, and I closed my eyes to breathe them in. Really, this was everything right here. Everything I once had and yet never did.

Although we were in the middle of the city, my lot was a quadruple lot. There was a building on all three sides, tucked fairly close together. The building on the right was basically on top of my juice bar. The one to the left was further away, leaving an alley between the two so we could access the parking lot out back. And the building behind was far enough away that it didn't encroach on my parking lot.

I owned the buildings to the left and behind. One was a storefront, and the other was an office building. What no one saw was that the other quarter of a lot I owned was hidden behind what one presumed to be only trees. It was fenced in with high, old trees surrounding the perimeter. I'd always paid to have it maintained.

Recently, I paid to have it landscaped, too. It wasn't a huge lot. When there's a building on the lots, they tend to look so much bigger. But I was pleased with the way it turned out. The facelift was needed.

"Ready?" I asked.

"For what?" Kaiser returned, not pulling his face from my neck.

I understood not wanting to move. With the two of them in my arms, I could stay like this all day. But then, I had some fun and cozy things planned. One of which included snuggling close.

Gently, I urged them both back and kissed Kaiser when he

pouted. Taking his bottom lip between my teeth, he shivered around a groan, his eyes heating immediately.

He was out of his heat and over his heat spikes. But he was still an omega and their on button was more like a dimmer. Always nearly fully on.

If I didn't let his lip go, I'd end up with him against the wall and giving a rather inappropriate display for the neighbors. With a final lick, I kissed Marley's neck, making her giggle and push at me. Then I turned, grabbing both of their hands and dragging them along.

The trees weren't overly thick right here, but you could see a fence through them and that tended to deter anyone from getting curious. Especially since my little garden was hidden from the street without the gate readily visible.

We followed the fence until we reached the iron gate where I punched in a code. The lock released and I pulled open the gate. I took a quick peek inside before pulling Marley around and then Kaiser behind her, urging them inside.

"Wow," Kaiser said as they stepped through.

I shut the gate behind us, the lock catching as it secured. The grass was freshly laid sod. The area was cut in two, the perimeter lined with green foliage and flowers. There was a small pond with mini koi fish and a center statue of a dragon spitting water from its mouth.

The second half of the space was accessed through an arch of twisted dead branches. The ground was covered in crushed stone. There was a cozy seating area to one side and the other had a raised mini cottage. Three sides were closed in, and the roof was beautifully handcrafted. There was a gauzy curtain in the front that was currently held open by ties.

Inside was a little nest. A plush mattress covered in cushions and cozy blankets.

Under the raised cottage was a dry-locked cabinet with

snacks and two small mini-fridges filled with juice and water. A white projector screen fell over the wall and a projector hidden in the rafters would allow us to watch movies or stream shows.

I'd taken a look when I got home last night and stocked the fridge and cabinets with whatever I could find. This meant most of my cabinets were now empty. There was a delivery scheduled for this evening, so it wasn't a big deal. I planned to keep the two through dinner. I'd also bought a grill and patio furniture that were tucked away in my garage for now. Maybe one side of this stone area could be an outdoor kitchen. I'd have to contemplate it.

"What is this place?" Marley asked as she brushed her fingertips delicately over the petals of a purple flower.

"My garden."

"It's yours?" Kaiser asked from a few feet away where he was studying some of the hidden features within the foliage.

I nodded. "I own these four lots and rent two of them out commercially."

"You're just full of secrets!" he said, grinning as he bent to smell some of the flowers.

I followed them through the garden, letting them take their time to admire the flowers and pond. Marley went towards the arch first and paused.

"Kai, I think this is for you."

Kaiser stood from where he'd been grinning at the koi. He looked back at me first before following her. I was close enough that I saw his eyes widen and his lips part as he looked at the little nest.

Several minutes passed while he gaped. When he turned to me, his bottom lip was trembling and there were tears in his eyes.

"Is it really a nest?" he asked, his voice so quiet I almost missed it on the light breeze.

I nodded. My apartment wasn't big enough for a nest and I ached to give him one for as much time as he spent here. When the months grew colder, I'd make sure the outside nest was filled with heat so he could enjoy it year-round.

Kaiser swayed, rooted to the spot before he covered his face with his hands. Marley leaned into him, kissing him and nudging him towards me, before walking through the arch towards the seating area.

He walked into my chest with his hands still covering his face and I wrapped him in my embrace.

"You didn't have to do that," he whispered.

"I know," I answered, rocking him gently and purring softly. "I wanted to. I need you to know that I'm serious, despite all my screw ups. I'll give you anything, Kaiser. You and Marley. I'll make her a nest, too, if she wants one."

He chuckled, the sound coming with hiccups as he dropped his hands and wrapped his arms around me. "She'll tell you no, but I think she'd love that. Maybe a she shed."

"Okay, I'll make it happen. You want to help me design it?"

Kaiser nodded. He looked up at me, his face blotchy with trying to hold back his tears. "Thank you," he said. "You don't know how much this means to me."

The words were on my tongue, but I couldn't say them. I was sure it would kill me later if I did. Instead, I pressed my forehead to his before kissing him gently. "Go make sure you have enough pillows. There are more but I didn't want it to be too crowded. I'm going to get Marley."

"You're perfect," Kaiser whispered and I was sure that was his compromise to saying the words that I wasn't ready to say or hear.

"I'm not, but you make me want to be better. Go make that nest right. We'll be right over."

Kaiser nodded. He pulled away and wiped his face. I

watched as he stopped at the bottom of the stairs and gazed up at it for another minute before taking slow steps up, looking at every detail. It had been the truth. Kaiser made me want to be a better alpha. He made me want to be worthy of having him as my omega.

I turned to Marley who was also watching Kaiser with a small, fond smile. It was hard to convince myself that treating the two slightly differently was okay. My instincts said to smother the omega with things the omega craved. They also said to show the beta how special she was by treating her like she was an omega, but in a different way.

Not with nests but with day trips. Excursions. Treating her like she was precious and special and giving her everything as if she were the only one.

She looked up at me when I sat in the chair across from her. "I think you've just made his entire month," she told me.

"Is it okay?" I asked.

"Terence, it's amazing."

I smiled, reaching for her hand. She twisted her fingers with mine. "But is it okay?"

It was the second time asking the same question that she caught what I was really asking. "I'm not an omega. I don't need the same things."

"But do you want them?"

Her smile was sweet. But the slight flush that rose in her cheeks and the shyness that met her eyes said that she did. At least on some level. Instead of answering outright, she said, "I've always been content being a beta. I've never wished for anything more. But I think why so many betas would give their right leg to be an omega is because they're treated as if they're royalty. As if they're an only child, a soulmate. They're doted on and spoiled and *rare*. While a beta is as common as sand."

I slipped from the chair and knelt in front of her, bringing my free hand into her hair. She leaned her head into my touch, her smile softening.

"I already have what an omega has," she said quietly. "Alphas who love me and give me the world, protect me but let me have my freedom. None of you treat me any differently than you do Kaiser. The gifts aren't the same but the sentiments behind them are."

"If there's ever something he gets that you want, I don't care how you tell me, but do so. I hear what you're saying, but I've never had an omega and I'm just winging it based on what my instincts are telling me to do. It's only after I've done something that I'm left questioning whether you'll feel like I don't care about you as much."

Marley pressed her lips to mine. "It's beautiful and Kaiser is right in love. I don't need a nest, Terence."

"How about something that's all yours but not a nest?" I asked.

"Like my bedroom?" she asked, raising a brow.

"I had a nest built out here because there's literally nowhere for one in my apartment."

She kissed me again. I drew my tongue through her mouth, pressing it over hers as I tightened my hold in her hair. I wanted more. But knew it wasn't the time.

"Come on," I whispered, getting to my feet and pulling her up, too. "Let's cuddle with Kaiser for a while."

Marley nodded.

I kept her hand in mine and decided I needed to pay extra attention to any comments she made on whatever I gifted Kaiser. Maybe I needed to duplicate whatever I bought but make sure it was distinctly separate. Like a nest for an omega. But a sunny, cozy den for Marley.

Kaiser had shifted everything around so that the cushions made a little wall and were lined more thickly at the back. He had his shoes off and sitting on the mat I'd intended for them. His shirt was also slung over a hook. It was private back here in that no one could see us. Not in noise. And yet, I didn't think I cared in the least.

He was smiling as we climbed in with him, his eyes filled with glassy awe. Marley and I boxed him in, curling up around him and for a while, we just lay there. Kaiser continued to look around, a smile never leaving his lips.

When he finally turned to me, I thought he was ready to explode. I grinned, waiting for his onslaught of excitement.

"Purr," he whispered.

As if his word was a command, I purred loudly. His smile climbed as he rested his hand on my chest.

"Thank you," he said. "Not for the purr, but I need that, too."

"I really will give you anything," I told him.

"All I want is you," he answered, his words careful and quiet. "Since the moment I saw you at the gym."

I chuckled. "You mean when I looked at you like you were a dragon? Or a slug? And ran like a chicken?"

Kaiser laughed. Marley hid her smile on his shoulder.

"Yes. And every time since."

I traced my thumb over his bottom lip as I stared into his eyes. It was right there on the tip of my tongue, creating so much pressure in my chest I couldn't take a full breath.

"When I run, follow me," I told him, the words sounding choked even to my own ears.

He nodded. "You can't keep me away," he answered, sliding in closer. He reached behind him and pulled Marley against his back.

I took a deep breath, filling my lungs with his perfume and the more subtle hints of Marley's scent right behind it. Leaning in, I brushed my cheek against his, feeling the way he melted into me, his hand gripping my shirt to hold me there.

Behind him, Marley smiled, picking her head up to kiss my lips. I held her there, still nuzzling softly against Kaiser, layering my scent on him, while I tried to take Marley's breath for my own.

When I rolled back, I pulled them both with me, draping them over each other and on my chest. These two were mine. I needed them. But that meant it was time to ease into other things. More serious areas.

"Tell me about your alphas," I said into the quiet, feeling how they both tensed under my hands.

CHAPTER THIRTY-ONE

Marley

K aiser had told me about how Terence asked about his pack the first time they went to dinner. He'd sensed even then that it was a bad idea and had sidestepped that conversation. He'd been right. Terence had tried to end it there.

But this was surely different. We were laying in a nest for Kaiser that Terence had made for him. On his property. And based on what he'd said, the only reason it was outside was because it wouldn't fit inside.

That meant things were different now, right? This could be a safe subject?

Kaiser winced under me, his hand sliding up Terence's chest to tangle in his hair. Since my hand was lying on Kaiser's arm, I could feel that he was gripping Terence tightly.

Terence didn't repeat the request. And he remained calm and relaxed under us while we processed it.

"Really?" Kaiser asked after several minutes had gone by.

"Really," Terence confirmed. Kaiser and I both looked up at the note of amusement in his voice.

"What do you want to know?" Kaiser asked.

"Based on your bites, there are two alphas or just two that have claimed you?"

"Two only," Kaiser said. After another pause, he added, "Adrian and Phynn."

A smile grew on Terence's face when Kaiser didn't elaborate. "And?"

Sighing, Kaiser pulled himself from between us and climbed more firmly on top of Terence, straddling his hips, and looking down at him with a frown. Terence kept his gaze locked on Kaiser, even as he pulled me tighter to them both.

"This is a good thing?" Kaiser asked. "You're not trying to talk yourself out of this again?"

Terence grinned. "Believe it or not, I was never trying to talk myself out of it." He wavered his head back and forth. "Not in the sense you mean, anyway. Yes, it's a good thing. Tell me about your alphas."

Kaiser bit his lip and looked at me. "You have to start. You were with them first."

I nodded, mimicking Kaiser and taking my bottom lip between my teeth for a minute. And then I pushed myself up so that I was kneeling, facing Terence. Kaiser pulled me close so that I leaned into his side.

How much was I supposed to tell?

"Okay, so Adrian and Phynn were childhood friends. They grew up together, within the same neighborhood. They played sports together. But then Phynn moved away for college. I met Adrian in college, but we both attended local state college. I wanted to remain at home, but I think Adrian just didn't have direction or drive, so he took a guaranteed ticket. Followed a degree his parents set for him. We'd been kind of seeing each other for a while without really making it a thing. I think it was Phynn's moving home that kind of propelled us to examine our relationship more thoroughly."

I paused to continue to study Terence. His expression was open, a light smile on his lips as he listened. When I stopped talking, he shifted his hand to rest on my knee and nodded for me to continue.

"Phynn and I had an instant connection. It was stupid and cliché and idiotically sweet. Like a reality version of insta-love." I smiled wistfully. "The three of us were almost always together. Within a month of Phynn coming home, we had the conversation to become a pack. Adrian bit me as soon as we agreed that we were an official pack. Phynn waited a while longer, just because we'd only started seeing each other. They're really good men. They treated me like I was their omega, in all the ways I've seen them treating Kaiser since he joined us. Eight years ago, after we'd visited one of their friends' packs who had a real omega, the conversation came up as to whether we wanted to list our pack. They left that decision up to me, saying they didn't need anyone more than me."

"They didn't," Kaiser said. "I saw that as soon as I walked in the door that first time."

I smiled at him, leaning my head against his shoulder. "Hush. Not to you yet."

Kaiser grinned, gripping my wrist gently.

"Anyway. It was a lie, even if they didn't lie outright. An alpha needs an omega. And as much as they loved me, I was never going to fulfill the place an omega would. So, I agreed on the stipulation that we needed a male omega. We registered with the Pack Listing the following day, knowing that I'd basically just cut the chances of giving my alphas an omega to complete our pack by five-sixths."

"And yet, here I am," Kaiser said, grinning down at her. He

rocked in his happiness, leaning down to look at my face and resting his hand on Terence's stomach.

Their easy familiarity and comfort with each other were another point of jealousy in me. I wasn't there yet. But now, as I'm telling Terence about our meetings, I realized that maybe that was how Kaiser had felt coming into our pack. The situation had been reversed. The alphas were already mine and had been for a couple years. Kaiser was new and learning us all at the same time.

"Your turn," I told him.

"About time," he muttered playfully. He turned his attention to Terence with a wide smile. "I already told you some. You know I'd been looking at packs since I was sixteen because the world is a fucked up, terrifying place for an unclaimed omega. And because I was dreading a heat without a pack. For a long time, I tried to look at the packs objectively. I didn't want to make a decision based on what's expected of me. I wanted a pack that would let me live. Not lock me away so I'd never see the outside world. Have you ever looked on the Pack Listing site?"

Terence nodded. I swear, there was a brief flash of something there, but it vacated almost immediately. The touch of a smile returned to his lips.

I glanced up at Kaiser. I couldn't tell if he noticed or not. But he continued, nevertheless.

Kaiser mimicked Terence's nod. "They're thorough and yet vague at the same time. After more than a year of just skimming through the overwhelming number of packs, I decided to try some filters. My favorite was dropping my results to just show those who wanted a male omega. The list was still stupid long, but it was far more manageable to sift through. And then I searched for those who had a beta in their pack. Further filters of 'small pack,' 'minimum age: 25,' 'maximum age: 35,' and 'female present' shortened my list even further. But that's where my success ended. Objective was no longer working. On paper, they all looked good. So when my body started pointing to signs that I was going to be getting my first heat within a year, I ordered a whole slew of scent cards."

"Angrily ordered them," I added.

Terence chuckled. "Okay, hold on. How did you know your heat would come in a year? And why angrily?"

"I was getting to the age where my body was going to kick into final maturity. Heats are commonly first had between ages nineteen and twenty-three. But the real telling thing is the fevers. Like my preheat spikes? For almost an entire year before the first heat comes on, we get random fevers. Not like the spikes, just fevers where we burn up for an hour or two. And let me just tell you, that first one had me shaking in terror that I was going to choose a pack too late. Those fevers didn't come with arousal, thankfully. But there are other nuances with them. The way my head fogged. The need of wanting something that I wasn't getting. My irrationality and heightened emotions. I come from a family with a long line of omegas, so they knew right away what was going on."

I nuzzled into Kaiser's side, and he wrapped his arm around me. Even his memory of that time was enough to have his heart beating faster.

"And angry because I couldn't find a way to choose a pack without bringing in a biological response. My mother had told me that I could just line up a bunch of meetings. Packs would come to me, line up for me, and I could even choose from a distance with their voices modified by recordings, so I didn't even hear them. My family indulged me and my hatred of what I was. But of course, they did. Imagine how pissed I was when I realized they didn't just indulge me because I was their son, but because I was their *omega* son and to a handful of alpha fathers, indulging me was the only answer."

I grinned, hiding it in his chest. Terence smiled at him and covered his hand.

Kaiser sighed, calming himself down again as he rolled his eyes. "Anyway. The entire thirty packs of scent cards in the first batch that came I sent back. In the second batch I ordered, I set up a meeting with one. But I went to them at my family's persuasion. You know, to see the nest. There were three alphas, two males, a female, and a male beta. The house was big with a whole lot of yard space, pools, rooms that weren't used. And three nests. They were nice, looking at me like I was the answer to everything. There was a silent plea in their gazes that made me tense. I didn't give them an answer when I left, but I told the Guardian that accompanied me that it was a no. It felt wrong. I didn't want to be looked at like that."

"I met two others and didn't like them either. I was starting to get a little more frantic when my second fever hit. It was short-lived at twenty minutes, but it was enough to terrify me. I didn't even smell the last set of scent cards before I let the Guardian know I wanted to meet them all. Hell, I'd meet every fucking alpha pack at this point because I was terrified. I nixed the first three almost as soon as I walked in their door. I ignored as much of my biological reaction as I could. But not my gut reaction. Two of those three freaked me out. But the pheromones of the third one made me cringe and gag. Based on the way they looked at me with wide eyes and tried to stay away, I was sure they didn't appreciate my perfume, either."

"I never imagined what kind of a process this could be," Terence said.

"I think it might move more smoothly with an omega who didn't hate being an omega."

Terence picked himself up, curling with the muscles of his

abs to do so until he could kiss Kaiser. Kaiser moaned into Terence's mouth as he leaned in to mold his body to Terence's, rocking his hips on instinct alone. I smirked, shaking my head.

"It's not so bad being an omega, is it?" Terence murmured through his purr against Kaiser's lips.

Kaiser shivered. For a minute, he looked like he was dazed, his body slightly swaying, his eyes nearly closed. Terence grinned, licking his tongue across Kaiser's mouth, and winking at me. I giggled.

The sound caused Kaiser to suck in a breath and his eyes opened. He glared at us both. "Yes! Look what you do to me."

"Are you saying you want me to stop?" Terence asked, his voice low and sultry.

Kaiser shivered. "No."

"Are you suggesting you don't like when I kiss you?"

Kaiser pressed his lips together before he shook his head.

"Then it can't be all that bad."

Kaiser huffed, pushing gently at Terence's chest to make him fall back within the cushions. Terence laughed quietly, a sound that made Kaiser and I both shiver. It was like an instant high.

"Being an omega with the alphas and beta I share my life with isn't bad," Kaiser admitted. "I almost like it. Almost."

Terence accepted that. "Continue."

"The next meeting was with my pack. I smelled their cards on the way over and choked, they smelled so good. I rubbed them all over my face, almost licking them to taste these two alphas. Everything in me was on fire with things I couldn't even fathom. So, I walk in and am already panting with lust and such a deep need I can't identify what it is. Talk about omega biology at its finest. They were kind, sweet, and respectful. They spoke to me like a damn human. Marley was gorgeous – well, they all were. I didn't want to leave when my visit was over. I kept trying to find reasons to stay longer. Ask more questions. As soon as I got to the car, my Guardian said, 'that's your pack, isn't it?' I could only nod, a whine stuck in my throat. 'Want to go back?' she asked. I stilled immediately and told her I did. Well, I ran back to the door and rang the bell like eight times until Adrian opened the door. I think I asked something pathetic like 'can I be your omega?' He offered me his hand and pulled me to him. Pretty sure I bit him as I tried to crawl into his chest."

"You did bite him," I said, giggling.

Kaiser grinned. "They surrounded me. Betas in a pack don't get scent cards but as soon as Marley was close and I smelled her, I licked her face. I swear, I was a damn animal."

"Yes, you did that, too," I said.

"So, I was scared for a while that I had suddenly been tricked by my biological need for a pack with this kind of match and they'd expect me to be a boring omega and lock me away. But they don't. They let me be who I want to be. Do what I want to do. They still treat me like an omega, but they don't force me to be one. And they like to pretend that some of what they do isn't a response to me being an omega when it is. It makes me happy that they try though."

"They sound great," Terence said.

Kaiser nodded, his focus far away with a wistful smile on his lips. Then he sighed and focused on Terence. "So, this was still a good conversation?"

Terence smiled. "Yes. I'm glad they're good people. I'm glad they treat you both like they do."

"They'd like to meet you," Kaiser said.

I sucked in a breath at his declaration and stared at Terence. He started to nod before his phone interrupted us. Kaiser wiggled down his legs so Terence could reach into his pocket and pull it out. He frowned at the number before opening it.

"Hello?"

His voice was cautious. I looked up at Kaiser. He was staring at Terence with anxiety. The last call Terence got while Kaiser was there had been the reason he was sent home and miserable for his heat. He was holding his breath. But then, so was I.

Terence must have been too. His expression softened as he smiled up at Kaiser. Kaiser and I both relaxed.

"I'll be right there," Terence said and hung up the phone. He sat up, using those amazing abdominal muscles to sit. "Furniture is here. Want to help me tell them what to do?"

Kaiser grinned as if the furniture was for him. "Yes!" He scrambled from Terence's lap and moved to the edge of the nest to slip his shoes back on.

Terence leaned into me, kissing me lightly. "Not a bad phone call," he said. "Everything is fine."

I smiled, not even upset that he called us out on our nerves. He kissed my nose and nudged me towards my shoes.

Terence sent us upstairs to get the apartment ready while he supervised the unloading of furniture. Kaiser stripped the bed of all his bedding and put it on the couch while I emptied Terence's drawers. Was it awkward to be handling his underwear before I'd actually seen them on him? Not exactly, but my imagination was filled with images of what he might look like in them.

"Sexy as fuck," Kaiser told me, likely feeling my interest piqued through our shared bonds as I brought handfuls of them to the couch. He winked at me on the way by.

I bit my lip and set them on the couch. We were just finishing emptying the living room console onto the table when

Terence came upstairs with two men. One brought a wine rack that had Kaiser grinning like a child.

Terence removed the TV from the console and set it in the kitchen on the counter. The men removed the console before returning for the dresser. With those two pieces out of the way, Terence removed the mattress from the bed.

It was several hours before we had the small space back together. Although the amount of furniture hadn't changed, Terence had brought in bigger furniture with more storage. The dresser had a larger wardrobe piece against the wall for hanging garments. The bed was filled with drawers underneath. Even so, Terence pushed it against the wall, making two of them unusable.

By the time I had the TV console arranged, Terence put back his clothing, and Kaiser had rebuilt his nest on Terence's bed, we were all sprawled out at the foot of the bed with the setting sun peeking in through the crack in the curtains.

"So," Kaiser said, rolling over so he was on top of Terence again. I knew that grin. My heartbeat began to race just seeing it before he continued. "I think we should break in this new bed, alpha."

A smile grew up on Terence's face, his tongue poking out to trace his bottom lip. "Is that what you want?"

Kaiser nodded eagerly, rocking his hips against Terence's. "Yes. Please."

Terence looked at me and I wondered what he saw. My flush? Me trying to hide my timidity? My desire for him, too?

I think it was the last. When he sat up, he didn't grab Kaiser to bring him in for a kiss. He tangled his fingers into my hair and pulled my mouth to his.

We'd kissed plenty of times and I loved every minute of it. But none of them had been like this. Kaiser groaning next to me as he ground his hips into Terence's lap only heightened the dizzying feeling as it swept through me.

He was a beautiful poison that made my insides burn.

"You okay with this?" Terence asked against my mouth before feathering his lips across my cheek. Along my jaw. Over my neck, making me shiver and turn instantly wet at the same moment. He didn't even need to ask. I was sure he could smell my arousal now.

"Yes," I told him anyway. I think we both needed to hear my agreement.

Kaiser moved from Terence's lap before he started pushing at both of our clothing. "You have to go first," he said, excitedly. "Or you'll have to wait hours to ride him. It's not a ride you want to miss, Mar."

I flushed and swatted at him. Damn Kaiser.

Terence chuckled, laying back to let Kaiser pull at his pants. He tucked his hands under his head as he let Kaiser strip him, lifting his hips when Kaiser finally succeeded at the buttons.

I was not at all prepared for the size of him. Funny, since I was pretty sure he was right in line with Adrian and Phynn, yet he was huge.

"Wait till you feel his knot," Kaiser said, making my face burn again.

Fucking hell, omega.

"You take a knot?" Terence asked, surprised.

I shook my head.

"No, no," Kaiser said, looking up with a wide, hungry grin as he traced Terence's erection with his fingers. "But she likes them all the same."

I sighed, shoving him playfully until he looked at me with a pout. "Sorry," he said, dropping his eyes.

Shaking my head, I pulled his face to mine and kissed him

hard. Reminding him that he's mine. My omega. My beautiful, boundaryless omega.

"Take your clothes off," Kaiser breathed against my mouth. "Or I'm enjoying him on my own."

I grinned and slowly started to pull my clothes from my body. I remained flushed, feeling Terence's eyes on me. I watched Kaiser rub on Terence through his briefs while I shed my protective layer of clothes. I wasn't always shy, but I'd only been kissing Terence to this point.

Oh, I was ready for this. Don't get me wrong. But I was still nervous.

When I was fully undressed, I glanced up to Terence. His green-gold eyes were trained on mine, as if he hadn't even looked at my body at all. He was studying my face. He was so beautiful. So relaxed. Waiting for us to call the shots.

"I know," Kaiser said as if he'd heard my thoughts. Sometimes, I swear he did. He pushed Terence's briefs down finally, relieving his ridiculous cock. Gorgeous. Thick. Long. And Kaiser wasn't wrong. That fucking knot, man! Jeezus.

"Suck him while I get you ready, Mar," Kaiser said, already shifting me to hover over Terence's dick. The man had no idea.

Terence did, though. "Easy, Kaiser. Let Marley settle, babe."

Kaiser preened at the affectionate name. He nodded and sat back. I smiled at Terence, but I knew my omega. The man was not patient. And certainly not when it came to sex. So, I nodded at him, pulling his lips to mine again.

I loved his kisses. He was always a little sloppy, using his tongue a whole lot. But he tasted divine.

"Love you," he whispered against my lips. "I don't mean to push."

"I know," I answered. "Love you, too. Ready?"

"I was literally born ready," Kaiser said, sighing. His eyelids drooped with his irritation at it.

I grinned, pecking his lips again, and crawling in front of him. He actually didn't like to be behind me. He'd rather be on top of me. But if he wanted me sucking dick, that was the direction he had to take.

I grinned again when I felt him sigh, his hands gently rubbing on my ass. Nope, he didn't want to be behind me.

"What about if I'm on my back and you ride me. Terence can stand over us for you to suck?" Kaiser asked.

I laughed, dropping my head to look back at him. He was pouting.

"Come here, Marley," Terence murmured. I looked up to find an amused but heated smile touching his lips. "Lie down."

I shifted along his body until I could lie next to him. He brushed my face, tilting my head so I looked up at him. "You don't actually have to suck."

I raised my hand before Kaiser could say anything. I heard his lips pop closed in response. "I don't have any objections to it, actually. Can I squeeze your knot?" Heat flamed over my cheeks as I asked.

Terence smiled wider, full of wild sex and sin. "As much as you want."

"She doesn't like cum in her mouth," Kaiser said.

I sighed.

Kaiser winced. "Sorry. I was trying to be helpful that time."

"I know, love," I told him, still held in Terence's gaze.

"No coming in your mouth. Not a problem," Terence told me.

"Even if she squeezes your knot?" Kaiser asked. This time it was genuine curiosity more than anything.

"Even then," Terence agreed. He moved up the bed, turning onto his side so his dick was in my face.

I shifted too, so I could twist my body and touch him. Big. Hard like stone. I swear, it was pulsing in my hand. I licked my lips.

"This is much better," Kaiser murmured as he moved to push himself inside me. But as knot hungry as he was, when he wasn't quite so wrung up, he enjoyed touching. So, I wasn't in the least bit surprised when it wasn't his dick that he pushed in me but two of his fingers.

He wasn't actually aiming for pleasure when he touched. He was exploring. He always told me that he knows a man's body inside and out. He had one. But a woman's was fascinating and he just wanted to touch.

I flicked my eyes up to Terence's as he smiled down at us both. Patient. Beautiful.

I pulled my hand down his length, ending my hand at his knot before bringing it back up. Just to feel the way his skin moved over the ridiculous rigidity underneath. And then I wrapped my hand around his knot. It was bigger than both Adrian and Phynn's. Was it harder? Kaiser suggested it was.

I squeaked when Kaiser stopped playing and pushed himself inside me instead. "Mmm," he murmured, rocking his hips slowly. I glanced at him to see his eyes closed as he moved in the few experimental thrusts before he was ready to move in earnest.

If I didn't grab onto Terence's dick now, Kaiser would have me moving all around the bed with his Wildman ways.

I wasn't disappointed. As soon as I latched my mouth around Terence's head, earning myself a quiet breath from him, Kaiser started lunging into me for real. I grunted around Terence, gripping his knot almost more to hang on than anything. His hand cupped the back of my head, cradling it as Kaiser went to town.

He was quick to release in almost any position. He filled

me in no time as he fell over me. I knew I only had a few minutes to truly stay under him before he was going to carry on. Only a knot could truly satisfy him. And the only time Kaiser ever fully gave into his omega nature was during sex.

I didn't think it was so much a choice as it was a need he couldn't escape. Something that turned painful quickly.

"So good, baby girl," Terence murmured.

My heart fluttered in response. Kaiser filled me again, grunting as he started to slow.

"Okay," Kaiser muttered. "Switch. You're warmed up."

I giggled as I pulled from Terence's dick.

Kaiser's face was a mix of high arousal and profound longing. He looked at me with a bit of stress. "I'm sorry. I'm awful at threesomes."

I laughed. Terence and I reached for him at the same time, showering him with kisses.

"Go ahead," I murmured. "I'm happy to stay around you."

Kaiser whined but shook his head. "No. I need you to enjoy our alpha, too."

I realized then why he was going to be insistent about this. He knew I'd been jealous. Jealous enough that I didn't feel comfortable sharing his heat spikes with him. He didn't want me left out. And right now, there was no way I was going to convince him otherwise.

I hugged him tightly and he pulled away, moving further across the bed and half burying himself within the pillows. He didn't want to see. He did, but it was only going to make him worse. This was why he was one of the best people I've ever known.

Terence pulled me to him, kissing along my jaw and neck. His lips stopped at my ear where he whispered low enough that I knew it was just for me. "I promise, I'll make this quick one up to you. Hearing him whine is not something I can physically ignore for long."

I smiled, nodding. "I know," I answered just as quietly. "No alpha can."

"I'll spend hours worshiping you another time, Marley. You have no idea how badly I want to."

His words made me swallow. He rolled, bringing me with him. Because we both knew that soon the quiet, choked sound that Kaiser was making would be turning into a whine he would no longer be able to contain, no matter how hard he was trying, Terence didn't draw it out.

He kissed me slowly as he arranged me over him, spreading my legs as he rubbed his hard length between my folds. I was already trembling by the fourth pass when he adjusted to press his head into me.

He was big. Kaiser wasn't wrong when he told me it was different than our alphas. Nor did I miss the difference of his knot when he was so thoroughly seated in me. My eyes were rolling.

But he was still kissing me. Rubbing his hands over my ass cheeks, digging his fingers in as he slowly rolled his hips up.

I saw stars as I gasped, the hard bulge of his knot hitting my clit. Yep, this was going to be quick. The second time he rolled so his knot hit my clit, I gasped, little spasms of pleasure shooting through me.

I refused to come in three seconds. What the hell was that?

Kaiser's whine escaped before he swallowed it, growling into the pillows with effort. Terence shivered under me, but he didn't change his rhythm or speed. He continued the long, slow rocking that rubbed me in all the right ways. His lips stayed on mine as our tongues occasionally met for a wetter kiss.

Trying to hold off my orgasm meant that it suddenly exploded out of me when I wasn't expecting it. I almost screamed through a moan as lights burst behind my eyes, leaving little spots dancing. I was barely coming out of it when Kaiser dug himself out.

His skin was flushed. A slightly mad look danced in his eyes. He was visibly trembling. "Knot," he said, his voice quiet but miraculously devoid of a whine. "Please. Knot, alpha."

"Come here," I said, reaching for him.

Kaiser stumbled his way across the bed, letting me cup his face. He rubbed into my palm as he tried to focus on me. His skin was warm again. Not a heat thing. Just an omega thing. And he was most certainly shaking.

I looked up at Terence as I climbed off. He smiled, bringing my lips to his, making my heart flutter. "Stay close. You're going to be the cherry on top."

I shivered as I pulled away.

"Get on, omega," Terence purred, and Kaiser moved to do so. Terence had him turn around so he was sitting reverse as Kaiser wiggled his ass to get Terence to hurry up with his dick. I giggled, appreciating Terence's endless patience with him. The smile on his face said he enjoyed it.

Kaiser wasn't happy until he took Terence's knot completely. Terence sat up, rubbing his hand over Kaiser's swollen dick and balls. With an open hand, he rubbed his length, kissing his neck in a sensual dance of teeth and tongue.

"You're doing so good, Kaiser," he murmured. "Feel how good this is?"

Kaiser nodded, his head tipping back and to the side. Giving Terence his neck. Terence dragged his teeth across, causing Kaiser to buck his hips. The movement made him cum with a gasp.

"Beautiful," Terence said, bringing his hand up to lick. "So good, baby."

He lay back, bringing Kaiser with him. Kaiser's eyes

widened to saucers as he squirmed at the new position. The way it pulled and tugged and made him arch. It was hot. One of the most erotic things ever was seeing an omega knotted.

"Ready for Marley, too?" Terence asked.

"Marley," Kaiser grunted, nodding.

Terence held his hand to me, and I took it. Cherry on top. I grinned as I climbed on. It was like riding a horse way up here. I slid down Kaiser's wet length, making him howl in another orgasm as he trembled between us.

Terence wrapped a hand around my ankle and a hand around Kaiser's neck.

"What do you think, sweetie," Terence purred in Kaiser's ear, his eyes glinting up at me. "I think we should try for six more orgasms. Think you got that in you?"

Kaiser shuddered, moaning. "Yes, alpha."

"That's my good boy. Let's see how many we can achieve, our perfect little omega."

CHAPTER THIRTY-TWO

Adrian

Once again, I watched as Kaiser's nervous excited behavior reminded me of a teenager readying for a date. But not just any date. One akin to meeting the parents. I leaned against the door and watched his jittery pacing back and forth as we waited for Marley.

She was a quieter version of Kaiser right now. I was sure her nerves were amplified because she was feeling Kaiser's.

Finally, I pulled Kaiser to a stop and made him focus on me. "You're going to make us all need a Valium if you don't calm down, Kai."

"Sorry," he said. He closed his eyes and took a breath, letting the motion sweep through him and fill him with a brief semblance of calm.

Very brief. It wasn't long before he was almost bouncing again.

"We need to go before his apprehension makes me need a drink," Marley said from the door.

Kaiser gave her a sheepish look. "I know it's going to be fine. But I can't help but worry. Is it too soon for him?"

"Terence agreed," Marley said, coming into the room and stopping at my side. She held my arm and watched Kaiser with sympathy. "You know he wouldn't agree unless he thought he could handle it."

He sighed. "I know."

"Let's go," Phynn called from downstairs. "Or I'm leaving you all behind and I'll have dinner with your alpha alone."

Kaiser's eyes widened and I chuckled. "Come on."

The car ride was quiet. I could almost feel Kaiser's leg bouncing in the back seat, even as Marley tried to make it stop.

I recognized him as soon as we pulled in. A tall man with a body shaped like a wrestler. Yet the cut of his clothing made him look like a casual businessman. His hair was a bit windblown from being on the longer side. He was scruffy with a bit of facial hair.

Kaiser pushed the door open as soon as the car stopped and launched himself towards Terence's arms right away.

"It's a good thing I'm not prone to jealousy," Phynn said with amusement. "I can't remember the last time he flung himself on me like that."

"Heat," Marley and I said together.

Phynn chuckled as we watched the two of them through the windshield.

Kaiser had slowed down before he plowed into Terence, his steps turning into something like a skip until Terence held his arms out. Then Kaiser lifted his restraint and fell into Terence's arms.

I was relieved to see that the alpha looked completely relaxed. His smile was easy, and he held our omega like the treasure he is. Sweetly. Reverently. Adoringly.

They exchanged some words before Terence looked up.

Kaiser twisted their bodies so he could peek shyly at us. They were far enough away that I couldn't see his coy smile hidden behind Terence's bicep, but I knew that look and that it was there.

"He's so fucking adorable," Phynn said, shaking his head. "He'd have us eating out of his hand if he was that kind of man."

I chuckled because he wasn't wrong. If Kaiser actually played his omega card as some do, we'd be groveling at his feet. Or never releasing our knots. Either one.

"Go, Marley," Phynn said quietly.

Marley leaned over the seat and kissed his cheek before pushing out of the car. She didn't run. Our pretty little beta was too reserved for that. She also didn't demand a hug without Kaiser involved.

Terence held his arm out and Kaiser shifted to give her room, bringing her into their hug. He kissed the top of her head, his arm tightening around her in an embrace that was meant just for her.

"They look happy," Phynn noted. "All three of them."

"I hope that means this is going to go well," I said.

Phynn nodded, sighing. "Yea. Me too."

When their hold began to loosen, Phynn and I climbed out. Terence didn't remove his attention from Kaiser and Marley as Kaiser talked. His jitters were still pouring out of him, this time in his rambling. I smiled, shaking my head.

Phynn tangled his fingers in Kaiser's hair, gently digging his fingers into Kaiser's scalp. He'd recently had his hair cut so it was no longer at the length that we could get even a teasing hold of it. Terence's smile ticked up as Kaiser blushed and stopped talking, giving in to letting Phynn gently pull his head back.

"I'm a little nervous," Kaiser admitted, looking at Terence.

Terence grinned at him this time. "Are you?"

Kaiser pressed his lips together, the exchange making Marley giggle. Terence touched his thumb to Kaiser's jaw, smoothing it across Kaiser's skin for an inch or so before he met Phynn's eyes. Then they flickered to mine.

Marley did the introductions.

Unsurprisingly, Terence's grip was strong. Surprisingly, I had an odd visceral reaction to his scent this close that was only amplified by his touch.

Maybe because I was used to my omega and beta coming home smelling like him. I was used to his scent now. I actually enjoyed the way it mingled with theirs.

At the subtle cocking of Phynn's head, I guessed that he was either responding to my reaction or experienced one similar. However, there was no indication on whether it affected Terence at all.

"Ready to go in?" I asked.

Terence nodded. Marley moved to my side, and I slid her hand in mine. Kaiser put himself under Terence's arm but took Phynn's hand, too. He was going to eat up having us all together. An omega wanted their entire pack around. And the two had already determined that Terence was pack from the moment they met.

I had made the reservation, so I checked us in with Marley still at my side. Now that we were alone, I could feel her nerves. She was better at managing them.

We were shown to a round booth. Phynn slid in first, followed by our omega and beta on either side of him. I took the seat next to Marley, knowing that Kaiser would want Terence on his other side. I was right, but his foot immediately found mine under the table. He grinned at me as he settled in.

A happy omega.

The server was at the table almost as soon as we sat, taking our drink orders. I was amused to find that Kaiser ordered wine for Terence. When the server left, Terence squeezed Kaiser's wrist.

He met my eyes. "I don't drink much wine. I tend to defer to whatever Kaiser says is good."

I nodded. "He's got good taste."

"I do," Kaiser said, grinning broadly. I was sure he wasn't just talking about the wine.

Between Kaiser and Marley, the conversation flowed smoothly with no overly long quiet moments. And though the two knew a bunch about Terence, there was an entire part of his life that wasn't touched on.

They knew his likes and dislikes. His interests and hobbies. There were even a few bits about places he'd traveled to as a child.

But all of this was either far off history or very present. When Phynn or I brought up something closer to home, Marley or Kaiser would steer us in a different direction. Most of the time, Terence let it happen with an amused smile. Sometimes he'd actually answer.

There was definitely something in his past that he didn't want to talk about and the two had learned which avenues to avoid. I pushed a little more anyway. Just to see what I could find without being overly aggressive.

"Where'd you grow up?" I asked him.

"California," he said. "Mid-state. Delano until college."

"Nice. We're actually from right here. Phynn and I grew up together."

Terence smiled, his gaze dropping to Marley. He already knew that. Marley smiled back at him.

"Where'd you go to college?" Phynn asked, maybe seeing where I was headed with this.

"University of Denver. And then the University of

Colorado School of Medicine. I'd intended to become a Radiologist. I stopped at emergency medicine during rotations and never left."

"Wow. High-pressure job," Phynn said.

He chuckled. "As long as you know how to separate yourself, it's not so bad."

Curious. "You stayed in Colorado after graduation?" I asked.

Marley and Kaiser exchanged looks again. I could feel both of their anxiety like a leash as they tried to reel me in.

"For a while."

"But he's made for juices," Kaiser said before I could ask another question. "You should taste his protein shakes. And they don't even make them at the juice bar."

Terence looked at him, once more with that amused smile. Fond and indulgent. I knew it well since I wore it often.

"Oh! Nora was all for adding a protein shake line," Kaiser told me. "She said she was going to have to do some research and get some mixes in to let her best Juice Artists experiment. There's going to be some free drinks until they find things they like!"

"I didn't think you liked protein shakes," Phynn said.

"I don't usually. They're chalky. Terence's aren't chalky."

"Just need strong enough flavors around the mix. It doesn't take away from the protein," Terence told him.

"You could add protein to most smoothies," Marley said. "Maybe Nora should hunt down a good quality mix that's mostly tasteless."

"I'll make sure she gets the suggestion," Terence said.

I tried a few more attempts to get some more personal information from him without being overly obvious I was prying. He knew I was. And he also intentionally left answers vague when he didn't want to answer.

His questions in return weren't quite so plentiful. I gathered that Kaiser and Marley had recently talked to him about Phynn and me, or he was letting this meeting stay in our hands. I couldn't determine which was the answer, but I let it carry on.

In reality, Kaiser and Marley kept the meeting headed mostly in the direction they wanted. This was a fun, carefree meeting. Anything serious could be discussed at the next. Their goal was to make it so a 'next time' happened.

That meant, light and leisurely right now.

After a couple more attempts at getting something outside of the trivial, Marley pushed past it while Kaiser gave me an exasperated look. I chuckled, raising my hands, finally giving in, and letting them control the direction of our dialogue for the remainder of the evening.

They instantly relaxed and the conversation remained friendly. Terence wasn't a bad guy. And though he didn't often let that side of him show, he was highly intelligent. I only caught a few rough hints at it, primarily based on his vocabulary more than the actual response itself.

I relaxed as I watched my pack. Phynn was laughing at a story Terence was telling them of college. I wasn't really listening but admiring those I loved and how this new alpha fit in pretty seamlessly.

And then the restaurant suddenly shook, a loud crunching crash accompanying it. A chorus of screams went up through the room as the lights flickered. Marley turned her face into my chest, and I wrapped my arm around her, every hair on my body standing on end.

We looked around the restaurant as the servers tried to reestablish calm. Sirens filled the air a moment later, getting louder as they got closer.

Kaiser's hand was over his face as he sank into the bench

between Phynn and Terence. Phynn already had his phone out, trying to figure out what the cause of the commotion was.

The power continued to flicker until it went out entirely. It was early enough in the day that the sun was still shining, even as it approached dusk.

"Everyone, please remain calm," one of the servers said. "There was an accident at the street corner. A car ran into the telephone pole."

Murmurs rose around the room as everyone shared their thoughts and assumptions.

"The police have arrived on the scene. There are people trapped inside the vehicle. We don't know anything else right now. Please remain calm."

"How awful," Marley whispered as she peeked towards the window behind Phynn.

"I hope they're okay," Kaiser said, sitting up and trying to see outside. "I can't imagine..."

His words trailed off and I glanced at him. He was looking at Terence, who had gone white as a ghost. His pupils were dilated as he stared at nothing. I wasn't sure he was even breathing.

A wave of anxiety rushed through me from Kaiser as he stared. He didn't speak. He didn't even move. In the corner of my eye, Marley gently touched Phynn's arm to get his attention. Phynn looked up and then followed the direction we were looking.

When Terence finally took a breath, it was a gasping inhale. A violent shudder went through him, and he stood. His hands were shaking as he pulled out a wad of cash and dropped it on the table. He didn't look at any of his as he muttered, "I can't do this. I'm sorry."

We watched as he took off, almost stumbling in an effort to run outside.

Kaiser climbed up on his knees to press his face to the window. But we knew Terence wouldn't come this way. The accident was blocking the end of the street. He'd have had to turn in the opposite direction.

Kaiser's anxiety took a sinking turn into sorrow as he turned to look at me, tears in his eyes. He made a solid effort to keep himself together as he took a seat on the bench again. He pressed his lips together as he looked at the empty seat where Terence had once been.

We finished dinner in silence, dropping cash onto the table for the server and pocketing Terence's to return to him at a later time.

"Can we-?" Kaiser began.

Phynn shook his head as he wrapped our omega in his arms. "Not tonight, love. Whatever triggered him, I think he needs the night to himself."

A whine stuck in Kaiser's throat as he tried to hold himself together.

His hold faltered for a few seconds as the evening carried on.

Over the next couple days, we stopped by his apartment several times. He didn't answer the door no matter who knocked on it. Marley checked with Nora at Juice Me, but she said she hadn't seen Terence in a couple days.

He didn't answer texts from either Marley or Kaiser.

When he did, three days after he ran from the restaurant, the answer had Kaiser disappearing to his nest and burying himself in the pillows as he tried not to cry. Marley handed me Kaiser's phone, her face pink from suppressing her dismay.

[Terence] You didn't do anything wrong. You're a perfect omega. An amazing man. I'm so sorry, Kaiser. I can't do this right now. I'm sorry.

I frowned, showing the text to Phynn. Phynn shook his

head. I clicked the phone off as Phynn began drumming his fingers on the table. I pulled Marley to me. She sagged, shaking as she tried to hold in her tears.

"I'm going to check on Kaiser," Phynn said quietly. "Then I'm going to see what I can find out."

CHAPTER THIRTY-THREE

Phynn

I hadn't been watching it unfold and I kicked myself for missing the shift. I'd been staring at my phone, scanning the news channels boards for some information. By the time I looked up, Terence was already deep in whatever trauma had surfaced.

Was it the lights flickering? The loud noise? The accident? The screams? Fuck, if I'd only been watching, maybe I'd have more to go on.

For three days we tried to reach him but outside the single text he sent to Kaiser, and one similar to Marley, there was silence. I'd called a friend who frequents the gym that Terence uses to let us know if he shows up. Marley has been in touch with Nora at Juice Me.

But so far, he had just vanished.

Not really vanished. If I had to guess, he had locked himself in his apartment. But maybe not. If he needed to be alone, in a tiny apartment that I was sure was saturated with my omega's perfume, he wasn't going to get away from it.

Maybe that wasn't what he needed though. It wasn't to get away from Kaiser. It was to deal with his suffering alone. And I was sure 'alone' was the key, based on what Marley had told me about a conversation she'd had with him not long ago.

Adrian and I traded off tending to Kaiser and Marley. Marley had finally given in to her own sorrow. She didn't have a nest to lock herself in, but she curled up in the big cushy chair in her room, wrapped in a plush blanket, and stared out the window with tear stains running down her face.

I wish they'd mourn together. It's difficult to be pulled in different directions. Our drive was to spoil them both. To nurse them and snuggle them and do anything we could to make them feel better.

But we knew what that would be. Finding an answer to the puzzle that was Terence.

Seeing the close down first hand had been telling and yet, still puzzling. He wanted Kaiser and Marley. There was no doubt in my mind. To see them together, the three of them, it had been so insanely clear I couldn't unsee it.

And this wasn't an intentional snub. Even Adrian, stressed over how upset Kaiser and Marley were, wasn't mad at Terence this time. He desperately wanted Terence to answer, if for no other reason than to put Kaiser and Marley's minds at ease. But we both saw that it was out of his control. He'd hardly been present enough to speak as he ran out the door.

Indicative of a past trauma, triggered by something in that moment. But it didn't seem to matter what I searched; I wasn't finding anything. I searched his name in Denver and Delano. There was nothing. Not even a parking ticket.

I found a mention of him on the Dean's list for undergraduate studies. I found a high school picture of him with a group of guys and girls at what I thought might be a football game. The photo and the mention were enough to confirm that those were truthful facts about him. He'd been in both places.

Maybe he was in the military. I sent an email to a friend in information asking him to look into Terence Andersen's military record. See if there was one. Or any kind of civil service. He was an ER doctor, maybe something had happened at the hospital.

That seemed to be the most likely of possibilities since he doesn't work in medicine now.

I got up and headed into Kaiser's nest. He was asleep, his phone gripped in his hand. The screen was on with a picture of him and Terence curled up in what I thought was a nest. They were both bare chested and I could see the affection for Kaiser in Terence's embrace. His light smile. The way he was curled around him.

I flicked the screen off and brought a blanket over Kaiser's shoulders. His cheeks were tear stained. Even in his sleep, he looked like he was ready to cry.

For a minute, I sat with him, my hand on his shoulder. Under my touch, he relaxed a little. Not enough that his sleep turned peaceful, but enough that I knew he felt that I was there.

This wasn't the same level of distraught that he'd been in previously. The incident that triggered his heat aside, Kaiser's burden felt different. He knew he wasn't the cause. There was a note of hope in there that it wasn't permanent. I wasn't sure if that was based on a pattern or a conversation they'd shared.

I kissed his forehead before I backed out of the room.

Down the hall, there was a soft lamp on in Marley's room. She was alone. I was sure that Adrian was cooking something for dinner.

She looked up when I stepped inside and gave me a sad smile.

I knelt in front of her, resting my face in her lap. Marley sighed. "You know. I understand that it's far too early and not appropriate, but I really just wish we shared a bond with him. That way we'd know what he needed."

That was a sentiment I understood.

"I know he says he needs to be alone but what if that's really the worst thing for him right now?" she asked.

"We will keep trying," I told her. "Kaiser said Terence needed him to be an alpha when he was lost in panic mode. Obviously, our omega is not quite built to be that, but we will do what we can to make sure Terence knows we're here if he needs us."

She nodded. Her fingers slipped into my hair as she turned back towards the window. She let her head rest against the side of the chair with a sigh.

"I worry that maybe he won't know he needs someone," she whispered.

I left Marley after a few more minutes. I'd meant to go downstairs to head to Terence's apartment and try his door again. But I heard Kaiser's soft whimper from the cracked door of the nest and turned back.

He was awake, his glossy eyes staring at nothing as he quietly whimpered. I dropped into the nest with him, and he looked up.

"I'm sorry. I'm trying to be-"

"Shh," I murmured, laying with him so we were facing each other. "I don't need you to try and be anything right now. We'll let him have his space but keep making sure he knows that he's not alone."

I watched as relief lit his eyes. He closed them for a second before looking at me. "I know what he told me," he whispered.

"But I keep thinking that maybe this is the time that he won't make it out of that state and he's not coming back."

I touched my fingertips to his cheek as he shivered. His skin was cool, so he wasn't feverish. Even under stress, it was too soon for another heat. But if our omega's fear was founded, I wasn't sure we could pull him from his misery before another heat was brought on by this duress.

"He built you a nest," I told him. "For you and you alone. He bought all new furniture so there was more room for you to spend time there. He buys you gifts every time he sees you. Honey, I can't imagine he's willing to walk away. Something happened to him and whatever it is, causes him a great deal of pain. Sometimes those moments are ugly, and we all deal with them in our own way. Like you preferring the comfort of your nest when you're upset."

"I hear your logic. But my fear is screaming louder," he said.

I smiled, sliding closer so I could hug him to me. He nestled in, his fingers fisting tightly in my shirt.

"I think he loves me," Kaiser said quietly. "It hurts more when I think that."

Bringing my knee up, I draped it over his hip and wrapped him securely into my chest in a grip that was vice tight. He gasped as tears soaked my shirt. I didn't know how to fix this, but I fucking needed to figure it out.

He fell back asleep again. I held him for a while longer, trying to deliver him the peaceful rest that he hadn't been getting. When I let him go, I headed downstairs.

Adrian was leaning against the counter with his head bowed and his eyes closed, likely in response to the sudden surge of renewed hurt from Kaiser. It was almost a physical pain to feel our omega like this. To know he was so upset and be helpless to fix it. What good was being an alpha if we couldn't deliver rainbows and laughter to our omega? What was there for us to do to make his pain go away?

I stopped in front of him, walking into his chest and resting against him. He didn't respond for a minute but then his hands moved to my waist, and he took a breath.

"I've never felt this helpless," he muttered. "I don't know what to do."

I dropped my face against his shoulder before turning into his neck. Adrian and I had been friends for a really long time. When one of my fathers got sick when I was a child, it had been Adrian that had been there to comfort me. I attribute that to being the reason he's always smelled like comfort to me. He was always home. Falling into a pack with him had been easy. Without his little beta, it might have happened a lot slower than it did. But everything just fell into place.

And it kept falling into place when Kaiser called on us. Even with the rockiness that Terence had been, I was sure he'd be falling into place too.

But this... I didn't know what to do with this. How do you comfort someone when you just don't know what to do? Marley was right – a bond would certainly be helpful right now.

Or so crippling that it would drive us insane.

"What are the chances that they're going to eat something?" Adrien asked as he slid his hands around my waist.

I kissed softly at his neck, nipping the skin until I felt his shiver. "Zero. I don't even feel like eating so I can't imagine either of them will."

"That's why I hadn't actually started cooking," he said, sighing. "Should one of us try again? See if he answers? Maybe get Nora to check on him?"

I shook my head. "Definitely not an employee. I don't think he'll appreciate that. And I don't know. I was debating dropping in again, too. But then I circle back to maybe he just needs a night to be left completely alone. Maybe the morning will look better."

"Which part of that moment did he react to?" Adrian asked, leaning his face against mine and slowly rubbing his cheek on mine.

I smiled a little. As kids, alphas cringe at the idea of wearing another alpha's scent. But fuck, it was a turn on. Being claimed by another alpha. The battle for dominance, both play and real. The sting of teeth and the flare of the bond.

We'd traded bites, just because we couldn't come to an agreement on who would wear the other's. I liked it best this way and how it spread the bond between us wide was a different kind of high. Especially when we were fucking.

"As an emergency doctor, it could have been any of those moments," I said. "The fact that he's not practicing anymore supports that there'd been something too tragic there for him to return to that kind of work."

Adrian nodded, still rubbing his skin on mine.

We remained in silence for a long time. Adrian gave up any pretense of actually cooking and headed upstairs to check on our pack. I wandered around downstairs for a while, looking for something to distract me.

As the sun reached its orange fingers to the horizon, I admitted defeat and returned to my room.

I brushed my hand over my face as I sat back at my computer. My information buddy had sent back an email with an attachment. I skipped the body of the email in favor of the attachment, opening it on my screen.

Chills broke out all over my body as I stared in horror at the headline. The image was just as gruesome. I read the article dated one year ago today as a crippling pain spread through my chest and tears filled my eyes.

Everything fell into place.

Terence was a strong fucking man to be dealing with this burden of loss and guilt on his own. I hit print as I slipped into my shoes. Grabbing the paper from my printer, I headed for the garage as I sent Adrian a text. 'I know what's wrong. I'll be back in a bit.'

The second floor of his building was dark. I climbed the stairs and knocked, waiting for him to answer. Every few minutes, I'd knock again. This time, I wasn't going away. I wasn't going to leave him alone.

CHAPTER THIRTY-FOUR

Terence

"Mr. Andersen?"

I almost told the voice he had the wrong number. I was too distracted, reaching for bonds that I couldn't find. Absently, I said, "Yes."

"This is Officer Marks with the Roanak County Police Department. There's been an accident, Mr. Andersen."

I'll never be able to explain the first tendrils of dread and despair as I fell to my knees, tears filling my eyes. I held my breath, trying to keep the sobs in as he continued to speak. I wasn't sure I actually heard his voice and yet his words were burned into my memory.

"Your pack is in critical condition at Melview Hospital in Roanak. I need you to get here as soon as you are able."

My body shook as my vision blurred, tears streaking down my face as I fell further to the ground. This time I couldn't keep the sobs in. Because I knew, even if he wasn't allowed to say over the phone, I knew by the hollow empty bonds – the remnants of which were starting to fade.

My pack wasn't in critical condition. They were dead. All of them.

I don't know how I made it to the hospital, and I'll never forget looking down at their broken bodies. They at least had the decency to put them in the same room. This was my hospital, and the doctors were gracious enough that they didn't interrupt or rush me as I spent hours sobbing over their bodies, begging them that they wake up.

I didn't care if it was a sick trick. I'd forgive them if they'd just wake up. I'd do anything if they'd open their eyes. Fuck, even for a goodbye. They couldn't leave me like this.

Why hadn't I gone with them? Why hadn't I been in the car, too? How dare they not take me with them! What was I supposed to do without them? They couldn't possibly expect me to live in our house, our lives, our promises that were now gone.

I wasn't sure if it was their bodies, cold and still before me covered in lacerations and dry blood, or the massive void inside me that had once been filled with their bonds that broke me completely.

Another sob wracked my body as I leaned over Zack's body and cried desperately for him to come back. I wanted to shake him, hit him, yell and scream until he barked at me to stop.

I'd never hear his bark again. I'd never feel his purr. I'd never feel the warm walls of his steady love in my head. It was all gone.

They were gone.

————

DAYS WENT by in which the only thing I truly recalled between crying was choosing their tomb. I refused their individual stones.

Refused individual plots. I didn't care how much it cost. I wanted them together. Miles and Ronan in the middle somehow. Emery and Foster below them, holding them, and Zack on top, protecting them. Shielding them. I didn't think that's how they'd end up, but that's how I wanted them. Their bodies had shifted but not enough that I couldn't still imagine them that way.

And me, draped over their bodies forever as I mourned their loss.

The funeral was big as six families came together. Countless friends and acquaintances. I didn't let anyone in my house. Their lingering scents were all I had left, and I couldn't bear the idea that someone could muffle that with their own.

I didn't speak to anyone. I wasn't sure I'd even stopped crying.

When everyone finally left me in the room with their temporary caskets, I sank to the floor in the middle of them, wrapping my arms around my middle as the tears overtook me. I cursed whatever higher being there was that they would cause someone this much pain. Taking part of a pack shouldn't be allowed. All or nothing. That should be a universal law. Making someone live like this was a punishment no one deserved.

But it didn't matter how loudly I screamed at the sky; it didn't bring my pack back. They didn't open their eyes one last time to look at me. I didn't hear their voices brushing my ear or their touches ghosting over my skin.

They were gone.

———

I OPENED my eyes in the darkness of my room. I'd have given anything to feel them again. To hear their voices, the sound of their laughter. Just their hands in mine. I didn't care what I got. I'd take anything.

I've heard that people often see their loved ones in dreams. Sometimes they get messages. I've heard of loved ones haunting someone they left behind.

My dreams were memories. Maybe that's why they hurt so bad; the reminder that I'd never get to make more memories. If it was something new that came to me when I slept, I could pretend that they were still here with me. I could say that they hadn't really left. That they couldn't bear to leave me any more than I could stand that they were gone.

But they weren't new. They were little moments picked from our lives together. Most of the time, things that I hadn't thought of in ages. Moments that were ordinary or had seemed trivial at the time. Now they stung like little knives burrowing in deeper and deeper. Ripping open the wounds wider with each new memory.

As if I needed more punishment for not climbing in that car with them. Karma kept throwing blades at me, reminding me of every tiny thing that I would never experience again. That first taste of soup as Emery tried seasoning it right. Ronan's tanking video as he laughed at the lack of views. Zack's new entrepreneurial purchase that he was already shaking his head at. Foster's laughter as he watched the same episodes of *Friends* every evening. Miles's smile every time he looked at me.

Never any new dreams. Not my pack visiting me while I sleep. Just my subconscious reminding me that I would never have them again. And that bank of little moments that I took for granted would never be added to.

Nor was I haunted by their ghosts. Aside from the periodic knock on my door or the occasional notification on my phone, my apartment was silent. It was even rare that a noise from the outside penetrated my walls loud enough for me to hear.

Silence. No sounds. No voices. No movement.

It was just me as I gasped for breath.

I rolled, burying my face in the plethora of pillows, and breathing in Kaiser's perfume. It settled me. Calmed my struggle to breathe and slowed my pulse. I hugged a pillow to me, squeezing my eyes shut as I focused on filling my lungs with his scent.

It wasn't fading. Even days later, his pine and cinnamon was strong enough to wear. My head ached. My sinuses felt like they were going to burst from all the pressure of crying. And somehow, being surrounded by Kaiser's scent gave me a bit of reprieve from the storm.

Knowing that I was already going through a shit storm mentally, I didn't allow myself to concentrate on more than the relief of how his perfume calmed me. I knew that would be an entirely new can of emotional torture that I didn't think I'd get through in one piece if I let myself think about it for even a minute.

I took a deep breath through my nose and held it, letting it fill me with something warm. Letting it touch the cavity that had once been thick with the bonds of my pack. It wasn't an immediate revulsion anymore. I'd been letting the two parts of my life mingle and connect more and more over the last few weeks.

My body ached. My muscles were stiff and protesting from laying in bed for so long. I felt sluggish with dehydration. The thought of moving through the apartment was too much effort though.

The sudden knock on the door made me jump. But when I picked my head up, it was gone. Or I'd imagined it. I listened for a minute, for any noise at all. Footsteps. Breaths. A voice. There was nothing.

Until I laid my head back down and the knocking came again.

For a breathless moment, I tricked myself into thinking that maybe my pack was trying to talk to me from beyond the grave. But when the knock came again a few minutes later, I knew it was just someone at my door.

It took an embarrassing amount of effort to force myself from bed. I staggered into the kitchen and opened the fridge. With a bottle of water, I headed back for my bed, ignoring the knock as it continued every handful of minutes. They'd go away.

My body protested as I lowered myself to sit again. I sipped my water slowly as I stared at the door.

Knock. Knock. Knock.

More water. Silence. Close my eyes.

Knock. Knock.

More water. Silence. Deep breath.

Knock. Knock. Knock.

"Go away," I called, though my voice was probably too quiet to hear.

But then the noise changed. Something slid. Quietly. Scratching. I narrowed my eyes as I leaned over, looking at my door. The light of the setting sun through the crack in my curtains made the folded piece of paper glow.

Okay. Obviously, I needed to see what it was. To humor them and then push it back and tell them to go away again. I wasn't done yet. I needed to be alone.

The paper was folded in half, and I picked it up. I flicked on the light so I could read it and my breath caught.

FREAK ACCIDENT TAKES THE LIVES OF ENTIRE PACK, LEAVING ONE BEHIND

I'd never actually seen the article. I'd never seen the car. But there it was in a pixelated black and white photocopy dated one year ago.

Bile rose in my throat as I tried to breathe.

I fumbled with the door as tears stung my eyes. Maybe I

shouldn't have drunk the water. Now there was something in me to cry out.

I expected Kaiser or Marley. But it was neither. As I flung the door open, Phynn stared back at me. He held my gaze as my vision of him was slowly lost behind the build up of tears. My jaw shook at the effort to keep in the sob that was building.

He didn't speak as he looked at me. As my chest began to tremble, Phynn reached for me and pulled me in.

It was the comfort I'd needed since the moment the police officer told me there'd been an accident. As if the moment was happening all over again, I bawled. The grief crashed over me like a tidal wave. Slamming into my chest and making me cry out as the pain overtook me.

Phynn held me like I might fall through the ground if he let go. His grip was almost painful from being so tight and I welcomed the feeling. He still didn't say anything as I made a mess of his shirt and neck.

He didn't rock me or make sounds to try and ease my pain. He did exactly what I needed him to. Nothing and everything while I shared this moment of debilitating pain with him. The devastation of losing everyone I loved in the same instant. The unbearable emptiness of their bonds as they left no trace behind. An empty echo in my soul was the only reminder that they'd been there at all.

Maybe he understood why I was such a mess. Maybe he wouldn't be angry when I buried myself in my hole and didn't come out again. Maybe he could explain to his omega and beta why I wasn't what they deserved or needed.

Breathing was hard. My lungs wouldn't take in a full breath of air as my sobbing died down. I tried to take a breath over and over again until I was slumping in Phynn's arms in exhaustion.

He finally spoke, his tone quiet and gentle. "Sometimes, even an alpha needs to be taken care of so they can heal."

CHAPTER THIRTY-FIVE

Terence

Maybe there was magic in his words. Maybe his words were the pinnacle for what I needed to catch my breath. My lungs unlocked as I pulled in a deep breath. Several more and my sinuses had cleared a bit.

My head ached. It hurt to open my eyes.

"Can I come in?" Phynn asked.

I nodded and he pushed me backwards, easing me one shuffling step at a time until he could shut the door. He sat me on the couch and moved through my apartment like he'd been here before. He flicked the bathroom light on and came out a moment later with a box of tissues.

I cringed at the mess I left on his shirt. He handed me the box and went to my fridge as I cleaned up my face. This time when he came back, he sat next to me on the couch and held the bottle of water to me.

Dropping my head into my hand, I took it from him. When I didn't drink it, he took it back, opened it, and pushed it to me again. I imagined that he'd have already barked at me to drink it, but since we were still basically just meeting, he was avoiding doing so.

He didn't look around but watched me as I drank. Only when I'd managed to swallow half the bottle was he satisfied to let me take a break from it by offering me the cap.

I leaned back on the couch, looking at my ceiling.

"I won't pretend to know how to help you," Phynn said quietly. "But I don't think *this* is helping."

I let out a mockery of laughter through a quiet breath and blinked, my eyelids moving slowly as if I couldn't bear to move at my regular speed for even that.

Phynn slid down the couch until he was in the corner. "Come here," he ordered. I was too tired and weak to care if it was a demand. I complied. When I was within reach, he pulled me down so my head was on his thigh. His fingers went into my hair, and I closed my eyes.

With the soothing gesture, my body slowly began to relax as I forced one breath in at a time. I closed my eyes to try and let in the comforting assurance he was offering me. I kind of wanted the hug again. But I was too tired to move and ask for it.

When I opened my eyes, my face was pressed into Phynn's stomach. I'd apparently fallen asleep. Still, I didn't move for a while as I breathed in his scent. What was it – cherries? He was the cherries that were always lingering on Kaiser and Marley. But there was something else. Something that made my mouth water. Almonds. The combination together made me salivate. I smirked in amusement.

I glanced up to find Phynn watching me. A soft smile touched his lips. His hand was still in my hair, gently massaging my scalp and twisting in the strands.

"Feeling better?" he asked.

I nodded. "Thanks."

Phynn nodded. "What do I need to say to convince you to come home with me?"

I flinched and turned my face back down, pretending he didn't ask that as I buried my face in his stomach again. He chuckled, moving the hand I hadn't realized was on my shoulder down to rest on my ribs.

"I've been thinking," he said quietly. "And I think I understand why you're trying to do this alone. I'm not going to tell you I can even fathom what it feels like to-" I squeezed my eyes shut, tensing at the words that were coming next. But he didn't finish that sentence. He skirted around it instead. "I'm not going to tell you that I think a year is long enough to get over your pain, Terence. I don't think it is. But I do think it's time to let someone in. A therapist at the very least. If not a stranger, maybe Kaiser. Marley might be a little more level and the kind of calm that will help more, but Kaiser will help you get lost in him, holding you until all you can do is breathe him in."

It was like he knew that's what I'd been doing in my bed. I chuckled, shaking my head. "I don't want to talk about it."

"I won't make you."

"Nothing I say will bring them back," I whispered, feeling the sting of tears in my eyes. I forced a breath out and waited until the sensation settled. I needed a break from crying. My head was going to explode.

"No," Phynn agreed when I relaxed again. "And I imagine you tried everything."

I laughed bitterly, nodding. "Every plea, promise, and curse. Yes. I tried."

Phynn gently pushed me off him and I rolled until I could sit. He headed for my bathroom again and I thought he was going to use the toilet. But after a minute of cabinets opening, he returned with a bottle of pain reliever.

Picking up my water and handing it to me, he offered me two capsules.

"It's like you're in my head," I muttered.

"I'm both trying to be and trying not to be," he agreed, offering me a smile.

I swallowed the capsules and then downed the rest of my water. Phynn left the bottle of pain relievers on the table and pulled another bottle of water from the fridge before retaking his seat and pulling my head back into his lap.

Rolling back into him, I closed my eyes and let his scent fill me this time. There were only little hints of Kaiser on him. Subtle notes of Marley. A much stronger residue of a third scent – crisp ice. That must be Adrian.

He went back to rubbing my head and I let my mind remain blank as I lay there. A blanket fell on me, and Phynn arranged it so that it was covering most of my body. It was only then that I realized I'd been shivering.

And when he started to purr, I closed my eyes and fell asleep.

There were no dreams this time. I just floated in the peace and comfort that I knew was Phynn. I could smell him. Feel him around me. It was almost as if he were keeping away my pain.

Not by telling me it wasn't warranted but agreeing that it was justified. Necessary. Completely and totally real and deserved. He was telling me it was okay to feel this awful. It was acceptable to not have healed. He didn't think less of me nor was he angry that I'd run from them the way I did. And neither would Kaiser and Marley be.

When I awoke, Phynn's fingers were still moving rhythmically in my hair. He was still purring. And the sun was peeking through the curtains.

He'd stayed with me all night. It was the first night I'd slept in days.

I shifted so I could look up. His head was back, and his eyes closed. His phone was on the armrest. When I continued to look at him, a smile touched his lips and his eyes cracked open.

I hadn't looked too closely before, but Phynn was a hot man. There was a couple days' worth of scruff over his face that gave him an unpolished look. His light golden hair looked like there was always sun glowing in it. And even through the slit of his eyes, they were bright blue. His body was lean and strong. And his damn fingers were magic.

"You didn't have to stay," I said.

The touch of a smile turned into a smirk. "You weren't going to let me back in if I left. I'm still hoping to convince you to come home with me."

"Mm," I answered but I kept my focus on his face. Not just because he was gorgeous, but because I barely knew this man. Watching his reaction was a good way to start learning him. "I haven't slept in days."

He nodded, picking his head up to look down at me more fully. "You slept soundly last night."

Sighing, I pushed myself up and rubbed my head. My headache was back. Maybe that's why I woke up. I was tired enough that I could probably sleep the entire day away.

As if he read my mind again, Phynn moved from the couch to bring me more pain relievers. I smiled, shaking my head, and plucked the bottle of water from the floor to swallow them with. When he joined me on the couch again, it wasn't by sitting back in the corner. He sat behind me, his back leg bent up along my side, and wrapped his arms around my chest.

I closed my eyes as it both opened the wound wider but also helped stitch it together. As if he were spreading the two edges to clean it before pulling them close to run a thread through them.

I'd had enough of crying. Everything about me ached and protested at the prospect of another sobbing fit. So, I let all thoughts slide away and I leaned back into him, letting my head fall onto his shoulder.

My body obeyed in that I didn't start crying. But I wasn't anywhere near done grieving. I shook like I was in withdrawal. My breaths were short and labored.

Phynn hugged me until I was still and breathing regularly again. He didn't let me go until I moved away. He ran his fingers through my hair as he got up.

"Shower," he told me, and I watched him with a brow raised as he entered my kitchen and started looking through my fridge and cabinets. When I didn't move, he looked at me over his shoulder. Waiting for me to challenge him.

I had absolutely no desire to do so. Pulling myself to my feet, I watched him on my way by, giving him a shrewd look as I went. I didn't miss his smirk of satisfaction.

I stripped at the bathroom door and tossed my clothes into the hamper. Shutting the door behind me, I turned the water on as I stepped into the shower. The shock of icy water made me shiver until it heated up. Then I stood there as the water rushed over me.

Everything in me was exhausted, including my mind. Even little tendrils of sadness couldn't take root right now. There wasn't enough strength to hold onto it.

When I opened my eyes, I was looking at Kaiser's body wash and shampoo. Smiling, I used them both instead of my own before getting out of the shower. I used his towel, too. It still smelled like him, like so many other surfaces in my house. Marley hadn't been here enough to truly leave her mark behind. It would come in time.

I stepped out with the towel around my waist. A last minute effort to remember to be modest. Despite sharing my personal demons with him, Phynn was still essentially a stranger. I dressed and returned to the kitchen in time to find him setting a plate with eggs, bacon, and toast on the table.

He looked at me, ready for me to challenge him on this, too. He'd find that I wasn't much for challenging. If he really wanted the bigger bark, he could have it. I had no energy or interest in that battle.

Convinced I was eating, he rounded behind me, heading for the bathroom as he pulled his shirt over his head. "You're welcome to whatever clothes," I told him on the way there. "Kaiser's are in the top right drawer."

I wasn't looking at him, but I was sure I felt his smile.

I had the dishes done when the shower shut off. I'd downed two bottles of juice and was working on another bottle of water when Phynn stepped out in my clothes. I watched him as he neared me.

"Kaiser's are too small," he said.

I nodded, continuing to watch him as I finished my water. When I set the bottle down, Phynn closed the distance. He stood close enough that I felt his body heat brush against me as he stared into my eyes.

"Are you going to be angry if I demand you come home with me?" he asked.

I laughed, bowing my head. Since he was standing with a complete disregard for personal space, my forehead landed on his shoulder. He brought his arms up, but this time his hug wasn't harsh. It was light and lulling. Just like the rest of him.

"If I go with you, they're going to need an explanation," I said.

"Yes," he agreed.

"That means I'm going to need to talk about it," I pointed out.

"Yes," he agreed again.

"I don't particularly want to talk about it."

"I know. But Kaiser and Marley deserve to know. I don't want to lay this burden on you, Terence, because you don't need nor deserve it. But they're devastated at your silence and absence. I think if they know why, their suffering will be alleviated, and you can take the time you need without them bothering you."

"They don't bother me," I said quietly.

"They've been here no less than half a dozen times apiece. I have no idea how many texts Kaiser has sent."

I released a breath. He was right in that they didn't deserve to suffer with me. Knowing that they were only added to the mountain of pain inside.

"Come with me. Tell them. I'll let you sleep again, and I'll make sure it's as peaceful as I can make it. And then if you want to leave, you're welcome to. I'll drive you back myself."

"I don't suppose you could just let them read the newspaper," I suggested. I still hadn't read the article. The headline and grainy black and white image had been more than enough.

"If that's what you want, then yes. I'd really still like you to come with me."

"Are you ordering me?"

Phynn paused. The truth was, I needed to tell them. I wanted to do as he suggested. But I wasn't strong enough to make that decision on my own. I swallowed, waiting for Phynn to answer. His fingers dug into my back as he pulled me more securely to him and I knew he'd figured me out.

"Yes," he said, his voice low. And the next words held his bark. "You're coming home with me and telling my pack what happened to yours. Then you will sleep. From there, we'll revisit your next course of action, Terence. Understand?"

I let his words settle over me, feeling the way his demand made me shiver in both irritation and relief. I shuddered, took a deep breath, and nodded.

"Yes, alpha," I murmured, a smile touching my lips as the words left my mouth.

I forgot how much I enjoyed saying those words.

CHAPTER THIRTY-SIX

Adrian

Phynn's sudden departure and following silence had me a little nervous. What had he found? And how was he going to reach Terence who refused to answer his door or phone? Hours passed without a word.

Marley and Kaiser hadn't noticed him missing yet. He was still very much present in the bonds, sending us all a calm reassurance and warm affection. Nothing had changed. Not even when he figured out what was bothering Terence.

His text came late in the evening. A link to an article and his words 'don't say anything to them, please.' The newspaper article had me gagging in horror. A cold fell over my skin, making me shiver as tears stung my eyes. The thought of losing all of my pack and living without them was unbearable. No wonder Terence was such a wreck.

And now I felt like the lowest form of scum for being so angry at him.

Well, I was justified in my irritation for him. This was my

omega and beta we're talking about. But I was wrong to think that he just needed to pull his head out of his ass. This wasn't a drive by night type of trauma. There was nothing worse than this.

I sent Phynn back a message that said nothing more than 'take your time' because I couldn't find any other words to say. And then I split the night between wrapping around Kaiser and Marley since they chose to be in separate rooms. I almost demanded they choose one so I could have them both within reach. After the article, it was hard not to have my whole pack close.

It was morning when Phynn called. I almost dove for the phone.

"He's in the shower," Phynn said, the muffled sound of grease frying in the background. "I'm going to try and push him to come home with me. Whatever progress he'd made in the last month or so has been undone in these last few days. He's falling further into a black hole."

"Phynn, I-"

"I know, Adrian," Phynn said quietly. "We've actually spoken very little. Every time I think I find something sympathetic or assuring, I just imagine if that would be enough for me to hear. If I'd appreciate it or if it would upset me more. At this point, I think everything would upset me further, so I don't say anything."

"Bring him here," I told him. "Let me know when you convince him. Those two will need a shower."

Phynn chuckled. "So do I."

I smiled and closed my eyes. "Hurry home."

Phynn hung up and I stood there staring at the back of my eyelids for another minute. I'd never concentrated too much on the idea that I could lose one of my packmates. But now that's all that I could think about since reading the article. I wanted to wrap them in bubble wrap and lock them in padded rooms to keep them safe. Phynn being out of the house right now where literally anything could happen was making it impossible for me to find my calm.

His text came twenty minutes later. They were on their way. I sighed in relief before moving to the stairs. I pushed open the nest door to find Kaiser staring blankly at nothing.

"Come here," I told him.

His gaze shifted to me, his pupils narrowing to focus. He blinked slowly and gave me a pout, but he didn't move.

"It wasn't a suggestion, Kaiser."

I didn't bark either time but this time he flinched. "But Adrian-"

"Up," I said, still without bark.

Kaiser looked like I'd spanked him and not in the way he liked. He struggled to get to his hands and knees, pausing there for a minute before pushing himself up. He moved into my outstretched arm, and I pulled him through the door and down the hall.

Marley had likewise not moved since last I left her. She was still curled in the chair looking out the window. Her attention shifted to us when I pulled Kaiser in. I didn't make her get up but took her chin in my hand to assure she was paying attention.

"Phynn's on his way home," I told them, feeling confusion flutter through both of them. "He's bringing Terence."

Identical looks crossed their faces. Surprise. Hope. Anxiety.

"Shower and be downstairs in ten minutes. Understand?"

A chorus of 'Yes, alpha' met my ears and they both moved away. My body was still covered in goose flesh, the chills not stopping. A new dread settled within the pit of my stomach. Anything could take them from me.

I closed my eyes as I heard Marley's shower turn on. Taking a deep breath, I eased calm through me. A constant state of near panic was not going to prevent accidents and it would end up driving me insane.

If for no other reason than to try and give strength to Terence when he arrived, I needed to get my shit together and my new anxiety under control. Besides, my pack *did not* need to feel that as a constant backdrop through our bonds. That wouldn't be healthy for any of us.

Back in the kitchen, I looked around for something to do. No one had eaten in this house for twenty-four hours, but I couldn't imagine they'd eat anything right now. I was sure, based on the sounds in the background, that Phynn had made Terence eat before coming. I'd wager a guess that he'd had a few bites while preparing Terence food, too.

Maybe tea? Coffee? Juice?

It wasn't long before Kaiser and Marley were downstairs, both standing in the entry to the kitchen and watching me. Their stares were heavy, and I didn't meet them right away.

"Adrian?" Marley asked.

With a deep, steadying breath, I faced them, hoping that I was keeping my fear under wraps. They were both looking at me with nervousness. I held my arms out for them, and they tucked themselves under, one on each side of me. It was almost twin time as they simultaneously nuzzled their faces into my chest and neck.

"It's going to be okay," I told them. For us, it would be. I wasn't speaking for Terence.

"Phynn is really bringing Terence here?" Kaiser asked.

I nodded as the front door opened on the other side of the house. The three of us looked in that direction. Before they could move away, I gripped their arms. "Listen to me," I said quietly. "I need you both to have a seat in the den and only after Terence says it's okay can you go to him. Understand?"

They looked at me with renewed anxiety.

"Understand?" I pressed.

"Yes, alpha," Marley whispered.

I didn't receive words from Kaiser, but he nodded, his emotions bright in his eyes.

"Good. Go to the den. We'll be right there."

I let them go and watched as they moved down the hall. When I was convinced they'd done as I said, I turned towards the foyer.

Terence was leaning against the front door with his eyes closed, Phynn's hands on his chest. He was murmuring something to Terence in words too low for me to discern. Terence nodded subtly. If it hadn't been for the distress on Terence's face, I'd have thought it looked almost intimate.

"Time to go in," Phynn said, a subtle note of command in his voice.

I raised my brow in curiosity as he leaned back from Terence, waiting for the other man to open his eyes. Terence did and Phynn held his hand out. Terence pressed his lips together but grabbed Phynn's hand before he could take it back.

Ah. Terence didn't want to do it alone. He wanted to be told to.

Otherwise, he'd probably not do it at all. Yet, I watched as Phynn gently pulled him along, Terence's breathing eased, even as his shoulders tensed for what was to come.

Phynn met my gaze, giving me a half smile. He stopped at my side and Terence finally took note of me. He swallowed and I did the same. What was I supposed to say? Would anything I say be comforting?

"Terence has something to tell us," Phynn said, removing the option from me.

I relaxed a little. Putting it off for ten minutes was better than trying to come up with something now and putting my foot in my mouth.

"Den," I answered quietly, turning to lead the way.

Kaiser and Marley were sitting ramrod straight on the hassock. Kaiser's eyes widened in alarm when Terence walked in being guided by Phynn. Marley's expression fell into commiseration.

Phynn brought Terence to the couch and sat with him, keeping close so Terence was almost in his lap. He buried his fingers in the back of Terence's hair, purring softly. I watched, almost fascinated, as Terence fought to keep his composure against the pressure of having to say the words out loud.

When minutes went by and he didn't speak, I joined them on the couch, mirroring Phynn. To my surprise, Terence turned his face against mine and leaned in. He was trembling. My instincts were to wrap around him and purr, trying to lend him my strength and comfort. When I flickered my eyes to Phynn, he nodded, so I did just what my alpha nature was telling me to do.

Terence relieved a breath and buried his face into my neck. I could almost physically feel his pain seep into me.

"Do you want me to tell them?" Phynn asked gently.

Terence shook his head. A minute later, he shifted enough to look at Kaiser and Marley. I didn't need to look to see that they would both have tears in their eyes to see Terence like this. Even if they didn't know the details, they could see Terence's pain.

"I had a pack before I moved to Ocean City," Terence whispered. "Three alphas and two betas. A year ago-" His words cut off on a choke as tears fell. He took several breaths before he could force the words out. "A year ago, I lost them all in a car accident. All five of them."

A sob broke free and he closed his eyes as it overtook him. He shook as he tried to hold himself together. I met Phynn's eyes over Terence's head in a reflection of what he was likely seeing in me. Sharing an unimaginable pain.

On the hassock, Marley's quiet tears mingled with Terence's. Kaiser stared, frozen, as tears streaked down his cheeks. His lips kept moving as if he were trying to find the right words to say.

When Terence shifted, I picked my head up. He looked at Kaiser, giving him the smallest hint of a nod. That was all our omega needed. He dove into Terence's lap and wrapped around him as tightly as he could.

Terence settled an arm around him before looking at Marley. Never forgetting our beta. Wanting her close, too. Marley was slower to join, settling herself within Phynn and Terence's laps. Terence wrapped his arms around both of them. Still an alpha holding close those who had his love. As if they were the ones needing comfort.

Then he leaned into me again, turning so his face was in my neck. I tried to bury the urge to rub my skin on his. Leaving our scent on someone wasn't just a means of claim. Not only an advertisement to let others know that they already belonged to an alpha.

It was also a means of comfort. An alpha's scent will always settle their omega and beta's anxiety in times of stress and pain and fear. It was an innate hunger. Just as it was an instinctive craving of an alpha to deliver that comfort to them.

But Terence wasn't my omega or my beta. He wasn't even my alpha. But when he tried to shift into me further, I lightly rubbed my cheek against him. Not enough to truly scent mark him. But still trying to offer him some form of comfort.

When I stopped, he pushed against me further, so I continued. Slowly, he relaxed into me, though his grip on

Kaiser and Marley didn't loosen. No one spoke for a long time as we tried to heal this broken alpha.

"Remember what I said came next?" Phynn asked quietly.

Terence nodded. "Sleep."

Phynn smiled. "Good. You want to curl up on the couch or upstairs in a room?"

Terence didn't answer. After a minute, he peeked out to meet Phynn's eyes. Phynn nodded and slowly extracted himself, gently pulling Marley with him. "Get up, alpha. We're going upstairs."

Kaiser picked his head up and looked at Phynn with horror. He just barked at Terence, even with his voice low and soothing. I rested my hand on Kaiser's shoulder, trying to reassure him that it was okay. Whatever dynamics they'd worked out back at Terence's house were carrying over here.

Terence didn't answer verbally but nodded. And being the good alpha he was, he pulled Kaiser to him and kissed him softly, telling him it was okay, too. He was choosing to listen.

Kaiser got up, holding his hands out to Terence. Terence gave him a tired smile and accepted his hands though he didn't pull on our omega at all. Phynn led the way upstairs and into Kaiser's room. I wasn't surprised. Terence and Kaiser were already developing a deep bond. Being surrounded by his omega's scent would help to settle him.

Phynn looked at me and then to the giant puff chair. Before I sat, he pulled at my shirt and then my pants. Taking the hint, I stripped to my underwear and arranged myself in the chair. Then he did the same to Terence.

Terence was slower to comply but followed Phynn's nonverbal instructions, stripping to his boxer briefs. Phynn nudged him to the chair before pulling at Kaiser's clothes, too. I turned away from our omega to let Terence settle into me. He was a big man, but somehow managed to curl at my side so his face was in my neck.

And then Kaiser was crawling on our laps, settling in, too. It wasn't long before a mostly naked Phynn and Marley joined us with a couple blankets.

Though it was still early in the morning, not yet ten, we settled in and hunkered down to let Terence sleep. Terence fidgeted until I rubbed my cheek against him, and Phynn and I both began to purr. Kaiser and Marley clung to Terence, and Terence held them in return just as tightly. As if they were the ones hurting.

As if they were his deceased pack and he was getting in one last cuddle.

The thought brought tears to my eyes again and though I concentrated on not interrupting my purr or stopping brushing my skin against his, I let my tears fall at last. I told myself I was crying for Terence. And maybe I was.

But I was also shedding tears for a possibility that I hoped would never come.

CHAPTER THIRTY-SEVEN

Marley

I'd never experienced true grief or sorrow, but I was so heartbroken and devastated for Terence that I was rendered speechless. There was nothing more horrible than this. I couldn't imagine what he was going through.

For an entire year, he'd been suffering with this pain. Alone.

I knew what he was going through from a scientific perspective. I'd been fascinated by psychology and the way our minds work. Especially where designations were concerned. But within that study, we went through the whole episode that was the trauma of loss and severe grief.

He wasn't just upset about his pack. As the lone survivor, I was sure a lot of what he was experiencing was survivor's guilt. With his entire pack gone and him left behind, as the lone member of his pack, I couldn't fathom what blame his mind was laying on him.

All those times he'd told Kaiser he was a shit alpha. It broke me. He was a damn good one, even through the mental strain he was carrying. I was amazed by how normal a life he'd been able to lead for the past year. At least the past couple months that we'd known him.

Terence slept for six hours. The four of us never moved. My alphas never stopped purring. Kaiser didn't stop clinging to him, his grip never slacking. And I don't think I stopped shaking.

Even when he woke, the four of us didn't change how we lay with him. He'd slept like the dead, his arms tight around Kaiser and me. I hadn't realized his fingers were twined with Phynn's over my arm until he started to wake, and I felt Phynn's fingers flex in Terence's against my bare skin.

He pulled in a deep breath and held it. Kaiser's eyes opened, gazing into mine. When Terence released his breath, he sagged a little before twisting as if stretching.

"This is strangely a comfortable and uncomfortable chair," Terence murmured.

Kaiser grinned and looked up at him. "When you lay in it alone, it basically wraps you in a cocoon."

"Perfect for an omega. I see," Terence said.

Kaiser nodded. His smile softened as he studied Terence. There was a question on the tip of his tongue that he bit down. I thought it was probably going to be along the lines of 'are you okay?' The answer would be 'no,' of course, so he didn't ask.

Instead, the question he asked was, "Are you hungry? Thirsty?"

Terence's fond smile graced his lips and my stomach jumped. There was the alpha we knew peeking out.

He sighed. "I don't know. Am I?"

"Yes," Phynn answered when Kaiser looked at Terence confused. "Stay with Adrian. I'll make dinner and then you'll eat."

Kaiser eyed Phynn, squinting at his tone. There wasn't a bark in it but we both knew that was a tone we didn't argue with. The one that came before the bark.

But Terence nodded. "Okay, then I'm hungry."

His question had been for Phynn. I had no idea what to make of that.

Phynn nodded. He released Terence's hand where it rested on me and brushed his hair back. But that tender gliding of his fingers tangled into Terence's shaggy strands and tipped his head back until Terence was forced to meet his eyes.

Neither spoke. When Phynn nodded and released him, caressing the side of his face as he stood, I thought that maybe he was trying to read something in Terence's gaze. Terence watched him walk out with hooded eyes and a bemused smile before turning his attention back to Kaiser.

The look Kaiser was giving him made Terence grin and chuckled. "I don't want to think," he said quietly. "I'm letting a stronger alpha do that for me."

"You're the strongest alpha I know," Kaiser whispered, his voice slightly wobbly.

Terence smiled, letting his head fall back into Adrian. He didn't answer but he didn't need to for us to know he didn't agree.

"Do you need anything right now?" Adrian asked.

Terence shrugged and shook his head. "Just this. Maybe some purring."

Adrian smiled and started purring again. He adjusted into the big chair so that he was further tucked under Terence and Kaiser, bringing the three of us more squarely on his chest. If we were any more horizontal, this would be a pile. Terence and Kaiser on top of Adrian, and me perched on top of them.

But it was somewhat comical because Terence was a big

man. Neither of my alphas were small, but Terence was a tank from his endless hours of working out.

It finally clicked why he spent so long at the gym. Trying to chase away any kind of thoughts at all. Concentrate on something mundane and fill his body with a different kind of pain and exhaustion. One that left him too drained to truly have time to think.

My heart swelled with an aching again and I closed my eyes. Terence's fingers moved to my hair, and he slowly started twirling it around. I sighed, shifting so I could nuzzle in further. I couldn't offer the comfort of an alpha with a purr. Nor the soft, yielding heart of an omega. But somehow, the alphas that were in my life still treated me like I was special to them. Both like an omega and also with my own kind of distinct treatment.

Even without the constant praise and low-key envy from my family, I knew how lucky I was to have this. We remained where we were while the increasing aroma from the kitchen drifted upstairs with the backdrop of Adrian's purr. Terence felt calm. His scent had regulated to his normal yummy toasted coconut and mineral oil.

Phynn called us downstairs while I was in the middle of trying to memorize each slight change in the note of Terence's scent. I sighed as I stood, and I abruptly remembered that we were all almost naked. I flushed but the men didn't seem to notice at all.

Actually, that's not entirely accurate. Kaiser took a long look at all three of us, his cock thickening in his shorts and an appreciative smile touching his lips. I know Adrian at least didn't pay it attention since our omega was always slightly on. Terence might have been too mentally distracted to notice.

We didn't dress and it took my modest ass a few minutes to accept that I was walking around with my pack and the alpha I was dating in the equivalent of a bikini before the flush would go away.

I wasn't sure how Phynn had managed to throw together the feast he had. There were baked potato wedges with ham and cheese melted on them. Two pasta salads. A whole slew of roasted vegetables. Fresh biscuits. And braised beef tips. And I didn't miss the slightly sweet hint of sugar in the air. That meant there was dessert.

Adrian rested his hands on my shoulders and kissed the back of my head before pushing me forward to take my plate. Phynn and Adrian always dished plates and handed them out. It was a toss-up as to whether they made me take mine first or Kaiser. Whenever I think I've figured out why they choose one of us, it's disproved at the next meal.

Phynn kissed my cheek as I took my plate from him and headed for the nook. Adrian slapped Kaiser's ass to make him move forward. Kaiser narrowed his eyes as he took a few steps closer to Phynn as our alpha finished loading a plate for him.

I watched shamelessly as Kaiser walked over, his gorgeous lean body on display and the outline of a partially hard, generous cock in his tight shorts. He scooched on the bench next to me and kissed my cheek as Phynn had. He was feeling better now that Terence was here. So was I. Even despite the truth of his life having been devastating.

Adrian coaxed Terence towards Phynn next as Phynn piled food onto another plate and handed it to Terence. He didn't let the plate go until Terence met his gaze. A smile touched his lips and Phynn released him.

He sat next to Kaiser, looking beyond him to me for a minute. I offered him a reassuring smile. Terence sighed and sat back, looking down at his full plate. Emphasis on full. If he hadn't eaten much in the last handful of days, I was pretty sure that was too much food.

Our alphas joined us a minute later, Phynn moving in to sit next to me and Adrian taking the outside. It was always our alphas on the outside. I loved being boxed in by them.

We ate quietly. I was sure, like me, my pack was trying to find a topic that might be appropriate. Was talking about books too mundane a subject and silly to bring up in the shadow of learning that Terence's pack had been killed a year ago? Was the current political state too serious?

In the end, no one spoke more than to compliment Phynn's food. Adrian returned the dishes to the dishwasher while Phynn brought over chocolate mousse. Then the five of us put away leftovers and straightened the kitchen again.

That brought Phynn to step inside Terence's personal space. Terence didn't seem to mind as he stood there watching Phynn. He was sad. His shoulders dropped slightly. It felt like a cloud surrounded him.

"Are you ready to make a decision or no?" Phynn asked, his voice quiet and gentle.

The corner of Terence's lips lifted in answer. Phynn nodded. "You understand that I'm telling you what I think you need when you defer, right? It's not necessarily based on what I or my pack want."

Terence nodded, a subtle bob of his head.

"Okay, choose a room and take a shower. Relax for a bit. Then we'll regroup in Kaiser's room to sleep. And if you're not ready for sleep, Marley will read to us. Understand?"

Once more, Phynn's tone was that which fell just before his bark entered his voice. I was surprised when Terence said, "Yes, alpha," in response. A thrill went through me at his words. It was echoed by a sudden burst of arousal from Kaiser within our bonds; the air beginning to become saturated by his perfume. I tried to hide my smirk.

"Take your time in the shower. I'm going back to your place to grab you some clothes."

This time, he left the statement open for argument. But Terence nodded, his gaze shifting to Kaiser as his head tilted. Responding to Kaiser's perfume, no doubt. Kaiser flushed, covering his face. "Sorry."

Terence chuckled, bowing his head and taking a deep breath.

"Go," Phynn said, stepping away from Terence after he touched his arm softly.

Terence nodded and walked towards the stairs while the four of us watched him. I wondered what room he would choose. Which shower. I was betting it would be Kaiser's. An alpha will always find comfort in their omega's scent. And Kaiser was basically his, too.

When he had disappeared, Phynn headed for the door before stopping and looking down at his lack of attire. He glanced back at us with amusement. "Get dressed, Mar. You're coming with me."

I nodded and rushed for the stairs. I was surprised when it was Adrian's shower on and paused to consider this. Phynn stepped up behind me and kissed the back of my head. "I'm betting one of two reasons," he said, answering my unasked question. "Either Adrian's scent and/or presence reminds him of someone in his pack and he's taking comfort in that. Or he knows Adrian is our head of house, either by your conversations with him or by instinct, and is taking comfort in that. Maybe a combination."

"Maybe he just likes Adrian's scent," I stated, looking up at him over my shoulder.

"It is a sexy scent," Phynn agreed, nipping at my nose. "Dress, love. Let's go and get back."

I threw on a dress and slipped into sandals since it was the quickest assemblance of garments I needed. Phynn had thrown on shorts and a shirt with sneakers and met me in the hall. The drive felt long but I found Terence's gym bag and started piling clothes in it before pulling his toiletries. The drive back was shorter.

Phynn took his bag upstairs where Adrian's shower was still running, and I went to Kaiser's room where he was readjusting the bedding. Moving a pillow or cushion somewhere and then moving it again. It was a nervous tick more than a true need to nest. I stopped behind him, crawling on the bed until I could pull him against my chest.

Kaiser sighed. "He's going to be in my bed. Mar, I'm a fucking *omega*. Despite knowing how broken up he is inside, my body doesn't respond like that. It's not taking a hint. He said 'yes, alpha' and I was ready to jump him right then."

There was a plea in his voice. I hugged him to me and rubbed my cheek to his. It didn't have the same effect as when one of our alphas did it, but he settled a little bit. "We don't have time for me to ride you until it's out of your system," I teased.

"Hmph," he said, glaring at me.

I grinned. "Honey, you'll be alright. You're not a slave to your biology. You've always been the first to remind us of that."

"I know. But recently, I've let myself be the omega," he whispered. "I'm having a hard time pulling it back."

"Adrian and Phynn will be here, too. They won't have any trouble making sure you behave yourself."

Kaiser smiled.

We both turned when the three alphas walked in, still just in underwear. I swear, we were very lucky, Kaiser and I. There were never three more striking men that had cocks with knots to envy.

Terence glanced around the room before his gaze settled on

the bed. His lips ticked up into a half smile as Kaiser looked at him with anxiety. He stopped at the edge and held his hand out to Kaiser. "Come here," he whispered.

Kaiser moved from my hold and stopped at the edge, just shy of touching Terence. There was a whine in his throat that he was trying to keep in. "Are you nervous?" Terence asked.

Kaiser nodded. "I just- I want to be good but I'm just- having a hard time." His face reddened as he looked down.

Terence drew his finger up Kaiser's stomach, his chest, until he could tilt Kaiser's face to him. "You're a perfect omega," he whispered. "But you don't have to be an omega right now if you don't want to."

"I don't want to," he said. "But I think that maybe you need me to."

"I just need you to be here, Kaiser. I need to feel your heart and smell your perfume. That's all I need."

Kaiser nodded. He lost one of his many struggles and quickly closed the distance between him and Terence, wrapping his arms around Terence's neck and pressing his lips to his alpha's. Terence was his alpha, even if it wasn't an official thing. There was no doubt about that.

Terence sighed, leaning in to kiss him a little deeper before drawing his mouth back. And then took Kaiser's lip in his teeth when Kaiser tried to apologize. "Hush," he whispered. "Get in bed with me."

A whine slipped from his lips, and he flinched. This time he didn't apologize, but only because his jaw was tense as he forced his mouth shut. He moved into the bed, getting closer to where I was still kneeling, and Terence followed. They curled together and I watched with happy contentment.

Terence's eyes moved to our alphas, searching for Phynn this time instead of Adrian. Phynn nodded at the silent request and moved behind Terence where he could spoon the larger alpha.

Adrian climbed in behind me, bringing me down at Kaiser's back. We laid in silence as Phynn's quiet purr filled the room. Terence's hand covered mine where it laid on Kaiser's hip and he twisted our fingers together. I smiled, closing my eyes.

I hoped he'd never leave.

CHAPTER THIRTY-EIGHT

Terence

"Get up," Foster murmured in my ear.

I grumbled as I rolled over. "What's wrong?"

"Nothing. Get up. Come with me."

Cracking my eyes, I peered at him in the dark. But once my eyes were open even that much, other senses came back to me. Light flashed outside, followed by a rumble of thunder. Heavy rain splattered the tin roof. It was a lulling feeling and I wanted to do anything but get up.

There wasn't urgency in his face. Just the touch of a smile as he implored me to get out of bed. In the middle of the night. I was pretty sure I'd been having a good dream.

The smile grew as I threw my covers back and swung my legs over the side. Ronan and Miles were sound asleep in the middle of the bed, draped over each other. I made sure they remained blanketed before following Foster from the room.

He pulled me into Ronan's empty room before turning to me with a playful smile. "Remember the day we met?" he asked, his voice low so it wouldn't carry. With all the noise the rainstorm made, I'd be surprised if anyone heard him talking in a normal tone.

"Yes, you stalker," I answered.

Foster grinned and turned to continue walking through the room. Two of the bedrooms in the house had small balconies and we gave them to our betas. The tiny attic room had a widow's walk out one of the windows, but that was dedicated for a nest should we need it. Right now, it was just an empty space.

He stopped at the door and unlocked it. Waiting until I stopped at his side, Foster pulled open one of the doors and pulled me into the pouring rain. I glared at him, shutting the door behind me.

Foster wasn't generally the romantic type. He enjoyed leaving thoughtful gifts around, pretending that it wasn't any big deal and that they'd been purchased on a whim instead of planning. We knew that to be false. He put a lot of dedication into gifting us little things.

He pulled me to him, wrapping his arms under mine and around my waist. His lips on mine were warm. Overhead, lightning streaked across the sky, followed by thunder so loud I could feel it in my bones. But with Foster kissing me, I barely noted it.

His kiss was wet and languid, full of tongue and sensuality. I wrapped my arms around him, pressing fully against his wet flesh.

"I think of you every time it rains," Foster murmured. "And I swear, whenever I'm down, the skies open and all I can do is smile. Because I have you. And with you came a pack I'd do anything for."

Part of me wanted to tease him on the sentimentality of it because it was so out of nature for him. But I didn't. I loved this little confession.

"Love you, too, alpha," I said against his lips.
"More than life," he answered.

I AWOKE GASPING, looking around frantically to figure out my surroundings. The room was too big. Too dark. Too open.

Jerking from the bed, I stumbled to the closest door as bile rose in my throat. Tears stung my eyes as I tried to take a breath. There was something on my chest. Something heavy and sharp. Something that filled my stomach with lead, making me gag.

Falling to the floor in front of the toilet, I leaned in and dry heaved until the motion nearly made me sick all on its own. My stomach muscles protested until I fell back on the tile floor, shivering and panting.

I hadn't realized I wasn't alone until a wet hand landed gently on my bare shoulder. I jumped, looking above me into Adrian's warm brown eyes. His hair dripping on me was a triggering moment as it fell on me like rain. I lurched forward again and dry heaved some more.

Adrian ran his fingers through the back of my hair, scratching gently on my scalp. I was still shaking violently. As my stomach settled into the knot of black misery I had grown accustomed to, I leaned back again, my back hitting Adrian's legs.

He gave me a minute to catch my breath before forcing me to regain my feet. I didn't fight him. I didn't have the strength to. He pulled me towards the shower. Only then did I realize it was still running and the room was filled with steam.

"Sorry," I whispered.

"Don't be," he answered.

His fingers slipped to my underwear and pushed at them,

indicating he wanted me to take them off. I complied, nearly tripping as they circled my ankles. Then he pulled me into the steaming hot water.

He moved behind me, wrapping his arms around my chest and leaning his cheek against mine, his chest to my back. In his tight embrace with the steam of the scalding water falling on me, I leaned my head back to try and hold myself together.

Minutes passed. Maybe a lot of them.

"Nightmare?" Adrian asked.

I shook my head. "Just memories," I whispered. "Little moments that I might never have thought about as being important. Or damning."

Adrian didn't answer. He remained in the shower with me, and I used his strength to hold me up. Otherwise, I was sure I'd have been on my knees, still trying to vomit my stomach up. He washed my hair, but then we stood there. Waiting until I was in one piece.

Finally, I nodded. "I'm good," I told him, picking my head up and opening my eyes. "Thanks."

He nodded, reaching around me to shut the water off. He handed me a towel after he stepped out. I dried and meandered back into Kaiser's room. Phynn and Marley had packed me a variety of clothing. I was glad to see there were gym clothes in there. Not that I thought I was up to the gym right now but because they were the more comfortable option.

Adrian had left the room, likely going to his own to get dressed. I stepped into the hall and almost plowed Marley over. She giggled as I caught her. The sound of her laugh drew a smile to my lips.

"Good morning," she said. "Where you headed?"

I shrugged.

Marley took my hand and pulled me towards the stairs. I

anticipated she was bringing me to the kitchen but I found myself drawn outside instead.

The backyard was beautifully landscaped. Simple yet still elegant. It was alive with greenery and only a light smattering of flowers. There was a little stream that wound its way through the yard, little bridges crossing it as it snaked around the property.

She brought me to a covered patio, all four sides draped with viney flowers that provided a curtain of delicious scents. I closed my eyes as we stepped in, just to let its soothing scents fill me.

"I like it out here when I need to clear my head," she said, pulling me towards the bench.

I sat, tugging her into my lap. Marley smiled at me, a touch of shyness on her face. Leaning my head against hers, I sighed. Our relationship had only just begun. I'd been seeing Kaiser longer so having Marley see me like this was rough. Kaiser was bad enough but Marley-

And then there were their alphas who were basically scraping me off the ground. Talk about horrifying. And yet, I needed this. Aside from the last little memory that surfaced while asleep, I'd slept a whole lot of hours since Phynn had come to my apartment a day and a half ago.

We weren't on the patio long before the rest of Marley's pack found us. Kaiser grinned widely before sitting on the ground in front of us, crossing his legs under him and looking up at me. Adrian sat with him, but Phynn sat on the bench next to Marley and me.

He crowded in, one of his legs bent and the other practically over mine as he got close. His hand went into the back of my hair as he pressed his lips, mouth open to my skin, right in front of my ear.

I closed my eyes for a minute, waiting for whatever it was

he was going to drop on me. It didn't come until I relaxed and leaned into his touch. His inviting scent. The security of his alpha pheromones.

His voice was calm, even, and quiet when he spoke. "It seems to me that as long as you're not alone, you tend to be okay. But as soon as you're left by yourself, you allow the memories to seep back in. Memories that aren't bad but should be good. Am I close?"

I hadn't thought about it in these terms, but he was completely accurate. I nodded.

"I want you to try something that you might find a little difficult at first but that I think will help in the long run. You're running from your memories because they hurt, knowing that those who fill them are no longer here. I think there are two sides of you fighting. One that wants to remember, hang on to every moment you can recall, no matter how trivial. And one that wants to forget because remembering is too painful. I want you to remember them, Terence. Start by telling us about your pack."

I shuddered, squeezing my eyes closed. Phynn moved in closer, bringing me into his chest. My grip on Marley became tight enough that my arms ached. She didn't complain, though I tried to let her go.

"Take your time," Phynn whispered. "But I want you to tell me about each of them. Since I think giving you direction helps, let's start with something basic. Tell me how you met."

I swallowed, trembling in his arms. I didn't open my eyes as I let the memories fall over me like a shower.

"I met Miles when we were seven," I said quietly. "Even at seven, I hated sports, but my parents thought I needed to be a well-rounded alpha. They signed me up for baseball. Because I didn't want to let them down, I put some effort in. As much as a seven-year-old can, anyway. I was in the outfield when a fly ball came my way but several dozen feet to my right. I ran, keeping my eye on it as I did, and ran headfirst into a beta. We tumbled to the ground though I was already scrambling to my feet to get the ball. I retrieved it and headed back for the beta I'd run into, pulling him up and handing him the ball. He stared at me with wide eyes before throwing it. Miles and I were inseparable from that day on. He loved sports. I just enjoyed throwing balls.

"He lived close, so we were together all the time. He was my best friend. As we grew, the hunger of those wanting an alpha's attention became more prominent. It drove me crazy. I was nice. Miles always said too nice since my rejections never truly discouraged anyone. It wasn't until we were twelve that I found that if I claimed I already had a beta and wasn't looking for another, I could get myself off their radar for the most part. Conveniently, I had a beta that didn't mind pretending. We were still watched through a magnifying glass, just in case there was trouble in our relationship, and I might be in the market for a new beta."

Miles's smile flashed before my eyes, and I shivered. His smile had always given me chills. Beautiful. Innocent. Enthusiastic. Adoring.

"It wasn't until we were in our late teens that I realized that I'd been in love with him for years. When I told him, he just laughed at me, telling me 'it's about time you realize you love me.' I wasn't impressed with this reaction, nor was it the one I wanted. But his smile softened, and he said, 'Silly alpha. I've been in love with you since you handed me that baseball.'"

I smiled at the memory, remembering how his face had softened. Reading what I had always thought was just the devotion of my best friend for what it really was. My beta's love for me.

"I bit him that week. It was stupid and sloppy of me to, but we never regretted it. It was a handful of years later when we met Zack. We were both going to school and working. Ironically, he worked at a juice shop." I cracked my eyes to see Kaiser grin at me before closing them again. "Miles came home one day and said, 'There's an alpha that keeps coming around.' As you can imagine, I was not happy. I stormed in after class the next day, and sure enough, there was an alpha at the counter watching my beta. When I stopped at his side with my arms crossed over my chest, he looked at me with a sexy ass grin. 'Ah. You're the delicious coconut I smell on him,' he said. I shivered, glared, growled, and fucking Zack smiled all the more. I'm still not sure how it happened, and I used to try and figure it out often. But Zack was in our pack in short order. Hell, the second alpha *made* our pack."

He was the alpha we both needed. I didn't want to be an alpha. Okay. I guess that's not quite true. I didn't *not* want to be an alpha. I just didn't want to alpha. I wanted to be. To live. To enjoy my pack and provide for them. I didn't want to make decisions or keep my pack in line. Zack was good at all of it. And he had a pierced dick and pierced nipples. That was fun.

"Foster was next. I was doing Christmas shopping in the pouring rain. I'd already been to three stores and was grouchy because I was sopping wet. I'd spotted him at each place but until I glanced at him following me as I walked down the street, I hadn't realized it hadn't been a coincidence. I let it carry on for an hour until I finally had enough. The rain was making me irritable. I rounded a corner into an alley and waited for him. He stepped around and I slammed him to the wall with my hand around his neck. He grinned at me, not in the least threatened. He wanted to catch up. Wanted to be caught. When I let him go, frowning at him, he lunged. Spinning us around so I was against the wall as he shoved his tongue down my throat."

Fucker knew how to kiss, too. I'd been so damn irritated

that I was enjoying it. He tasted like mint. Addictive and beautifully refreshing.

"I brought the son of a bitch home with me that evening, making sure he knew that if my alpha and beta didn't like him, he was out. Jerk just shrugged. I was both glad and irritated when Zack and Miles liked him. Foster brought us Ronan shortly after. 'I have a friend you should meet.' By friend, he meant his own beta. I was pretty sure what made me love Foster was how he treated Ronan. Just like I doted on Miles."

Ronan and his obsession with social media. Making videos and gaining a rabid following. He'd just started being contacted by companies who wanted to pay him to subtly drop their products in the background.

"We were five for a long time. Emery showed up for employment at one of Zack's many endeavors. Zack was always buying businesses. Most of the time he'd turn them into something profitable before selling them again. This one, in particular, he was regretting almost as soon as he walked into the building. We were always sniggering because he kept coming home griping about us letting him buy that place. Emery was one of his first hires. But I don't think Emery was interested in the company once he met Zack. He kept showing up at our house for odd things. Eventually, we called him out and he grinned at us, shrugging. 'Yep. I don't give a fuck about the business. I want the pack attached to it,' he told us. Initially, I think Zack was just flattered. But Emery grew on all of us. He became pack within the year."

And thus, our pack was whole.

"We were happy," I whispered. "Spent as much time together as humanly possible. We didn't want more. We tossed around the idea of kids sometimes but as much as we wanted some, we didn't particularly want to hunt down someone we all liked. It seemed too daunting. Too impossible. And though we registered with the Pack Listing, we were realistic about it. There were thousands of packs and so few omegas. Sometimes we tossed around the idea of surrogacy as an answer but the conversations hadn't gotten serious."

I opened my eyes and looked down at Marley. She was still curled up in my lap, both of us tucked into Phynn's chest. My arms had relaxed to be reasonably snug around her instead of strangling. I touched under her chin, guiding her face up to look at me.

"They'd have loved you. All of them."

She smiled, leaning into my touch.

Looking over her head, I met Kaiser's eyes. "You really are the perfect omega. They'd have loved you, too. You'd have had them eating out of your hands in no time."

He beamed at me from where he was lounging in Adrian's lap.

"Actually, they'd have loved all of you. You're an amazing pack," I said, closing my eyes and leaning into Phynn once more as I let the memory of them fall around me like a warm, familiar blanket. I could almost smell them.

CHAPTER THIRTY-NINE

Terence

I'd been at Kaiser and Marley's home for almost a week. Phynn had been right – when I was alone, the world caught up to me and sorrow settled in. I'd been pushing it off for so long, the grief was no longer content to idle in the background. But it seemed when I was distracted with whatever or whoever was around me, it wasn't quite so heavy.

We continued to talk about my pack. Little things, but memories all the same. I didn't stop dreaming about them and I'd still wake up gasping and filled with a renewed grief. But I hadn't run from bed to heave over the toilet since my first morning waking up here.

I enjoyed talking about them. It felt good to tell someone. And they acted very interested, asking questions, and reveling in the sweetness of my memories with me.

I roamed from minute task to inconsequential assignment as the days wore on. I knew that someone, probably Phynn, had made several trips back to my apartment. More and more clothes showed up, as did food from my fridge and cabinets. My water bottles and protein shake mix. My toiletries.

Most of the living items ended up in Kaiser's room. An empty drawer mysteriously appeared with my clothing neatly folded inside. And then a section of his closet for some of my nicer things. My toothbrush was in his bathroom, lying in the drawer next to his. My shampoo combination was in the shower next to his.

Though I wore my own clothing and used my own toothbrush, the shampoo changed depending on which bathroom I ended up in. Generally speaking, that was Kaiser's. But I found I was pushed between his bed and Adrian's when the nights came on. I hadn't noticed until two days ago. I was pretty sure they were choosing depending on how rough the day had been for me. If I was surviving somewhat lowkey, I was fit enough for cuddling with Kaiser. If it had been stressful, I was nestled into Adrian's.

It was a pack affair when we went to sleep. Both alphas wrapped the three of us tightly in their embrace for the night. It was a strange kind of comfort. One I wasn't sure what to make of.

I was keenly aware I might have passed out from starvation at this point if Phynn hadn't demanded his way into my apartment. The same despair that had nearly made me roll over and crawl under a rock until death took me too when I found my pack was dead had come calling again.

But this time, it might have succeeded. I had no true debt to speak of. My business, as long as Nora was there, could run itself. Everything I had was on autopay and I didn't have much. Zack had owned Juice Me outright. I'd already liquidized everything else my pack had owned before moving to Ocean City. It was now sitting in various accounts all over the place.

Phynn had probably saved my life. I was thankful for it but

the guilt at that thought was heavy. My pack was gone. A very substantial part of me wanted to join them. And yet, I found that I no longer wanted to welcome that idea in my head. I wanted to live. I had a reason to live, even as guilt-ridden as the idea made me.

I felt Phynn's approach before he'd gotten close. I wasn't sure why or how. It was like the air was charged. His presence brushed against me. Maybe because he'd seen me at my lowest. He'd witnessed my breakdown when he came to my door and let me blubber all over him.

I tried not to think about it. Not that he'd seen me that way–that was bad enough–but that I'd basically soaked him with tears and snot. Crying was a disgusting habit full of body fluids that were not the fun kind.

"Hey," he said as he paused next to me.

Phynn always stood close, which was fine with me since I usually ended up leaning into him. I stood staring out the window at their backyard. It reminded me so much of the one I'd helped my pack design and yet very different. It was wide open with lots of nooks and greenery. Offering serenity and privacy. But that was where the similarities stopped.

Often, I'd look outside. There was nothing like the promise of a backyard and all it could expand into. A spa for the family. A garden to grow with. Safety and fun for children. It was the dream of a future that could hold any shape, bend to any mold.

He leaned against the wall with his hip, his chest barely touching my shoulder. I glanced his way with a smile touching my lips. He smelled like all things relaxing and filled with comfort. But there was an underlying element of seduction, too. Just a trace but that whiff was growing.

"Hi," I answered.

"You doing alright?"

For days, no one asked me how I was doing. I was sure they

all knew it wasn't well. But no longer was that question meant as a weighted question. How was I doing right this second compared to before they'd left me alone.

I nodded. Leaning in, I took a breath. Deeply inhaling his scent and filling my lungs with air.

The alphas didn't always touch me more than to let me lean into them. Even when leaning into them consisted of me sticking my nose in their neck to drown out the world. When one of them did touch me, it was usually Phynn.

As he did now, with his hand resting lightly on my lower back. It was comfort and it was heat. Not that he'd ever given me any indication that he was interested in anything other than my sanity and my attraction to his omega and beta.

Phynn leaned in, pressing his forehead to the side of my head. When I didn't react, he brought his other hand around to rest on my hip across my body, turning me sideways until he could push my back to the window. He didn't press against me fully or hard, just enough that I could almost consider it an embrace.

"You know, no one was ever trying to replace them," Phynn murmured in my ear. I shivered at the words and closed my eyes. "I understand your guilt, Terence. But you have to know that they wouldn't want you to spend the rest of your life alone. No pack would."

I took a deep shaking breath and held it. His hands moved to my hips again, resting gently against me as he stepped more firmly into me.

"Whatever you feel for anyone outside of your pack is not a betrayal to them."

That he was hitting everything on the head made me tense up. My breath came out in a rush as I closed my eyes.

"Do you understand that, or do you disagree?"

"It doesn't change how it feels," I answered.

"I know. But you understand it as truth, right?"

I nodded, though I wasn't sure I did. Maybe a part of me did. But not the part that was usually in the forefront of my mind.

"Would they want you to be alone to mourn over their absence for the rest of your life?"

I grimaced. "No."

I felt his smile against my skin. "Of course, they wouldn't."

His lips moved to my jaw, and I finally picked up my hands. For a moment, there was a bit of panic when I didn't know where to touch him. Fuck, when was the last time I touched someone?

Frowning, I mentally rolled my eyes at myself. Not long ago. It had been more than a week since I'd actually really touched Kaiser or Marley, but I wasn't a blushing virgin, that was for sure.

My hands landed on his stomach when he drew his lips along my cheek until they very softly covered mine.

I waited for the panic. For the guilt. For the crushing sorrow. For a weight to land on my shoulders for me to stumble under.

They didn't come. So, I turned my face more fully into him, letting him kiss me as he pleased. Phynn wasted no time bringing his hand up my body and over the back of my neck to press in my hair. He wasn't going slow, though he waited for me to respond before he continued.

I responded by parting my lips, groaning when his tongue surged forward to dance around mine. When I met his tongue with my own, Phynn pressed harder against me, trapping one of my legs between his.

Despite the near-constant contact with one of them, it had been more than a week since I'd been touched. Since I'd touched. Too lost in my misery to feel much of anything else, it had become a nonissue again. But now I was on fire. I groaned against him. Phynn growled in response.

The hand that wasn't at the back of my head, commanding my mouth for his own, ran up my stomach and chest before slowly dragging south again. He shifted to the side, his fingers pausing at the waistline of my jeans. I dug my fingers into his skin, silently cursing him for stopping, as I jerked my hips against his.

His hand dropped, cupping my dick in his hand. He squeezed me gently at first before rubbing along my hardening length through my pants.

I chased his tongue, trying to catch it. His growl was almost constant. I jumped when he tightened his hold on my dick.

The sound of my phone pinging made me jump again, ripping my mouth from his. It was sitting on the sill, and I glanced down at it, expecting to see Nora's name flash at me. Phynn's teeth along my neck had me moaning again and my eyes fluttered shut.

But there was something about the message. An unknown number but there was something in the message itself that made me pause. I reached for it, pulling it up and swiping at the screen.

The movement made Phynn pause and shift, giving me room. I had installed an app on my phone years ago that immediately shoved all unknown callers into a SPAM folder within my phone, keeping their calls and messages from bothering me. It meant I didn't get phone calls from people unsaved in my phone. Nor did I get text messages.

I'd had to turn it off in recent months because my phone number was all over the place with vendors for my new store. Until they learned that Nora was the contact, something I reminded them every time they called or messaged me, I'd had to attend to some things.

Usually, business took place in calls. I don't know what possessed me to open it. I wasn't sure what caught my attention in the preview. But I brought it up and my breath caught before leaving me completely.

There was an image of the car wreck that took my pack. I knew it wasn't a generic stock photo because I recognized the plates. I knew that shock of white-blonde hair that I could barely catch a glimpse of within the shattered windshield as Zack's – caked in blood.

I almost didn't get past the photo. Who would send me such a thing? Why?

But then there were the words.

[Unknown] You should have been in the car, alpha.

I choked on air as the phone left my hand. A vice tightened around my chest, preventing me from breathing as the room dimmed. Guilt fell like a pit in my stomach as I sank to my knees in despair.

CHAPTER FORTY

Terence

Tears filled my eyes as I gasped, my hands fisted at the side of my head. The horror of what I'd been doing started to consume me. My pack was everything. And here I was, betraying them.

I was suddenly hauled to my feet, my face tucked into a neck. I struggled until Phynn demanded I stand still and breathe. His bark was just sharp enough that I flinched, growled in protest, and swallowed the objection.

It took many deep breaths before I stopped trembling. His clean cherry almond scent trickled its way through my mind, easing my muscles and dulling my pain. But the guilt - that didn't go away.

"Terence," Phynn said.

I grunted in acknowledgment.

"Please know I'm not saying this to be harsh and unsympathetic. They're not coming back. You are allowed to begin moving on."

The idea made bile rise in my throat.

"I'm not ever going to ask you to stop loving them. In fact, I don't want you to stop. You will love them every single day and I will never stop asking about them. I want to know them. Even though they're not here, they will be a part of this."

I wasn't sure if it was his tone, his words, or what they implied. A breath escaped me and with it went the dead weight of guilt and betrayal. The sorrow and horror of the text image remained. I clung to Phynn, digging my fingers in, and biting into his shoulder through his shirt.

It took many long minutes before I was composed enough that I backed away. Phynn studied me for several heartbeats before he was satisfied that I wasn't going to lose my shit. Then he bent to pick up my phone.

I looked away. I couldn't look at that image again. It was one thing seeing the car. It was another seeing my alpha inside it. If he hadn't been dead already, he was dying. And I hadn't been there. The text was right; I should have been in the car. Because I was supposed to go with them. But I'd stayed behind to finish some work.

"Terence, have you reported these?"

I looked at him, a frown forming on my face. "I just got it. You were standing right here, witnessing my breakdown."

He looked up with his bright eyes and smiled softly. He kissed my lips, letting the pressure linger for just a second. "You can break down all you need to. Believe me when I tell you, we will never judge your pain."

Fuck, I didn't deserve this pack. I hung my head until he forced me to look up at him again with a hand gently tangled in my hair.

"These texts. Have you reported them?"

When it was obvious I didn't know what he was talking about, Phynn turned my phone to me. I flinched away but he didn't let me go. I watched through a cringe as he started to scroll back before the image and today's text.

There were a couple more messages.

Where are you, alpha?

You can't run or hide from me.

Phynn closed out of that message and opened the one right below it.

We will find you.

And the next number.

You should have died, too.

I narrowed my eyes as he continued to open one after another. Shaking my head, I took the phone. There were dozens of them from different numbers. The latest wasn't the only one with the picture of my pack's crushed car. I was careful not to look at those. Zack's blonde hair wasn't the only evidence of my pack in those images. It was just the most easily seen.

"I don't open my texts," I admitted, looking up at him. "I typically reply when the notification window pops on my phone without actually opening the message app."

"And these continuously popping up didn't ever become alarming?" he asked.

I barked a laugh and closed the app before scrolling through my settings to find what I wanted to show him. Handing back my phone, I watched as Phynn took in the functions.

"This is both disturbingly and impressively well-made technology," he answered.

"If it managed to keep me from seeing the taunting texts, I'd say impressive," I countered.

Phynn's expression when he looked at me with a brow raised said he disagreed. His lips pressed together as he considered me. "Terence, these aren't taunting texts. These aren't people just being heartless assholes. They're threats. You were supposed to be in the car with them that day, weren't you?"

My shoulders tensed as I nodded. "We were going away for four days. Not far but just a long weekend that we could spend together. We took them a lot. But I had a couple reports I wanted to finish, and I was running late. I told them to go without me and I'd meet them there."

Phynn sighed, leaning forward to press his cheek against mine. He rubbed against me lightly, gently. It wasn't meant as a marking. He just figured out why my survivor's guilt was as fucking deep a wound as it was. Because I *was* supposed to die with my pack.

And someone figured out too late that I hadn't been in the car. My pack still died. And I was left behind.

"Wait," I said, pulling away to look at Phynn with a new horror. "Are you saying that this wasn't an accident? My pack wasn't in an accidental collision? It was planned?"

Phynn didn't answer as he looked down at my phone in his hands. "Let's get Marley." Before I could ask why, he continued. "She did a few internships in Criminal Investigation. I don't want to tell you something that might be inaccurate."

We didn't just get Marley. With Marley came Adrian. And so Kaiser didn't feel left out and like we were hiding something from him, Phynn called him down, too. Marley had my phone as she stared, scrolling through texts.

I hadn't realized how many there were until twenty minutes went by before she looked up. "Terence, these started seven months ago. You didn't see any of them?"

I shook my head, sighing. "I understand closing out life is unhealthy and someday, maybe I'll be stable enough for you to lecture me on it. But what I want to know is whether my pack was murdered."

"What?!" Kaiser asked in alarm as he nearly shot out of his seat.

Marley glanced at Kaiser with sympathy before her gaze met Adrian's. She returned her attention to me shortly after. "It appears that way. It sounds as though you were supposed to be in the car, and someone isn't happy you weren't and disappeared before they could finish the job."

The panic in Kaiser's eyes as he looked between us might have been what made me keep my head. My pack hadn't accidentally been in a car wreck. Someone had set that up with the intention that we all die.

Oddly enough, that was a bit of a comfort. They didn't leave me behind. They were taken from me. They weren't supposed to die without me.

I closed my eyes and bowed my head as I let that settle around me. The guilt of still living didn't go away. The truth didn't change the fact that my entire pack was gone, and I was still left here, expected to carry on through life without them. The hollow place inside me where their bonds had once been still echoed with the remnants of what had been there. But those echoes weren't from someone on the other end. They were whispers of memories like everything else that lived on inside me.

"I'm not sure if I should concentrate on being pissed that someone had my pack killed or concerned about how I apparently shut out that someone has been threatening my life," I admitted.

Phynn shook his head. "No. Honey, we should be focused on finding *who* has been threatening your life. How you feel about it is inconsequential at this point. You can think about that later."

"While I hear you, all I can think about is how fucked up I am that I hadn't checked that app in at least seven months. What have I been doing?"

"Growing muscles," Kaiser said.

I looked at him. The near panic hadn't left his gaze, even as he tried to make light of the situation. I held my hand out and he tripped over himself to get close. If I hadn't known better, I'd have said it was *his* pack that had been murdered.

Murdered. If it wasn't an accident, that meant it was planned. That meant my pack didn't just happen to die. They were killed.

There was someone who had gotten away with the murder of my entire pack and the world thought it was an unfortunate accident.

I met Phynn's eyes and he smiled, relaxing back into the chair. Satisfied that I was paying attention to the part that was important. The people who had killed my pack were still out there. Still running around loose and free. And intending to kill me.

And no one was any wiser.

"They're aware that Terence hasn't handed this information over to the police," Marley said after a while. "They've stopped changing numbers quite so frequently. But at least it doesn't appear that they've known where you were all along."

"You don't think we should bring them in now, do you?" Adrian asked.

Marley shook her head. "Not yet. I think they'll need to be notified once it's clear that these men know where Terence is, but since they've been texting Terence for months and he's still alive, I would hazard a guess that they haven't found him yet."

"Which is stupid," I said, frowning at her. "I haven't

changed my name. I might have moved across the country, but I still own one of Zack's businesses under my name."

"Juice Me belonged to Zack?" Kaiser asked.

I nodded, looking down at where he was curled at my side, his head buried into my ribs. "Yea. He liked to buy dying businesses and resurrect them before selling them again."

"A flipper," he said, looking up at me with a grin.

I smiled in return. "Yea. I kept Juice Me because it was in a location far as fuck away, there was an apartment over it, and he was slightly obsessed with juicing things. When you want me to scare you into sleeping, I'll tell you some of the awful things he made us drink."

Kaiser laughed, nodding. But there were still stress lines on his forehead. His shoulders were still stiff. His heart still beat quickly.

"I have a friend," Marley said, bringing us back on topic. "They should be able to track this person down. With this many burner numbers, there must be something out there. Like why you have a target over your head."

"Before you ask, I think there had to have been a mistake. We worked and we messed around with each other. There was never a time when we weren't together."

Adrian, Phynn, and Marley stared at me.

I smiled, nodding. "Okay, I get that you might not believe that or think I'm naïve. That's fine. When I say we were together all the time, I mean that. Every waking moment if we could help it. I suppose it wouldn't be impossible for someone to fuck up in something, but I can't believe it was enough to make someone want to kill our entire pack."

"Can I take your phone?" Marley asked as she got to her feet. "I promise I won't go through it or delete anything off it."

"You can go through it if you want but please don't delete anything," I countered. "Where are you taking it?"

"A friend of mine is a private investigator with Westman Enterprises in Captain's Knoll," she answered.

"That's a beta-only firm," I said.

Marley smirked, tilting her head to the side. "*I am* a beta, Terence. You're not inquiring. I am."

I sighed. "If they tell you no-"

"They won't," she said, moving to the front of me and crouching down so her eyes were level with mine. She kissed me tenderly and I realized I hadn't kissed her since before the restaurant fiasco. Someday I'd get my shit together. "Jaal owes me a favor."

"Jaal is an ex-lover," Adrian told me as he crossed his arms with a smirk.

I watched Marley's smile creep up to mischief. "And that's why my alpha is not going to let me go alone. He thinks I'm going to leave him for a beta." She said the word beta as if it were a curse.

Kaiser laughed, turning his face to hide in my thigh and drown out his amusement at Marley's teasing.

Adrian was quick when he crossed the room. Even with his growl in the air, Marley didn't have enough time to even get to her feet before he had her off the ground. She squealed as he buried his teeth in her neck, her hands yanking on his hair to pull him away. Her body wriggled madly as she laughed.

"They're cute, huh?" Kaiser said quietly.

I smiled, nodding.

When Adrian was done torturing Marley, he put her down and she kissed us all goodbye. Adrian rested his hand in my hair before gently pushing my head back so I had to look up at him as he hovered over me.

"We won't let anyone touch you," he said.

I nodded, the corner of my mouth raising a little. He nodded in return before following Marley out, his hand slapping her little ass with a sharp *clap* that made her squeak and swat at him.

We were left in the quiet and I sighed. Kaiser got to his knees and moved behind me where he rubbed my shoulders. I let my head fall forward, allowing him this moment to dote on me. Marley said he liked to take care of them when they'd allow it. Most of the time, they did because it made him happy. I wondered if Kaiser knew that they allowed it as another form of pampering him.

His fingers dug into my muscles in the most delicious way. A quiet groan left my lips. It wasn't long after that that with each effort to dig his fingers in, his body rocked forward, pressing his ever-hardening cock into my back.

A smile grew on my face though I didn't comment.

Eventually, Kaiser paused. I could hear the flush in his breathless voice when he spoke. "Sorry. It's frustrating how I can never turn it off."

Silly man. As if his hard dick was ever going to bother me.

In the corner of my eye, I could see Phynn shake his head. "Come here, omega," he said, his voice a low purr. Kaiser shivered behind me, leaning in more heavily before scrambling to his alpha.

With Kaiser standing in front of him, Phynn pulled at his pants until he could get them open. I had a perfect angle of seeing Phynn take Kaiser's cock into his mouth, placing both his hands on Kaiser's hips.

Kaiser moaned loudly, dropping his head back as Phynn worked his length into his mouth. Further. Deeper. Until his lips met Kaiser's stomach.

I knew when Kaiser got off for the first time by the sound he made and the way his body twitched. I also had the pleasure of seeing Phynn's throat contract as he swallowed it down. Kaiser's perfume filled the air with a sweet cinnamon that burned as it coated me. Sweet fuck, it elicited an instant hard-on.

Kaiser whined and I knew what was coming before the words left his mouth. His fingers tangled in Phynn's hair as he bit his lip, trying to keep the demand in. This was one of those moments where he was frustrated with what he was. He didn't want to give in.

But then he reached his tipping point as Phynn sucked another orgasm from him. "Knot," he whined. "Please, alpha. Knot me."

Phynn smiled around his mouthful of dick before pulling him out slowly. "Why don't you see if Terence wants a taste while I get my clothes off, Kaiser." His voice was a velveting purr that nearly had me falling from the couch. Damn, that was good.

Kaiser's heated eyes met mine and I nodded. He almost tripped over his pants before Phynn helped him climb out of them. He stopped in front of me, his dripping cock level with my face as he held his shirt up.

I slid forward on the couch, too distracted with the treat in front of me to acknowledge Phynn taking his clothes off. "Shirt," I told Kaiser and he immediately pulled it over his head. "Good boy," I whispered, making him shiver in appreciation.

His hands landed on my shoulders as he leaned forward so I could take him in. With my hands on his hips where Phynn's had been, I leaned back, pulling him with me. He lost his balance, his body colliding into mine, driving his dick down my throat until I'd reached the end, something I was absolutely prepared for.

Kaiser wasn't. He cried out, "Coming," a second before he was pouring down my throat.

The one disadvantage of having him in all the way was that

I didn't really get to taste him like this. Just the phantom tang of cum with a hefty dose of cinnamon sugar.

When his hips jerked, I felt Phynn behind him, easing himself into the omega between us. I continued to sloppily suck on Kaiser, only pulling him out long enough to take a breath before swallowing him whole again.

It was no time before Phynn had him howling, a constant stream of releasing coating my throat, nearly making me choke as I tried to keep up swallowing it all. But fuck, if I drowned in it, it'd still be a happy day.

CHAPTER FORTY-ONE

Terence

I found myself with a lot of free time. Marley was taking care of my juice bar and Nora. There was a home gym in the basement. And a blender and juicer in the kitchen. I had no reason to leave their house.

Strangely enough, aside from the brush of guilt that swept through me from time to time, I found I didn't really want to leave their house. I was content here. Ready to lose myself in one of their companies if the world got too heavy.

As such, I found that I had a lot of time to consider life. With a borrowed laptop in hand, I went in search of Kaiser. At this point, I didn't think I was going to go home without Kaiser and/or Marley. Hell, I didn't think I'd go without all four of them. My apartment wasn't big enough for five people, but I was sure we'd find a way to fit.

Therefore, there was at least one more thing I needed to do.

I found Kaiser in the den with his phone in hand. I could tell by the way he was concentrating with just the tip of his tongue sticking out that he was playing a game. I loved this look. The carefree grins and happy light in his eyes.

He glanced up before pausing and giving me his attention, a wide smile on his lips.

"Hey," I said. "You busy?"

Kaiser shook his head, clicking his phone off and tossing it onto the table. He unfolded himself, waiting to see what I wanted.

What I wanted was for him to know my pack. I was loving how this pack circled around him while not letting him in on it. Giving him his space while still tending to any whim he mentioned off-hand. I was sure heats were a blast.

If I closed my eyes, I could just imagine him in the center of my pack during a heat. Sometimes, I saw both of our packs together around him. That was a lot of bodies. A whole lot of knots. But damn, the idea was intoxicating.

Or it would have been if half of that fantasy wasn't encased in stone.

It was a sobering thought.

I entered the room and sat next to him. Kaiser immediately cuddled close. As soon as I opened the laptop, I wrapped an arm around him and purred. He loved to be purred to. Just as I was remembering how much I enjoyed it, as well. Not just purring for him but being purred to.

"So, remember when we talked about building Marley a she shed for my garden?" I asked.

I could almost feel his giddiness well up. "Yes!"

"Want to help me plan it?"

He looked at me with such pure joy, I couldn't help but wonder how people could actually bring themselves to hurt an omega. There was never a look or feeling that was better than the way he was watching me. And knowing that I'd put that look there was powerful.

We chose a style that was full of eclectic touches. The entire structure was made out of reclaimed windows put together like Tetris. Inside was a big couch and a couple crystal chandeliers. There were tables and a couple chairs. Shelves. It was built on a deck with a birdbath and a couple urn planters.

A week later, it was set up at my house by the same company who'd constructed the little nest for Kaiser. After promising Adrian a short trip so we wouldn't be late for dinner, I grabbed the two of them and loaded them into my car. I wasn't even going to ask how it got there at this point. So many of my belongings had shown up. Not there when I went to sleep but magically there in the morning.

I parked in the garage and closed it before taking both their hands and dragging them into the trees that quickly swallowed us from sight. The way it softened the city noise was like magic.

Kaiser and I hadn't told Marley what the plan was. Only that we wanted to check on the garden and maybe get a little bit of a snuggle in before eating. She didn't question it. Like so many other things in this pack, Marley assumed we were indulging Kaiser. And this time, Kaiser was happy to play along.

As much as Kaiser enjoyed receiving gifts, he also loved being part of the giving of them. He loved the thought process that went in and the little touches that made it perfect. He was nearly bouncing out of his skin by the time I ushered them inside my little oasis.

Marley immediately slowed and took a deep breath of the flowers. I nodded Kaiser along, telling him we'd be there in a minute. I didn't want to rush Marley as she enjoyed the peace of the garden.

"Who feeds the fish?" she asked as we paused at the little koi pond.

"They're small enough that they feed on the plants," I said.

"But if I were ever away for an extended period of time, I'd have a company come in to make sure they're tended to every week."

She nodded, touching the surface of the water with her finger. I could see Kaiser waiting impatiently on the other side of the arch and grinned. Offering my hand to Marley, I pulled her to her feet and led her in.

Her eyes landed on the nest first before sweeping the rest of the hidden area as she took a few steps towards it. Then she paused, staring at the new structure that Kaiser was standing in front of with a beaming smile.

"What's this?" she asked, tilting her head to the side.

"A she shed," I answered.

A breath left her as she looked at it. Then she turned to me with wide eyes. "A she shed?"

"For you. Kaiser has a nest. And you have a she shed."

"I- but you- when did-?"

Her stutterings were adorable. I cupped the side of her face and kissed her softly. "Want to look?"

Marley nodded. "Why?" she whispered.

"Because you deserve to be spoiled as much as Kaiser and I didn't want you to forget that."

Her eyes glossed over with moisture as she looked at me. "Thank you." She wrapped her arms around me, kissing me with fervent passion. I picked her up, humming into her mouth as I wrapped her legs around my waist, and walked towards the shed.

"I think I should have responded like that, too," Kaiser said thoughtfully. "Marley does everything better."

Marley giggled, releasing my lips and glancing over her shoulder at him. "Sweet omega. I can already tell you were in on this."

Kaiser grinned, shrugging.

I let her down and watched as the two of them explored it together. I wondered if this was what it was like to have kids. Seeing their wonder and feeling their excitement at something you've done for them.

A lot like Miles whenever I'd bring him a new hat. The man had enough hats to fill a room.

We didn't get to stay long since we were on a promised deadline with Adrian. Kaiser promised we could come back and curl up on the couch as the sun went down one night, using the light of the chandeliers to watch the world go quiet.

I led them out, listening to them talk. Locking the gate, I stopped short before we broke through the trees into the parking lot.

I wasn't sure what it was that made my hackles rise. I raised my arm, blocking the path for Kaiser and Marley to break the protective covering of the trees that kept the three of us hidden within the shadows.

"Wha-?"

"Shh," I whispered, hushing Kaiser before he could speak.

He fell silent as I tucked them both behind me and further pushed them backwards so that we were well hidden. My little secret garden was just that – a complete secret. Unless you had the plot of the land or flew a drone over, it wasn't readily found. It was surrounded by buildings on all sides but even moving around them, it was tucked away enough that any onlooker would think that it was a tiny pocket backyard of one of the neighboring buildings.

I waited, hoping that maybe my unease was unfounded. But then the door that led to my stairs opened, and a figure came out. He was big but as I lifted my nose into the air, I knew he was a beta. How did he think he was going to get into an alpha's apartment lowkey?

And then the door opened again, and two more men trailed

him. I could feel Kaiser press hard into me, his heart racing in his chest as he peered around. Those were alphas. I watched them as they scouted the garage door and all the cars of my employees in the parking lot.

The beta came back around and stopped at the garage door. Not the big one for the car but the one we walk in from the outside. In broad daylight, he broke the lock and walked in, one of the alphas following him.

These fuckers had found me. Whoever they were, they found me. And apparently, they intended to kill me in the middle of the day. With my juice bar below, filled with my employees and the public, right under my feet.

Who were they? How were their balls so big that they thought they could get away with this? How did they think they were so untouchable to just walk into my apartment and take me out?

I kept absolutely still so that no hint of movement caught the second alpha's attention. When he turned away, looking down at his phone and typing, I urged Marley and Kaiser back until we were no longer within sight of my building.

I kept pushing them backwards until we were at the gate of my garden on the far side. "Back in," I told them. "Do not make a sound and do not come out until I get you."

Kaiser's eyes widened in fear. Marley's only reaction was to frown at me, pressing her lips into a thin line.

"Don't argue," I whispered. "Turn your phones on silent and text your alphas. Ask them to pick us up at Bay Street Optics as soon as they can."

Marley nodded as I tugged at Kaiser's hoodie. "Let me borrow this, babe."

His eyes widened and despite his fear, he grinned as he pulled his zipper down and shrugged out of the hoodie. It wasn't going to fit me. I was going to stretch it out so badly that I'd need to replace it. Fuck, I'd buy him a dozen new hoodies.

"Stay here and keep quiet," I whispered, kissing them both. I shut them inside. I hadn't ordered them. Not really. If I thought they wouldn't obey my instructions, I would have, but as afraid as Kaiser was, and displeased as Marley was, I thought they'd listen.

When they were safely hidden, I headed to the back of the building that abutted my parking lot. This section of the city was a little weird. Between the two parallel roads were buildings three deep. The buildings that lined Walker (where the juice bar was) and the streets that lined Bay had an entirely separate set of buildings running between them with no streets connecting. I owned one such building. My garden was on the second middle lot that I owned.

There was no street between. Most of the buildings had easements and right of ways, sharing parking with a building on either side of them. Rounding the middle building at the one that sat on the Bay until I could check out the alley between Juice Me and the store next to it opposite the door to my apartment.

That's where their SUV was parked. Nondescript black. There wasn't even a make or model, and the plate was hidden in one of those reflective plastic sleeves. I didn't creep close enough to get any better look and was glad when I'd made the unconscious decision to remain hidden where I was, even though I really wanted to mark it. The driver's door opened, and another man came out.

Four men. They sent four men after me.

I caught my breath when I remembered that my house smelled heavily like omega. They might not have noticed Marley's scent since she hadn't been there nearly as many times as Kaiser. And besides that, I've literally knotted him all over my apartment.

All. Over.

And then there was probably Phynn's lingering scent. At least near the couch where he'd been for a solid ten hours.

Fuck.

The slight scrape of shoes on packed gravel was the only warning that someone was coming. I slinked behind a dumpster as one might see in any crime movie and waited. At least with a dumpster, it should be strong enough to mask most of my scent.

It wasn't anyone I knew and when he rounded the corner away from my building, I didn't think he was with the people scoping out my apartment. I watched until the man who'd stepped out a moment ago returned to the car and shut the door. Then I turned back to retrieve my beta and omega hiding in my garden.

Kaiser launched into my arms when I reappeared. He was trembling. I kissed the top of his head and held my finger to my lips as I backed us back into the tiny path that led from my garden around the surrounding buildings. Marley locked the gate behind us. When they were both within reach, I led them to Bay Street Optics.

Marley pointed to Phynn's car as it pulled up and we climbed in before he came to a complete stop. The windows were dark, so I felt safe asking him to round to the front of the juice bar. Phynn followed an old lady driver who cut him off instead of pulling around, so we had a minute to scope out the situation. When I watched the beta walk out of the juice bar with a smoothie, a different dread filled me.

"Marley, are your PIs making progress?" I asked.

She shifted in the seat to look at me. "They're making connections as fast as they can but there's nothing yet."

"Do I call the police?" I asked, more to myself than her.

"No," Phynn answered. "I imagine they'll want you to meet them at your apartment and I'm not letting you go back there."

There was a bit of a bite in his words that made me smirk. Instead, I dialed Nora.

"Hi Mr. Andersen," she said, and I didn't miss the relief in her voice. I'd had her dealing with Marley as much as possible, so I didn't have to talk to anyone. Cowardly maybe but there you go.

"Nora, listen closely. Without causing any kind of panic or drawing concern from anyone, I need you to close the shop. Send everyone home. Stay out of that building until I tell you otherwise. You'll all continue to be paid."

"But-"

"Don't argue with me, Nora. Get out of there as soon as possible. Do you understand? Shut down and lock up." I was really regretting not having an alarm. We were a juice bar. We didn't carry expensive technology nor merchandise. The most we ever hand on hand for cash was $1500 since most people paid with cards these days. What were they going to steal, a pineapple? Some bananas?

"Okay," she answered.

"Call me when you're all gone. Make sure everyone drives away. And Nora, if you see anyone out back that doesn't belong there, pretend you don't see them. Don't acknowledge them. And make sure no one else does either."

Nora didn't answer for a minute. "Are you in trouble, Mr. Andersen?" she asked, her voice low and calm.

I smiled, leaning back into the seat, and looking through the dark window as the city passed me by. "Not in the way you're thinking. I haven't actually done anything to warrant trouble. But there's something going on and I need to make sure you're all safe."

"Okay," she answered. "I'll take care of everything and call you back."

Nora was efficient. She returned my call thirteen minutes later letting me know she was the last one to pull out and that there were three men hanging around my garage, watching them as they left.

"Kaiser, call the police on an anonymous tip. You think the owner is away on vacation because you frequent the shop and it's closed. There are suspicious people hanging around that have you concerned," Phynn said. "And I know you're going to hate it but play up your omega."

Kaiser smirked at him before turning eyes made dark by the heavily tinted windows to me. Playful and heated. "Sure. I'll play omega for you."

CHAPTER FORTY-TWO

Phynn

Kaiser's laugh through the wall made me smile. He was many things these days aside from his usual sweet, stubborn, horny self. He was genuinely and thoroughly happy that Terence was here. His smile never left his face.

But he was also afraid. Just as a smile was never far from his lips, neither was the hint of fear in his eyes. Seeing the strange men at Terence's house had really shaken him. Knowing that they weren't there for a friendly purpose.

It was one thing to watch crime shows, either based on reality or complete fabrication. It was a touch more real when we'd discovered the whole slew of threatening text messages on Terence's phone. Kaiser's fear was real then.

Seeing men who were very likely there to kill Terence had truly upset Kaiser. Once they got home and everything settled, when he'd had a chance to reflect on what had happened, Kaiser had been utterly freaked out.

Even so, that was ten days ago. The text messages that had come through since hadn't given any indication that they'd found Terence's apartment. His car was still parked in his garage and the shop was still closed. Nora continued to move forward with the second shop, but she did so quietly and from her own home as much as possible.

Terence had asked some neighboring businesses to give him a call if they saw anything suspicious around his place. He hadn't actually thought they would. People don't like to be involved. By the time the police got there, the men had left. There was minor property damage and no sign of breaking and entering other than the fact that the lock was broken.

Marley's PI hadn't come back with anything useful as far as I knew. My business was advertising for large companies. Putting together packages, selling the packages, and then making good on my promises. I wasn't in any position to know how to help. But once again, I reached out to the friend who'd found the article on Terence's pack and asked him to keep an ear out for anything regarding him or his packmates.

Adrian had even fewer contacts. He was in pharmaceutical sales. And he was fucking brilliant at it.

I leaned over my desk with my hands in my hair as I stared at the tablet in front of me. I had a love-hate relationship with the package that included billboards. They were great money, but I hate designing them. I was only all too eager to let in whoever knocked.

I spun in my chair as Marley walked in. She was so soft footed that if I hadn't turned to see her, her presence would have gone completely unnoticed. Her smile was shy and soft, just as she was. Her hair fell like a curtain, partially obscuring her face.

She shut the door quietly and crossed the room until she could lean against my desk.

"Beautiful woman," I purred, pulling a smile to her lips and a blush to her cheeks. My very favorite expression on her. Well, outside of orgasm. There was nothing more beautiful than the face my Marley made during an orgasm.

Marley sighed and all too soon that smile and flush faded. "So, I heard back from Jaal," she said. "And it's not a pretty picture."

I tensed. Waiting for her to tell me the bad news.

"The group after Terence is Decrescenti."

I flinched at the name. As far as organized crime went, they were the kingpin. The boss. Their reach was far and wide and frightening. They weren't above the law, but they may as well own it.

It wasn't just your regular crime that they ran – street drugs, theft, etc. It was the most terrifying corruption of all. Abducting and selling of omegas. Assassins for hire. And a drug company unlike any other. Drugs like you can't fathom.

"From what Jaal can find, Terence isn't guilty of anything. He hasn't crossed their paths at all. He's guilty by association. His packmate got tangled in something with Decrescenti half a decade before he had even met Terence's pack. He bailed on his end of whatever agreement he'd made with Decrescenti. It wasn't enough just to kill him. They wanted to kill his entire pack."

I sighed, a pit forming in my stomach as it churned. These people knew how to hurt someone. But what was the point in carrying it out now? Terence didn't know this information. If he had, he wouldn't have brought Kaiser and Marley into danger. I knew that for a fact. No alpha would put their omega in danger. And Kaiser sure as fuck was his omega.

"There's more," Marley said, her voice dropping lower. She glanced at the door. "Nothing that's here nor there, but a truly terrifying thing Jaal found. Emery, Terence's alpha who got tangled with Decrescenti, had agreed to be a delivery agent for one of their new products. It's called Obey. Basically, it's a drug to make an alpha respond to a beta as if the beta had a bark. It only works for a short period but in that period, they're inclined to do as they're told."

I frowned at her. That was just stupid. Once that alpha came out of it, he was going to rip some heads off. Marley was worrying her lip, so I knew there was more to this than she was saying. I waited for the other shoe to drop.

"You don't see the implications?" she asked.

"I see a pissed off alpha," I answered.

She smiled, shaking her head. "Phynn, they're selling bites in the same way they're selling omegas. Think about it. Betas have the same biological craving for a pack that omegas and alphas do. But they're not nearly as wanted, and they can't form their own. Now, if you're a beta with enough money, you can essentially buy an alpha. They're advertising it as 'buying a bite.' When an alpha is drugged with Obey, they do as they're told as if they don't have a choice. Including biting whoever they're instructed to. Even if they come out of it ravenous, they now have many betas tied to them irrevocably."

The whole thing made my blood run cold. What the fuck was wrong with people? This was disgusting. Horrendous.

"I don't even have words," I muttered, lowering my head to rest on her thigh.

Her fingers brushed through my hair gently for several minutes as she sighed. "Anyway, I don't think all this stuff needs to be disclosed. Just who is after him but even then, I'm not sure it's going to do us any good."

"Let's keep Emery's involvement quiet if we can," I said. "I don't want him to have any negative memories concerning his pack if I can help it."

Marley nodded. "The real question is how do we protect him? Decrescenti isn't going to go away. And they don't forget."

I shook my head. "I think it's time for a family meeting to decide where to go from here."

Marley nodded again. We didn't move for several minutes as I let this new weight settle on top of me. I'd keep Emery's involvement sealed within me. He had enough pain to deal with. I couldn't imagine how much more it would hurt to know this.

But what if he asked why? What had his pack done to draw their attention? To kill his entire pack? To continue to hunt him until he, too, was dead?

Adrian was rolling out cookies in the kitchen. I left Marley with him so she could tell him what she'd just told me while I gathered Terence and Kaiser. They were nestled in Kaiser's nest, fully clothed, but wrapped around each other. I could smell them both as if there was someone in front of me spritzing their scents directly in my face relentlessly.

They weren't talking right now. Terence's eyes were closed but Kaiser was looking at him. Watching him. A look that could only be described as puppy love bright on his face.

I almost didn't want to interrupt. Actually, I *didn't* want to interrupt. But this was important.

I pushed the door open, causing them both to look up at me. I really liked that they both smiled. I hadn't kissed Terence again. I had been waiting for him to make the next move, but I forget that Terence was not about making moves at all. He'd told our omega to be an alpha because he couldn't be one. A beta might have been able. But not our omega. He wanted to. But stress and then his heat right on top of it had made him almost regress into a traumatized child for a short period.

Terence didn't know the extent of that either. Our goal wasn't to hurt him but build him back up to someone he wanted to be. To be happy. To take care of our omega and beta with us. And if that meant perhaps forming relationships with Adrian and/or I, then good. Otherwise, just a packmate was also fine.

We would get there. But we had one giant hurdle to get past first.

"Come downstairs for a bit. We have to talk about something," I said.

Kaiser nodded, already moving to do as I said. Terence looked at me warily as he got to his feet a whole lot slower. I watched as Kaiser skipped ahead, already on his way down the stairs. Terence paused next to me in the door. Could I kiss him now? Would it be inappropriate?

"It's not good, is it?" he asked, his voice low enough that it wouldn't carry beyond where we stood in the doorway.

I didn't answer. Anything outside of the truth would make the blow that much worse.

Maybe he'd accept a hug? I inhaled a deep breath and turned so that I could walk into him. He let me, his eyes on mine until I'd moved close enough that it would have pulled our necks in awkward positions to hold eye contact.

Terence liked to be against Adrian or I while he slept. He liked that we'd purr against him, rub him with our scent, hold him like he was our omega. I was inclined to believe that he much preferred to be the quieter side of an alpha. He didn't want the bark or responsibility. His reflexes were to take care of Kaiser and he loved to do so, but outside of that, he wanted to be demure. Especially now that he'd been staying here and there were other alphas around.

I brushed my cheek along his, slowly drawing my lips to his ear. "I promise you, we won't let anything happen to you. We will do whatever it takes to keep you safe."

I felt his smile against my neck as he dropped his face into my shoulder. "It really isn't a good talk, is it?"

"There will be better talks," I conceded.

Terence chuckled.

In a drawn out, soft movement, I rubbed my cheek against his, purring softly. It was only at night that he wanted these acts, but then, Kaiser and Marley kept him occupied most of the day. He sighed, allowing his body to relax into me. I took that as permission to continue and wrapped my arms around him, too.

"I guess we should go downstairs so you can tell me what you're not telling me," Terence murmured.

Unless Kaiser or Marley had him worked up, Terence was damn good about keeping his scent regulated. There was no spike in emotion outside of the night I presented him with the truth he was keeping to himself and the following day. Otherwise, his control was admirable. It made his toasted coconut and mineral oil scent easy and lickable.

I pulled back from him enough to look at him. There weren't new stress lines or concerns yet. Resignation. He was expecting the worst. Because he'd already had everything taken from him.

My gaze dropped as he licked his lips. His hands lifted to rest on my stomach. When I pressed my lips against his, he smiled. I swear, there was amusement in his kiss as I pressed into him harder.

I didn't let it last long. We were expected downstairs. Just long enough to taste him and bite his lip as I was pulling away. The flex of his fingers against my stomach made my cock twitch in excitement.

Releasing him, I took a step back. He still wore a touch of laughter on his lips as he stared at me. "How long have you been waiting to do that?" he asked.

Narrowing my eyes, I watched as the hint of a smile turned into a grin. He leaned into me this time and said, "I tried to make your omega be my alpha. Don't expect anything from me. Be the alpha, Phynn. I won't be."

I growled slightly because I'd *just* been thinking about that. He squeezed my wrist as he walked by, brushing his shoulder against mine. Fuck. I'm pretty sure that was consent to pursue him.

I turned on him like a predator watching as he reached the top of the stairs and started down them. It was stupidly difficult to watch him walk away. Everything in me said *chase. Catch. Bite.*

Obviously, that was getting a little aggressive. So, I waited until he was completely out of sight before I followed.

When I reached the den, Terence was just taking a seat with Marley and Adrian. Kaiser had a bowl of chips in his lap as he watched, his ever-present smile dancing on his lips. I was going to hate to see it slip away.

I nodded at Marley as I took a seat with Kaiser, bringing my arm behind his shoulders so he'd tuck into me.

"My PI found something," Marley said, shifting so she could look at Terence. I could tell from the tension in Adrian's shoulders that she'd managed to tell him before Kaiser and Terence had come down. "Decrescenti has issued a death sentence for your pack. You slipped through the cracks but they're apparently not willing to let that go."

Terence frowned at her. I was just waiting for the question. *Why?*

He didn't ask. Kaiser did. My hand was already on the bowl of chips, and I pulled it away as his hands started to shake. "Why are they trying to kill Terence?"

"A lot of Jaal's information was not directly tied into Terence," Marley answered.

Marley's non-answer wasn't lost on Terence, but he didn't care enough to ask. The why doesn't really matter. When they want something, Decrescenti doesn't stop until it's done.

Adrian rubbed his face before slipping from the couch. I expected him to stop at Kaiser's side to comfort him. His perfume was expanding like a room spray, but now brightly acerbic with his fear.

Instead, Adrian knelt in front of Terence, bringing Terence's face close. "I swear to you, we'll figure this out. We won't let anything happen."

Terence smiled a little. "Your obligation is to your omega and beta. Their protection-"

"Trust me, alpha. No one will touch my pack. And no one will touch you. We will find a solution, so they back off."

I appreciated his assurance, but I had no idea how we were going to make that happen. We weren't just talking about a mountain to climb. This was like trying to get to the moon on roller skates.

CHAPTER FORTY-THREE

Terence

I wasn't going to lie. Everything about Adrian's declaration had me deeply conflicted. Aside from the nearly suffocating sense of betrayal towards my pack and the grief that plagued me, there was now a deep fear of being murdered.

I was surprised that I wasn't welcoming it. Once not long ago, I'd have just handed myself over to Decrescenti so that they could kill me. They'd satisfy whatever stupidity has gotten into them regarding my pack and I'd be reunited with my pack.

But when I met Adrian's eyes, felt Marley's grip on my hand, felt Kaiser's fear for me flooding the room, and remembered Phynn's lips against mine, I realized that I no longer wanted to invite death in.

For the first time in over a year, I wanted to live. I'd deal with the emotional conflict of that realization later. Right now, I needed to figure out how to make this happen while putting Adrian's pack in as little danger as possible.

They knew where my apartment was. I was confident that they didn't know where I was currently, or they'd have already been here. But that couldn't last. They would know I was close.

"Are you listening to me?" Adrian asked.

Nope. I hadn't been. The corner of my lips raised as I looked at him. He sighed, his fingers gently rubbing my scalp. He was a good man.

I wasn't prepared for the strength of his bark. "You're staying here, Terence."

The force of his bark made everything in me stand up and want to fight. It had taken me years to convince myself to obey Zack's bark. Submitting to another alpha wasn't easy. Especially not when you're partially convinced that your bark is harsher.

My muscles tensed, despite my efforts to keep them loose. My jaw clenched as I stared at him. Adrian kept my gaze, and I was sure as he did, he could see it as clearly as I could feel the struggle that I was trying to agree.

I was stronger. That became clear when the struggle to submit to him raged in my eyes as he stared at me.

But I didn't want to be.

I closed my eyes, coaxing every last bit of resistance out of me until I could open my mouth and be assured I wasn't going to tell him off. Or lay him out.

"Yes, alpha," I murmured. The words were stiff and not at all convincing. At least not to the two alphas in the room. But my compliance had both Marley and Kaiser relaxing.

"Good," Kaiser said. "What do we do next? Or first...?"

Adrian held my gaze, waiting until he was sure that I really wasn't going to challenge him. I made myself relax back into the couch but try as I may, there was no way I was going to drop my eyes. I may not want to play alpha, but that didn't make me anything else.

He was satisfied with my reaction though. Adrian pulled back, his gaze swinging to Phynn. I was sure there was an unspoken conversation in that quick look. Phynn pulled Kaiser closer to him and kissed the side of his head.

"Don't worry about anything. We'll take care of it," Phynn told him.

I was sure neither Kaiser nor Marley was totally assured of his declaration. Decrescenti was a name you knew growing up. There was no darker fairy tale. Nothing scarier to threaten to get your kids in line.

I truly couldn't fathom what my pack could have done to gather their attention. I wouldn't say it was impossible that one of them did something behind the rest of our backs, but I just couldn't believe it. We spent every waking moment together outside of work. There wasn't time for that.

Whatever it was, I didn't want to know. I didn't care. They'd already killed my pack. They couldn't take anything else.

And yet, they could. As Adrian and Phynn continued to assure Kaiser that everything would be fine, I knew that now I had a whole lot more that I could lose. But whatever my pack had done, whatever I had done, this pack didn't deserve to be in the crosshairs.

"We will figure it out," Marley said, her voice quiet.

I looked at her, meeting her startlingly beautiful sapphire eyes. There was nothing demure or shy about her right now. This was the alpha side of the mesmerizing beta. Looking at Marley, I was sure there should be a fourth designation. Something that encompassed all three. Because that's what Marley did.

After her very alpha-like declaration, she snuggled into my side like Kaiser does. Just like an omega who wanted comfort. I smiled, turning my attention to watching the two alphas try to ease Kaiser's increased fear.

If I closed my eyes, I could convince myself that I was listening to Zack and Foster comforting Ronan about something. It was Miles tucked into my side. And Emery was making food because, after every upset, you soothe it away with something delicious.

————

THE REVELATION WAS a few days ago. It wasn't quite the weight on my shoulders as I thought it might be. Nothing would be heavier than carrying the loss of my pack. Feeling the emptiness inside me where their bonds had once filled. And the new guilt of falling for another pack in their absence was perhaps the crowning burden.

His sweet cherry almond scent swirled around me a moment before Phynn stepped up behind me. His arms came around my waist, taking a grip of the railing and pinning me in. His mouth pressed against the back of my shoulder.

And then he leaned his body against mine, his arms moving closer together to wrap around me. I closed my eyes, letting a smile touch my lips.

"You're not thinking about going out and doing something stupid and dangerous, are you?" Phynn asked.

I laughed, shaking my head. "I'm not delusional enough to think I can make this go away by striking out on my own. All that's going to do is deliver me to their hands and grant me the death they're promising."

"They won't kill you," he said.

I was a little amused to know that he had almost promised something he didn't have any control over. An alpha was careful about their promises. We didn't like to break them and so we rarely made them.

"I mean, they will if they find you," he amended. "But we're not going to let that happen."

"Phynn, I'm like eighteen miles from home. The only thing you're doing by keeping me here is putting your whole pack at risk," I told him.

"Yes, we know that. We're working on it."

"When are you going to let me in on your plans?"

"That depends." He kissed the side of my neck. The sensation made my entire body tingle. "Do you want to be an alpha or do you want to pretend you're not one?"

I laughed again, leaning back into him. Phynn removed his hands from the rail and spread them across my torso. One going up my chest and the other around my waist. The grip pressed the length of his body against mine. I closed my eyes, reveling in his touch. The hard planes of his body. His mouth on my neck.

"I'd rather not be an alpha," I told him, something he already knew. "But I also don't want you doing something reckless to keep me safe and putting your pack at risk. You know that if you get in the way, they'll kill you too."

"Yes, I know. We've got some feelers out to determine our options. They don't know where you are yet."

"You think that, but maybe they're just waiting for me to walk out of here."

Phynn didn't answer. He shifted his attention to kissing my neck, raking his teeth along my skin, making my dick harden as he did. He pressed his teeth into my neck, closing his mouth around the muscle there and sucking on my skin until I groaned.

He sighed. "We won't stay much longer," Phynn told me. "We're just waiting on some paperwork before we leave."

I stilled at his words.

"I think you should make Nora your power of attorney. Set her up with a bank account to finish the stores and manage the finances. Make her the acting CFO. When it's safe to come back, we will."

Chills went down my spine, making the little hairs on my arms stand on end. I knew they'd been thinking about this and talking it over between the two of them. I hadn't realized they were leaning towards disappearing entirely.

"Phynn-" I started but I had no idea where I was going with that. Disappear. I'd already run away once. I wasn't sure I could do it again.

"We know there are risks involved, mainly to Nora. But we don't think it'll be too bad since you were pretty absent most of the time anyway. All they have to say is that yes, you own the juice bar but the most they see you is to come in for a smoothie. And even then, they haven't seen you in weeks. It's all the truth, anyway."

I flinched, making Phynn flex his arms tighter for a moment. Yep, I was a deadbeat owner.

"I don't want to put Nora at risk. She has a family. Hell, I don't want to put any of my employees at risk. They're good people."

"The only other options would be to close it permanently until we get this taken care of or sell it and walk away."

I frowned, shifting until he loosened his arms so I could look at him. "This is one of the few businesses I kept of Zack's. I'd rather not do either of those things."

He kissed my cheek, his mouth touching the corner of my lips. "I am by no means encouraging either option. Despite how little you like to be involved with Juice Me, I know you love it. I'd rather see you put Nora in charge. I think we can work it so it's convincing."

Sighing, I turned back around to stare out over the side yard. They had security cameras. Something I appreciated. And they were always monitored, both by them and by a company.

Our conversation was interrupted when Marley came out the door with my phone in her hands. I'd not taken it back, even knowing it was here. Marley kept up with Nora's progress and relayed anything that the two of them thought I needed to be involved in or made aware of. And Marley kept whatever technology in the background running as it should to send the information to her PI buddy. I didn't care what they did with my phone as long as they didn't erase anything on it.

But the horror in her eyes shone brightly. Marley didn't speak as she handed me the phone. A text message was up with a short clip. Whoever was recording the video had been standing a couple lots down within the center column of buildings with the camera pointed at my parking lot.

I hit play. It was a six second clip showing that my garage door had been blown out from the inside. Meaning that it was probably my car.

Six seconds. That's all.

As I held the phone, a text came through.

If you keep hiding, we will make this slow and painful.

"How can they possibly think I've been hiding?" I growled. "They killed my pack. I ran because I couldn't take the pain of being in my home without them. It's not hiding, fuckers. It's called unimaginable, crippling grief."

I hadn't actually meant to say the words out loud. I only knew I had because Marley's eyes filled with tears in the same instant that Phynn's arms tightened around me in a vice grip. Sighing, I closed my eyes. In the next second, my phone rang. But I was already anticipating the call from the police.

Before I could answer it, Marley took the phone from me

and shook her head. "Jaal said not to use your phone outside of texting. We don't want it connected to satellites for long, giving Decrescenti time to trace your location."

"I should ignore the police reporting my car's explosion?"

Marley nodded. "They'll call Nora. You've already given her power when you set up for her to take over the construction of your second site. And I've already coached her to say that she'll send you an email since that's your only form of communication right now."

"When did you coach her to do this?" I asked, narrowing my eyes.

She gave me a shy smile. "When you got here. I thought you were already dealing with enough stress that you didn't need anymore."

I reached for her, pulling her into my arms. Phynn adjusted his hold on me to encompass Marley, too. I don't know what I did to find myself surrounded by such an amazing pack, but I knew how incredibly fortunate I was for them.

"So, really, my power of attorney is already set with Nora," I said. "Something you knew."

Phynn had the decency to sound sheepish when he answered. "Yes. I knew."

I shook my head as he kissed my neck again. "We have a safe house to go to for a while. We're waiting for the paperwork we need to disappear."

"Make sure Nora can get in touch. I don't care how. I'm fine turning my phone off but know that I won't get rid of it."

"I'd never ask you to. Does this mean you agree?"

"Depends. Are you giving me a choice?"

Marley's fingers dug into my ribs. I don't think she'd ever heard me turn a question around on Phynn. And I hadn't since they both knew that my bark wasn't actually as submissive as I've been playing it up. So now, would he order me? He had no problem doing so when he thought I wasn't a strong alpha. When he thought that my hesitation was what any alpha's would be when being ordered by another alpha. Knee jerk defiance.

"No," Phynn said at last. "When our paperwork is finished, we're leaving. And you're coming with us."

There was no bark in his tone, something that made me grin. Giving me an order, demanding my obedience, without actually trying to enforce it.

What he was doing was giving me what I wanted without challenging my impulses to respond.

I sighed, letting my weight fall against him so that he was holding me up. His quiet snort of laughter made me grin. It also made him purr. He rubbed his cheek against me as Marley rubbed her face against my chest.

"Answer me," Phynn purred. "Do you understand?"

Still no bark. I licked my lips, nodding. "Yes, alpha."

His purr turned into a growl of approval for a second before he continued to purr. But it was Marley's arousal that met both of our noses, making Phynn and I groan together.

CHAPTER FORTY-FOUR

Marley

This wasn't something I was doing behind my pack's back *exactly*. I told my alphas that I was going to leave work early and head into Captains Knoll to see if Jaal could take another look at Terence's phone. I wanted him to transfer service to a burner and continue to monitor the texts while we shut off his actual service. Or at least pause it so the GPS isn't trackable.

They'd agreed on the condition that I stayed far away from Juice Me. I had no reason to go there except curiosity. I wanted to see if there was someone hanging around. I wanted to see the damage in person.

But we all knew someone would be watching the shop. Someone would expect Terence to come around and check it out.

He'd given strict orders to Nora, whom we called on a burner phone of our own, to make sure she told all employees that they were absolutely not allowed anywhere near the shop until further notice. They would continue to be paid unless otherwise notified.

I wasn't sure how much money Terence had, but he didn't seem concerned about their pay and the lack of revenue coming in to offset it.

So, this wasn't a secret trip in itself. Adrian, Phynn, and Terence all knew that I was going to see Jaal about Terence's phone. That wasn't a lie at all. I would talk to him about the phone, leaving it with him while I did the side errand I asked him to set up.

Jaal and I had been dating when I met Adrian. I'd kind of ghosted him without really meaning to when things got serious between Adrian, Phynn, and I. I'd reached out shortly after I had Adrian's bite to tell him what had happened and apologized profusely. He'd said we were good.

I hadn't known if that was the case until I reached out to him for this. We were good. And I was thankful for it. Not only because I wasn't usually that much of an awful person but because he was a good guy. And I was incredibly thankful for the connection.

"This is kind of a stupid idea," Jaal said as he strapped some new tech to my body. I had a single shot round within a single barrel that extended at the flick of my wrist. Out of the same compartment was a solid metal blade.

And the other hand was magic torture. Seriously, I was afraid to use it.

They were all favors Jaal had pulled in from the agency he worked for. After he'd gone over how they operated for the dozenth time, he stared at me like this might be the last time he sees me. It probably would be. If I came out alive, I would be going off grid with my pack in the coming days.

"This is really stupid," he repeated, not lessening the blow this time. "They'll likely kill you and you're giving away the pack he's hiding in."

"And that's why if this goes bad, you call Adrian and tell them to run now."

"He's going to kill me," Jaal said, frowning.

"Then you run, too."

"Marley, I'm serious."

I sighed. "I know, Jaal. But unless someone can appeal to these assholes, we're never going to be able to come out of hiding. We'll constantly be moving around, trying to stay off their radar. And I can't bring another life into this."

The confusion that crossed his face turned comically alarmed. "Oh no. You're not going in there-"

I laughed. "I'm not pregnant right now. But we've always wanted kids. I can't bring a child into a life where we're always running from death, looking over our shoulder."

He took a deep breath. "Let's go. Before I change my mind. This is stupid. I shouldn't have set this up."

There were three other betas in the car when Jaal led me down to the garage and I climbed in the back. They'd not accompany me inside, but they'd be there.

I'd asked Jaal to find a representative, one with influence within their crime syndicate, and set up a meeting. Terence was innocent. I knew that for a fact. They'd already killed their target. And seriously, their idea of punishment was skewed. If you're trying to hurt someone for betraying you, killing them and everyone they love isn't going to punish them. Sure, they'd be dead. But keeping them alive and killing everyone they loved was true torture. Terence was proof of that.

We were still within the city as I climbed out in front of a warehouse. Yes, cliché but there we are. Jaal walked me inside and to the room that he'd been instructed to deliver me.

It felt like he was handing me into the arms of death. But I took a breath and walked in.

There's a term in our society called designation fluid. It refers to when a beta has strong attributes of all three designations and can use them all. Their bark doesn't really carry the magic that makes a beta and alpha obey, but it is just barely not there. And they don't give off perfume that makes an alpha crazy like an omega.

But their personalities, bodies, and instincts carry the characteristics of all three designations. For this reason, betas who are designation fluid tend to find themselves in packs.

Growing up, there was another beta who was labeled this. Her name was Philla. She and I became quick friends during the later parts of primary school. We remained close through middle and high school. Our correspondence remained intact for the first couple years of college. And then life happened, and we lost touch.

I'd found myself an amazing pack. Apparently, Philla had gotten herself tied up in Decrescenti. The room was filled with five big beta men and a single woman. I knew she recognized me by the slight raising of her brows when I walked in. I took them all in one at a time as Jaal shut the door, confining me in a room with murderers.

I raised my hands as I walked in, turning in a slow circle as Jaal had instructed me to do so they could see that I was there unarmed.

"Look at you," one of the big men said, grinning.

It was a look I'd seen frequently throughout my life. I had the initial look of an omega. And right now, I likely smelled like one since Kaiser had been cuddled up with me this morning on the couch. Betas didn't react to omegas like alphas did, but some still reacted to me as if they were alphas.

As with the asshats in the park the day Terence found me

surrounded by three betas, their response was to try to possess the smaller beta who was clearly something different. Something special. Their reaction to me would be like a feral alpha coming across an omega in heat. Maybe not quite so drastic, but their behavior would have escalated. It wasn't the first time I'd been in that situation.

Philla's size and structure was a lot like mine. She was small, petite, with classically shy beauty. At first glance, she was always pinned as an omega.

"You wanted this meeting," one of the men prompted

"Terence Andersen," I said, knowing damn well I just sold his whereabouts. "You're trying to kill him and he's innocent."

"He should have already died. Little sneak wasn't where he was supposed to be."

"Believe me, that guilt has never left him. Again, he's innocent. Whatever you want with him is unfounded."

"Sounds to me like you know what we want," another said.

"I know the transgression against Decrescenti," I admitted. "Not only is the alpha dead who didn't follow through, but so are a whole lot of innocent people. And Terence knew nothing about it. He didn't know Emery's involvement and he still doesn't."

It was clear by the way they looked at me that I wasn't convincing them. These people had no conscience. But I'd known that coming in. I glanced at Philla again before looking at the last man who spoke.

"What will it take to convince you to ignore his existence and pretend like he's already dead?" I asked.

"Trade yourself," the first man said with that predatory grin. "Your life for his."

"Really? A beta's life for an alpha's?" I challenged.

He shrugged. "A life for a life."

I knew by his expression that he wouldn't kill me. Not right away at any rate. He had other, nastier plans. I knew his kind.

"Just so I'm clear, will you accept only my life in trade, or will anyone's do?" I asked.

"Anyone's," he agreed, telling me that they'd already agreed upon a plea deal. "A life for a life."

"A life for a life," I agreed. I moved before there could be any other caveat. I lifted my hand, flicking my wrist out to extract the single barrel. He didn't even have time to widen his eyes as I squeezed, and the projectile impaled into his forehead. Not center but just above his left eye.

He fell to the ground, and I turned back to the other men as I let the barrel drop to the floor. "So, this satisfies the life for a life, right?"

The corner of Philla's lips curled up briefly. But then there was sudden movement as two more betas came at me. Two at once. Of course.

The one on my left reached me first, gripping my neck with his hand. I wrapped my hand around his bare wrist and squeezed the pressure triggers on the glove. His hair stood on end as he was jolted with electricity.

Unfortunately, I felt it too since his hand was on me. I shuttered, my jaw shaking. He dropped hold of me and collapsed. He wasn't dead. He continued to try and get to his feet as the second beta reached for me.

I flicked my right wrist again and the blade popped out. Gripping it tightly, I let his body weight and velocity drive it into his ribs. This time I was careful that his hands weren't on me before I wrapped my left hand around it and sent more electricity through him. This time, I wrapped it around the handle of the solid metal blade that was sticking out of his ribs.

I let him go when he began to smell like burning flesh. Then I pressed my hand to the face of the first man who was looking at me snarling. He fell after a good struggle and didn't get back up.

Heaving with fear-filled energy, I looked at Philla and the two remaining betas on her sides. "Three men for the life of one. Pretty sure I did you a favor."

Laughter glistened in Philla's eyes, but she didn't address me. "Leave us," she told the two men. They looked at her like she was out of her mind. Like I'd set my taser glove on her and they watched in horror.

Philla sighed. "Just stand outside the door while I talk to this woman. Make friends with the PI contact, hmm?"

Reluctantly, they agreed. Their gazes were hard on me, but they didn't make any move toward me. Whatever position she'd found herself in within Decrescenti meant that she was important.

The door shut and Philla broke out into a grin. "Damn, Mar. Where have you been? And when did you turn so badass?" She stepped over a body and wrapped her arms around me. Being careful not to touch her with my taser hand, I hugged her back. It was only as she backed away that I realized I'd just opened myself up to allowing her to put a knife in my back. Literally, not figuratively.

"I found a pack that I love more than anything. And we found Terence. Please tell me the lives of these goons is enough to clear him. They weren't specific on who's life I traded for his."

Philla laughed jovially. "I'll make it work," she said, waving her hand.

"What about you?" I asked, narrowing my eyes. "How'd you get caught up in Decrescenti?"

She sighed, rolling her eyes. "Actually, I married the boss's son. Mind you, I didn't know anything about his ties to this mess when I married him. It was something he clued me into after our honeymoon. I love the asshole and believe it or not, he's insanely good to me. Worships me like I'm an omega." She grinned, winking at me. But then she frowned as she looked at the bodies on the floor. "I've been trying to convince him that we should find some, you know, upstanding things to do with our power, money, and reach. So far, I've gained trust with his father and it allows me to get involved sometimes."

"Why did you get involved in this one?" I asked.

She smiled. "Accidental, I assure you. I heard my husband talking about it and when he mentioned your name, even though I knew it was a long shot and there must be dozens of other Marley's in the world, I told him I wanted to be in on this one." Her smile turned wicked. "They know that means someone usually gets a lightened sentence, but since I only insert myself in occasionally, and his father wants grandchildren to spoil, they tend to indulge me."

"I'm both horrified by your life and so ridiculously relieved."

Philla grinned. "I'll take care of this. Probably still run for a bit. A month or so. But then you'll be fine. Need to give the world time to spread the word that Terence can be left alone, you know. And when you come back, let's do lunch. I'm dying to catch up."

"Please tell me you understand my hesitation with getting close to Decrescenti in any incarnation of it," I said, cautiously.

She laughed, taking my hand that was not lined with taser tips. "Mar, honey. There is no safer place for you and your pack than to reestablish our friendship."

Yes, I believed that. Besides, I'd always liked Philla.

I turned my hand over. "Give me your number. I'll call you when we get back. We can have lunch and follow it up with shopping."

Philla smiled brilliantly. She pulled a card from her pocket and tapped her finger over one of the numbers. "They're all mine, but this one is the number I carry around." As if to prove it, she lifted her cell phone and wiggled it in the air. "One month. If I think you need longer, I'll get word to you."

"You know where we're going?" I asked warily.

She shook her head. "No. But I'll find you if I need to."

I wasn't sure how I felt about that, but I accepted her hug again and opened the door. Jaal was waiting, standing between the two betas that Philla had sent out. I was actually surprised to find them chatting as if they'd taken Philla's order to befriend them seriously.

Jaal smiled at me in relief and hurried to my side. I waved to Philla, and she grinned in return. I wasn't sure how I was going to convince my pack that it would all blow over within a month and we could go home, but it was a weight off my shoulders.

Now to tell my alphas without them getting mad at me. Maybe it could wait a while.

CHAPTER FORTY-FIVE

Terence

I had no idea where we were, but I didn't exactly ask nor pay attention when we were driving. This was one of three stops we'd be making over the next month. Marley insisted that after a month, we could return to our lives per usual. But she was secretive as to why she was convinced of that.

Neither of her alphas had persuaded her to disclose information further than that she was sure. And I'd been there for a few of their barks. I was fascinated that she managed to resist the urge to spill it all. However, all they got out of her was that they needed to trust that she'd taken care of it.

I was both horrified that she might have put herself in danger for me and ready to worship her bravery; after scolding her disregard for her own safety. Whatever she had done, I was sure that Adrian and Phynn wouldn't be alone in their fearful anger at her actions.

Which was probably why she was keeping it to herself.

The house we were in was small. Three bedrooms, the smallest of which we reserved for a nest. It wasn't the right shape or size, too big and open with tall ceilings and massive glass windows that were impossible to cover to Kaiser's preference, but he didn't complain. We only knew he didn't care for it since he didn't go into it.

Kaiser loved his permanent nest. His only fear about leaving home was that Decrescenti would find their house and blow it up like they had my car. And then his nest would be gone.

He was still afraid, but he trusted Marley at her word. Trusted that his beta had taken care of what his alphas hadn't been able to. But we were hiding. Despite trying to make it like a family vacation, Kaiser knew better. Even if he was outwardly trying to accept it and play it up with that view, he was an omega.

It was only as the days progressed and I was with them all the time did I start to see Kaiser's true personality. I'd only caught glimpses of it before, but now that he was settling, it was coming out more clearly.

He was obstinate. A bit of a brat. But he was smart and happy. Marley was right. He loved to work on his abs. He cared little about any other part of his body, but he loved his stomach. His favorite things were his nest, a few choice gifts from us, and quiet time where he could cuddle up against someone.

He wasn't prone to whine and didn't care much for being waited on. I was sure he'd cook for himself if he could find the passion to cook. He liked gaming on his phone, sudoku puzzles, and teasing Marley.

Kaiser was a perfect omega even when he was just being himself. What he failed to realize was that the traits that came with being an omega were not what made an omega. It was how a pack comes together around an omega. A pack can be a pack without one. And a damn good, happy pack at that. But there was a different element involved when there was an omega in the pack. Something that fed a deeper, more carnal part of an alpha.

All Kaiser had to do was be there. He could embrace or refuse the things about his designation as he chose. All it took was his smile and contentment that made him a perfect omega.

We'd been in this house for a few days and since we were trying to vanish from life, we weren't working. That meant we were spending a lot of time together. I felt like this was a sink or swim moment with me and this pack. I'd spent every possible moment with mine – never getting tired of them and always craving more. Even though I knew that no pack would provide to me what mine had been, I would never be satisfied with anything less than that.

Three days in and we'd barely left the bed. We were curled up, watching movies. Only leaving for food or showers. I was constantly against Adrian's chest or Phynn's and always with either Kaiser or Marley in my arms. The others were pressed up tightly to us as well.

We talked and shared and just remained quiet. As the hours passed and I settled more deeply into them, I thought that maybe this was a home for me. The guilt that came with that thought felt like a hippo on my chest.

I was anticipating our quiet camaraderie was about to end. We'd been in bed for three days with very minimal touching. And our omega was getting restless with need. An omega is always on, after all. And this omega hadn't been pleased in days.

He was the one in my arms right now with Phynn behind me. Kaiser was getting fidgety. His perfume started to fill the air with a slightly sweet note in it. I was just waiting for the word. Waiting for him to tell me what he wanted.

Finally, he groaned and sighed in exasperation. His voice was nearly a whine when he spoke. "If someone doesn't touch me, I'm going to lose my mind."

"But I am touching you," I said, squeezing him in my arms.

"Me, too," Marley said, her voice sweet and innocent as she looked over her shoulder at him with wide eyes.

Kaiser growled at us both. But he was too hungry to keep up his irritation. His growl turned to a whine.

His whine grabbed me by my throat, and I rolled on top of him, covering his mouth with mine so I could swallow the sound.

It didn't stop but turned needier as it transformed into something with claws. They raked down my skin. Or maybe that was his hands trying to tear at my clothing.

I had a feeling we were skipping the warm up.

I pulled off him and Kaiser snarled at me before the sound broke up. He blinked up at me, startled, before Phynn burst out laughing.

Kaiser flushed. "That was awful. What the fuck?"

I chuckled, pulling my shirt over my head, and distracting him. I didn't miss Marley's eyes on me. Nor the blatant sweet note that bloomed within the cherry almond scent as it filled the air next to me from Phynn.

"Kaiser," I purred, making his entire body shiver in delight, and filling the room with his sweet cinnamon roll perfume. "Present for me, my sweet omega."

He stared with wide eyes, desire and need shining through like a beacon. He was still for a solid five seconds before he was pulling at his clothing and trying to get on his hands and knees at the same time. I took mercy on him and assisted with the clothing removal.

And then his ass was high in the air, waiting for me. He wiggled, making me growl.

"Beautiful," Adrian said quietly.

I nodded, gently dragging my fingers over his smooth skin. "So soft. So tight," I added.

Kaiser wiggled again, shifting so he could look at me.

"How do you want to do this?" Phynn asked as I started to pull down my pants again.

I glanced at him, brow raised. I wanted my knot in his perfect ass. But I knew what he was asking. "You're giving me options?" I asked.

"Depends. Name it and we'll see."

I licked my lips as I slid from my gym pants, bringing my briefs with them. Phynn's bright eyes dropped, heat rising brighter in their depths as he brought them to mine.

"Marley below," I said. "With Kaiser so I can make them both moan. Adrian first. Then you."

"Chain?" Marley asked, perking up as she slid out of her clothes. I shivered at the arousal thick in her voice.

"Uh, yea. But not quite what I meant."

"I didn't peg you for a bottom," Adrian noted.

I smirked, getting on my knees to line up with Kaiser so his whining would stop making me want to drown the sun. "I'm not," I said. "Things change."

Neither alpha argued as I pushed inside the omega beneath me. He sighed in relief before groaning in pleasure. I eased in, rocking in him with slow deep thrusts. I slowed to a stop as Marley shuffled under him.

I gave them a minute to get situated. In the stillness as Kaiser came off me almost fully to dive into Marley, Adrian moved behind me. His touch was gentle with all the strength and assurance of a pack alpha. I swallowed as I adjusted my position to push back into Kaiser.

"Knot, Terence," he whispered. "Please."

He rarely said my name in these moments. It was always

'alpha.' I loved this even more. I leaned over him, kissing his cheek as Adrian worked cold lube around and into my ass. I hadn't asked for that, but thank fuck.

I took my time with my knot, ever so slowly, easing in bit by bit. Kaiser's hurry was gone as Marley's steady rocking beneath him distracted him from his impatience. I only started to push my knot into him in earnest when Adrian started pushing his dick into me.

Closing my eyes, I focused on Kaiser beneath me and keeping my muscles relaxed. It wasn't so bad until I remembered just how big alphas were. My jaw tensed as I waited for him to finish his intrusion. The sting was there. Oh, the sting. I shivered at the memory.

I'd bottomed for all my alphas and betas once. Exactly once each. I had never been a fan.

So why did I suddenly decide I wanted a role reversal? No fucking idea. But I was set on this. This was what I wanted. This was where I needed to be.

"Easy, alpha," Adrian murmured, rubbing his hands down my back to my shoulders. "That's it." He pulled back before slowly entering me again. I shivered. "There you go."

There was something to be said about being praised during sex. It felt fucking good. Kaiser agreed, even though the words weren't meant for him. He sighed happily, wiggling his ass as he worked himself around my knot.

It made the Adrian invasion less mentally chaotic as my mind and body battled as to whether we wanted to keep this up.

Adrian didn't remain with me long. It was as if he were loosening me up and I suddenly thought that maybe I should have examined those two before I suggested this setup.

But it didn't matter. This was what I wanted.

While they switched positions, I let my body fall more fully on Kaiser and Marley. "You okay, Mar?" I asked.

"Mhm," she said. "Perfect."

"Yes, you are," I agreed, moving my hand to gently tangle in her hair.

And then Phynn was there, and it was lights out again as the aching in my ass increased anew, around a different cock. And this time, Phynn didn't ease in quite as slowly as Adrian. His quiet growl singing my praises, encouraging me to take him, was like an aphrodisiac all on its own. I found myself thrusting gently, my knot making Kaiser gasp and moan as he filled Marley again and again.

Phynn stilled for a minute. When he groaned, low enough that it sounded like a growl, I glanced back to see Adrian had taken up position behind him. I smirked, looking down at Marley. "Chain," I mouthed.

She grinned hugely, nuzzling her face into Kaiser's neck as he shook through another orgasm. Oh, to be an omega.

When Adrian and Phynn got themselves situated, my thoughts slowly drifted away and Phynn leaned over me, murmuring in my ear how good I felt. There was a moment of our bodies moving on our own, making the movements short and jerky. But then we synced up and the whole thing became a beautiful movement of sounds, slick, and intense pleasure.

After my second orgasm as Phynn leaned more heavily on me, I reached back and grabbed the back of his head. "Bite me, alpha," I whispered.

Phynn stilled. They all froze at my words. Maybe this required a longer conversation.

"Really?" he asked.

I grinned at the surprise in his voice.

Nodding, I flexed my fingers against his hair. "If you'll have me, I want to be here."

"No more running," Adrian said.

"No more running," I agreed. "You already know my darkest skeletons. I have nothing left to hide."

Phynn took a deep breath, bringing his lips to my neck. "Do you know, I've wanted to make you mine since I first kissed you."

"You mean before or after I freaked out?"

He chuckled. "Both. Before, because I knew you belonged to me. And after, so I could give you the strength and comfort you needed. As it turns out, it's frustratingly difficult without a bond."

I grinned. "As with everything, I'm waiting for an opportune time to talk about these things. Bite me, Phynn. Make me yours."

He didn't need any more convincing. His teeth sank into my flesh right where his mouth rested. At first, it was just the sting of the bite. And then the rush of him inside me, filling all the echoing emptiness with warmth and affection. Security. And as he promised, strength and comfort.

Behind him came the others more quietly. It was easy to figure them out. Adrian was relaxed, somewhat aloof, and a wall of fortification, there to shelter me from anything. Marley was quiet, shy, and a glowing beam of happiness.

Kaiser was blissful, almost jittering. And an undercurrent of constant arousal that made my dick twitch.

Phynn chuckled as I grunted in response to the heat that came pouring in from Kaiser. "Yep, welcome to life with an omega."

"Sorry," Kaiser whispered.

I nipped at his neck. "Don't be. I wouldn't change a thing about you, my adorable little hornball."

Kaiser grinned as we all slowly rolled away from each other. Gently disentangling our bodies. Except for Kaiser and me. With the continuous influx of hot arousal, I was not going to soften anytime soon.

But that was fine. I was content to lay with my pack surrounding me as I learned them through their bonds. Perfect alphas. Perfect beta. And a perfect omega. They were mine.

The window shattering had us all jumping. Marley's scream made my blood run cold. I jerked upright and was rewarded with a bullet grazing my shoulder.

"Fuck," muttered as I shoved us all towards the far edge of the bed and onto the floor.

I was still locked within Kaiser, and he whimpered, trying to wrap around me so I wasn't pulled out of him harshly. It wouldn't be long before I could pull out at this rate. Glass rained down as another of the windows broke, the rapid-fire of a machine gun littered the air.

"Marley," Adrian hollered.

"I need a phone," she yelled back as she tried to head for the hall.

"Stay," I barked and everyone around me stilled as if their bodies were programmed to do exactly as I said.

Kaiser's fear as he clung to me was a fantastic dampening agent. That was probably the shortest time it had ever taken for my knot to recede. I slipped out of him as bullets continued to pepper the room. I kissed his cheek and set him in Adrian's lap.

"Don't move, Marley," I said, putting a whole lot of bark in my voice.

She looked at me with desperate eyes as her whole body stilled as if she were icing over. I turned away and yanked the bed off the wall. Where the bullet grazed my shoulder stung like a bitch. It was only the sudden burst of that pain that made the way my new bite ached more prevalent.

Only as I thought about it was I tuned into my bondmates' presence. Their fear. Their surprise. Their anxiety.

With the bed away from the wall, I heaved it up like I had the giant tractor tire time and time again until it was resting on its side like a wall. It gave us more cover, though a mattress wasn't going to slow down bullets.

A canister hit the floor and I spun around swearing.

"Into the hall," I ordered them.

Phynn got to the canister first and chucked it back through the window as he jerkily did what I demanded and exited into the hall. There was commotion outside as the canister exploded causing chaos while they regrouped. That gave us a few precious seconds to get away from the room and find better cover.

"Wait," Adrian said, gritting his teeth. "Fuck, Terence. Let me go."

I wasn't actually touching him. But I nodded, my command over him falling away. He glared at me for a minute before turning to the night table. He pulled the door open, bending down in time to barely miss a bullet to his temple. Someone outside was up again. I gritted my teeth as I waited. This better be worth it.

Adrian pushed a rifle behind him. Before I could grab it, Marley pulled it from me. I watched as she checked the chamber, pulled a bullet in, and then rolled away to take aim around the bed.

I was startled enough with her efficiency and familiarity with the rifle that I didn't speak before she was already firing back. Another round of yelling commenced outside when the rain of bullets was returned to them.

Adrian shoved another in my hand, asking me if I knew how to use it while he dug out a couple more.

"Enough," I told him. It had been a long time since I'd held a gun and it was only for target practice.

"Now can we get in the hall?" I asked, opposed to ordering.

Adrian smiled at me, inclining his head and giving me a sarcastic grin. "Yes, alpha. Tell me what you want."

I growled at him.

"No time for hanky panky," Marley chided. "I need a fucking phone."

We both looked at her with brows raised as she got on her hands and knees and glared at us. We watched her naked ass crawl out while there was confusion outside.

"She's sexy as all fuck when she gets bossy," Adrian said.

My dick agreed.

We followed her into the hall and Marley continued down it for the other room. Before she made it inside, the window from the room exploded inward. She swore, backing up again.

"Okay, in full disclosure, I'm getting my plans from watching Foster and Ronan play video games," I said as I hunkered down with Kaiser behind me. Phynn snorted. "I anticipate that we're going to receive some grenades or knock-out gas at the very least. Try to redirect them into one of the rooms or back at whoever threw it. And be ready at all entrances with a gun trained."

As I spoke, we heard the splintering of the front door.

"Seriously," Marley said in exasperation. "A phone. I can fix this with a phone!"

"How?" Adrian demanded.

"Now is not the time for that discussion," she said shrilly.

Adrian sighed in irritation. I turned when his gun went off in time to see he shot a man as he came up the stairs. Behind me, Kaiser yelped. I turned in time to see him scramble to his knees and toss something back into the room we'd been fucking in. By the explosion that followed, it wasn't a canister of gas but a grenade or bottle rocket.

"How much ammunition do we have?" I asked.

"There's a bunch stashed through the house," Adrian said.

"Later, when you get me a phone, I think we're going to need to have a few family confessions," Marley said.

I grinned as a chorus of footsteps started clomping on the stairs. I turned towards the stairs with Adrian.

"Let's go, Mar," Phynn said. "While our alphas have them occupied, we'll find a phone."

"No, wait," Kaiser said as he tried to curl himself into mine and Adrian's backs.

"Just stay there and stay low," Phynn said gently. "And be ready to use that amazing arm again, babe. That throw was phenomenal."

"Incredible," I agreed as I took aim at the man peeking over the stairs.

I'd not seriously shot a gun in a long time. But at close range and somewhat large targets, missing would have been comical. And deadly, but we weren't going to address that.

Phynn and Marley disappeared into the nest room. Kaiser threw another incoming from the room we left away but this time, he hurled it down the stairs. There was a whole lot of cursing before it detonated.

I cringed, thinking of the hole in the stairs.

Adrian laughed. "Brilliant, omega. You cut off their access that way."

"I hope we got insurance on the house," Kaiser said in return. He looked a little green.

And then it all stopped. The shots. The footsteps. The voices. All of it. Ended, just like that.

Adrian and I exchanged a look before I scrambled forward and pulled the earpiece out of the head of a man who'd made it up the stairs. It was just his torso left but it looked like these were wireless anyway. When I got it to my ear, there was a woman yelling.

"I told you to cease fire. I'll have all your heads for this insubordination. The target has been removed. Cease fucking fire. This is what you get when you don't have complete control over your employees. When there's no consequences, Rion. Your interview process needs to be better."

And then the line went dead. Like this yelling woman had hung up a phone.

I turned my gaze back to Adrian with my brows raised as Phynn and Marley came out of the room on their feet, Marley holding a phone. I fell back against the wall and closed my eyes.

"What did you hear?" Kaiser asked.

"A woman screaming. Apparently, the target was called off me, but someone had it in their heads that they were going to go through with this anyway. She was not happy."

"Hm. Imagine that," Phynn said, looking at Marley with a brow raised.

Marley smiled, leaning against him like a rag doll. "If it's all the same to you, I'd like to empty my stomach of its contents in a toilet before you yell at me."

I cracked my eyes open to see the queasy look on her face.

Adrian slid against the wall next to me as Kaiser crawled into our laps. I rubbed his face with a sweaty hand before grabbing the mess of Adrian's long hair and bringing it to my neck.

He laughed, shifting around so he could better nuzzle against me. "I think you've got a bark that you've been hiding."

Kaiser snorted. "It felt like I was a marionette."

I chuckled. "Miles always said I had a bark that never fully left my voice. But I think I lost the will to use it when they died." They didn't answer, both of them rubbing their faces against me. I sighed. "He wasn't wrong, but I also never wanted to be the alpha of our family. Though I'll admit, I didn't quite revolt against it like I do now. I was happy to defer to Zack. I made sure he knew it and I never challenged him.

Mostly because I knew I never needed to. I trusted him explicitly."

"You still don't want to be alpha," Kaiser said quietly, more in observation than anything else.

I shook my head. "No. I never wanted to be alpha. I'm happy to be an alpha but I don't want to *be* one. You understand that, don't you?"

Kaiser nodded. "Yes. Very much."

"But I think I lost my will even more since they died. I don't want to bite; I'd rather be bitten. I don't want to command; I'd rather do as I'm told – which, I know is a little more difficult since I'm not fully settled with you yet, but I know it'll come. Now," I said, tightening my hold in Adrian's hair and bringing his mouth back to my neck. "Bite."

He laughed, pushing away from me gently. "Terence, I don't have to bite you for you to be part of our pack."

"I know. Bite me."

His warm brown eyes met mine with a soft smile on his lips. "Yea?"

I nodded.

"It's not necessary."

"Just bite him already," Kaiser said. "I want to feel more of him."

Adrian looked at Kaiser with the fond indulgent smile that I felt in my very soul. I'd always looked at Miles that way. And then Ronan. And now Kaiser and Marley.

"You have to make our omega happy," I said, shrugging.

Adrian's grin was as beautiful as it was arousing. He leaned in, stroking along my collar bone with his tongue until he chose a spot that would mostly always be covered if I chose it to be. He sank his teeth in. I gritted my teeth as I let my head fall back against the wall.

I could already feel Adrian through the new bite I had from

Phynn. But that little echo doubled, tripled, until it was loud and firm. Taking a strong hold and settling around me like a solid foundation.

His teeth pulled from my skin, and he began to gently lick at my bite, tending to it and healing it. As he did, sirens filled the air.

About fucking time.

CHAPTER FORTY-SIX

Adrian
Seven months later

I wrapped my arms around his shoulders, pulling his back to my chest. He was trying very hard not to pout or be upset. This was a big day for Terence. A huge step for us as a pack. Kaiser knew that. He was as excited and nervous for it as Terence was.

But Kaiser was dismayed because Terence hadn't bitten him yet. He'd become even more hurt by it because Terence had bitten Marley in the last month and still wasn't ready to bite Kaiser.

"He loves you," I murmured. "You're his omega even without his bite."

"But why?" he whispered, a whine caught in his throat. "What did I do?"

I sighed. "If he hears you say that, you know he's going to be making you recite that you're a good omega."

He grunted, crossing his arms as he watched Terence with Marley and Phynn. They were standing in front of a long window, Marley cradled between the two of them as the two alphas shared a long, languid kiss.

Kaiser's jealousy rose by the second. It was only because he was trying so hard to muffle it that I was maybe partially convinced that Terence didn't feel it. But he shared three bonds within our pack now, so I know his long distant bond with Kaiser was fairly clear.

It was why I knew that Terence was holding off for a reason. He made extra sure that he paid Kaiser a whole lot of attention. Showered him with presents and orgasms. And for a while, it satisfied Kaiser.

But he hadn't knotted our omega in almost four days now. And it had been about that long since he'd given Kaiser a gift. I had no doubt that he loved our omega. As such, I had no doubt that he was working through something that prevented him from being close to Kaiser.

Today was a big day though. A monumental step for Terence especially.

I turned Kaiser to look at me. "We can talk to him later. Tomorrow. But today, you need to be 1000% supportive and understanding. Have a stupid amount of patience. Alright?"

Kaiser nodded, the distress on his face lightening. He glanced at Terence and sympathy took root instead. He was already anticipating an influx of pain from Terence, even through the diluted bond.

Today, we were visiting Terence's pack's grave.

"Yes," Kaiser whispered, tears already stinging his eyes.

"Ready?" Phynn asked the room, though no one answered. This was Terence's show.

Terence nodded, giving him a smile. He kissed the top of Marley's head and let her go. On the way to the door, he wrapped an arm around Kaiser's waist and pulled him along. Kaiser wasn't good about hiding his distress or his hurt. I *knew* Terence had a reason. And it better be good because he really was hurting Kaiser right now.

"Give him time," Phynn said, bringing Marley between us as we watched the two head out the door. "I'm sure he has a purpose."

"I hope it's a good one," Marley whispered.

The drive from the hotel was quick and soon, we were driving into a massive cemetery. It was beautiful, filled with pine trees and little ponds. There was a quiet, somber tone but there was no doubt that the place was filled with splendor. Calm. Serenity.

I was not at all prepared for what Terence stopped us in front of. The sobbing angel that hung over the top alone was enough to gouge your heart and bring tears to your eyes. It did mine. I didn't miss the tear streaking down Marley's cheek, either. Or how Kaiser brought a hand to cover his mouth.

But Terence stood back looking at it as if seeing it objectively for the first time. He sighed and moved closer, until he could fall to his knees in front of it. He placed his hand over the stone with the names of his packmates engraved and bowed his head.

His sorrow built slowly in me before it took concentrated effort to pull in a breath. As if I took a breath for him, Terence released one slowly and looked up at the angel weeping over the top.

"Was it too much?" he asked.

I wasn't sure if he was talking to us or not.

"No," Kaiser answered, his voice hushed. He was staring at

the angel with his own particular brand of pain, looking at it in awe and sadness. "Not at all."

Terence smiled lightly, turning his attention back down to the names. He turned his gaze to me, and I got closer, crouching down to be next to him. He removed his hand from the stone to take mine, pressing it flat where his hand was and keeping his over it.

"You know what Zack would have liked most about you?" he asked. I shook my head, looking at him out of the corner of my eye while moving my focus to where Zack's name was carved into the stone. "That you are slightly offended that my bark is bigger than yours, but I refuse to use it."

I chuckled, bowing my head a little.

Terence grinned. "He started out offended, too. Especially since he found that Miles was right, in that mine was usually lacing my everyday conversational tone. It drove him crazy."

"And how did he get over it?" I asked.

He sighed, leaning into me a little. I wrapped my other arm around him, kissing the side of his head. "Because he loved me and when it came down to it, an alpha will take care of all his packmates."

I nodded, smiling. "Got it. I'll take note."

Terence smiled, moving his fingers to trace over the Z. "Miles would have called you debonair. Mostly because of your hair and the way you hold it back with a length of suede instead of an elastic. And Ronan probably would have hidden them on you, just to grin at your irritation and wait for his punishment."

He dropped his hand, and I took that as my time with them was up. I kissed him softly, letting my lips linger on his forehead, before standing. I squeezed his shoulder gently as I moved away.

Terence spent a minute alone before Phynn joined him. He placed Phynn's hand on their names as he did mine and they spoke quietly. When he moved on to Marley, I realized that he was introducing us to his pack. It both warmed and broke my heart.

I hadn't realized how incredibly strong a man he was until this moment. This wasn't just an emotional step for him. This was part of a goodbye. He was ready to accept his life moving on without the pack that he was entirely devoted to with every cell in his body.

I was close enough to hear him gently scold Marley while he introduced her to his alphas. I had the distinct impression he was telling on her.

"Foster would have punished you relentlessly for going behind our backs and meeting with Decrescenti on your own," Terence said. Marley flushed, his hand covering hers completely. "He'd have praised you for being such a badass and killing three men to free me of their attention. And in the same breath, he'd have edged you to orgasm until you were begging for release."

Marley's flush turned bright red as she stared at the stone. I was sure she was staring at Foster's name in particular.

She'd finally told us the lengths to which she went through in her attempt to clear Terence's name. We were understandably horrified. There was yelling and arguments and a whole lot of reverence for our little beta.

We had continued our month-long tour of staying off grid while Philla finished cleaning out ranks and having anyone who disregarded her eliminated. She'd gotten in touch with Marley when she was finished, telling her it was safe for us to return home.

And now Marley had a best friend who was dangerous as fuck. You'd never know by looking at her, because Philla was a doll, just like Marley. But damn, knowing that a rain of wildfire would fall if Philla demanded it was a whole new set of traumas.

"Zack would have spanked you until your ass was as red as Rudolph's nose," Terence said, smirking. At this point, I was sure Marley was going to remain beet red.

"And Emery?" Marley asked.

"He would have fed you, so you still had the energy for Zack and Foster's punishments. He was a team player like that."

I shook my head, grinning all the while.

Terence took a few minutes to himself before inviting Kaiser to him. Unlike the rest of us, he didn't let Kaiser kneel beside him. He brought our omega into his lap. Although I tried to keep my distance and give them space, I had a feeling this was going to be the hardest one for him. An omega represented a lot in a pack.

He didn't speak for a few minutes as he rested his hand over Kaiser's on the stone.

"We had thought that what we really wanted was babies to fill our yard," Terence said. "But not ever enough that we actually put any effort into finding a woman. Although babies would have made us happy, what we'd have been missing all along was you."

Kaiser sucked in a breath.

"You're exactly what we've always wanted, and we'd have happily given up any idea of a future with kids if you'd have been in our life. Your complete disregard of designation norms would have thrilled Ronan more than you can imagine. He was happy being a beta, but it truly pissed him off how everyone looked at him and treated him. But Miles would have indulged you and still turned around and bought you the world. He was beta through and through, but he craved to be a caregiver and not let you be any wiser that you were being taken care of. It was his best kept secret talent and took me years to figure out what he was doing."

"They've always sounded amazing," Kaiser said. "I swear, I can see them grinning at me."

I didn't know if he meant now or in general. But he leaned his head against Terence's as he settled into him.

"You know, so much of my guilt is because I feel like I'm betraying my pack by loving others. Yet, every day, I find another reason why my pack would have loved you, and you them. I've finally come to the realization that this was never about replacing them or their love. I'm sure that we'd have grown into one big pack. So, that's what I'm doing. Expanding my pack."

"I love that," Kaiser whispered.

"You want my bite, omega?" Terence asked, his voice low.

Kaiser shifted to look at him with wide eyes. I sighed at the tears that formed. I'd gotten closer. When my shoulder brushed Phynn's, I realized he and Marley were standing close, too.

"Yes," Kaiser said, his voice choked. "I thought you-"

"Hush," Terence said, cutting him off. "Tell me."

The demand came with no bark, but Kaiser flushed all the same. "I did nothing wrong," he said, keeping his gaze on Terence, otherwise Terence would make him repeat it until he was looking directly into his eyes. "I'm a perfect omega."

Terence nodded. "I'm sorry," he said, brushing his lips over Kaiser's. "I'm still working out some kinks and not the fun kind." Kaiser flashed him a smile. "I've wanted to bite you since we met. But I haven't been able to bring myself to. Not because I don't want you. Or because I have doubts about this. Or because I don't love you. I do. I don't. And I do. But to claim my omega, I need to be with my whole pack. I know you can't really feel them, but-"

His words cut off abruptly as he closed his eyes. Kaiser

looked up at me with panic, not knowing what to do. I silently urged him to remain still and let Terence work through this.

Terence opened his eyes and released a harsh breath. "Some things are easier to think than say," he mused.

"I love you," Kaiser said quickly before rocking back like the words had shocked him. His eyes went wide, his pupils dilating as he stared at Terence.

Terence grinned, bringing the hand that wasn't pinning Kaiser's to the stone behind his head and pressing his lips firmly to Kaiser's. It was a long kiss in which the emotions from both of them filled our bonds in a collision of fireworks.

"Yes, bite me," Kaiser said. He leaned into the stone, pressing his weight on his hand as if that would bring him closer to Terence's pack.

Terence's smile was soft as he dragged his lips feather-light across Kaiser's jaw and down his neck. I'd had a suspicion that he would bite Kaiser right where the world would see. Where it would be impossible to hide. And he didn't disappoint. He buried his teeth into the front of Kaiser's neck, right beside his trachea.

Kaiser gasped, tangling the fingers of his free hand into Terence's hair to hold him there. The smile on his face was euphoric. I was sure their knot fasting was over once we returned to the hotel.

Terence tended to his bite for several minutes, their hands never leaving the stone of our extended pack. When they finally stood together and Kaiser started to move away, Marley thought she needed to extend the moment.

"Wait. One more thing I'd like for us to share with your pack. Our pack," Marley said.

The way Terence looked at her was as if she were the angel weeping over the grave come to life. He smiled, nodding.

Marley pulled us all forward and placed her hands on the

stone. We followed suit, our hands overlapping so that we were touching each other and all five names.

"So, I've known about this for a couple weeks now, but I also knew we were coming here. I didn't know you were going to claim Kaiser here or I'd have left this moment for him," Marley said.

Kaiser smiled, shaking his head. "Family time." He moved his hand to hers and squeezed it. "I'm happy to share all my moments with you, Mar."

She smiled, leaning her head on Phynn's chest. "Well, we're expanding a little more. I'm due in six months."

Silence fell around us until I dumbly asked, "Due?"

Marley grinned up at me. "Yes. Our child is due to enter this world in six months."

We all stared at Marley as she looked between us. "I hope this is a good silence."

Kaiser reacted first. I was sure, any other time, that he'd have pulled her away and swung her around. Instead, he turned her around and pressed her back to the stone before kissing her breathless. Then he fell to his knees, one hand still flat on the stone, and pressed his face to her stomach.

I was sure, if Terence hadn't already been in love with both of them that day, he was now. We stayed at the grave for a while longer, sharing in the pleasure of each other and Terence talking to his pack as if they were there, though at the same time, at their memories of them. Not like they were standing there. But as if he were telling us a memory that could have been reality right now.

I watched as the four of them started towards the exit. My hand still rested against the stone. I slid it over the five names before I stopped over Zack's.

"I promise we'll take care of him. And we'll love him like you do."

Another minute went by before I pulled my hand away. I took a step and paused, my hand twitching as if someone had touched me. I brought my hand up and looked at the stone. The phantom touch brushed my skin again and I smiled.

I was glad they accepted my promise.

ACKNOWLEDGMENTS

Hello my lovelies. Thank you so much for reading my very first omegaverse. I know, it was a little touch and go there with the heartache and whether or not Terence would be able to make it out of his grief. I'm glad he did!

I hope you enjoyed the introduction to this world. I'm not going to lie, if you're in any of my groups, you probably noticed that I'm a little omegaverse obsessed. More will be coming in various forms!

I'd like to thank my wonderful patron who have constantly been encouraging me and supporting me! Jennifer, Lauren, Sarah, Shyla, and Chelsi, thank you for all that you do! I love spoiling you with extra goodies and treating you to sneak peeks!

And of course, there's my amazing beta team, my ARC team, my rockstar PAs, and most importantly, my readers. Thank you for making my dreams of writing a possibility.

ABOUT THE AUTHOR

Crea lives in upstate New York with her dog and husband. She has been writing since grade school, when her second grade teacher had her class keep writing journals. She has a habit of creating secondary, and often time tertiary, characters that take over her stories. When she can't fall asleep at night, she thinks up new scenes for her characters to act out. This, of course, is how most of her meant-to-be-thrown-away characters tend to end up front and center - and utterly swoon-worthy! Don't ask her how many book boyfriends she has...

When not writing, Crea is an avid reader. Her TBR pile is several hundred books high (don't even look at her kindle wish list or the unread books on her tablet). Sometimes, she enjoys crafting; sometimes, exploring nature; sometimes, traveling. Mostly, she enjoys putting her characters on paper and breathing life into them. Oh, and sleeping. Crea *loves* to sleep!

THANK YOU

Thank you for reading *Alpha Hunted* and joining Terence as he navigates healing. It's a tough road but I'm so glad he found what he needs to be able to live again.

Would you be so kind as to take a moment and leave a review? Reviews play a big role in a book's success and you can help with just a few sentences.

Review on Amazon, Goodreads, and Bookbub

Thank you!!

Crea Reitan

PS - If you find any errors, spelling or the like, please do not use your kindle/Amazon to mark them. Amazon's algorithms pull the book! Instead, please reach out to me on Facebook at https://www.facebook.com/Crea.Reitan or via email at LadyCreaAuthor@gmail.com. Thank you!!